A Middy of the Sl

A Middy of the Slave Squadron: A West African Story

by Harry Collingwood

Copyright © 2/5/2016
Jefferson Publication

ISBN-13: 978-1523898978

Printed in the United States of America

Table of Contents

Chapter One.

A sound through the darkness.

"Phew!" ejaculated Mr Perry, first lieutenant of His Britannic Majesty's corvette *Psyche*, as he removed his hat and mopped the perspiration from his streaming forehead with an enormous spotted pocket-handkerchief. "I believe it's getting hotter instead of cooler; although, by all the laws that are supposed to govern this pestiferous climate, we ought to be close upon the coolest hour of the twenty-four! Just step aft to the skylight, Mr Fortescue, and see what the time is, will ye? It must surely be nearing two bells."

"Ay, ay, sir!" I dutifully answered; and, moving aft to the skylight, raised the canvas cover which had been placed over it to mask the light of the low-turned lamp which was kept burning all night in the fore cabin, and glanced at the clock which, screwed to the coaming on one side of the tell-tale compass, balanced the barometer which, hung in gimbals, was suspended on the other side. The clock marked the time as two minutes to five a.m., or within two minutes of two bells in the morning watch.

Dropping the canvas screen back into place, I was about to announce the time to my superior officer, when I thought I caught, through the faint creak of the ship's timbers and the light rustling of the canvas aloft, a slight, far off sound, like the squeak of a sheave on a rusty pin. Therefore, instead of proclaiming the time aloud, I stepped quietly to the side of the first luff, and asked, almost in a whisper—

"Did you hear anything just then, sir?"

"Hear anything?" reiterated Mr Perry, unconsciously lowering his usually stentorian voice in response to the suggestion of secrecy conveyed by my whisper; "no, I can't say that I did. What d'ye mean, Mr Fortescue?"

"I mean, sir," I replied, "that I thought I caught, a moment ago, a sound like that of— ah! did you hear *that*, then, sir?" as a voice, uttering some words of command, apparently in the Spanish language, came floating to us, faint but clear, across the invisible water upon which the *Psyche* lay rolling almost imperceptibly.

"Ay, I did," answered Mr Perry, modulating his voice still further. "No mistake about that, eh? There's a craft of some sort out there, less than a mile distant, I should say. Did you catch the words? They sounded to me like some foreign lingo."

"No, sir," I replied, "I did not quite catch them, but, as you say, they appeared to be foreign, and I believe they were Spanish. What about striking two bells, sir? It only wanted two minutes—"

"On no account whatever, Mr Fortescue," hastily interrupted my companion. "On the contrary, have the kindness to slip for'ard and caution the watch not to sing out, or make the slightest noise, on any account, but to come quietly aft if they happen to have anything to report. And when you have done that, kindly go down and call Captain Harrison."

"Ay, ay, sir!" I answered; and, kicking off my shoes, lest the sound of them upon the deck should reach the stranger through that still and breathless atmosphere, I proceeded upon my twofold errand.

But it is time to tell the reader where the *Psyche* was upon this dark and stifling night; what she was doing there; and why the precautions above referred to were deemed necessary.

As has already been mentioned, the *Psyche* was a British man-o'-war. She was a sloop, armed with fourteen long 18-pounders; and carried a crew which had originally consisted of one hundred and thirty men, but which had now been reduced by sickness and casualties to one hundred and four, all told. She was a unit in the somewhat scanty Slave Squadron which Great Britain had stationed on the West African coast for the suppression of the infamous slave-trade; and when this story opens—namely, about the middle of the year 1822—had been upon the station nearly two years, during the whole of which period I, Richard Fortescue, hailing from the neighbourhood of the good town of Plymouth, had been on board her, and now held the responsible position of senior midshipman; being, at the above date, just turned seventeen years of age.

The *Psyche* was a fine, stout, roomy, and comfortable craft of her class; but about as unsuitable for the work upon which she was now engaged as could well be, for she was a converted merchant ship, built for the purpose of carrying the biggest possible cargo that could be packed into certain prescribed limits, and consequently, as might be expected, phenomenally slow. To commission such a vessel to chase and capture the nimble craft that were usually employed to transport the unhappy blacks across the Atlantic was simply a ghastly farce, and caused us, her unfortunate crew, to be the laughing-stock of the entire coast. Yet, considering all things, we had not done so very badly; for realising, early in the commission, that we need never hope for success from the speed of our ship, we had invoked the aid of strategy, and by dint of long practice had brought the trapping of slavers almost up to the level of high art. Consequently the *Psyche*, despite the disabilities arising from her astonishing lack of speed, had acquired a certain reputation among the slave-dealing fraternity, and was as intensely detested by them as any ship on the station.

At the moment when the reader first finds himself a member of her crew the *Psyche* was lying near the mouth of the Benin river, some two miles off the shore and about twice that distance from the river's mouth, at which point we had arrived at midnight; having made our way thither in consequence of "information received," which led us to believe that a large ship was at that moment in the river taking on board a full cargo of blacks. We had drifted down to the position which we then occupied under the impulse of the last of the land-breeze, which had died out and left us becalmed some two miles short of the precise spot for which we were aiming. Still, we were near enough for all practical purposes, or believed that we were; for we thought that if a thoroughly smart look-out were maintained—and we had grown to be adepts at that sort of thing—it would be impossible for a slaver to attempt to slip out of the river without our becoming cognisant of the fact. And now, to return to my story.

Having first stolen forward and warned the watch that a craft of some sort was within hearing distance of us, and that they were therefore carefully to avoid crying out, or making any other sound that might betray our presence, I returned aft, in the same cautious manner, and was on the point of descending the companion ladder to call the captain, when *ting-ting* came the soft chiming of a ship's bell, mellowed by distance, from somewhere in the offing, evidencing—or so it seemed to me—the fact that the stranger had not as yet discovered our proximity.

The skipper, accustomed to being disturbed at all hours of the night, awoke at the first touch of my knuckles upon his cabin door.

"Yes!" he called; "what is it?"

"There is a strange craft not far from us, sir," I answered; "and Mr Perry considered that you should be apprised of the fact. We know nothing whatever about her, except that she is there; for the night is so intensely dark that we have been unable to catch the faintest glimpse of her, but we have just heard them strike two bells aboard her. We have not struck our own bell, sir, thinking—"

"Yes, of course, quite right," interrupted the skipper, as he landed with a soft thud on the floor of his state-room. "Tell Mr Perry that I'll be on deck in a brace of shakes."

He followed close at my heels up the companion ladder, having paused only long enough to slip into his nether garments, and came groping blindly out on deck.

"Phew!" he muttered, as he emerged from the companion; "it's as dark as the inside of a cow. Where are you, Mr Perry?"

"Here I am, sir; close alongside you," answered the first luff, stretching out his hand and lightly touching the skipper's arm. "Yes," he continued, "it certainly *is* dark, unusually so; so dark that I am in hopes of keeping our presence a secret from the fellow out yonder until you shall have decided what is to be done."

"Mr Fortescue tells me that you have not seen anything of him thus far," remarked the captain. "Whereabout is he, and how far off, do you reckon?"

"Somewhere away in that direction," indicated the lieutenant, with a flourish of his arm. "As to the distance—well, that is rather difficult to judge. Sound travels far on such a night as this; but I should say that the craft is not more than half a mile distant, or three-quarters, at the utmost."

"Um!" commented the captain meditatively. "I suppose it is not, by any chance, the craft which we are after, which has slipped out of the river in the darkness, eh?"

"I should scarcely think so, sir," answered Perry. "A man would literally have to be able to find his way about blindfolded to attempt to run out of the river on such a night as this. No, I am inclined to think that it is some inward-bound craft, becalmed like ourselves. We caught the sound of some order spoken on board her when we first became aware of her presence, and Mr Fortescue here was of opinion that the words used were Spanish, although the distance was too great to enable us to distinguish just what was said."

"Ay," responded the skipper; "two out of every three slavers doing business on this coast are either Spaniards or Portuguese. Now, the question is, What are we to do with regard to our unknown friend out yonder? Either she is, or is not, the craft that we are on the look-out for. If she *is*, we must take her, by hook or by crook, before the sea-breeze sets in and gives her the chance to run away from us; and that means a jaunt in the boats. On the other hand, if she is not the craft that we are after, she is still in all probability a slaver, and in any case will doubtless pay for an overhaul, which again means a boat trip. Therefore, Mr Perry, be good enough to have the hands called, and the boats got into the water as silently as possible. If the men are quick we may be able to get away, and perhaps alongside her, before the dawn breaks. I will take charge of this little pleasure-party myself, and you can stay here and keep house during my absence."

"Ay, ay, sir," answered Perry, in tones which clearly betrayed his disappointment at the arrangement come to by the skipper. "I will put matters in hand."

"Yes, do," returned the skipper; "and meanwhile I will go and dress. It shall be your turn next time, Perry," he chuckled, as he turned away to go below again.

"Ay," grumbled the lieutenant to himself, but audibly enough for me to hear. "Same old yarn—'your turn next time, Perry.' This will make the third time running that I have been left behind to 'keep house,' but there's not going to be a fourth, I'll see to that; it is time that this child stood up for his rights. Now, Mr Fortescue, have the goodness, if you please, to pass the word for all hands to arm and man boats; and to be quiet about it, too, and show no lights."

"Ay, ay, sir," I briskly responded, as I turned to hurry away; "I'll see that our lambs don't bleat too loudly. And—I suppose—that I may take it for granted that—"

"That you will make one of the 'pleasure-party'?" interrupted the lieutenant, with a laugh, as he put his disappointment and ill-humour away from him. "Oh, yes, I suppose so. At all events there will be no harm in making your preparations; the captain is pretty certain to take you."

Still on my bare feet, I hurried forward and found the boatswain.

"That you, Mr Futtock?" I inquired, as I made out his burly form.

"Ay, ay, Mr Fortescue, it's me, right enough," was the answer. "I presoom, sir, it's another boat job, eh? You heard that bell?"

"We did, Mr Futtock; yes, we heard it distinctly, seeing that we don't 'caulk' in our watch on deck," I retorted. "Yes, it's another boat affair; so be good enough to have all hands called at once, if you please. And kindly make it your personal business to see that nobody raises his voice, lets anything fall, or otherwise creates row enough to wake the dead. This is going to be a little surprise visit, you understand."

"Ay, ay, Mr Fortescue, I understands," answered Futtock, as he moved toward the open hatchway; "I'll see that the swabs don't make no noise. The man that raises his voice above a whisper won't go. That's all."

"Just one word more, Mr Futtock," I hastily interposed, as the boatswain stepped over the coaming to descend the hatchway. "You may do me a favour, if you will. Kindly ask the armourer to pick me out a nice sharp cutlass, if you please. You can bring it on deck with you when you come up."

To this request the boatswain readily enough assented; and matters being thus far satisfactorily arranged I descended to the cockroach-haunted den wherein we mids. ate and slept, to find that little Tom Copplestone—who shared my watch, and who was a special favourite of mine because of his gentle, genial disposition, and also perhaps because he hailed from the same county as myself—having overheard the conversation between Mr Perry and myself, had already come below and roused the occupants of the place, who, by the smoky rays of a flaring oil lamp that did its best to make the atmosphere quite unendurable, were hastily arraying themselves.

"Murder!" I ejaculated, as I entered the pokey little place and got my first whiff of its close, reeking, smoke-laden atmosphere; "put out that abominable lamp and light a candle or two, somebody, for pity's sake. How the dickens you fellows can manage to breathe down here I can't understand. And, boy," to the messenger outside, "pass the word for Cupid to bring us along some cocoa from the galley."

"There's no need," remarked Nugent, the master's mate, as he struggled ineffectively to find the left sleeve of his jacket. "The word has already been passed; I passed it myself when Master Cock-robin there," pointing to Copplestone, "came and roused us out. And, as to candles, I'm afraid we haven't any; the rats appear to have eaten the last two we had in the locker. However—ah, here comes the cocoa. Put the pot down there, Cupid—never mind if it *does* soil our beautiful damask table-cloth, we're going to have it washed next time we go into Sierra Leone. And just see if you can find us a biscuit or two and some butter, will ye, you black angel? Here, avast there,"—as the black was about to retire— "produce our best china breakfast-set before you go, you swab, and pour out the cocoa."

The black, a herculean Krooboy, picked up when we first arrived on the Coast, and promptly christened "Cupid" by the master's mate, who, possibly because of sundry disappointments, had developed a somewhat sardonic turn of humour, grinned appreciatively at Nugent's sorry jest respecting "our best china breakfast-set," and proceeded to rout out the heterogeneous assortment of delf and tin cups, basins, and plates that constituted the table-equipage of the midshipmen's berth, poured out a generous allowance of cocoa for each of us, and then departed, with the empty bread-barge, in quest of a supply of ship's biscuit. By the time that Cupid returned with this, we had gulped down our cocoa and were ready to go on deck. I therefore helped myself to a couple of biscuits which, breaking into pieces of convenient size by the simple process of dashing them against my elbow, I crammed into my jacket pocket, and then rushed up the ladder to the deck, leaving my companions to follow after they had snatched a hasty bite or two of food; for there was now no knowing when we might get breakfast.

Upon my arrival on deck I found the hands already mustering under the supervision of the first lieutenant, and a moment later I encountered the boatswain, who handed over to me a good serviceable ship's cutlass—worth a dozen of the ridiculous little dirks which were considered suitable weapons for midshipmen—which I promptly girded about my waist. At this moment all was bustle and animation throughout the ship, yet so sedulously had we been trained to act in perfect silence that I am certain the stealthy footfalls of the men hurrying to their stations, and the whispered words of command, were quite inaudible at a distance of twenty yards from the ship. Within a minute or two, however, even these faint sounds had subsided, the crew were all mustered, and the first lieutenant, assisted by a quartermaster who carried a carefully masked lantern, was carefully, yet rapidly, inspecting each man's weapons and equipment, scrutinising the flints in the locks of the pistols, and otherwise satisfying himself of the efficiency of our hurried preparations. While the inspection was still in progress the captain came on deck, with his sword girded to his side and a brace of pistols thrust into his belt, and stood quietly looking on until the inspection was completed and Mr Perry had reported that everything was in order.

Then the skipper announced that he would personally lead the attack in his own gig, manned by eight oarsmen, a coxswain, and a midshipman—myself; while the first cutter, manned by sixteen oarsmen, a coxswain, and a midshipman—Jack Keene—was to be commanded by Mr Purchase, the second lieutenant; and the second cutter, with twelve oarsmen, a coxswain, and Nugent, the master's mate, was to be under the command of the boatswain. Thus the attacking party was to consist of forty-five persons, all told, which was as many, I suppose, as the skipper felt justified in taking out of the ship under the circumstances.

Then ensued a busy five minutes, during which the boats were being noiselessly lowered and manned, the oars muffled, and every possible precaution observed to enable us to take our unseen but doubtless vigilant enemy unawares. This was just then regarded as of especial importance, for at the time of which I am now writing the traffic in slaves was regarded as piracy, and rendered its perpetrators liable to capital punishment, in consequence of which almost every slaver went heavily armed, and her crew, knowing that the halter was already about their necks, resisted capture by every means which their ingenuity could devise, whenever they had the chance, and often fought with desperate valour.

As I hurried aft to attend to the lowering of the gig, which hung from davits over the stern, a hand was suddenly laid upon my arm, and, turning, I found myself confronted by Cupid, the Krooboy servant who "did for us" in the midshipmen's berth. His eyes were aglow with excitement, he carried a short-handled hatchet, with a head somewhat bigger and heavier than that of a ship's tomahawk, in his hand, and he was naked, save for a pair of dungaree trousers, the legs of which were rolled up above his knees.

"Mr Fortescue, sar, I fit for go in dem boat wid you, sar," he whispered eagerly.

"Yes, I quite believe it, Cupid," I replied. "But you know perfectly well that I cannot give you permission to join the gig's crew. If the captain had been anxious to have the pleasure of your company I feel sure that he would have mentioned the fact. Besides, if you should happen to be killed, what would become of us poor midshipmen?"

A suppressed chuckle, and a gleam of white teeth through the darkness, betrayed Cupid's appreciation of the compliment subtly conveyed in the suggestion that the budding admirals inhabiting the midshipmen's berth aboard H.M.S. *Psyche* would suffer, should he unhappily be slain in the impending conflict, but he hastened to reassure me.

"No fear, sar," he whispered. "Dem slaber no lib for kill me. I, Cupid, too much plenty black for see in de dark; an' if dey no see me, dey no kill. Savvey? *Please*, Mr Fortescue, sar. I no lib for fight too much plenty long time."

"Look here, Cupid," I replied. "It is no use for you to ask me for permission to go in the gig, for I cannot give it you. But,"—meaningly—"if you were to stow yourself away in the eyes of the gig it is just possible that the captain might not notice you until we had got too far from the ship to turn back. Only don't let me see you doing it, that's all."

"Dat all right, sar," answered the black, with a sigh of extreme content. "If you no look for dem Cupid you no see um." And he turned and ostentatiously walked away forward.

The boats having been gently and carefully lowered into the water without a splash, or so much as a single tell-tale squeak from the tackle-blocks—the pins and bushes of which were habitually overhauled at frequent intervals and kept well lubricated with a mixture of melted tallow and plumbago—the crews took their places, each man carefully depositing his drawn cutlass on the bottom-boards between his feet, and we shoved off with muffled oars, the three boats pulling abreast, with about a ship's length between each; so that if perchance we should happen to be seen, we should present as small a target as possible to aim at.

8

We pulled slowly and with the utmost caution, for the twofold reason that we had not yet caught sight of our quarry and only knew in a general sort of way that she was somewhere to seaward of us, and because we were anxious to avoid premature discovery from the splash of our oars. It was of course perfectly right and proper that we should observe all the precautions that I have indicated; for if we could but contrive to creep up alongside the stranger without being detected, it would undoubtedly mean the prevention of much loss of life. But, personally, I had very little hope of our being able to do so; for the night was so breathlessly still that, if any sort of look-out at all were being kept aboard the stranger—and slavers usually slept with one eye open—they must surely have caught some hint of our proximity, careful as we had been to maintain as complete silence as possible while making our preparations. Besides, as ill-luck would have it, the water was in an unusually brilliant phosphorescent condition just then, the slightest disturbance of it caused a silvery glow that could be seen a mile away; and, be as silent as we might, the dip of our oars and the passage of the boats through the water set up such a blaze as could not fail to betray us, should a man happen to glance in our direction.

At length, when we had pulled about half a mile, as nearly as I could judge, I detected a slight suspicion of a softening in the velvety blackness of the sky in the eastern quarter. It brightened, even as I looked, and a solitary star, low down in the sky, seemed to flicker, faintly and more faintly, for half a dozen seconds, and then disappear.

"The dawn is coming, sir," I whispered to the skipper, by whose side I was sitting, "and in another minute or two we ought to—ah! there she is. Do you see her, sir?" And I pointed in the direction of a faint, ghostlike blotch that had suddenly appeared at a spot some three points on our port bow.

"Where away?" demanded the skipper, instinctively raising his hand to shade his eyes; but he had scarcely lifted it to the height of his shoulder when he too caught sight of the object.

"Ay," he exclaimed, "I see her. And a big craft she is, too; a barque, apparently. Surely that cannot be the craft that we are after? Yet it looks very like her. If so, she must have slipped out of the river with the last of the land-breeze last night, and lain becalmed all night where she is. Now what are the other boats about that they have not seen her? Parkinson," to the coxswain, "show that lantern for a moment to the other boats, but take care to shield it with—ah! never mind, there are both their lights. Give way, men. Put me alongside under her mizen chains, my lad. Either side; I don't care which."

While the captain had been speaking the faint, ghostly glimmer that I had detected had resolved itself into the spectral semblance of a large ship clothed from her trucks down with canvas upon which the rapidly growing light of the advancing dawn was falling and thus rendering it just barely visible against its dark background of sky.

In the tropics day comes and goes with a rush, and, even while the skipper had been speaking, the object which had first revealed itself to me, a minute earlier, as a mere wan, ghostly suggestion had assumed solidity and definiteness of form, and now stood out against the sky behind her as a full-rigged ship of some seven hundred and fifty tons burthen, her hull painted bright green, and coppered to the water-line. She was lying stern-on to us, and sat deep in the water, from which latter fact one inferred that she had her cargo of slaves on board and had doubtless, as the skipper conjectured, come out of the river with the last of the land-breeze during the previous night, and had remained becalmed near us, and, we hoped, quite unaware of our proximity all night. She was now within a cable's length of the boats, but, lying as she was, dead stern-on to us, we in the gig were unable to see how many guns she carried, which was, however, an advantage to us, since, however many guns she might mount on her broadsides, she could bring none of them to bear upon us. We saw, however, that she carried two stern-chasers—long nine's, apparently—and now, in the hope of dashing alongside before those two guns could be cast loose and brought to bear upon us, the captain stood up in the stern-sheets of the gig and waved his arm to the other boats as a signal to them to give way—for, with the coming of the daylight we could not possibly hope to remain undiscovered above a second or two longer.

Indeed the boats' crews had scarcely bent their backs in response to the signal when there arose a sudden startled outcry on board the ship, followed by a volley of hurried commands and the hasty trampling of feet upon her decks. But we were so close to her, when discovered, and the surprise was so complete, that her crew had no time to do anything effective in the way of defence; and in little over a couple of minutes we had swept up alongside, clambered in over her lofty bulwarks, driven her crew below, and were in full possession of the *Doña Isabella* of Havana, mounting twelve guns, with a crew of forty-six Spaniards, Portuguese, and half-castes, constituting as ruffianly a lot as I had ever met with. She had a cargo of seven hundred and forty negroes on board, and was far and away the finest prize that had thus far fallen to the lot of the *Psyche*. So valuable, indeed, was she that Captain Harrison decided not to trust her entirely to a prize crew, but to escort her to Sierra Leone in the corvette; and some two hours later, having meanwhile made all the necessary dispositions, the two craft trimmed sail with the first of the sea-breeze and hauled up for Sierra Leone, where we arrived a week later after an uneventful passage.

Chapter Two.

In the Fernan Vaz River.

While we were awaiting the formal condemnation of the *Doña Isabella* by the Mixed Commission, and the trial of her crew upon the charge of piracy, Captain Harrison, our skipper, busily employed himself, as was his wont, in hunting up information relative to the movements, present and prospective, of the slavers upon the coast. And this was not quite so difficult to do as might at first be imagined; for, Sierra Leone being the headquarters, so to speak, of the British Slave Squadron, the persons actually engaged in the slave-trade found that it paid them well to maintain agents there for the sole purpose of picking up every possible item of information relative to the movements and doings of that squadron. For it not unfrequently happened that, to those behind the scenes, an apparently trivial and seemingly quite worthless bit of information, an imprudent word dropped by an unwary officer respecting one of our vessels, enabled the acute ones to calculate so closely that they often succeeded in making a dash into some river, shipping a cargo of slaves, and getting clear away to sea again only a few hours before our cruisers put in an appearance on the spot. And in the same way our own officers, by frequenting, in disguise, the haunts of the slavers and their agents, very often succeeded in catching a hint that, carefully followed up, led to most important captures being made. It was, indeed, through a hint so acquired that we had been put upon the track of the *Doña Isabella*.

Now, our own skipper, Captain Harrison, was particularly keen upon this sort of work, and was exceptionally well qualified to achieve success in it. For, in the first place, he was a West Indian by birth, being the son of a Trinidad sugar-planter, and he consequently spoke Creole Spanish as fluently as he did his mother tongue. Also his physical characteristics were such as to be of the greatest assistance to him in such enterprises; for he was tall, lean, and muscular, of swarthy complexion, with thick, black, curly hair, and large, black, flashing eyes, suggesting that he carried a touch of the tar-brush, although, as a matter of fact, he had not a drop of negro blood in him. He was a man of dauntless courage, knowing not the meaning of fear, and absolutely revelling in situations of the most extreme peril, yet gifted with quite as much discretion as was needful for a man entrusted with heavy responsibilities involving the lives of many of his fellow-men. He never sought danger for danger's sake alone, and never embarked in an enterprise which his reason assured him was hopelessly impracticable, but, on the other hand, he never hesitated to undertake the most perilous task if he believed he could see a way to its successful accomplishment. It was his habit to assume a variety of disguises in which he would haunt the third and fourth rate taverns of Freetown, especially patronised by the slave-dealing fraternity, and mingling freely with these gentry, would boldly express his own views, adopted, of course, for the occasion, upon the various matters affecting the trade, or discuss with them the most promising schemes for baffling the efforts of the British cruisers. He had noticed, very early in his career as an officer of the Slave Squadron, that it was always the *British* who constituted the *bête noire* of the slavers; the French they feared very little; the Americans not at all.

These little incursions into the enemy's territory Captain Harrison conducted with consummate boldness and skill, and with a considerable measure of success, for it was quite a favourite amusement of his to devise and suggest schemes of a particularly alluring character which, when adopted by the enemy, he of course triumphantly circumvented without difficulty. There was only one fault to find with this propensity on the part of our skipper, but in my humble judgment it constituted a serious one. It was this. Captain Harrison's personality was a distinctly striking one; he was the kind of man who, once seen, is not easily forgotten; and I greatly dreaded that some day, sooner or later, the reckless frequenter of the low-class Freetown taverns would be identified as one and the same with the captain of H.M.S. *Psyche*, who was of course frequently to be seen about the streets in the uniform of a British naval captain. Indeed I once took the liberty of delicately hinting at this possibility; but the skipper laughed at the idea; he had, it appeared, the most implicit faith in his disguises, which included, amongst other things, a huge false moustache of most ferocious appearance, and an enormous pair of gold earrings.

We had been at Sierra Leone a little over a fortnight, and our business there was just completed, when the skipper came aboard on a certain afternoon in a state of the highest good-humour, occasioned, as soon transpired, by the fact that he had succeeded in obtaining full particulars of an exceptionally grand *coup* that had been planned by a number of slavers in conjunction, which they were perfectly confident of pulling off triumphantly.

It appeared, from his story, that intelligence had just been received of the successful conclusion of a great slave-hunting raid into the interior by a certain King Olomba, who had recently returned in triumph to his town of Olomba, on the left bank of the Fernan Vaz river, bringing with him nearly three thousand negroes, of whom over two thousand were males, all in prime condition. This information having reached the slavers' agents at Sierra Leone through the mysterious channels by which news often travels in Africa, an effort of quite exceptional magnitude was to be made to get at least the two thousand males out of the country at one fell swoop; the present being regarded as an almost uniquely favourable opportunity for the accomplishment of this object, for the reason that the *Psyche* was just then the only ship which could by any possibility interfere with the scheme. And in the event of her happening to put in an inopportune appearance on that part of the coast at the critical moment—as she had a knack of doing, in the most unaccountable manner—she was to be decoyed away from the spot by the simple process of dispatching to sea a certain notorious schooner well-known to be in the trade, but which, for this occasion only, was to have no slaves or slave fittings or adjuncts on board, and after a chase of some two or three hundred miles to the southward, was to permit herself to be caught, only to be released again, of course, after an exhaustive overhaul.

It was an admirable scheme, beautifully simple, and could scarcely fail to achieve complete success, but for the fact that Captain Harrison had contrived to obtain full particulars of it, and therefore knew exactly how to frustrate the plan. His plot was as simple as that of the slavers: he would proceed in the *Psyche* to the scene of operations, and when the decoy schooner made her appearance she would be permitted to go on her way unmolested, while a boat expedition would be dispatched up the river to the town of Olomba, where the vessels actually engaged in shipping the two thousand blacks would be captured *flagrante delicto*.

Naturally we were all thrown into a high state of jubilation at the receipt of this intelligence; for it promised us a slice of good luck of such magnitude as very seldom fell to the lot of a single cruiser. To convey two thousand negroes across the Atlantic at once would necessitate the employment of at least three large ships, the value of which might be roughly calculated at, upon the very lowest estimate, ten thousand pounds each, or thirty thousand pounds in all, besides which there would be the head-money upon two thousand negroes, amounting altogether to quite a nice little sum in prize-money for a cruise of probably less than a month's duration. Oh, how we chuckled as we pictured to ourselves the effect which the news of so magnificent a *coup* would create upon the minds of the rest of the Slave Squadron. The *Psyche*, from her phenomenal lack of speed, and general unsuitability for the service upon which she was employed, had, with her crew, become the butt and laughing-stock of every stupid and scurrilous jester on the coast, and many a time had we been made to writhe under the lash of some more than ordinarily envenomed gibe; but now the laugh was to be on our side; we were going to demonstrate to those shallow, jeering wits the superiority of brains over a clean pair of heels.

Of course we were all in a perfect fever of impatience to get to sea and make the best of our way to the scene of action, lest haply we should arrive too late and find the birds flown; but the skipper retained his coolness and would permit nothing to be done that could by any possibility suggest to the slavers the idea that the faintest hint of their audacious scheme had been allowed to get abroad. He insisted that we had plenty of time and to spare, and actually remained in harbour three whole days after the information had reached him. Then, on the morning of the fourth day, we weighed and stood out to sea, beating off the land against the sea-breeze until we ran into the calm belt between the sea-breeze and the trade-wind. Here we remained motionless for more than an hour until the trade-wind gradually ate its way inshore and reached us, when we ran right out to sea until we had sunk the land astern of us. Then we hauled up to the southward on a taut bowline, and, under easy canvas, made our leisurely way toward the mouth of the Fernan Vaz river, off which we arrived five days later, making the land from the masthead about an hour before sunset.

All that night, the whole of the next day, and all the night following we remained hove-to under topsails, jib, and spanker, dodging to and fro athwart the mouth of the river, with a man on the main-royal yard, during the hours of daylight, to give us timely notice of the appearance of the craft which was to play the part of decoy; while with the approach of nightfall we made sail and beat in to within a distance of some three miles of the coast, running off into the offing again an hour before daylight. At length, when we had hung upon the tenterhooks of suspense for close upon forty hours, and were beginning to fear that the captain, in his resolve to cut matters as fine as possible, had overdone the thing and allowed the quarry to escape, we were gladdened by the hail from aloft of—

"Sail he! A large schooner just comin' out o' the river, sir."

"Ay, ay," answered the first lieutenant, whose watch it happened to be. "Just keep your eye on her, my lad, and let me know how she steers when she is clear of the bar."

We were heading to the southward at the time, and were about three miles south of the river entrance, and some sixteen miles off the land; by pretending therefore not to see her for the next quarter of an hour or so, and keeping the *Psyche* still heading to the southward, we should afford the stranger an excellent opportunity to secure a sufficient offing to make good her escape. Then we would heave about, make sail in chase, drive her off the coast, and work in as close to the river's mouth as we dared venture, when the ship was to be brought to an anchor, and the boats manned, armed, and dispatched into the river.

Meanwhile, as previously arranged, Captain Harrison was aroused, and informed of the fact that the decoy schooner, or what was assumed to be such, had made her appearance and was now fairly at sea, steering a little to the northward of west under a heavy press of sail; and close upon the heels of the returning messenger the worthy skipper himself appeared. He sprang upon a gun-carriage and peered intently shoreward under the shade of his hand; but only the upper canvas of the stranger was visible from our deck; and he impatiently hailed the look-out aloft to give him a detailed description of the vessel. The fellow in the cross-trees happened, however, to be a poor sort of unintelligent fellow, and could say very little about the craft beyond stating the fact that she was a schooner, painted black; that she sat deep in the water, showed an immense spread of canvas, and appeared to be very fast.

"I have no sort of doubt that yonder schooner is the craft whose duty it is to draw us off the coast and leave the way clear for the other fellows to get out to sea," he said. "But I should like to have a somewhat better description of her than that 'sodger' up aloft there seems able to give."

He glanced round the deck and his eye fell upon me.

"Ah, Mr Fortescue," he exclaimed, "you will doubtless be able to do what I want. Just slip down into my cabin; you will find my glass hanging above the head of my bunk. Throw the strap of it over your shoulder, and shin up alongside that fellow in the cross-trees; take a good look at the stranger; and report to me any peculiarities that you may detect in her, will ye."

"Ay, ay, sir," I replied, touching my hat; and five minutes later I was sitting in the main-topmast cross-trees, with the long barrel of the telescope steadied against the topmast-head, and my eye glued to the eye-piece. From this elevation I commanded a complete, if distant, view of the low land about the river entrance, with its fringe of mangrove trees running away inland, the sand hummocks, sparsely clothed with coarse, reedy grass and trailing plants, and the endless line of the surf-beaten African beach. Also through the skipper's powerful lenses I obtained a most excellent view of the strange schooner, from her trucks to her water-line, including such details as I could have discerned with the naked eye at a distance of about half a mile. I saw, for example, that, as the look-out had already reported, she was a large schooner—I estimated her to be one hundred and eighty tons burthen at the least; I verified the statement that her hull was painted all black from the rail to the top of her copper; that she showed an enormous spread of canvas; and that she sat very low in the water. But I noticed a few other peculiarities as well; I saw that her bowsprit was painted black, while her jib-booms were scraped and varnished; that her foremast, fore-topmast, and fore-topgallant and royal-mast were varnished, while the mast heads were painted black, and that the whole of the mainmast, from the cap down, was painted *white*, which was a peculiarity that ought to have been sufficient to identify her as far as one could see her. And so it was; for the moment that I reported it the skipper hailed—

13

"Thank you, Mr Fortescue; that will do; you may come down. Or—hold on a minute. Is the stranger far enough out of the river to enable her to get clear away, think ye?"

"She is fully a mile from the mouth of the river, sir," I answered.

"Ah, that will do, then, thank you; you may both come down," answered the skipper. And as I swung myself down through the cross-trees to the topmast rigging, I heard him give the order to "Wear ship and make sail."

Five minutes later the *Psyche* was heading to the northward, close-hauled on the port tack, under all plain sail to her royals, doing nearly seven knots, and laying a course that, with nice steering, would just enable us to fetch the river's mouth handsomely without breaking tacks. The schooner, meanwhile, was romping along at a pace of at least twelve knots per hour, on the starboard tack, throwing the spray over her weather bow to half the height of her lower yard, and shaping a course which would enable her to pass us at a distance of fully eight miles dead to windward. We allowed her to go on her way unmolested.

It was just noon when, having arrived off the mouth of the river, we made a flying moor of it, letting go the first and then the second bower anchor in ten fathoms, at a distance of about one and a half miles from the shore, and at a spot from which the river mouth and perhaps half a mile of the river itself were in plain view. The town of King Olomba, it was understood, was situated at a distance of about thirty-two miles from our anchorage; and as the captain was anxious that the journey should be made at an easy pace, so that the men might arrive comparatively fresh, and in fit condition for the rather stiff bit of work that lay at the end of it, eight hours were to be allowed for the passage of the boats to their destination. And as it was highly undesirable that the expedition should be unduly exposed in the boats to the pestiferous effects of the miasmatic night-fogs which gather upon most of the West African rivers after sunset, it had already been arranged that the attacking party should not start until the following morning, at an hour which would enable us to reach the scene of operations in time to make a reconnaissance and arrange the plan of attack by nightfall. The remainder of that day was therefore employed in getting the boats ready, stocking them with three days' rations of provisions and water, overhauling the boat guns and slinging them ready for lowering, filling the ammunition boxes, sharpening cutlasses, fixing new flints to the pistols, where necessary, and generally completing our preparations. We also sent down royal and topgallant yards and housed the topgallant-masts, in order that, should it by any chance come on to blow heavily from the westward during our absence the ship might ride the more easily at her anchors. We also made preparation, in view of the foregoing contingency, for backing the bowers with the two stream anchors, and otherwise made every possible preparation for the safety of the ship during our absence; for the expedition in which we were about to engage was one of very considerable importance, and the task which we had set ourselves to perform was so formidable that, in order to insure success, it would be necessary to employ practically the entire ship's company, leaving the vessel in charge of the second lieutenant and only enough hands to keep a look-out and perform such tasks as, for example, the letting go of the stream anchors in case of necessity, the paying out of the additional amount of cable, the keeping of the ship reasonably clean, and so on.

On the following morning, having washed decks and partaken of breakfast, the hands were mustered and inspected, the boats lowered, guns secured in the bows of the launch, pinnace, and first and second cutters, ammunition boxes passed down, masts stepped, sails cast loose, yards hooked on, and, in short, everything made ready for a start. Then we went down over the side and took our places in the boats to which we were severally appointed, the captain going as usual in his own gig, while Mr Perry, the first luff, was in command of the launch; Mr Hoskins, the third lieutenant, commanding the pinnace; Mr Marline, the master, having charge of the first cutter, while Mr Tompson, the gunner, commanded the second cutter. The skipper took me, as he generally did, in his own boat, but the other three mids. were left on board the *Psyche* to keep Mr Purchase company. For the rest, Nugent, the master's mate, went with the first lieutenant, while Peter Futtock, the boatswain, accompanied the third lieutenant in the pinnace.

We mustered ninety all told, and were none too many for the work that we had undertaken to do, which was—to capture three, if not four, large ships; capture and demolish the shore batteries which the slavers very frequently erected for the defence of their strongholds; and also, most likely, fight King Olomba and a whole flotilla of war canoes. The task was indeed a formidable one; the more so that we, the attacking party, would be, at least at the beginning of the fight, huddled closely together in boats, while our antagonists would have all the advantage of roomy decks to move about on, and steady gun platforms from which to pour in their fire, to say nothing of a tremendous superiority in point of numbers. We thought nothing of all this, however; we were going to have a change from the monotony of shipboard life; we should be certain to see new sights of a more or less interesting character; there was the excitement and exhilaration of a stiff fight awaiting us at the end of our journey; and, finally, there was the prospect of a pocketful of prize-money as a wind-up to the whole affair. What more could any reasonable individual desire?

Like most African rivers, the Fernan Vaz has a bar, but the sea breaks upon it only when the wind blows fresh from the north-west, owing to the fact that as far up as the town of Olomba the river flows parallel to the line of coast, being separated from the open Atlantic by a low, sandy peninsula, varying from one to three miles in breadth, terminating in a spit which ordinarily shelters the bar from the rollers, leaving a narrow channel of unbroken water, wide enough to enable a couple of craft of moderate tonnage to pass each other comfortably.

And well was it for us that this was the case; for as we approached the river's mouth we saw that the ground-swell was rapidly increasing in weight, and that the surf was breaking upon the beach with such violence that if it happened to be also breaking upon the bar it would be quite useless for us to attempt to enter the river. Indeed, so formidable did the appearance of the surf at length become that the captain ordered the rest of the boats to heave-to, while we in the gig went ahead to reconnoitre and inspect the condition of the bar. This was a bit of work for which the gig was peculiarly well adapted, for she was a beautifully modelled boat, double-ended, with a long flat floor—a splendid sailer, and a boat which would claw off a lee shore in almost any weather, the skipper having had her fitted with a good, deep, false keel.

The wind was blowing a moderately fresh breeze from the westward at the time, thus, the rest of the boats having hove-to, it did not take us very long to run in far enough to get a sight of the bar. This was a rather trying experience for the nerves of us all; for the surf was pounding on the beach ahead of us in a constant succession of towering walls of water, that reared themselves to a height of fully thirty feet ere they curled over and broke in thunder so deafening that we presently found it impossible to make our voices heard above its continuous roar. But the skipper, standing up in the stern-sheets, soon detected the smooth, narrow strip of unbroken water, and directed the coxswain to shift his helm for it. I sprang up on a thwart and waved a small white flag as a signal to the other boats to fill away and follow us; and as soon as we had reached the very middle of the channel we rounded-to and lowered our sail, remaining where we were to act as a guide to the other boats.

Keeping our position with the aid of a couple of oars thrown over to enable us to stem the out-flowing current, which we now began to feel, we allowed the other boats to pass in over the bar and reach the smooth water before us; then, hoisting our sail again, we followed them in and presently resumed our position at the head of the line.

The change from the scene of wind-flecked blue sea, stately march of the swell, and thunderous roar and creaming froth of the breakers outside to the oil-smooth, mud-laden, strong-smelling river, with its tiny, swirling eddies here and there, its mangrove-lined banks, and its silence, through which the roar of the surf came to us over the intervening sand spit, mellowed and subdued by distance, was so marked that, although this was by no means my first experience of that kind of thing, I found myself rubbing my eyes as though I were by no means certain that I was awake; and I noticed others doing the same. A sharp word from the skipper, however, cautioning all hands to maintain a smart look-out, soon brought to us the realisation of our surroundings; for the river here was narrow, being not more than half a mile wide, with a number of small islets dotted about it, any one of which might prove to be the hiding-place of a formidable foe. When at length we had passed these without interference, and had reached the point where the river began to widen out somewhat, we were no better off, but rather the worse; for here the stream was encumbered with extensive sandbanks, to avoid which we were compelled to approach the margin of the river so closely that a well-arranged ambush might have practically annihilated us before we could have effected a landing through the thick, viscid mud and the almost impenetrable growth of mangroves that divided the waters of the river from the solid ground of the shore. Fortunately for us, the slavers appeared unaccountably to have overlooked the admirable opportunities thus afforded for frustrating an attack; or possibly, as we thought, it was that they had fully relied upon the power of the decoy schooner to draw us away from the coast, and thus leave the way free for them to escape.

The passage of this part of the river occupied us until noon, and was rather trying to the nerves of all hands, for not only were we constantly exposed to attack by the slavers, but there were the natives also to be reckoned with; and these, as we all knew, had a most objectionable habit of using poisoned arrows, the slightest wound from which was invariably followed by death after some eight to twelve hours of dreadful suffering. Shortly after noon we emerged from these natural entanglements into a long reach of the river where the stream expanded to a width of some three and a half miles, with a narrow deep-water channel running about midway between the banks. Here we were quite free from any possibility of ambush of any kind; and with a sigh of intense relief the captain gave the word to pipe to dinner.

About four o'clock in the afternoon we arrived at a point where the river again narrowed to a width of about a mile; but some two miles farther on it again widened out, and changed its direction, trending away almost due east, or about at right angles to its former course; and this, according to the information in the skipper's possession, indicated that we were nearing our destination. Drawing from his pocket a sketch chart which he had already consulted several times during our passage up the river, he again studied it intently for several minutes, carefully comparing the configurations delineated upon it with our actual surroundings; then, apparently satisfied with the result, he refolded the paper, returned it to his pocket, and directed the coxswain to bear away a couple of points toward a projecting point—which we afterwards discovered to be the western extremity of an islet—on the far side of the river. As we approached the spot for which we were heading it became apparent that there were two islets instead of one between us and the river bank; and a quarter of an hour later the gig, with the rest of the flotilla following her, glided in between these two islets, and, lowering her sails, made the signal for the other boats to anchor.

The boats were now completely concealed from all possible observation, for we soon saw that the islets between which we were anchored consisted merely of mud-banks thickly overgrown with mangroves, and absolutely uninhabitable even by natives; for there did not appear to be an inch of ground upon either of the islets sufficiently solid to support even a reed hut, while the mangroves were tall enough and grew densely enough to hide the boats from all possible observation from the mainland. The only question which now troubled us was whether the presence of the boats in the river had already been observed. If the slavers had placed absolute confidence in the success of their plan to draw us away from the coast by means of the decoy schooner, they might not have troubled to keep a look-out; but if they were as cautious as such gentry usually are, and had left nothing to chance, it would be scarcely possible for the approach of the boats to have passed undetected. This was the question to which the captain was now going to seek an answer.

Chapter Three.

At the Camma Lagoon.

Distant about a mile from our hiding-place, there was, according to the captain's rough sketch map, a small peninsula enclosing a little bay, or creek, at the inner extremity of which was situated King Olomba's town; and it was here that we were led to believe we should find the slavers busily engaged in shipping their human cargoes. And truly, as seen from the boats, the ingenuity of man could scarcely have devised a more perfect spot whereat to conduct the infamous traffic; for the configuration of the land was such that boats, entering the river merely on an exploring expedition, without having first obtained, like ourselves, special information, would never have suspected the existence of the creek, or of the town which lay concealed within it. Nor would it have been possible to detect the presence of slave craft in the creek; for the peninsula which masked it was thickly overgrown with lofty trees which would effectually conceal all but the upper spars of a ship, and these would doubtless be struck or housed while she was lying in the creek.

The skipper having explained to the officers in command of the other boats what he intended to do, and given them instructions how to act in the event of certain contingencies arising, the gig's crew manned their oars, and we pulled away in the direction of the peninsula, which we reached in the course of a few minutes. Now our real troubles began, for our object was not only to reach the peninsula but also to land upon and walk across it until a spot could be found from which, unseen ourselves, we could obtain a clear view of the creek and everything in it, and upon approaching the shore of the peninsula we discovered that, in common with as much of the river bank as we had yet seen, it consisted, first of all, of a wide belt of soft, fathomless mud overgrown with mangrove trees; the mud being of such a consistency that to attempt to walk upon it would mean being swallowed up and suffocated in it, for a sixteen-foot oar could be thrust perpendicularly into it with scarcely any effort, although when one of the men incautiously tried the experiment, it was only with the utmost difficulty that he was able to withdraw the oar, so tenaciously did the mud cling to it. Yet it was not sufficiently liquid to allow of the gig being forced through it, even if the thickly clustering mangrove roots would have permitted of such a proceeding. The only alternative left to us, therefore, was to endeavour to reach solid ground by clambering over the slippery mangrove roots, with the possibility that at any moment one or another of us might lose our footing, fall into the mud, and be swallowed up by it. However, "needs must" under certain circumstances, the skipper and I therefore scrambled out of the boat—taking Cupid with us to search out the way and carry a small coil of light line in case it should be wanted—and proceeded cautiously to claw our way like so many parrots, over and among the gnarled and twisted roots of the mangrove trees, the Krooboy leading the way, leaping and swinging himself with marvellous agility from tree to tree, while we followed

17

slowly in his wake, as often as not being obliged to make a slip-rope of the line to enable us to cross some exceptionally wide or awkward gap. In this manner, after about half an hour's arduous toil, with the perspiration pouring out of us until our clothes were saturated with it, while we were driven nearly frantic by the attacks of the mosquitoes and stinging flies that beset us by thousands, and could by no means be driven away, we contrived at length to reach soil firm enough to support our weight, and, some five minutes later, the solid ground itself.

But, even now, our troubles were only half over; for after we had crossed the peninsula we still found it impossible to discover a spot from which the interior of the creek could be seen without laying out upon the roots of the mangrove trees that bordered the inner as well as the outer shore of the peninsula, the wearisome business of crawling and climbing had therefore all to be gone over again, with the result that the sun was close upon setting before we had reached a spot from which a clear view of the entire creek could be obtained. And then we had the unspeakable mortification of discovering that the expedition must result in failure; for, save a few canoes, the creek was innocent of craft of every description—*there were no slavers in it*! Moreover, the so-called town of King Olomba consisted only of about fifty miserable native huts in the very last stage of sordidness and dilapidation; and there was no sign that a slave barracoon had ever existed near the place.

The captain stared across the water as though he found it quite impossible to believe his eyes. Then he drew the sketch map from his pocket and once more studied it attentively, muttering to himself the while. Finally he sat himself down upon a knot of twisted roots, with his back against the trunk of the tree, and, spreading the sketch wide open on his knee, beckoned me to place myself beside him.

"Just come here and look at this map, Mr Fortescue," he said, and he spoke with the air and in the tones of a man who is so utterly dazed with disappointment that he begins to doubt the evidence of his own senses. "Just give me your opinion, will ye. I cannot understand this business at all. This map, although only a free-hand sketch, seems to me to be perfectly accurate. There, you see, is the mouth of the river, just as we found it; there are the little islets that we passed immediately after getting inside; there are the dry mud-banks; and there, you see, the river widens out, in precise accordance with our experience; here it narrows again at the bend; there is where the boats are lying concealed; and this," laying his finger upon a particular part of the sketch, "is the creek that we are now looking at; and there is the town of Olomba. It all seems to me to be absolutely correct. Does it not appear so to you?"

"Certainly, sir," I answered. "The sketch answers in every particular to what we have seen since entering the river—answers to it so perfectly, indeed, that it might have been copied from a carefully plotted survey."

"Exactly," assented the skipper. "Yet it is nothing of the kind; for with my own eyes I saw it drawn from memory by a man whom I happened to meet in one of the third-rate hotels in Freetown, which are frequented by the masters and mates of palm-oil traders and the like. I happened to hear him mention that he had been in and out of the Fernan Vaz at least a dozen times, in his search for cargo along the coast, so I waited until the people with whom he was talking had left him, and then I entered into conversation with him, finally inducing him to furnish me with this sketch."

"And was it from him, sir, that you also obtained the information upon the strength of which you determined upon this expedition?" I asked.

"Oh, no," answered the skipper. "I had that from quite a different source, in a very different kind of house. The people who told me about King Olomba's raid, and the plans laid by the slavers for carrying off the prisoners, were slavers themselves; and they told me of the scheme because they believed me to be the master of a slaver waiting for information from the Senegal river. The cream of the joke was that these fellows should have told me—*me*, the captain of the *Psyche*—that the scheme had been carefully planned with the express object of putting the *Psyche* upon a false scent and so getting her out of the way while the negroes were being shipped."

"Yet there seems to have been something wrong somewhere, sir," I ventured to suggest. "But it is not with your map; that appears to be marvellously accurate for a mere free-hand sketch; there is no attempt at deception apparent there. This creek that we are looking at is undoubtedly the one shown on your map, and there is King Olomba's town, precisely in the position indicated on the sketch; the assumption therefore is that the man who drew the map for you was dealing quite honestly with you. The misleading information, consequently must, it appears to me, have come from the others; as indeed is the case, seeing that they led you to believe that you would find at least three or four large ships in the creek, whereas there are none."

"That is perfectly true," concurred the skipper. "Yet I quite understood my informants to say that they were the persons who had formulated the scheme."

"I suppose, sir," said I, giving voice to an idea that had been gradually shaping itself in my brain, "it is not possible that the people who were so singularly frank with you happened to recognise you as Captain Harrison of H.M.S. *Psyche*, and gave you that bit of information with the deliberate purpose of misleading you and putting you upon a false scent, in order that while you are searching for them here they may have the opportunity to carry out their scheme elsewhere? Their story may in the main be perfectly true, but if by any chance they should have happened to recognise you it would not be very difficult for them to substitute the name of the Fernan Vaz for that of some other river, and to mention King Olomba instead of some other king."

"N–o–o," said the skipper dubiously; "it would not. Yet I cannot see why, if they had recognised me, they should have gone to the trouble of spinning an elaborate yarn merely to deceive me. It would have been just as easy for them to have knifed me, for there were seven of them, while I was quite alone. No, I don't quite see—"

"Do you not, sir?" I interrupted with a smile.

"I do. I see quite clearly two very excellent reasons why they did not resort to the rough and ready method of the knife. In the first place, these fellows attach a ridiculously high value to their own skins, and never seem to imperil them when an alternative will serve their purpose equally well; and although they were seven to one, if they really recognised you they would know perfectly well that, while the ultimate result of a fight would probably be in their favour, you would certainly not perish alone; and I suppose none of them were particularly anxious to accompany you into the Great Beyond. And, apart from that, they would know quite well that were the captain of a British man-o'-war to go a-missing there would be such a stir among their rookeries that soon there would be no rookeries left. Oh, no, sir! glad as they might be to put you quietly out of the way if they had the chance, depend upon it the last thing that they would dream of would be to attempt anything of the sort in Sierra Leone."

"Well, well, well, perhaps you are right, young gentleman, perhaps you are right. You seem to have quite a gift for reasoning things out," replied the skipper, as he pocketed his map and hove himself up into a standing position. "But it is high time that we should get under way, for the sun is setting, and we shall have all our work cut out to find our road back to the boat. Do you think you will be able to find the gig, Cupid?"

"Yes, I fit, sar," answered the Krooboy. "But we mus' make plenty haste; for dem darkness he come too much plenty soon, an' if we slip and fall into dem mud we lib for die one time."

"Ay, ay," answered the skipper, with an involuntary shudder at the hideous fate thus tersely sketched by Cupid; "I know that, my lad, without any telling; so heave ahead as smartly as you like."

And therewith we started upon our return journey with all speed; striding, leaping, slipping, and scrambling from root to root, Cupid leading the way, I following, and the skipper bringing up the rear, until at length we stood upon solid ground once more. But by this time not only had the sun set but the dusk was gathering about us like a curtain, while star after star came twinkling out from the rapidly darkening blue overhead, and the foliage of the trees that hemmed us in on every side was changing, even as we stood and watched while recovering our breath, from olive to deepest black. Now, too, we were beset, even more pertinaciously than before, by the myriads of mosquitoes, sand flies, gnats, and other winged biting creatures with which the islet swarmed; to say nothing of ants; indeed it almost seemed as though every individual insect upon that particular patch of soil and vegetation had scented us out and, having found us, was quite determined that we should never escape them alive. When presently we again began to move, it seemed impossible to take a single step without tripping over a land-crab's hole, or treading upon one of the creatures and hearing and feeling it crackle and writhe underfoot. Ugh! it was horrible.

All these unpleasantnesses were sharply accentuated by the darkness, which fell upon us like a pall; for now the stars began to be obscured by great black clouds that came sweeping in from seaward, while the increasing roar and swish in the boughs overhead seemed to indicate that the wind was freshening. Progress was difficult enough, under such conditions, while we were traversing solid ground and had no special need to pick our footsteps; how would it be, I wondered, when it came to our re-crossing the belt of mangroves and mud that lay between us and the gig? Then, to add still further to our difficulties, the dank, heavy, pestilential fog that rises from the tropical African rivers at nightfall began to gather about us, and in a few minutes, from being bathed in perspiration from our exertions, we were chilled to the bone, with our teeth chattering to such an extent that we could scarcely articulate an intelligible word.

"Plenty too much fever here come," remarked Cupid, while his teeth clattered together like castanets. "Sar, you lib for carry dem quinine powder dat dem doctor sarve out dis morning?"

"Certainly, Cupid," jibbered the skipper. "M–m–many thanks for the hint. M–m–m–mister Fortes—ugh! t–t–take a p–p–pow-ow-der at once."

I did so, and handed one to the Krooboy, who simply put it, paper and all, into his mouth, and swallowed the whole. Having done this, Cupid announced, as well as his chattering teeth would permit, that in view of the fog and the intense darkness it would be simply suicidal for us to attempt the passage of the mangroves without a light, and that therefore he proposed to make his way alone to the gig, not only to reassure her crew as to our safety, but also to procure a lantern. And he enjoined the skipper and me to remain exactly where we were until he should return. After an absence which seemed to be an age in duration, but which was really not quite three-quarters of an hour, he reappeared, accompanied by the coxswain of the boat and two other seamen, who brought along with them a couple of lighted lanterns. Thus reinforced and assisted, we got under way again, and eventually, after a most fatiguing and dangerous journey, reached the boat and shoved off into the stream. The gig was of course provided with a boat compass, and we knew the exact bearing of the spot where the other boats lay hidden; but we already knew also how complicated and confusing was the set of the currents in the river, and how hopeless would consequently be any attempt to find our friends in that thick fog. We therefore did not make the attempt, but, pushing off into the stream until we were clear of the mosquitoes and other winged plagues that had been tormenting all hands for so many

20

hours, let go our anchor in one and a half fathoms of water, and proceeded to take a meal prior to turning-in for the night.

Never in my life before, I think, had I spent so absolutely uncomfortable a night. What with the rats, cockroaches, fleas, and other vermin with which the ship was overrun, to say nothing of the complication of stenches which poisoned the atmosphere, the midshipmen's berth aboard the *Psyche* was by no means an ideal place to sleep in, but it was luxury compared with the state of affairs in the gig. For aboard the *Psyche* we at least slept dry, while in the boat we were fully exposed to the encroachments of that vile, malodorous, disease-laden fog which hemmed us in and pressed down upon us like a saturated blanket, penetrating everywhere, soaking our clothing until we were wet to the skin, chilling us to the very marrow, despite our greatcoats, so that we were too miserable to sleep; while it so completely enveloped us that, even with the help of half a dozen lanterns, we could not see a boat's length in any direction. As the foul water went swirling away past us great bubbles came rising up from the mud below, from time to time, bursting as they reached the surface, and giving off little puffs of noxious, vile-smelling gas that were heavy with disease-germs. Yet, singularly enough, when at length the morning dawned and the fog dispersed, not one of us aboard the gig betrayed the slightest trace of fever, although, among them, the other boats mustered nearly a dozen cases.

Our first business, after once more joining forces, was to pull into the creek and call upon his Majesty, King Olomba; but, upon interviewing that potentate, through the medium of Cupid, who acted as interpreter, it at once became evident that our worthy skipper had been made the victim of an elaborate hoax—even more elaborate, indeed, than we at the moment expected; for the king not only vigorously disclaimed any propensity toward slave-hunting or slave-dealing, but went the length of strenuously denying that the river was ever used at all by slavers; also he several times endeavoured to divert the conversation into another channel by pointedly hinting at his readiness to accept a cask of rum as a present, to which hint the skipper of course turned a deaf ear. Then, having got out of the old boy all the information that we could extract—which, when we came to analyse it, amounted to just nothing—we carefully searched the bush in the neighbourhood of the town, to see if we could discover anything in the nature of a barracoon, but found no trace whatever of any such thing.

Having drawn the creek blank, the skipper next determined to search a spot known as the Camma Lagoon, some twelve miles farther up the river; and, the sea-breeze having by this time set in, we stepped the masts and made sail upon the boats, creeping up the river close to its northern bank in order to dodge the current as much as possible.

Upon reaching the lagoon we found it to be in reality a sort of bay in the north bank of the river, some five and a half miles long by about three and three-quarter miles wide, with an island in the centre of it occupying so large an extent of its area that at one spot the creek behind was barely wide enough to allow the passage of a vessel of moderate tonnage. The eastern extremity of this creek, however, widened out until it presented a sheet of water some two miles long by about a mile and a half in width, with a depth of water ranging from two to three fathoms. Furthermore, the island itself and the adjacent banks of the river were thickly wooded, affording perfect concealment, behind which half a dozen slavers might lurk undetected; and altogether it wore, as seen from the river, the aspect of an exceedingly promising spot. We therefore lowered the boats' sails, unshipped their masts, and, keeping a bright look-out all round us, pulled warily into the lagoon at its eastern extremity.

For the first mile of our passage we detected nothing whatever of a suspicious character; but upon rounding the eastern extremity of the island and entering the widest part of the lagoon we sighted two large canoes paddling furiously up the creek, about a mile ahead of us. The captain at once brought his telescope to bear upon these craft, and with its aid discovered that each canoe was manned by about forty black paddlers, while the after end of each craft was occupied by some ten or a dozen men in European dress, most of whom appeared to be armed with muskets. These men had the appearance of being either Portuguese or Spaniards, and their presence in such a spot could mean but one thing, namely, that there was a barracoon somewhere near at hand. The skipper accordingly gave the order to chase the two canoes, to which the boats' crews responded with a cheer, and laid themselves down to their oars with such a will that they almost lifted the boats out of the water. But we had scarcely traversed a distance of half a dozen boats' lengths when, upon opening up a little indentation in the shore of the mainland, we saw before us a substantial wharf, long enough to accommodate two fair-sized craft at once, with a wide open space at the back of it upon which stood some eight or ten buildings, one of which was unmistakably a barracoon of enormous size.

With another cheer the course of the boats was at once diverted toward the wharf; and we had arrived within less than a hundred yards of it when the deathlike silence which had hitherto prevailed ashore was pierced by a shrill whistle, in response to which the whole face of the bush bordering the open space at once began to spit flame, while the air around us hummed and whined to the passage of a perfect storm of bullets and slugs, among which could be detected the hum of round shot, apparently nine-pounders, the gig weathered the storm unscathed; but upon glancing back I saw that the other boats had been less fortunate, there being a gap or two here and there where a moment before a man had sat, while certain of the oars were at that moment slipping through the rowlocks to trail in the water by their lanyards a second later. Here and there, too, could be seen a man hastily binding up a wounded limb or head, either his own or that of a shipmate.

The skipper sprang to his feet in the stern-sheets of the gig, and drew his sword.

"Hurrah, lads!" he shouted. "Give way, and get alongside that wharf as quickly as you can. Then let every man run his hardest for the shelter of the buildings, carrying his musket and ammunition with him. One hand remain in each boat as boat-keeper, who must crouch down under the shelter of the wharf face. Mr Fortescue, stick close alongside me, please; I shall probably want you to carry messages for me."

"Ay, ay, sir," I answered; and the next moment the voice of the coxswain pealed out: "Oars! rowed of all!" followed by the clatter of the long ash staves as they were laid in on the thwarts, and the gig, still leading the other boats, swept up alongside the low wharf and hooked on.

With a yell of fierce delight, and eyes blazing with excitement, Cupid, the Krooboy, bounded up on the wharf, and extended one great black paw to assist the skipper, while in the other he grasped his favourite weapon, an axe, the edge of which he had carefully ground and honed until one could have shaved with it; in addition to which he wore a ship's cutlass girded about his waist. Moreover he had "cleared for action," by stripping off the jacket and shirt which he usually wore, and stowing them carefully away in the stern-sheets of the boat; so that his garb consisted simply of a pair of dungaree trousers rolled up above his knees and braced tight to his waist by the broad belt from which hung his cutlass.

In a second the gig was empty save for her boat-keeper, and her crew were racing for the shelter afforded by the barracoon, where, as I understood it, the captain intended to announce his arrangements for clearing the enemy out of the bush. But when we had accomplished about half the distance between the edge of the wharf and the barracoon there came a sudden splutter of fire from the windows of the other buildings—which were so arranged as to enfilade the whole of the open space—and in a moment we once more found ourselves in the midst of a storm of flying bullets. The skipper, who was a pace ahead of me, stumbled, staggered a pace or two, and fell headlong upon his face, where he lay still, while his sword flew from his grasp with a ringing clatter. At the same moment the two cutters dashed up alongside the wharf, and their crews came swarming up out of them, to be met by another murderous discharge from the enemy lurking in the bush.

I came to a halt beside the skipper, and looked round me. A couple of yards away stood Cupid, who, it seemed, had just caught sight of the captain as he fell, and had pulled himself up short.

"You, Cupid," I shouted, "come back here, sir, and lend me a hand to get the captain back into the gig."

The fellow came, and stooping over the skipper's body raised it tenderly in his arms.

"All right, Mistah Fortescue, sar," he said; "you no trouble. I take dem captain back to de gig by myself, and find Mistah Hutchinson," (the surgeon). "But it no good, sar; he gone dead. Look dere." And he pointed to a ghastly great hole in the side of the skipper's head, just above the left ear, where a piece of langrage of some description had crashed its way through the poor fellow's skull into his brain. It was a horrid sight, and it turned me quite sick for the moment, accustomed though I was by this time to see men suffering from all sorts of injuries.

"Very well," I said; "take it—the captain, I mean—back to the gig, anyway, and do not leave him until you have turned him over to Mr Hutchinson; who, by the way, is in the launch, which I see is just coming alongside. I will find Mr Hutchinson and send him to you." And away I hurried toward the spot where I saw the launch approaching, for the double purpose of reporting to Mr Perry the news of the captain's fall, and dispatching the surgeon to see if life still remained in the body.

The first luff was terribly shocked at the news which I had to tell him; from a distance he had seen the skipper fall, but had hoped that it was a wound, at most. But this was not the moment for unavailing regrets; the fall of the captain at once placed Perry in command and made him responsible for the fate of the expedition. He therefore gave orders for the guns which were mounted in the bows of the launch, pinnace, and first and second cutters to be cast loose and landed, the men not engaged in this work being placed under the command of the third lieutenant, with instructions to load their muskets and keep up a constant fire upon the windows of the various buildings. Then, as soon as the guns were landed, two of them were loaded with double charges of grape, for the purpose of clearing the bush of the hidden foe, while the remaining two were double shotted and then run close up to the barricaded doors of the buildings, which were thus blown in, one after the other. As each door was blown in the building to which it belonged was stormed; the enemy, however, contriving to effect an exit by the rear as our lads poured in at the front. In ten minutes the whole of the buildings were ours, without further casualties on our side; after which we set them on fire and, waiting until they were well alight, retired in good order to the boats, in which we hauled off far enough to enable us to effectively cover the burning buildings with our musketry fire and thus defeat any attempt to extinguish the flames. An hour later the entire settlement was reduced to a heap of smouldering ashes; whereupon we pulled away round to the main stream once more by way of the back of the island, in search of further possible barracoons, but found none.

Our loss in this affair, considering its importance, was comparatively slight, amounting as it did to two killed—of whom one was the skipper—and seven wounded. But we were a sorrowful party as we left the lagoon behind us and found ourselves once more in the main stream and on our way back to the ship; for Captain Harrison was beloved by everybody, fore and aft, and we all felt that we could better have spared any one else than him.

Chapter Four.

The wreck of the Psyche.

Our journey down the river was a very different affair from that of our upward passage; for whereas in the latter we had been compelled to force our way against an adverse current, we now had that current favouring us; thus it came about that although the sun had passed the meridian when the boats emerged from the Camma Lagoon, after destroying the slave factory therein, it yet wanted an hour to sunset when the gig, still leading the rest of the flotilla, entered the last reach of the river and we once more caught sight and sound of the breakers beyond the bar.

Mr Perry, the late first lieutenant, who now, by the death of Captain Harrison, had automatically become acting captain of the *Psyche*, had turned over the command of the launch to the master's mate, for the return passage, and was in the gig with me; and as we drew nearer to the river's mouth I noticed that he rose in the stern-sheets of the boat and glanced somewhat anxiously to seaward. For a full minute or more he stood gazing under the sharp of his hand out across the sandbank as it seemed to glide rapidly past us, its summit momentarily growing lower as the gig swept along toward the point where the dwindling spit plunged beneath the surface of the water, and, as he gazed, the expression of puzzlement and anxiety on his face rapidly intensified. By this time, too, his action and attitude had attracted the attention of those in the boats astern, and, glancing back at them, I saw that Nugent, in the launch, and Hoskins, the third lieutenant, in the pinnace, had followed his example. Naturally, I did the same, wondering meanwhile what it was at which they were all looking so intently, when Mr Perry suddenly turned upon me and demanded, almost angrily—

"I say, Mr Fortescue, what has become of the ship? D'ye see anything of her?"

"The ship, sir?" I echoed dazedly—for, with the question, it had come to me in a flash that we ought by this time to be able to see at least the spars of the *Psyche* swaying rhythmically athwart the sky out over the low sandbank, if she still lay at anchor where we had left her;—"the ship? No, sir, I confess that I can't see her anywhere. Surely Mr Purchase cannot have shifted his berth, for any reason? But—no," I continued, as the absurdity of the suggestion came home to me—"of course he hasn't; he hasn't enough hands left with him to make sail upon the ship, even if he were obliged to slip his cables."

At that moment a hail of "Gig ahoy!" came from Nugent aboard the launch; and, glancing back at him, we saw him pointing at some object that had suddenly appeared on the ridge of the spit, away on our port quarter. It was a man, a white man, a seaman, if one might judge from his costume, and he was waving a large coloured handkerchief, or something of the kind, with the evident object of attracting our attention. While we still stood at gaze, wondering what this apparition could possibly mean, another man appeared beside him.

"Down helm, and run the boat in on the bank," ordered our new skipper. "I must see what this means."

"Flatten in, fore and aft, and stand by to let run your halyards!" ordered the coxswain, easing his helm down; and as he spoke I stepped upon the stern thwart with the object of getting a somewhat more extended view over the sandbank. But there was nothing to be seen—stay! why was the spray from the surf flying so much higher in one particular spot than elsewhere? And that spot appeared to be about abreast of that part of the bank where the two men were standing. I stood a moment or two longer, seeking an explanation of

24

the phenomenon, and then fell headlong over the man who was sitting upon the aftermost thwart gathering in the slack of the mainsail as the yard came down; for at that moment the gig grounded on the bank and shot a quarter of her length high and dry with the way that she had on her. As I picked myself up, rubbing my barked elbows ruefully, to the accompaniment of a suppressed snigger from the boat's crew, Mr Perry, with a brief "Make way, there, lads," sprang upon the thwarts and, striding rapidly from thwart to thwart, rushed along the length of the boat, placed one foot lightly on the gunwale, close to the stem head, and leaped out on to the sand, with me close at his heels.

Together we raced for the crest of the spit; but even before we had reached it the terrible truth lay plain before us. For there, about a quarter of a mile to the southward of us, on the seaward side of the spit, lay the *Psyche*, hard and fast aground, dismasted, and on her beam-ends, with the surf pounding at her, and her spars and rigging, worked up into a raft, floating in the swirl alongside the beach; while on the shore, opposite where she lay, the little company that had been left aboard to take care of her laboured to save such flotsam and jetsam as the surf flung up within their reach.

For a full minute the new skipper, thus by a cruel stroke of malicious fortune robbed of the command that had been his for such a few brief hours, stood gazing with stern, set features at the melancholy scene. Then he turned to me and said—very quietly—

"Mr Fortescue, be good enough to go down to Mr Hoskins, and request him, with my compliments, to take the boats back up the river until they are abreast the spot where the wreck lies, and there beach them; after which, leaving a boat-keeper to watch each boat, he will take the men over to the other side of the spit to assist in salving such matters as may come ashore. Having delivered this message, you will please join me yonder." And he pointed to where the little group of men were toiling on the beach.

"Ay, ay, sir!" I answered. And, touching my hat, I turned and hurried down to the river bank, alongside which the other boats were now lying, with lowered sails, evidently awaiting orders. Meanwhile Mr Perry strode off over the ridge in the direction of the wreck.

I quickly found Mr Hoskins and delivered my message, with the result that the entire flotilla pushed off again and headed up-stream, one of the men having landed upon the narrow spit and ascended to its ridge in order that he might notify the boats' crews when they should have arrived at the spot on the seaward side of which lay the wreck; while I, burning with curiosity to learn how the disaster had been brought about, hurried after the skipper. As he walked, while I ran, I managed to overtake him at the precise moment when Mr Purchase, who had been left by Captain Harrison in charge of the ship, met him at a little distance from the spot where the party of salvors were at work.

"Mr Purchase," said the skipper, as the two men met and halted, "I deeply regret to inform you that Captain Harrison is dead—killed this morning, with one other, while gallantly leading us to the attack of a strongly defended slave barracoon. We have both bodies in the boats, yonder, and it was my intention to have buried them at sea to-night; but that, I perceive, is no longer possible. And now, sir, perhaps you will be good enough to explain to me how the *Psyche* comes to be where I see her."

"Ah, sir!" answered Mr Purchase, removing his hat and mopping his forehead in great perturbation of spirit, "I wish I could tell you. All I know—all that *any* of us knows, so far as I have been able to ascertain—is that we were cut adrift—both cables, sir, cut through as clean as a whistle—and allowed to drive ashore!"

"Cut adrift?" reiterated the captain incredulously. "*Cut adrift*? Really, my dear Purchase, you must excuse me if I say that I utterly fail to understand you. How the mischief could you possibly be cut adrift from where you were anchored; and by whom? You surely do not intend to insinuate that any one of the ship's company—?"

"No—no; certainly not," interrupted Purchase. "Nothing of the kind. Let me tell you the whole yarn, Perry; then you will be as wise as myself, and can give me your opinion of the affair, which I admit is most extraordinary.

"Nothing in the least remarkable occurred for some hours after the boats left the ship yesterday morning. I stood aft and watched you through the starboard stern port until you had all safely crossed the bar and disappeared behind the sand spit; and then I set the hands to work upon various small jobs; after which I went round the ship and satisfied myself that everything was perfectly safe and snug on deck and below. Then, feeling tolerably certain that you would not return until to-day at the earliest, and that consequently it would be necessary for me to be up and about during the greater part of the coming night, I went below and turned in all standing, to get as much sleep as possible, leaving the boatswain's mate in charge of the deck, together with midshipmen Keene and Parkinson.

"The day passed quite uneventfully; everything went perfectly smoothly; the ship rode easily to her anchors; and there had been nothing to report. But about two bells in the first dog-watch I noticed that the sky was beginning to look a bit windy away down in the western quarter—nothing to speak of, you understand, or to cause any uneasiness; but it made me take a look at the barometer, and I saw that it had dropped a trifle since eight bells; and at the same time the wind was distinctly freshening and the swell gathering weight. All this, of course, meant more wind within the next few hours; I therefore kept a sharp eye on the barometer; and when at four bells I found it still dropping I decided to let go the two stream anchors, as a precautionary measure, while we had light enough to see what we were doing; and this I did, at the same time paying out an extra fifty fathoms on each cable, after which I felt that we were perfectly safe in the face of anything short of a hurricane."

The new skipper nodded his approval, but said nothing; and Purchase proceeded with his story.

"Well, as you probably noticed, shortly after sunset the wind breezed up quite strongly; but I was not in the least uneasy, for the barometer had ceased to drop before eight bells, and, although the sky was overcast and the night very dark, there was nothing threatening in the look of the weather, and it was only occasionally that we really tautened out our cables. Still, I made up my mind to remain on deck all night, having had a good spell of sleep during the day.

"As the night wore on and the wind held fresh but steady, I felt that after all I really need not have let go the streams, for the bowers alone would have held us quite easily against six times as much wind and sea as we had; you may therefore perhaps be able to picture to yourself my amazement and consternation when, a few minutes before six bells in the middle watch, I became aware that the ship was adrift and fast driving down toward the breakers!"

"How did you discover that the ship was adrift? Did you feel her cables parting?" demanded the skipper.

"No," answered Purchase; "we never felt anything of that kind; but I suddenly noticed that she was falling off and canting broadside-on to the wind and sea, so I knew at once that something was wrong—that in fact we had, in some incomprehensible way, struck adrift. I therefore sang out to Thompson, the boatswain's mate, to pipe all hands to make sail, intending to run her into the river, if possible. But by the time that we had got the mizzen and fore-topmast staysail upon her, and were loosing the main-topmast staysail, we were in the first line of breakers; and a moment later she struck heavily. Then a big comber came roaring in and broke over us, lifted us up, swept us shoreward a good twenty fathoms, and we struck again, with such violence this time that all three masts

26

went over the side together. After that we had a very bad half-hour, for every roller that came in swept clean over us, carrying away everything that was movable, smashing the bulwarks flat, and hammering the poor old barkie so furiously upon the sand that I momentarily expected her to go to pieces under our feet. To add to our difficulties, it was so intensely dark that we could not see where we were; true, the water all round us was ablaze with phosphorescence, which enabled us to discern that land of some sort lay about a couple of cables' lengths to leeward of us, but it was quite indistinguishable, and the water between us and it was leaping and spouting so furiously that I did not feel justified in making any attempt to get the men ashore, especially as we were then being swept so heavily that we had all our work cut out to hold on for our lives. About half an hour later, however, the tide turned and began to ebb, and then matters improved a bit.

"But it was not until daybreak that we were able to do anything really useful; and then all hands of us got to work and built a raft of sorts, after which we got up a good supply of provisions and water, sails to serve as tents, light line, and, in short, everything likely to be useful, and managed to get ashore without very much difficulty. But before I left the ship I had the cables hauled in through the hawse-pipes, and examined them most carefully. They were both unmistakably cut through—a clean cut, sir, evidently done with a sharp knife—at about the level of the water's edge."

"Most extraordinary!" commented Perry. "And I presume nobody saw anything, either immediately before you went adrift or afterwards—no boat, or anything of that kind, I mean—to account for the affair?"

"No," answered Purchase, "nothing. Yet I was not only wide-awake and on the alert myself, but I took care that the anchor watch should be so also; for I felt the responsibility of having such a ship as the *Psyche* to take care of, with only twenty hands, all told, to help me."

"Of course," agreed the skipper. "And did you succeed in getting everybody ashore safely?"

"Yes, thank God!" answered Purchase fervently. "We are all safe and sound, and very little the worse for our adventure, thus far."

"Ah! that at least is good news," remarked Perry. "Well," he continued, "there is one very melancholy duty demanding our immediate attention, Mr Purchase, namely, the interment of Captain Harrison and the other poor fellow who fell during the attack upon the barracoon to-day. I will see about that matter personally, by choosing a suitable spot and getting the graves dug, for we shall soon have the darkness upon us. Meanwhile, you will be good enough to get tents rigged and such other preparations made as may be possible for the comfort of all hands, and especially the wounded, during the coming night; for we have all had a very trying day, and it is imperative that we should secure a good night's rest. Mr Fortescue, come with me, if you please."

Now, during the progress of the foregoing conversation the boat party had not been idle; for, as soon as the fact of the wreck had become known to them, Mr Hoskins, the third lieutenant, seeing how matters stood, had grappled with the situation by causing the guns, ammunition, and stores of all kinds to be landed from the boats, and the craft themselves to be hauled up high and dry upon the beach on the river-side of the sand spit; and then, leading his men over the ridge, to where the others were at work upon the salving of wreckage from the surf, he had detailed a party to pick out from among the pile of heterogeneous articles such things as were most needed to meet our more immediate wants, and carry or drag them up the slope to the spot which Henderson, the surgeon, had already selected as the most suitable spot for a camp.

It was toward this party that Mr Perry and I now directed our steps; and when we had joined it the skipper, picking out a dozen of the most handy men, gave them instructions to provide themselves with tools of some sort suitable for the purpose of digging a couple of graves in the loose, yielding sand above the level of high-water mark; and while they were doing this, under my supervision, my companion wandered away by himself in search of a suitable site for the graves. As a matter of fact there was very little in the nature of choice, the entire spit, or at least that portion of it which we occupied, consisting of loose sand, sparsely covered, along the ridge and far a few yards on either side of it, with a kind of creeper with thick, tough, hairy stems and large, broad leaves, the upper surface of which bristled with hairy spicules about a quarter of an inch long. This plant, it was evident, bound the otherwise loose drifts and into a sufficiently firm condition to resist the perpetual scouring action of the wind; it was in this portion of the spit, therefore, that Mr Perry gave orders for the two graves to be dug; and presently my little gang of twelve were busily engaged in scooping out two holes, some twenty feet apart, to serve as graves. They were obliged to work with such tools as came to hand, and these consisted of splintered pieces of plank, the boats' balers, and some wooden buckets that had come ashore.

Under such circumstances the task of excavation was distinctly difficult, the more so that the sand ran back into the holes almost as fast as it was scooped up and thrown out; but at length, by dint of strenuous labour, a depth of some three feet was reached just as the sun's rim touched the western horizon and flung a trail of blood athwart the tumble of waters that lay between. Then, the exigencies of the occasion admitting of no further delay, the task was suspended; all hands knocked off work; and, the bodies having meanwhile been enclosed in rough coffins very hastily put together by the carpenter and his mate, we all fell in; the gig's crew shouldered the late captain's coffin, while six of his mates acted as bearers to the other dead man; and, with Mr Perry leading the way and reading the burial service from a prayer-book, which it appeared he always carried about with him, we marched, slowly, solemnly, and bare-headed, up the slope of the sand spit to the spot which had been selected for the last resting-place of the dead. Arrived there, the two coffins were at once deposited in their respective graves, when the new captain, standing between the two holes, somewhat hurriedly completed the ritual—for the light was fading fast; whereupon, after bestowing a final parting glance at the rough, uncouth box which concealed our beloved chief's body, we all turned slowly and reluctantly away to retrace our steps back to the apology for a camp which was to shelter us for the night, leaving a fresh party of workers to fill in the graves.

In neither arm of the British fighting service do men unduly dwell upon the loss of fallen comrades, for it is quite justly held that the man who yields up his life in the service of his country has done a glorious thing, whether he falls in a pitched battle deciding the fate of an empire, or in some such obscure and scarcely chronicled event as the attack upon a slave factory. He is, where such is possible, laid in his last resting-place with all the honourable observance that circumstances permit, and his memory is cherished in the hearts of his comrades; but whether his fame pass with the echo of the last volley fired over his grave, or outlives the brass of the tablet which records his name and deeds, there is no room for grief. Wherefore, when we got back to camp and had made the best possible arrangements for the coming night, there was little reference in our conversation to the tragic events of the past twenty-four hours; Mr Perry took up the reins of government, and matters proceeded precisely as they would have done had Captain Harrison been still alive and among us.

Our "camp" was, naturally, an exceedingly primitive affair; our living and sleeping quarters consisting simply of sails cut from the yards and stretched over such supports as could be contrived by inserting the lower ends of spars or planks in the sand and lashing their upper ends together. These structures we dignified with the name of "tents." The exigencies of the situation did not permit of the observance of such nice distinctions of rank in the matter of accommodation as exist under ordinary conditions, it therefore came about that we of the midshipmen's berth were lodged for the night in the same tent as the ward-room officers, and consequently we heard much of the conversation that passed between them, particularly at dinner. This meal—consisting of boiled salt beef and pork, with a few sweet potatoes, and a "duff" made of flour, damaged by sea water, with a few currants and raisins dotted about here and there in it—was served upon the *Psyche's* mizzen royal stretched upon the bare sand in the centre of our "tent"; and we partook of it squatted round the sail cross-legged on the sand, finding the way to our mouths by the light of four ship's lanterns symmetrically arranged one at each corner of the sail.

Naturally enough, Mr Purchase—now ranking as first lieutenant *vice* Mr Perry, acting captain—having told the tale of the happenings which had resulted in our becoming castaways, was anxious to hear full particulars of what had befallen the boat expedition; and this Mr Perry proceeded to relate to him as we sat round the "table." When he had finished there was silence for a moment; then Purchase looked up and said—

"Don't you think it very strange that your experiences throughout should have accorded so ill with the information that Captain Harrison acquired at so much trouble and personal risk? Hitherto it has always happened that such information as he has been able to pick up has proved to be accurate in every particular."

"Yes," agreed Mr Perry, "it has. I've been thinking a good deal about that to-day; and the opinion I have arrived at is that Harrison played the game once too often, with this result—" and he waved his right hand comprehensively about him, indicating the tent, the makeshift dinner, and our condition generally.

"What I mean is this," he continued, in reply to Purchase's glance of inquiry. "The poor old *Psyche*, as we all know, was a phenomenally slow ship, yet her successes, since she came on the Coast, have been greater and more brilliant than those of any other vessel belonging to the squadron. And why? Because she had a trick of always turning up on the right spot at the right moment. Now it seems to me that this peculiarity of hers can scarcely have escaped the notice of the slave-trading fraternity, because it was so very marked. I imagine that they must often have wondered by what means we gained our information; and when at length the thing had become so unmistakable as to provoke both conjecture and discussion it would not take them long to arrive at a very shrewd suspicion of the truth. When once the matter had reached this stage discovery could not possibly be very long delayed. Captain Harrison was undoubtedly a well-known figure in Sierra Leone; he was of so striking a personality that it could not be otherwise, and I am of opinion that at length his disguise was penetrated. He was recognised in one of those flash places in Freetown that are especially patronised by individuals of shady and doubtful character; and a scheme was devised for his and our undoing which has succeeded only too well. In a word, I believe that the whole of the information upon which he acted when arranging this most unfortunate expedition was carefully fabricated for the express purpose of bringing about the destruction of the ship, and was confided to him by some one who had recognised him as her captain. I believe, Purchase, that you were cut adrift last night, either by the individual who spun the yarn, or by some emissary or emissaries of his who have a lurking-place somewhere in this neighbourhood; and, if the truth could be got at, I believe it would be found that the schooner which we saw come out of this river on the day before yesterday—and which the captain was led to believe was a decoy intended to draw us off the coast—was actually chock-full of slaves!"

"By Jove!" ejaculated Purchase. "What a very extraordinary idea!"

"I don't think so at all," cut in Hoskins, before Mr Perry could reply. "It may seem so to you, Purchase, because it has just been presented to you, fresh and unexpectedly, as it were. But when we arrived at King Olomba's town yesterday morning, and found neither slaves nor barracoon there, I must confess that I was visited by some such suspicion as that of which Captain Perry has just been speaking, although in my case it did not take quite such a concrete and connected form. To my mind there is only one thing against your theory, sir," he continued, turning to the skipper, "and that is the existence of the factory on the lagoon."

"Yes," agreed the captain, "I admit that to be somewhat difficult to account for. And yet, perhaps not so very difficult either; because if the fellows who gave Captain Harrison the information upon which he acted happened to have a grudge against the owners of that factory they would naturally be more than glad if, while groping about in search of the imaginary slavers and barracoon, we should stumble upon the real thing and destroy it. All this, however, is mere idle conjecture, which may be either well founded or the opposite; but there is one indisputable fact about this business, which is—unless Mr Purchase is altogether mistaken, which I do not for a moment believe—that the *Psyche* was last night cut adrift from her anchors and wrecked by somebody who must have a lurking-place in this immediate neighbourhood; and I intend to have a hunt for that somebody to-morrow."

Chapter Five.

The Battle of the Sand Spit.

As the evening progressed it became evident to me that our new captain had developed a very preoccupied mood; he fell into long fits of abstraction; and often answered very much at random such remarks as happened to be addressed to him. He appeared to be turning over some puzzling matter in his mind; and at length that matter came to the surface and found expression in speech.

"Mr Purchase," he said, "I have been trying to put two and two together—or, in other words, I have been endeavouring to find an explanation of the puzzle which this business of the wreck of the *Psyche* presents. I can understand quite clearly that poor Captain Harrison was deliberately deceived and misled by certain persons in Sierra Leone in order that the ship might be cast away. But why *here* particularly? For if my theory be correct that the supposed decoy schooner actually sailed out of this river with a full cargo of black ivory, there must certainly be a barracoon somewhere close at hand from which she drew her supplies; and the people who planned the destruction of the sloop could scarcely have been so short-sighted as to have overlooked the fact that such a happening would leave us here stranded in close proximity to a slave factory which, presumably, they would be most anxious should remain undiscovered by us. That is the point which I cannot understand; and I have come to the conclusion that my theory with regard to the schooner must be altogether wrong, or there must be something else in the wind—that, in short, the wreck of the sloop is only a part instead of the whole of their plan."

"But what about the barracoon which you destroyed to-day, sir?" asked Purchase. "Might not that be the place from which those fellows draw their supplies of slaves?"

"It might, of course," admitted the skipper; "but, all the same, I do not believe it was. For the people who supplied Captain Harrison with false information would surely know enough of him and his methods to be certain that, failing to find anything in the nature of a slave factory at King Olomba's town, we should not leave the river again until we had thoroughly explored it; and if they knew the river at all they would also know that the factory on the Camma Lagoon could scarcely be overlooked by us. No; in my own mind I feel convinced that the factory which we destroyed to-day was not the one in which those fellows are interested; there is another one somewhere in the river; and I will not leave until I have discovered and destroyed it. But that only brings me back to the point from which I started, and once more raises the question, Why did they cast us away within a few miles of this other factory which I am persuaded exists? Is it that the place is so strongly fortified that they are confident of our inability to take it? Or is there something else at the back of it all, of which we have not yet got an inkling?"

Purchase shook his head hopelessly. "Upon my word, sir," he answered, "it is quite impossible for me to say. When you come to put the matter like that it becomes as inexplicable as a Chinese puzzle. What is your own opinion?"

"I haven't been able to form one at all," answered the skipper. "But the matter is puzzling enough to convince me that it would be folly on our part to assume that the casting away of the ship is the beginning and ending of the adventure; therefore we will neglect no precautions, Mr Purchase, lest we find ourselves landed in an even worse predicament than our present one. Our first and most important precaution must be to maintain a strict watch throughout the night. It need not be a very strong watch, but it must be a vigilant one; therefore each watch will be kept under the supervision of an officer who will be responsible for the vigilance of the men under him. Moreover, all hands must see that their muskets and pistols are loaded and ready for instant action; for it would not be a very difficult matter to surprise this camp of ours sometime during the small hours. Just come outside with me and let us take a look round."

The result of the above conversation and the "look round" was an arrangement that the night was to be divided into five watches of two hours each, beginning at eight o'clock in the evening and ending at six o'clock in the morning; each watch to consist of twelve men, fully armed, who were to act as sentries, half of them being detailed to watch the river in the neighbourhood of the boats, while the other half kept watch and ward over the land approach to our encampment, being stretched across the narrow isthmus in open order from the water's edge on the river-side to that on the sea-side. Each watch was commanded by an officer, with a midshipman under him; and the general orders were to fire a single shot at the first sign of anything of an alarming character, and then retire upon the camp, if an attack should threaten to cut off the outpost from the main body.

The first watch was taken by the captain, with me for his subordinate; and I was given the command of the party of six guarding the shore approach to the camp, while the skipper took the party mounting guard near the boats, as it was his opinion that if danger threatened it was most likely to come by way of the river.

My instructions were to march my men out to a distance of not more than two cables' lengths from the camp, and there take such cover as might be possible. At first sight it did not appear that there was the least bit of cover of any description available, for the spit or peninsula on which we were encamped was just bare sand for a distance of fully a mile from the spot whereon our camp was pitched, and then there began a growth of scrubby bush which gradually became more dense as one proceeded in a southerly direction; but I solved the difficulty by causing each man to scoop a little pit for himself in the loose sand, in which it was easy for him to crouch perfectly concealed particularly as there was no moon, and the light from the stars was not strong enough to reveal objects at a distance much beyond a quarter of a mile.

The first, second, and third watches passed uneventfully; but the fourth watch was little more than half through when—about a quarter after three o'clock in the morning—the whole camp was roused from its slumbers by the sound of musket-shots, one from the party guarding the boats and the river approach, quickly followed by three in rapid succession from the contingent that occupied the sand pits stretched across the neck of the peninsula. Then three or four more shots from the river party spurted out, and it began to dawn upon us that the matter threatened to be serious. Of course none of us had thought of discarding any of our clothing that night, the second shot therefore had scarcely pealed out upon the night air before we in the camp were upon our feet, with our weapons in our hands, and all drawn up in regular array ready for the next move in the game, with the skipper in command.

"Where are Mr Fortescue and Mr Copplestone?" demanded the captain, looking about him, as soon as the first momentary bustle was over.

"Here I am, sir," answered I, stepping forward and mechanically touching my hat; and "Here I am, sir," answered Tom Copplestone, suddenly appearing from nowhere in particular.

"Mr Fortescue," ordered the captain, "take to your heels and run out to Mr Nugent as fast as you can; ascertain from him the reason for the firing from his party; ask him whether he requires any assistance; and then return to me with his reply as quickly as possible. Mr Copplestone, you will run down to the boats with a similar message to Mr Marline."

Away we both went, as fast as we could lay legs to the ground, Copplestone down-hill toward the river beach, and I along the sand spit, making upward gradually toward the ridge as I ran. Running in that fine, heavy sand was, however, horribly exhausting work, especially to one whose only mode of taking exercise was to stump the lee side of the quarter-deck during his watch, and I was soon so completely blown that, with the best will in the world to hurry, I was brought to walking pace. But before I had made twenty fathoms from my starting-point two more shots rang out from the party by the boats, and a moment later one of the boat guns began to speak. I looked out over the river, striving to discover what the disturbance was about, and thought I could dimly make out several dark blurs on the faintly shimmering surface of the water, which I conjectured must be canoes, but I could not be sure; meanwhile my business was not with them, whatever they were, but with Nugent and his party, from whom, as I struggled along, two more musket-shots cracked out almost simultaneously. Then, down by the river-side, a second shot roared from a boat gun, and this time before the ringing report of the piece died away I distinctly heard a crash followed by loud shrieks and much splashing out somewhere on the surface of the river. A few seconds later, panting and gasping for breath, I staggered up to a figure which I had made out standing upright and motionless on the crest of the spit, and found it to be Nugent, with his drawn sword tucked under his right arm while with both hands he held his night glass to his eye.

"Who goes there?" he demanded sharply, wheeling round and seizing his sword as he heard the noise of my panting behind him.

"Friend!" I answered. "The sk——captain desires to know why you are firing, out here, and whether you require any assistance."

"Oh! is that Fortescue? All right. Just take my night glass, will you, and sweep the face of the spit carefully at about two hundred yards distance from here. Then tell me if you can see anything," answered Nugent. "And, if it comes to that, why are the others firing, down by the boats?"

"Can't say for certain," I answered, as I took the proffered night glass and raised it to my eye, "but I believe some suspicious canoes or boats have hove in sight, and they are just giving them a hint to keep their distance."

"Ah! just so," returned Nugent. "Now we are firing because, although we can't be absolutely certain in this darkness, we think that there is a body of men out there who would be not altogether disinclined to rush the camp, if we gave them the opportunity; so we are just potting at them—or what we fancy to be them—whenever we get a clear enough sight of them, just as a hint that we are awake. But as to assistance—n–no, I don't think we need any, at least not at present. Should we do so, later on, I will blow a blast on this whistle of mine." And he produced from his pocket a whistle possessing a particularly shrill and piercing note, with which he had been wont to summon Cupid to the midshipmen's berth aboard the *Psyche*, when that individual's presence had been needed with especial urgency.

"Well, d'ye see anything?" he demanded, after I had been peering through his glass for a full minute or more.

"I am really not at all certain whether I do, or not," I answered, still working away with the glass. "I thought, a moment or two ago, that I caught sight of something in motion for an instant, but it is so abominably dark, as you say, that—but stay a moment, what is that dark mass out there stretching across the ridge? I don't remember having noticed anything there before nightfall."

"Dark mass?" reiterated Nugent; "what dark mass d'ye mean? There is nothing out there, so far as I—"

"By Jingo! but there is, though, sir; I can see it myself now, wi' the naked eye!" exclaimed a seaman who was crouching in a sand pit a yard or so distant from where Nugent and I were standing. "There, don't ye see it, Mr Nugent, stretchin' athwart the back of the spit? Why, I can make it out quite distinctly."

"Give me the glass," demanded Nugent, snatching the instrument from me and applying it to his eye. For some eight or ten seconds he peered intently through the tube, then exclaimed excitedly—

"Ah, now I have it. Yes, by Jove, Fortescue, you are right, there *is* something out there; and it looks like—like—ay, and it *is*, too—a body of blacks creeping along toward us on their stomachs! Why, there must be hundreds of 'em, by the look of it; they reach right across the spit! Yes, we shall certainly want help, and plenty of it, to keep those fellows at arm's length. I thought it was only some twenty or thirty when I first made them out. Yes, cut away to the skipper, Fortescue, as hard as you can pelt; tell him what you've seen; and say that I shall be obliged if he will kindly send me as many men as he can spare. That disturbance down by the boats seems to have ceased, so he ought to be able to send us a pretty strong reinforcement."

"All right," I said; "I'll tell him, and then comeback with the men." And away I went back through the heavy sand at racing pace, and delivered my message.

The captain listened patiently to my breathless and somewhat disconnected story, and then turned to Mr Purchase, who was standing close at hand, and said—

"Mr Purchase, have the goodness to take the entire port watch, and go out to Mr Nugent's assistance. But do not allow your men to fire away their ammunition recklessly, for we have very little of it. Let no man pull trigger until he is quite certain of hitting his mark."

"Ay, ay, sir!" answered Purchase. "Port watch, follow me." And away he and his following trudged into the darkness. I was making to join them, but the skipper happened, unfortunately, to see me, and called me back.

"No, no, Mr Fortescue," he said; "you and Mr Copplestone will please remain with me. I may want one or both of you to run messages for me presently."

So we remained. But I at once ranged up alongside Copplestone, for I was anxious to hear the news from Marline, down by the boats.

"Well, Tommy," I said, "what was old Marline blazing away at? Whatever it was, he managed to hit it, for I heard the smash."

"Yes," answered Copplestone. "But it was more a case of luck than of good shooting, for it is as dark as a wolf's mouth. Some of his men, however, had eyes keen enough to see that there was a whole flotilla of boats, or canoes, or something of that sort, hovering in the river and manoeuvring in such a fashion as to lead to the suspicion that they had designs upon our boats, so he dosed them with a few charges of grape, which caused them to sheer off 'one time,' as Cupid is wont to remark. What was the row with Nugent?"

"Lot of niggers creeping along the spit on their stomachs toward him," I answered. "Got some idea of rushing the camp for the sake of the plunder in it, I expect. But now that Mr Purchase and the port watch have gone out to back him up I think we need not— hillo! that sounds like business, though, and no mistake."

My ejaculation was caused by a sudden cracking off of some six or eight muskets, one after the other, closely followed by a heavy if slightly irregular volley, and the next instant the air seemed to become positively vibrant with a perfect pandemonium of shrieks, howls, yells, and shouts as of men engaged in close and desperate conflict. The skipper pricked up his ears and clapped his hand to his sword-hilt; then he turned to where Tommy and I were standing close beside him.

"Mr Copplestone," he said, "take twenty men—the first you can pick—and go with them to support Mr Marline, for I fancy he will need a little help presently. The rest of us are going out to support Mr Purchase and Mr Nugent."

"Ay, ay, sir," answered Tommy. He picked out the first twenty men he could lay hands on and taarched them off to join Mr Marline's "picnic," as he expressed it, and the rest of us went off at the double to take part in the scrimmage that was proceeding in the neighbourhood of the sand pits. And a very pretty scrimmage it was, if one might judge from the tremendous medley of sounds that reached us from that direction. The firing was now very irregular and intermittent, but there was plenty of yelling and shrieking mingled, as we drew nearer to the scene of the fray, with sounds of gasping as of men engaged in a tremendous struggle, quick ejaculations, a running fire of forecastle imprecations, the occasional sharp order of an officer to "Rally here, lads!" dull, sickening thuds as of heavy blows crashing through yielding bones, and here and there a groan, or a cry for water. It was evident that the fight had resolved itself into a desperate hand-to-hand struggle; and it seemed to me that our lads were being hard put to it to hold their own. But the worst feature of the whole affair, to my mind, was that the darkness was so intense that it was almost impossible to distinguish friend from foe.

We reached the scene of the struggle so much sooner than I had expected that it was impossible to avoid the conclusion that our people were being steadily forced back in the direction of the camp; and this I afterwards found to be correct; but the appearance of the skipper with his reinforcements soon put another face upon the matter. It was evident that the foe—consisting of some hundreds of negro savages had been under the impression that they were fighting the entire strength of the British, but when we came up they at once discovered their mistake, which, with the knowledge that, for aught they could tell, there might be further reinforcements waiting to take a hand in the game, somewhat damped their courage. Not by any means at once, however; indeed it was not for perhaps two or three minutes after our appearance upon the scene that the first actual check upon their advance occurred. For they appeared to number seven or eight to every one of us, and moreover they were all picked warriors in the very prime of life, brave, fierce, determined fellows, every one of them, and well armed with spear, shield, war-club, and, in some cases, a most formidable kind of battle-axe.

"Spread out right and left, and cut in wherever you can find room," ordered the skipper as we plunged, stumbling and gasping, into the midst of the fray. And there was no difficulty in obeying this order; for, narrow as the sand spit was, it was yet too wide for Mr Purchase and the port watch to draw a close cordon across it; there were gaps of a fathom or more in width between each of our men, and those gaps were rapidly widening as some poor wretch went down, transfixed by a broad-bladed spear, was clove to the shoulder by the terrific blow of an axe, or had his brains dashed out by a war-club. But as our contingent arrived each man chose an enemy—there was no difficulty in doing that—and pulled trigger upon him, generally bringing him down, for we were too close to miss; after which it became literally a hand-to-hand fight, some using their discharged muskets as clubs while others flung them away and trusted to their cutlasses, and one or two at least—for I saw them close alongside me—depended entirely upon the weapons with which nature had provided them, first dealing an enemy a knock-out blow with the clenched fist and then dispatching him with one of his own weapons. As for me, I still had the brace of pistols and the cutlass with which I had provided myself when setting-out upon our ill-starred boat expedition up the river, and I made play as best I could with these, bowling over a savage with each of my pistols and then whipping out my cutlass. For a time I did pretty well, I and those on either side of me not only holding our ground but actually beginning to force the enemy back; but at length a huge savage loomed up before me with his war-club raised to strike. My only chance seemed to be to get in a cut or a thrust before the blow could fall, and I accordingly lunged out at his great brawny chest. But the fellow was keen-eyed and active as a cat; he sprang to one side, avoiding my thrust, and at the same instant brought down his club upon my blade with a force that shattered the latter like glass and made my arm tingle to such an extent that for the moment at least I was powerless in the right arm. Then, quick as thought, he swung up the huge club again, with the evident determination to brain me. Disarmed and defenceless, I did the on'y thing that was possible, which was to spring at his great throat and grip it with my left hand, pressing my thumb hard upon his wind-pipe. But I was like a child in his hands; he shook me off with scarcely an effort; and as I went reeling backward I saw his club come sweeping down straight for the top of my head. At that precise instant something seemed to flash dully before my eyes in a momentary gleam of starlight, a sharp *tchick* came to my ears, a few spots of what felt like hot rain spattered in my face, and the great savage, his knees doubling beneath him, reeled backward with a horrible groan and crashed to the sand, with Cupid's axe quivering in his brain, while the club, flying from his relaxed grasp, caught me on the left forearm, which I had instinctively flung up to defend myself, snapping the bone like a carrot, and then whirling over and catching me a blow upon the head that stretched me senseless. But before I fell I had become conscious that through the distracting noises of the fight that raged around me I could hear the sound of renewed firing spluttering out from the direction of the boats.

When my senses returned to me the day was apparently some three or four hours old, for the shadows of certain objects upon which my eyes happened to fall as I first opened them were, if anything, a trifle shorter than the objects themselves, which was a sure indication that the sun stood high in the heavens. I was lying, with a number of other people, in the large tent-like structure which the ward-room officers had used on the preceding evening; and Hutchinson, the ship's surgeon, was busily engaged in attending to the hurts of a seaman who lay not far from me.

This was the first general impression that I gained of my surroundings with the recovery of consciousness; the next was that my left arm, which was throbbing and burning with a dull, aching pain from wrist to shoulder, was firmly bound up and strapped tightly to my body, and that my head, which also ached most abominably, was likewise swathed in bandages. I was parched with thirst, which was increased by the sound of a man drinking eagerly at no great distance from me, and, turning my head painfully in the direction of the sound, I saw Jack Keene, a fellow-mid., administering drink out of a tin pannikin to a man whom I presently recognised as Nugent, the master's mate, who, poor fellow, seemed to be pretty near his last gasp.

"Jack," I called feebly, "you might bring me a drink presently, when you have finished with Nugent, will you? How are you feeling, Nugent? Not very badly hurt, I hope."

I saw Nugent's lips move, as though attempting to answer me, but no sound came from them, while Keene, glancing towards me, shook his head and laid his finger upon his lips as a sign, I took it, that I should not attempt to engage the poor fellow in conversation.

"All right, Fortescue," he said, in a low voice, "I'll attend to you in a brace of shakes."

He laid Nugent's head very gently back upon a jacket which had been folded to serve as a pillow, and then, refilling the pannikin from a bucket which stood close at hand, he came to me.

"Feeling bad, old chap?" he asked, as he raised my head and placed the pannikin to my lips. I emptied the pannikin before attempting to reply, and then said—

"Not so bad but that I might easily be a jolly sight worse. Bring me another drink, Jack, there's a good boy; that was like nectar."

"Ah; glad you enjoyed it," was the reply. "But you'll have to wait a spell for your next drink; Hutchinson's orders to me are that water is to be administered to you fellows very sparingly, as it is drawn from the river and is probably none too wholesome. What are your hurts?"

"Broken arm and a cracked skull, so far as I know," I answered. "What's the matter with poor Nugent?" I added, in a whisper. "He looks as though he is about to slip his cable."

Jack nodded. "Yes, poor chap," he whispered. "No chance of his weathering it. Ripped open by one of those broad-bladed spears. Can't possibly recover. Well, I must go and look after my other patients; I'm acting surgeon's mate, you know."

"Surgeon's mate!" I ejaculated. "Why, you surely don't mean to say that Murdoch has been bowled over, too, do you?"

"No; not so bad as that," answered Jack. "He's away with the rest in the boats. The skipper's gone to pay a return visit to those fellows who beat up our quarters last night. And now I really must be off, you know. Go to sleep, if you can; it will do you all the good in the world."

Go to sleep! Yes, it was excellent advice, but I did not seem able to follow it just then; the throbbing and aching of my arm and the racking pain of my sore head were altogether against it, to say nothing of the continuous groaning and moaning of the injured men round about me, and the occasional sharp ejaculations of agony extorted from the unfortunate individual who happened at the moment to be under the surgeon's hands. So, instead, I looked about me and endeavoured to form some idea of the extent of our casualties during the past night. Judging from what I saw, they must have been pretty heavy, for I counted twenty-three wounded, including myself, and I realised that there might be others elsewhere, for the tent in which we lay was full; there did not seem to be room enough for another patient in it without undue crowding. And even supposing that we comprised the sum total of the wounded, there must have been a large proportion of dead in so desperate an affair as that of the past night. I estimated that in so obstinately contested a fight as that in which we had all sustained our injuries, and against such tremendous odds as those which were opposed to us, there must have been at least half as many dead as wounded, which would make our casualties up to thirty-five; a very heavy percentage out of a crew that, owing to various causes, was already, before this fresh misfortune, growing short-handed. When to these came to be added the casualties sustained on the preceding day in the attack upon the barracoon, it seemed to me that our new captain would have little more than a mere handful of men available for service on this fresh expedition upon which he had embarked—for I did not suppose that he had gone off taking with him every sound man and leaving the camp and the wounded entirely unprotected and exposed to a renewed attack by the savages.

After about an hour's absence Jack came back to me again and gave me another draught of water, which so greatly refreshed me that the excitement and uneasiness under which I had been labouring since his first visit gradually subsided, my aches and pains grew rather more tolerable; my thoughts grew first more placid and then gradually more disconnected, wandering away from the present into the past and to more agreeable themes, my memory of past incidents became confused, and finally I slept.

I must have slept some three or four hours; for when I awoke it was undoubtedly afternoon; Hutchinson had completed his gruesome labours and was sitting not very far away entering some notes in his notebook, and a few of the less seriously wounded were sitting up partaking of soup or broth of some kind out of basins, pannikins, or anything of the kind that came most handy. The sight of these people refreshing themselves reminded me that I was beginning to feel the need of food, and I called out to the doctor to ask if I might have something to eat and drink. He at once rose up and came to me, felt my pulse, looked at my tongue, and prescribed a small quantity of broth, which Jack Keene presently brought me, and which I found delicious. I may here mention that several days later I became aware that this same broth—the origin of which puzzled me at the moment, though not enough to prevent me from taking it—had been prepared from a kind of tortoise, the existence of which in large numbers on the spit Hutchinson had accidentally discovered that very morning, and in pursuit of which he had sent out two of the most slightly wounded with a sack, and instructions to catch and bring in as many of the creatures as they could readily find.

While I was taking my broth the worthy medico stepped to where Nugent was lying and bent over the poor fellow, feeling his pulse and watching his white, pain-drawn face. Then, rising softly, he went into a dark corner of the tent, where, it appeared, his medicine-chest was stowed away, and quickly prepared a draught, which he brought and held to the lips of the patient, tenderly raising the head of the latter to enable him to drink it. Then, having replaced the sufferer's head upon the makeshift pillow, he bent over and murmured a few words in the dying man's ear. What they were I know not, nor did I catch Nugent's response, but the effect of the brief colloquy was that Hutchinson drew from his pocket a small copy of the New Testament and, after glancing here and there at its opened pages, finally began to read, in a clear voice and very impressively, the fifteenth chapter of the first epistle to the Corinthians, reading it through to the end. As he proceeded I saw poor Nugent slowly and painfully draw up his hands, that had lain clenched upon the sand beside him, until they were folded upon his breast in the attitude of prayer. And when at length Hutchinson, with a steady voice, but with the tears trickling down his cheeks, reached the passage, "But thanks be to God, which giveth us the victory," Nugent's lips began to move as though he were silently repeating the words. The chapter ended, Hutchinson remained silent for a few moments, regarding his patient, who he evidently believed was praying. Suddenly Nugent's eyes opened wide, and he stared up in surprise at the canvas roof over his head as though he beheld some wonderful sight; the colour flowed back into his cheeks and lips, and gradually his face became illumined with a smile of ecstatic joy.

"Yes," he murmured, "thanks be to God, which giveth us the victory—*the victory*—victory!" As he spoke his voice rose until the final word was a shout of inexpressible triumph. Then the colour ebbed away again from cheeks and lips, a film seemed to gather over the still open eyes, the death-rattle sounded in the patient's throat, he gasped once, as if for breath, and then a look of perfect, ineffable peace settled upon the waxen features. Nugent's gallant soul had gone forth to join the ranks of the great Captain of his salvation.

Chapter Six.

We find new quarters.

It was about half an hour after Nugent's death that young Parkinson, who had been engaged somewhere outside the tent, came in and said to Hutchinson—

"The launch, under sail, and with only about half a dozen hands in her, has just hove in sight from somewhere up the river. None of the other boats seem to be in company, but as she is flying her ensign at the peak,"—the launch, it may be mentioned, was rigged as a fore-and-aft schooner—"I suppose it's all right."

"It is to be hoped so," fervently responded the medico; "goodness knows we don't want anything further in the nature of a disaster; we've had quite enough of that sort of thing already. Could you distinguish the features of any of the people in the boat?"

"No, sir," answered the lad. "I hadn't a glass with me. Is there such a thing knocking about anywhere here in the tent, I wonder?"

"Yes," answered Hutchinson. "You will find Mr Nugent's somewhere about. It was picked up and brought in by the fatigue-party this morning. You might take it, if you can find it, and see if you can distinguish an officer in the boat. The glass ought to be somewhere over there."

Parkinson went to the spot indicated, and proceeded to rummage among the heterogeneous articles that had been recovered from the scene of the previous night's fight, and soon routed out the instrument of which he was in search, with which he went to the opening of the tent, from which the launch was by this time visible. Applying the telescope to his eye, he focussed it upon the fast-approaching boat and stared intently through the tube.

"Yes," he said at length, "I can make out Mr Purchase in the stern-sheets, with Rawlings, the coxswain, alongside of him; and there is Cupid's ugly mug acting as figure-head to the boat. The beggar is grinning like a Cheshire cat—I can see his double row of ivories distinctly—so I expect there is nothing much the matter."

Presently, from where I was lying, the launch slid into view, coming down-stream at a great pace under whole canvas, and driven along by a breeze that laid her over gunwale-to. She was edging in toward our side of the river; and as I watched her movements, her crew suddenly sprang to their feet, apparently in obedience to an order; her foresail and mainsail were simultaneously brailed up at the same moment that her staysail was hauled down, then her helm was put up and she swerved inward toward the beach, upon which she grounded a minute later. Then Mr Purchase rose to his feet, sprang up on the thwarts, and, striding from one to the other, finally sprang out upon the beach, up which, followed by Cupid, he made his way toward our tent. A couple of minutes later he stood in the entrance, waiting for his eyes to accustom themselves to the comparative darkness of the interior.

"Well, doc.," he exclaimed cheerily, "how have things been going with you to-day?"

"Quite as well as I could reasonably have expected, taking all things into consideration," answered Hutchinson. "Poor Nugent has passed away—went about half an hour ago—but the rest of the wounded are doing excellently. How have things gone with you, and where are the others?"

"Left them behind busily preparing quarters for you and your contingent," answered Purchase. "We have had a pretty lively time of it, I can tell you, since we left here this morning. Searched both banks of the river for a dozen miles or more, exploring creeks in search of the gentry who attacked us from the river last night, and who undoubtedly put the savages up to the shore attack upon the camp, and eventually found them snugly tucked away in a big lagoon about twelve miles from here, the entrance of which is so artfully concealed that we might have passed it within a hundred fathoms and never suspected its existence. Splendid place it is for carrying on the slave traffic; large open lagoon, with an average of about fifteen feet of water everywhere; fine spacious wharf, with water enough for ships to lie alongside; two spanking big barracoons; and a regular village of well-built houses; in fact, the finest and most complete slave factory that I've ever seen. Well-arranged defences, too; battery of four nine-pounders; houses loop-holed for musketry; and a garrison of about a hundred of the most villainous-looking Portuguese, Spaniards, and half-breeds that one need wish to meet. They were evidently on the look-out for us—had been watching us all day, I expect—and opened a brisk fire upon us the moment that we hove in sight. Luckily for us their shooting was simply disgraceful, and we managed to effect a landing, with only two or three hurt. But then came the tug-of-war. The beggars barricaded themselves inside their houses, and blazed away at us at short range, and then, of course, our people began to drop. But Perry wouldn't take any refusal; landed the boat guns, dragged them forward, and blew in the doors, one after the other, stormed the houses, and carried them in succession at the sword's point. After that it was all plain sailing, but very grim work, doc, I can tell you; our people had got their blood up, and went for the Dagoes like so many tigers. It lasted about a quarter of an hour after we had blown the doors down, and I don't believe that more than a dozen of the other side escaped. Of course we, too, suffered heavily, and there are a lot of fresh cases waiting for you, but Murdoch is working like a Trojan. And now I have come to fetch you and your contingent away out of this; there is a fine, big, airy house that Murdoch has turned into a hospital, where the wounded will be in clover, comparatively speaking; so, if you don't mind, we'll get to work at once and shift quarters before nightfall."

No sooner said than done. As I had surmised, a party of twenty unwounded men, under the boatswain, had been left behind by the skipper to look after the camp when he had gone away early in the morning, and these men were now called in to convey the most seriously wounded down to the launch, while the less seriously hurt helped each other; and in this way the whole of the occupants of the camp were got down to the launch and placed on board her in about twenty minutes. Then Hutchinson caused his medicine-chest to be taken down to the boat, together with such other matters as he thought might be useful; and, lastly, poor Nugent's body was taken down and reverently covered over with the ship's ensign, which had been saved, laid on a rough, impromptu platform on the thwarts amidships—the other poor fellows who had fallen in the fight had been buried before the setting-out of the boat expedition, I now learned. A final look round the camp was then taken by Purchase and Hutchinson; a few more articles that were thought worth preserving from possible midnight raiders were brought down; and then we got under way and stood up the river, keeping in the slack water as much as possible, in order to cheat the current.

It was within an hour of sunset when Purchase, who had been standing up in the stern-sheets of the boat, intently studying the shore of the right bank of the river for some ten minutes, gave the order to douse the canvas and stand by to ship the oars; and as he did so he waved his hand to the coxswain, who put down his helm and sheered the boat in toward what looked like an unbroken belt of mangroves stretching for miles along the bank. But as the launch, with plenty of way on her, surged forward, an opening gradually revealed itself; and presently we slid into a creek, or channel, some two hundred feet wide, the margins of which were heavily fringed with mangroves, and at once found ourselves winding along this narrow passage of oil-smooth, turbid water, in a stagnant atmosphere of roasting heat that was redolent of all the odours of foetid mud and decaying vegetation. This channel proved to be about a mile long, and curved round gradually from a north-easterly to a south-easterly direction, ending in a fine spacious lagoon about eight miles long by from three to four miles wide at its widest point, arrived in which we once more felt the breeze and the sails were again set, the boat heading about south-east, close-hauled on the port tack, toward what eventually proved to be an island of very fair size, fringed with the inevitable mangroves, but heavily timbered, as to its interior, with magnificent trees of several descriptions, among which I distinguished several very fine specimens of the *bombax*. Handsomely weathering this island, with a few fathoms to spare, and standing on until we could weather a small, low-lying island to windward of us on the next tack, we then hove about and stood for the northern shore of the lagoon, by that time some five miles distant, finally shooting in between the mainland and an island nearly two miles long, upon which stood the slave factory that our lads had captured earlier in the day. The whole surface of this island, except a narrow belt along its southern shore, had been completely cleared of vegetation; and upon the cleared space had been erected two enormous barracoons and, as Purchase had said, a regular village of well-constructed, stone-built houses raised on massive piers of masonry, and with broad galleries and verandahs all round them, evidently intended for the occupation of the slave-dealers and their dependants. A fine timber wharf extended along the entire northern side of the island, with massive bollards sunk into the soil at regular intervals for ships to make fast to; half a dozen trunk buoys occupied the middle of the fairway; and the whole settlement was completely screened from prying eyes by the heavy belt of standing timber that had been left undisturbed on the southern shore of the island. I had thought that the factory on the Camma Lagoon represented the last word in the construction of slave-dealing establishments; but this concern was quite twice as extensive, and more elaborately complete in every respect.

By the time that we invalids were landed it was close upon sunset, and under Purchase's guidance we were all conducted up to the largest house in the place, where, in one of the rooms, Murdoch was still hard at work attending to the batch of patients that were the result of that day's work. We, the new arrivals, however, were shepherded into another room, where fairly comfortable beds were arranged along the two sides, and into these beds the worst cases were at once put and turned over to Murdoch's care, while Hutchinson promptly pulled off his coat and took up Murdoch's work in what might be termed the operating-room. I, however, was not considered a bad case, and was accordingly placed in another smaller room, or ward, along with about half a dozen others in like condition with myself.

While these arrangements were proceeding, a fatigue-party had been busy at work in a secluded spot chosen by the skipper, at some distance from the houses; and before we, the wounded, had all been comfortably disposed of for the night, the dead Nugent included—were laid to rest with such honourable observance as the exigencies of the moment would permit.

The casualties in this last affair were, of course, by no means all on the British side; we had suffered pretty severely in the three affairs in which we had been involved since the departure of the boat expedition from the ship, our total amounting to eleven killed and twenty-six wounded; but the losses on the part of the enemy had been very considerably greater, their dead, in this last fight alone, numbering nineteen killed, while thirty-three wounded had been hurriedly bestowed in one of the houses, to be attended to by the surgeons as soon as our own people had been patched up; thus Hutchinson and Murdoch were kept busy the whole of that night, while Copplestone, Keene, and Parkinson—the three uninjured midshipmen—were impressed as ward-attendants to keep watch over our own wounded, and administer medicine, drink, and nourishment from time to time.

It was a most fortunate circumstance for all hands that this last factory had been discovered and captured; for we were thus provided with cool, comfortable living quarters, instead of being compelled to camp out on the exposed beach opposite the wreck; and to this circumstance alone may be attributed the saving of several of the more severely wounded, to say nothing of the fact that we now occupied a position which could be effectually defended from such attacks as that to which we had been exposed on the spit during the previous night. Moreover, it relieved the captain of a very heavy load of anxiety, since, but for the fortunate circumstance of this capture, he would have had no alternative but to have continued in the occupation of our makeshift camp on the spit, it being impossible for him to undertake a boat voyage to Sierra Leone with so many wounded on his hands. It is true that he might have sent away the launch, with an officer and half a dozen hands, to Sierra Leone to summon assistance; but his ambition was not to be so easily satisfied. We had done splendid service in capturing two factories and destroying one of them—the second would also, of course, be destroyed when we abandoned it—but the loss of the *Psyche* was a very serious matter, which must be atoned for in some shape or another; and he soon allowed it to be understood that he was in no particular hurry to quit our present quarters, where the wounded were making admirable progress, and the sound were comfortably housed, while provisions of all kinds were plentiful and the water was good. But this, excellent as it was in itself, was by no means all; with two such perfectly equipped factories as we had found upon the river it was certain that the slave traffic on the Fernan Vaz must have assumed quite formidable proportions; and it was the skipper's idea that before our wounded should be fit to be moved, one or more slavers would certainly enter the river, when it would be our own fault if we did not capture them.

The most careful dispositions were accordingly made, with this object in view; the gig, in charge of an officer, was daily dispatched to the entrance of the lagoon in order that, herself concealed, her crew might maintain a watch upon the river and report the passage of any vessels upward-bound for the Camma Lagoon, while, so far as our own quarters were concerned, everything was allowed to remain as nearly as possible as it was before it fell into our hands, in order that, should a slaver arrive at the factory, there should be nothing about the place to give the alarm until it should be too late for her to effect her escape. As a final precaution, a sort of crow's-nest arrangement was rigged up in a lofty silk-cotton tree which had been left standing in the screening belt of timber along the southern shore of the island, in order that a look-out might be maintained upon the approach channel during the hours of daylight, and timely notice given to us of the approach of slavers to the factory of which we were in occupation.

A full week elapsed from the date of our desperate fight on the sand spit, with no occurrence of any moment save that, thanks to the skill and indefatigable exertions of Hutchinson and Murdoch, all our wounded were doing remarkably well, two or three of them, indeed, having so far recovered that they were actually able to perform such light duty as that of hospital ward-attendants; while the unwounded had been kept perpetually busy at the scene of the wreck, salving such matters as were washed ashore, and transferring everything of any value to our quarters. Meanwhile, the ship had parted amidships, and was fast going to pieces, so that our labours in that direction were coming to an end, and in the course of another week or two there would be nothing more than a rib showing here and there above water, and a few trifles of wreckage scattered along the beach to tell to strangers the story of our disaster. The enemy's wounded also, who were sharing with us the attentions of the surgeon and his mate, were doing well upon the whole, although there had been some half a dozen deaths among them, and there were a few more, whose hurts were of an exceptionally severe character, with whom the issue still remained doubtful.

It chanced that among these last there was a negro who seemed gradually to be sinking, despite the utmost efforts of Hutchinson to save him; and this individual, named M'Pandala, had latterly evinced a disposition to be friendly and communicative to Cupid, our Krooboy, who had been told off for hospital duty in the house occupied by the enemy's wounded; and at length—it was on the tenth day of our occupation of the island, and I was by this time well enough to be out and about again, although still unable to do much on account of my disabled arm—this negro made a certain communication to Cupid which the latter deemed it his duty to pass on to me without loss of time. Accordingly, on the evening of that day, after Cupid had been relieved—he was on day duty—he sought me out and began—

"Mr Fortescue, sar, you know dem M'Pandala, in dere?" pointing with his chin toward the house in which the wounded man was lodged.

"No, Cupid," I answered. "I cannot truthfully say that I enjoy the honour of the gentleman's acquaintance. Who and what is he?"

Cupid grinned. "Him one Eboe man," he answered, "employed by dem Portugee to cook for and look after dem captain's house. He lib for die, one time now; and 'cause I been good to him, and gib him plenty drink when he thirsty, he tell me to-day one t'ing dat I t'ink de captain be glad to know. He say dat very soon—perhaps to-morrow or next day, or de day after—one big cauffle of slabe most likely comin' here for be ship away from de coas'; and now dat he am goin' to die he feel sorry for dem slabe and feel glad if dem was set free."

"Whew!" I whistled. "That is a bit of news well worth knowing—if it can be relied upon. Do you believe that the fellow is telling the truth, Cupid?"

"Cartain, Mr Fortescue, sar," answered the Krooboy, with conviction. "He lib for die now; what he want to tell me lie for? He no want debbil to come after him and say, 'Hi, you M'Pandala, why you tell dem white men lie about slabe cauffle comin' down to de coas'? You come along wid me, sar!' No, he not want dat, for cartain."

"When did he tell you this, Cupid?" I demanded.

"'Bout two hour ago," answered Cupid. "He say to me, 'Cupid, I lib for die to-night, and when you come on duty to-morrow you find me gone. So I want to tell you somet'ing now, before it too late.' And den he tell me de news, Mr Fortescue, sar, just as I tell it to you, only in de Eboe language, which I understand, bein' well educate."

"All right," said I. "In that case you had better come with me at once to the captain, and we will tell him the yarn. The sooner he hears it the better. Did he tell you where the cauffle was coming from, and which way?"

"He say," answered Cupid, "dat dem cauffle am comin' down from de Bakota country, where 'most all de slabe sent from dis place come from; and dere is only one way for dem to come here, t'rough de bush ober de oder side ob de water. Den dey bring dem across to de island in dem big flat-bottom punt dat lay moored up by de top end ob de wharf."

We found the captain in the store with Mr Futtock, the boatswain, overhauling the various articles salved from the wreck, and as soon as he had seen all that he desired, and was ready to leave the building, I got hold of him and repeated the yarn that Cupid had spun to me, the Krooboy confirming and elaborating my statement from time to time as I went on, and answering such questions as the skipper put to him. When at length we had brought the yarn to an end the captain stood for some minutes wrapped in deep thought, and then said—

"This is a very valuable piece of information that you have managed to pick up, Cupid: and if it should prove to be well founded I will not forget that we owe it to you. It is too late now, Mr Fortescue, to do anything in the matter to-night, for it will be dark in less than half an hour; but the first thing to-morrow morning you and Cupid here had better take the dinghy, pull across to the mainland, and endeavour to find the road by which the cauffle will come—there ought not to be very much difficulty in doing that, I should think. And, having found it, it will be well for the pair of you to proceed along the road on the look-out for some suitable spot at which to ambush the party, after which the rest should be easy. There is, however, another matter that needs consideration. How are we to ascertain the precise moment at which to expect the arrival of the slave-dealers? Because it will be hardly desirable to take a party out, day after day, and keep them in the bush all day waiting for the cauffle to come along. We are all doing excellently well here; but two or three days spent in the bush would very possibly mean half the party being down with fever."

Here Cupid, bursting with pride and importance at finding himself, as it were, a member of a council over which the captain was presiding, struck in—

"You jus' leabe dat to me, sar. Suppose you gib me leabe to go, I take ration for, say, free day, and go off by myself into de bush to meet dem cauffle. Dhen when I hab met dem I soon find out when dem expec' to arribe here, and I come back and tell you."

The skipper regarded the black doubtfully.

"But," he objected, "if you fall in with them, my man, the traders are as likely as not to shoot you; or, if not that, at least to seize you and chain you on to the cauffle. Then how could you let us know when to expect the beggars?"

"No fear ob dat, sar," answered Cupid with a grin. "I shall take care dat dem do not know I, Cupid, am anywhere near dem. Dem shall neber suspec' my presence, sar; but I shall be dere, all de same, and shall take partikler care to hear eberyt'ing dat dem say, so dat we may know exactly when to expec' dem. And when I hab learned dat piece of information, I shall hurry back so as to let you know as early as possible. I don' t'ink dat dere is much fault to find wid dat plan, sar."

"No," answered the skipper, smiling at the black's eagerness and excitement, "provided, of course, that you are quite confident of your ability to carry it through."

"You trust me, sar; I'll carry it through all right, sar," answered Cupid, in huge delight at being specially entrusted by the skipper with this mission. "You hab but to gib me leabe to go, and I will undertake to carry out de enterprise to your entire satisfaction."

"Very well," said the skipper, now struggling manfully to suppress his inclination to laugh outright at the man's high-flown phraseology; "let it be so, then. Mr Fortescue, I leave it with you to arrange the matter." And he turned away.

On the following morning, Cupid having called me at daylight, I snatched a hasty breakfast of cocoa and biscuit, and then wended my way to the wharf, where the Krooboy, in light marching order, with three days' rations—which he proposed to supplement on the way, if necessary—tied up in a gaudy bandana handkerchief, awaited me in the dinghy. Scrambling down into the boat with some circumspection—for my broken arm, although knitting together again nicely, was still rather painful at times, and very liable to break again in the same place if treated roughly—I took my place in the stern-sheets, whereupon Cupid, giving the little cockle-shell a powerful thrust off from the wharf wall, threw out the two tiny oars by which the boat was usually propelled, and proceeded with long powerful strokes to row across to the mainland, at this point a bare half-mile distant. As we went the black informed me that, with the view of ascertaining a few additional items of information of which he had thought during the night, he had looked into the ward wherein his friend M'Pandala had been lodged, but had discovered, as he indeed more than half feared, that the Eboe had quietly slipped his moorings during the night and passed on into his own particular "happy hunting grounds." But he added cheerfully that, after all, it really did not greatly matter; he would probably be able to obtain the required information in some other way.

Arrived at the other side of the inlet, it became necessary for us to search the shore for the spot at which the bush road debouched, and this we eventually found with some difficulty, for, like everything else connected with the factory, it had been very carefully arranged with the object of screening it from casual observation. But once discovered, our difficulties in that respect were at an end, for we found that it ran down into a tiny indentation in the shore, just sufficiently spacious to accommodate two of the large flats or punts at a time, with firm ground, sloping gently down into the water, affording admirable facilities for the rapid embarkation of large numbers of people.

Hauling the dinghy's stem up on this piece of firm sloping ground, and making fast her painter to a convenient tree, as a further precaution, Cupid and I set out along the firm, well-beaten path, some six feet in width, which had been cleared through the dense and impenetrable bush that hemmed us in on either hand, tormented all the while by the dense clouds of mosquitoes and other stinging and biting insects that hovered about us in clouds and positively declined to be driven away.

We walked thus about a mile and a half when we came out upon an open space, some ten acres in extent, through which the path ran. This cleared space had evidently been caused by a bush fire at no very distant date, for a few charred trunks and portions of trunks of trees still reared themselves here and there; but the undergrowth had all been burned away down to the bare earth, and was now springing up again, fresh and green, in little irregular patches, all over the open area. The spot would serve admirably for an ambuscade, for while it was sufficiently open to permit of straight shooting, there was cover enough to conceal a hundred men, or more, at need. But what made the place especially suitable for our purpose was the fact that away over in one corner of the clearing there grew a thick, dense belt of wild cactus, newly sprung up, fresh, tough, and vigorous, every leaf being thickly studded with long, strong, sharp spikes growing so closely together that nothing living would dare to face it, or attempt to force a passage through it—or, at all events, if they should be foolhardy enough to try it once they would not attempt it a second time. It immediately occurred to me—and Cupid promptly corroborated my view—that if our party could but find or make a way in behind this belt of cactus, they would be at once in a natural fort from which it would be impossible to dislodge them, and after further careful investigation a passage was found through the bush by which our lads could easily gain access to the interior of the cactus fort, and hold it against all comers. There was therefore no need to search farther; the place was admirably adapted to our requirements; and, once satisfied of this, I bade Cupid proceed on his way in quest of the approaching cauffle, while I leisurely wended my way back to the dinghy and, with a single oar thrown out over the stern, sculled myself back to the factory.

Chapter Seven.

La Belle Estelle.

My first act upon my return was, of course, to report the result of my reconnaissance to the captain, who, after hearing what I had to say, came to the conclusion that he would personally inspect the spot which I had selected as the scene of the proposed ambuscade;

and accordingly, ordering the second cutter to be manned, we pushed off, taking Mr Hoskins with us, and towing the dinghy, which was to be left on the other side for the convenience of Cupid, upon that individual's return.

When we at length reached the place the skipper was so pleased with it that he at once determined to set a strong party to work upon it, partly to keep the hands employed—there being by this time very little to do at the factory—and partly that the necessary preparations might be completed at the earliest possible moment. Accordingly he gave Hoskins, who was to have charge of the working-party, the most elaborate instructions as to how to proceed and what to do. The work was put in hand that same day; and when Hoskins and his party returned to quarters that night the former reported that the whole of the work absolutely necessary to insure the success of the ambuscade had been done, and that only about another hour's work, on the following day, was required to complete the whole of what the skipper had ordered.

The next day, accordingly, the party crossed to the mainland to complete the preparation of the ambuscade, returning, in good time for dinner, with the report that all was now done, and that the spot was ready for occupation at a moment's notice. As it happened, it was just as well that we had acted with such promptitude and expedition, for the men were still engaged upon their mid-day meal when Cupid was seen returning in the dinghy. The fellow had evidently travelled fast and far, for he was smothered in dust, and so done up that he could scarcely drag one leg after another—there is nothing that puts one out of walking condition more quickly than being pent up for long periods on board a ship.

But, despite his fatigue, he was puffed up with pride and importance, for he had accomplished the mission upon which he had been despatched, and in a very satisfactory manner, too. His report was to the effect that he had travelled at a good pace all through the preceding day, and that at nightfall, while still plodding forward, keeping his eyes wide open, meanwhile, on the look-out for a suitable camping spot, he had suddenly detected in the air a smell of burning wood and dry leaves, and, proceeding cautiously a little further, had become aware of a low, confused murmuring, as that of the voices of many people, together with a brisk crackling sound which he at once recognised as that of camp fires. A minute or two later, having meanwhile taken cover, he sighted the camp, which proved to be, as he had of course expected, that of the slave-traders and their unhappy victims.

The caravan, or "cauffle," had just camped for the night, and its members were busily engaged in preparing the evening meal, Cupid was therefore able to approach the camp closely enough to catch a great deal of the conversation of the slave-traders, as well as to make a pretty accurate guess at their number and that of their victims. Later on he was able to ascertain the exact number of the former, which totalled eighty-two, while the slaves he estimated to number from a thousand to fifteen hundred. Maintaining his concealment, but steadily working his way ever closer to the camp fire, the Krooboy ultimately wriggled himself into a position so close to the spot where the chiefs of the band had seated themselves that he was able without difficulty to catch every word spoken by them; and although his knowledge of the Spanish and Portuguese languages was exceedingly limited, yet by listening patiently to everything that was said during the somewhat dilatory progress of the meal, and afterwards while the leaders smoked and chatted prior to turning-in for the night, he was able to gather that the remaining distance of the journey was to be divided into three marches, the last of which was to bring the party to the shore of the lagoon pretty early in the afternoon of the day following that of Cupid's return to us.

Then, having learned this, the Krooboy had waited until the leaders of the expedition had bestowed themselves for the night, and the occupants of the camp generally were settling to rest after the hot and toilsome march of the past day, when he cautiously left his place of concealment and, mingling with the unhappy captives, had contrived to communicate to several of them the joyful news that in due time, and upon their arrival at a certain spot already fixed upon, the cauffle would be ambuscaded and the dealers and escort attacked and captured, after which the slaves would be released and supplied with food and water to enable them to return to their homes. He did this, he said, not only to comfort and encourage them but also to put them on their guard against falling into a panic at the critical moment and getting themselves hurt.

The skipper listened very carefully to this story, cross-examined the narrator upon several points, and then dismissed him to get food and rest. That same afternoon the captain, accompanied, as before, by Lieutenant Hoskins, again visited the place of ambush, and presumably made final arrangements for the capture of the cauffle, but what they were I did not know, for I was left behind, with Tompson, the gunner, in charge of the factory, with instructions to overhaul our stock of arms and ammunition, and see that everything of that kind was made perfectly ready for the next day's work.

When the next day arrived and all hands were mustered for inspection prior to the choosing of the ambuscading party, I learned to my disgust that I was to be left behind, with the other invalids, to look after the factory, Hutchinson having reported that I was not yet fit for duty, although, like a full dozen others who had been hurt in one or another of our recent fights, I was able to be up and about, and to attend to matters not requiring the use of both arms. But the slave-traders were known to be, as a general rule, determined fellows, and it was certain that, in the present case, with such a rich haul in their possession, they would fight desperately in defence of their booty. The skipper therefore determined to take only sound men with him, concluding that "lame ducks" would be more of a hindrance than a help to him.

With envious eyes I watched the departure of the skipper and his party—in three boats, namely, the launch and the first and second cutters—and then walked moodily away from the wharf to perform a duty inspection of the sick wards. The place wore an unnaturally quiet and deserted look, as I crossed the great open space between the wharf and the building which we had converted into a hospital; for there was nobody about excepting a round dozen or so of convalescents, well enough to sit out on the gallery under the shade of the verandah, and the solitary watcher, perched aloft in the crow's-nest which we had rigged among the topmost branches of one of the most lofty trees on the island, in order to maintain a watch upon the lagoon, and give us timely notice of the approach of a slaver.

Sauntering quietly along, for the heat was already intense, I entered the hospital building and proceeded with the usual daily inspection of the wards, which I found were to-day in Murdoch's charge, Hutchinson having been detailed to accompany the skipper's party. The invalids were all doing excellently, thanks, no doubt, in a great measure, to the fine, airy room in which they had been bestowed; some, indeed, were so far advanced toward recovery that Murdoch had given three or four of them permission to leave their beds and go into the open air for an hour or two, and these were now assisting each other to dress. I completed my rounds, both of this building and also of that in which the wounded prisoners were lodged, and was just leaving the latter when I caught sight of one of the convalescents hurrying toward me at a great rate, in the full glare of the sunshine, in direct defiance of the medico's standing order that none of them were on any account to leave the shadow of the verandah. But this man had a very excellent excuse for his breach of the rules, for the moment that he saw me he first took off his hat and waved it to attract my attention, and then flourished it in the direction of the look-out tree, glancing toward which I caught sight of the fluttering fragment of scarlet bunting which was the prearranged signal that a slaver had entered the lagoon and was approaching the factory! A moment later the look-out himself, having descended the tree, came hurrying along to make his report.

"Well, Edwards," I exclaimed, as the man came bustling up to me, and saluted, "I see you have made the signal that a slaver is approaching. What sort of a craft is she; and how far off?"

"She's a very tidy and smart-looking brig, sir, measurin' close upon three hundred ton, by the look of her; and she's headin' straight for the eastern end of this here island, clewin' up and furlin' as she comes. She was under topsails and to'ga'nts'ls when I shinned down out of the crow's-nest, yonder; and I reckon she'll reach the anchorage in about another twenty minutes or so," reported the man.

"Very good," I answered. "Now, go back to your look-out, and put that piece of red bunting out of sight as quickly as possible; for if those slaver fellows should happen to catch sight of it they may suspect something and be on their guard; which won't do; for, with only a few convalescents to help me, our sole chance of capturing them lies in the use of stratagem."

Then, as the man turned away and hurried back to his post, I crossed the open space between the wharf and the buildings, and, giving the convalescents instructions to arm themselves at once and to stand by to show themselves when called upon, I entered my own quarters and hastily shifted from my uniform into a somewhat soiled suit of "whites" and a pith hat that had doubtless once been the property of one of the former inhabitants of the place—and which I had appropriated in view of some such contingency as the present—and otherwise made such preparations as were possible for the suitable reception of our expected visitors.

We had only just barely completed our preparations when the strange brig, under topsails and fore-topmast staysail, came sweeping round the eastern extremity of the island, bracing sharp up as she did so and making a short "leg" athwart the anchorage, toward the mainland. Then, tacking very smartly, even under such short canvas as she was showing, she headed well up for the line of buoys which had been laid down as moorings, and, splendidly handled, presently came up head to wind, settling away both topsail-yards to the caps as she did so, and, while her crew clewed up the topsails and hauled down the staysail, glided, with the way which she still had on her, up to the weathermost buoy, to which a hawser was promptly run out and made fast. Then, as about a dozen hands climbed into the fore and main rigging and made their leisurely way aloft for the purpose of rolling up the topsails, a light, handsome gig was dropped into the water from the starboard quarter davits and presumably hauled alongside the gangway; but this I could not see, as she was presenting her port broadside to us—which, by the way, I noticed, was garnished with five grinning twelve-pounders. She was a most beautiful vessel, lying long and low upon the water, her hull painted all black, from her rail to her copper, relieved only by a single narrow white stripe running along her sheer-strake from her white figure-head to the rather elaborate white scroll-work that decorated her quarter. She was grandly sparred, with very heavy lower-masts, long mastheads, painted white, very taunt topmasts, topgallant and royal-masts, stayed to a hair, with a slight rake aft, and accurately parallel, and enormously long yards. The French ensign floated lazily from the end of her standing gaff.

As I stood under the shade of the verandah, admiring this sea beauty, the gig came foaming round under her stern, propelled by four oarsmen, and with a white-clad figure in the stern-sheets, and headed toward the wharf, alongside a flight of steps in which she presently ranged, and hooked on. Then the white-clad figure in the stern-sheets rose and, leisurely climbing the steps to the level of the wharf, revealed itself as that of a man somewhat over middle height, broadly built, with hair, beard, and moustache of raven black, and a skin tanned almost to the colour of that of a mulatto by long exposure to sea-breezes and a tropical sun. His age I roughly estimated as somewhere about forty.

With a swaggering sea roll he came striding across the wide arid space between the wharf side and the buildings, puffing at a big black cigar as he walked, and glancing about him curiously, as though he could not quite understand the utter quietude and deserted aspect of the place. Apparently, however, this was not sufficiently marked to arouse his suspicion, for he betrayed no hesitation as he made straight for the house under the broad verandah of which I stood in full view, watching his approach. As he came within speaking distance he slightly raised his broad-brimmed pugaree-bound Panama hat, for a moment, exclaiming, in execrable Spanish:

"Good-morning, señor! what has happened that I see nobody about? And where is Señor Morillo? I would have speech with him."

Raising my hat in reply, I answered, in the same language: "I deeply regret to inform you, señor, that Morillo is indisposed—down with a slight attack of fever, in fact; and, as for the rest, they are away in the bush on the other side, whither they have gone to help bring in the cauffle which is due to arrive this afternoon. But will you not step in out of the sun?"

"Thanks!" answered the stranger, ascending the gallery steps. "I am sorry to hear of my friend Morillo's indisposition. A *slight* attack of fever, I think you said. Is he too ill, think you, to talk business? If not, you will perhaps have the extreme kindness to tell him that Captain Lenoir of *La Belle Estelle* has arrived and would like to see him."

"Assuredly I will, señor," I answered politely. "Pray step inside here, out of the heat, and be seated, while I convey your message to Señor Morillo."

So saying, I flung open the door of an inner room, and stood aside for him to enter.

Quite unsuspectingly he stalked in through the open door, removed his hat and laid it upon the table, flung himself into a basket-chair, and, withdrawing an enormous silk pocket-handkerchief from his pocket, proceeded to mop the streaming perspiration from his forehead. At the same moment I whipped a loaded pistol from my pocket, aimed straight at his left eye, and, as he stared at me in amazement, said—

"You are a dead man, Captain Lenoir, if you move so much as a muscle. You are my prisoner, señor. No,"—as I saw by the expression of his eye that he had it in his mind to suddenly spring upon and disarm me—"not a movement, I pray you. To attempt what you are thinking of would be fatal, for upon your slightest motion I will pull the trigger and blow your brains out; I will, as surely as that you are sitting there." Then, slightly raising my voice, I called—

"Collins, bring your party into this room; and do not forget to bring along that length of ratline that I told you to have ready."

"Ay, ay, sir," answered Collins; and the reply was followed by the shuffling sound of several pairs of feet, the owners of which came shambling into the room the next moment, with naked cutlasses in their hands, while one of them carried, in addition, a length of some three or four fathoms of ratline.

Meanwhile, I had never for the smallest fraction of a second withdrawn my gaze from Captain Lenoir's eyes, or allowed the barrel of my pistol to waver a hair's-breadth from his larboard optic, for I knew that if I did he would be upon me like lightning. But although he dared not move his limbs he was not afraid to use his tongue, angrily demanding what I meant by perpetrating such an outrage upon one of Señor Morillo's best customers, and vowing that he would not be satisfied until he had seen me flogged within an inch of my life for my insolence. Then, when I explained to him the actual state of affairs—while Collins and another man securely lashed his hands together behind his back—his temper completely got the better of him, and he raved, and shrieked curses at us until we were perforce compelled to gag him lest his cries should reach the men in the boat and give them the alarm. However, we very soon secured and silenced him; and then, having marched him out at the back of the house and secured him in a remote hut by himself, I gave Collins fresh instructions, after which I sauntered across the open space of blistering sunshine to the edge of the wharf, and looked down into the boat. The four men had already made fast her painter to a ring in the wharf wall, and were now lolling over the gunwale, staring down into the deep, clear water at the fish playing about beneath them, and chatting disjointedly as they sucked at their pipes.

"It is thirsty work sitting there and grilling in the sun, is it not, lads?" said I in French. "Come up to the house and drink Señor Morillo's health in a jug of sangaree; and then Captain Lenoir wants you to carry down some fruit and vegetables that Señor Morillo has given him for the ship's use."

"*Bien*! we come, monsieur," they answered with one accord; and the next moment they were all slouching toward the house, a pace or two in my wake. I traversed a good three-quarters of the distance from the wharf to the house, and then halted suddenly and smote my forehead violently, as though I had just remembered something.

"Dolt that I am," I exclaimed in French, "I had almost forgotten! Indeed I have completely forgotten something—your mate's name. I have a message for him." And I looked the man nearest me straight in the eye.

"Ah!" he ejaculated; "monsieur doubtless means Monsieur Favart, our chief mate—"

"Of course," I cut in. "Favart is the name. Thanks! Go you on to the house and walk straight in; you will find your friends awaiting you. As for me—" I flung out my hand with an expression of disgust, and turned back as though to return to the wharf edge. But as soon as the quartette had fairly entered the house and I was assured, by certain subdued sounds, that they had fallen into the trap that had been set for them, I turned on my heel again, and presently found the four prisoners in process of being secured.

"I am sorry, lads," I said to them in French, "that I have been compelled to resort to subterfuge to make prisoners of you, but, you see, we are all invalids here, and not strong enough to take your ship by force; and therefore, since it is imperative that we should have her, I have been compelled to use guile. However, I will keep my word with you in the matter of something to quench your parched throats; and if you choose to be sensible, and make no foolish attempts at escape, you shall have no reason to complain of harsh treatment."

"Ah, Monsieur Anglais, if we had but known—" answered one of the Frenchmen, with a rather rueful smile. "However," he continued, shrugging his shoulders, "although you have contrived to get hold of us—and the captain—you have not yet got the ship; and before you can get her you will be obliged to use a great deal more guile than sufficed for our capture; for Monsieur Favart is a sharp one, I assure you, and not to be so very easily deceived."

"I can well believe it," I answered lightly. "All the same, I am very much obliged to you for the hint, and will do my best to profit by it."

Whereupon, as I turned on my heel to quit the house, the garrulous Frenchman's three shipmates fell upon him, figuratively, tooth and nail, heaping reproaches upon the unhappy man's head for having warned me against the chief mate's astuteness. I did not wait to hear how the matter ended, but, leaving the house briskly, as though I were the bearer of an important message, I hurried across to the wharf and, dropping into the dinghy, cast off her painter and sculled her across to *La Belle Estelle*, alongside which I coolly went, and, making fast the painter, ascended the gangway ladder and stepped in on deck before anybody condescended to take any notice of me. There were some twenty men, or thereabout, busying themselves about the deck in a very leisurely manner, taking off hatches, hauling taut the running rigging, and so on, under the supervision of a very smart, keen-looking man, dressed, like the skipper of the ship, in white. This man I took to be Monsieur Favart, the chief mate; so stepping up to him where he stood, at the break of the monkey poop, I raised my hat politely and said:

"Have I the pleasure to address Monsieur Favart, the chief mate of this vessel?"

"Certainly, monsieur," he answered, bringing his piercing black eyes to bear upon me. "And who may you be, my friend, that you find it necessary to ask such a question? I thought I had been here often enough to enable every dweller upon yonder island to at least know Jules Favart by sight. But I do not seem to remember ever having seen you before."

"You have not, monsieur," I answered. "I am quite a new recruit, and only joined just in time to witness the destruction of that pestilent British man-o'-war, the wreck of which you doubtless observed as you entered the river."

"We did," he answered; "and we guessed, of course, that it was the wreck of the *Psyche*. So that affair came off all right, eh? Well, I didn't very well see how it could possibly fail, for we all had a hand in the devising and arranging of it, and we chopped and trimmed away at the plan until I flatter myself that it was as perfect as human ingenuity could make it. But I take it that you did not come aboard here to discuss that matter with me?"

"No, indeed," I answered. "My business with you has reference to quite another affair. I bring a message to you from Captain Lenoir, who is at present discussing with Señor Morillo the matter of the expected arrival of the cauffle this afternoon. We find ourselves in something of a difficulty over that matter; and your arrival in the nick of time proves most opportune. For you must know that when the *Psyche* was cut adrift and came ashore, her crew were compelled to camp on the beach, yonder; and Señor Morillo considered that the opportunity to give the English a thorough drubbing was far too good to be let slip; he therefore attacked them in the dead of night, and punished them severely; but I regret to say that our side also suffered very heavily, with the result that a good many of our best men are at this moment on the sick list and unfit for duty. This puts us in a very awkward position; for the cauffle that is arriving is a big one, and rather difficult to handle—so we learn. Therefore, in order to avoid all possibility of trouble, Señor Morillo has arranged with Captain Lenoir that the latter shall land his crew to lend a hand in keeping the slaves in order when they arrive; and my instructions from the captain are to request that you will at once land, bringing all hands except the idlers with you."

"I understand," answered Favart. "Very well. When is the cauffle expected to arrive?"

"It may heave in sight at any moment," I answered. "Therefore it is advisable that you should lose no time in obeying Captain Lenoir's instructions."

"Trust me, I am not a man to lose time," answered Favart with a boisterous laugh. "Lenoir knows he may rely upon me. I suppose we ought to go fully armed?"

"Captain Lenoir said nothing about that," I answered. "No, I don't think there will be any need for you to arm yourselves. Anyhow, if weapons are needed we have plenty ashore."

"Very well; so much the better," observed Favart; "for it has just occurred to me that the skipper has the keys of the arms chest in his pocket, and we could not get at the weapons, even though we should require them ever so urgently. All right; you may tell the captain to expect me at once. But perhaps you would prefer to remain and go with us—I see that you are one of the lame ducks. Did you get that hurt in the fight with the English?"

"Yes," said I—"a broken arm. It is getting better fast, however; and I dare say I can scull the dinghy back, as I sculled her off, unless you will be charitable enough to give me a tow."

"Of course I will, with the utmost pleasure," answered Favart. And away he bustled forward, shouting an order for all hands to lay aft and get a couple of boats into the water. It was a very great relief to me to be rid of the fellow for a few minutes, for, truth to tell, the interview was beginning to get upon my nerves a bit; I could see that the French seaman's estimate of his chief officer was just, and that Favart was indeed "a sharp one." True, I had managed to hoodwink him, thus far, but I was in constant dread of saying or doing something that might awaken his suspicions, in which case all the fat would at once be in the fire; for I had placed myself absolutely in his power, and I judged him to be a man who would take a terrible revenge, should he prematurely discover that something was wrong. Moreover, if his suspicions should once be aroused, and verified, not only did we stand to lose the ship—which I was quite determined to capture—but with twenty stout seamen at his back he was fully capable of recapturing the factory and releasing all the prisoners, when we should find ourselves in a very pretty mess. Thus far, however, everything seemed to be going admirably, and I told myself that all I had to do was to keep my nerve and neither say nor do anything to excite suspicion; indeed it was this consideration that caused me to hang about aboard *La Belle Estelle* rather than hurry away ashore again as soon as I had delivered my message.

There was a great deal of fuss and bustle on board the brig, while the Frenchmen were clearing away and lowering the boats; then, with a vast amount of jabber, they went down the side, took their places, and shoved off, with me and my dinghy in tow.

Now came the critical moment when everything must be won or lost; for, personally, I had done all that was possible, and the rest depended entirely upon the intelligence of the little party of seamen to whom I had entrusted the carrying out of my plan; I had explained that plan to them, and directed them what to do and precisely when to do it, and I was also decoying the enemy into the trap prepared for them; but I foresaw clearly that if my men acted prematurely, and thus gave the alarm, or, on the other hand, allowed the psychological moment to pass before they put in an appearance, the whole affair was likely enough to end in a ghastly tragedy.

But while I reflected thus the boats traversed the space of water between the brig and the wharf, and ranged up alongside the landing steps. Then, with more excited jabber and shouting, the Frenchmen tumbled over the gunwales and up the steps to the top of the wharf, where they stood in a bunch, waiting for further orders. As the last of them ascended the steps, with me bringing up the rear, I glanced across the water toward the spot where I expected the cauffle to appear, and pretended that I caught sight of a cloud of dust rising beyond the trees. As a matter of fact there really was an effect of sunlight that might very easily have been mistaken for a dust cloud, and it was this appearance that gave me the inspiration to act as I now did.

"Look!" I exclaimed excitedly to Favart, pointing at the same moment across the water—"do you see that cloud of dust yonder? That is undoubtedly the cauffle coming along the road; and we must hurry with our arrangements, or we shall be too late. This way, Monsieur Favart, if you please. Come along, lads!" And I led them all at a rapid rate across the open space and into the compound belonging to the smallest barracoon.

"Straight across, and into the barracoon itself," I panted, making a great show of hurry and excitement; and the Frenchmen streamed through the gate like a flock of sheep. As the last man entered, I flung the gate to, dropped the bar into its place, and blew a piercing blast on a whistle which I carried. Then, replacing the whistle in my pocket, I drew forth a pistol, and placed my back against the gate.

At the first sound of the whistle the Frenchmen halted abruptly, instinctively guessing that it was a signal of some sort, while Favart turned in his tracks and flung a fierce glance of inquiry at me. Something in the expression of my face must have given him the alarm, I think, for after a prolonged stare he suddenly came striding toward me.

"Halt, monsieur!" I cried sharply, levelling the pistol at him. "Another step, and I fire! Look behind you."

He did so, and beheld eighteen English sailors, armed with muskets, cutlasses, and pistols, file out of the open door of the barracoon and draw up as if on parade.

"What does this mean, monsieur?" demanded Favart, glaring at me murderously.

"Simply that you and your men are my prisoners, monsieur," answered I. "Nay, do not move, I beg you,"—as the Frenchmen seemed to be preparing for a rush. "The man who moves will be shot dead without further warning. It is useless to dream of resistance, for my men are fully armed, while you are not; therefore, to save unnecessary bloodshed, I beg that you will at once surrender. You see the force of my argument, I am sure, Monsieur Favart?"

"I do," he answered grimly; "and of course we surrender, since there is nothing between that and being shot down. But, oh, if I had only suspected this when you were aboard the brig—! Well, what do you want us to do?"

"Have the goodness to march your men into the barracoon, monsieur," said I. "It is but for half an hour or so, until I can make other arrangements for your disposal. I assure you I have not the remotest intention of detaining you there."

Favart turned and said a word to his men, and the whole party then wheeled and shambled away across the compound and into the open door of the barracoon, which was immediately shut and locked upon them.

Chapter Eight.

Another stroke of luck.

Having captured the Frenchmen, the next item on the programme was to so arrange matters that they might be at once transferred to other and more comfortable quarters— thus leaving the barracoon free for the reception, if necessary, of the unfortunate slaves now close at hand without running any risk of their getting the better of my little band of invalids. This was not a very difficult matter, for there were plenty of slave irons about the place; and, having procured the necessary number of sets, I had the Frenchmen out of the barracoon, four at a time, ironed them, and then marched them out of the compound to a large empty shed which would answer the purpose of a prison most admirably. In less than half an hour I had the entire party secured and in charge of an armed guard of two men; and now all that remained to be done was to obtain possession of the brig.

To accomplish this, I chose the soundest eight of the party who had assisted in capturing the Frenchmen, and, leading them to the wharf steps, ordered them down into the French captain's gig, which was, of course, still lying alongside the wharf. Then, stepping into the stern-sheets myself, we pushed off and headed for the brig, which we boarded a few minutes later without let or hindrance, the small number of hands still remaining on board having apparently gone below and turned in the moment that they saw the chief mate clear of the ship. At all events when we ascended the gangway ladder not a soul was to be seen; our lads therefore quickly clapped on the hatches, beginning with the fore-scuttle, and the brig was ours. Then, having made sure that the half-dozen or so of prisoners down in the forecastle could not get loose again, I went up and hauled down the French flag, hoisting it again to the gaff-end beneath an English ensign which I found in the flag-locker. I thought that the sight of the brig, with the two ensigns thus arranged, would be an agreeable sight and afford a pleasant surprise to our people when they returned from capturing the cauffle.

It had just gone five bells in the afternoon watch when the skipper's party hove in sight at the spot where the bush path led down to the creek, and where their boats were moored. The brig, of course, at once attracted their attention, and, looking through the ship's telescope at them, I made out Captain Perry standing alone on a little projecting point, staring hard at her, as though he scarcely knew what to make of her; I therefore ordered four hands into the gig, and, rowing across to where he stood, explained matters. My story took quite a quarter of an hour to tell, for he continually interrupted me to ask questions; but when I had finished he was good enough to express his most unqualified approval of what I had done, winding up by saying—

"I may as well tell you now, Mr Fortescue—what indeed I had quite made up my mind to before the performance of this exceedingly meritorious piece of work—that it is my intention to give you an acting order as third lieutenant, Mr Purchase and Mr Hoskins moving up a step, as well as myself, in consequence of the lamented death of Captain Harrison."

Of course I thanked him, as in duty bound; and then he informed me that the ambuscade had been completely successful, the entire cauffle having been captured with the exchange of less than a score of shots; and that although three of the slave-traders had been killed and five wounded, not one of our own men had been hurt. But he added that the unhappy blacks were so completely worn out with their long march down to the coast that it would only be rank cruelty to release them at once, and that he had therefore decided to house them in the barracoons and give them a week's complete rest before starting them back on their long homeward march.

"And now, Mr Fortescue," he concluded, "since that English ensign aboard the prize has done its work, have the goodness to haul it down, and keep the French flag flying, if you please; I quite expect that we shall have two or three more ships here to help in the conveyance of this huge cauffle of slaves across the Atlantic; and I do not wish them to be alarmed and put on their guard—should they come upon us unexpectedly—by seeing a vessel riding at anchor with the signal flying that she has been captured by the English."

This was, of course, sound common sense, and I lost not a moment in returning to the brig and making the required alteration in the arrangement of the flags. That being done, it occurred to me that it would be a wise thing to clear the remainder of the French crew out of the vessel; and this I also did; afterwards assisting in transporting the miserable slaves across the channel to the island, and helping to arrange for their comfort and well-being during the night. They were, without exception, what the slave-dealers would doubtless have called "a prime lot"—numbering fifteen hundred and eighty-four, of whom less than two hundred were women; but they were all worn to skin and bone with the fatigue and hardship which they had been called upon to endure on the march from their own country down to the coast, and were so dead-beaten with fatigue that they appeared to have sunk into such a state of apathy that even the prospect of immediate rest, plenty of good food, and a speedy restoration to liberty seemed insufficient to lift them out of it. But after they had been made to bathe and thoroughly cleanse themselves from the dust and other impurities of the march, prior to being housed in the barracoons, they seemed to pluck up a little spirit,—a salt-water bath is a wonderful tonic,—and later on in the evening, when a plentiful meal was served out to them, they so far recovered their spirits as to begin to jabber among themselves. It was close upon sunset before the last batch had been ferried across to the island and lodged in the barracoons; and then, in accordance with an order from the skipper, I took a working-party on board the brig, and, casting her off from the buoy to which she had been moored, warped her in alongside the wharf and made her fast there.

The next two days were entirely devoid of incident; but we were all kept busy in attending to the unfortunate captive blacks, supervising the bathing of them in batches, inducing them to take a moderate amount of exercise in the barracoon compounds, feeding them up, and nursing the sick—of whom, however, there was luckily a singularly small percentage. But on the morning of the third day, before the gig had started upon her daily cruise of surveillance of the river, the look-out whose turn it was for duty in the crow's-nest had scarcely ascended to his lofty perch in the tree when he hurried down again with the intelligence that three craft—a ship, a barque, and a large brigantine— were in the offing and making for the mouth of the river. Whereupon Mr Purchase volunteered to go aloft, taking me with him as aide-de-camp, to keep an eye upon the strangers, and to transmit intelligence of their movements from time to time. The skipper promptly accepted the offer and, besides, arranged a system by which I was to write Mr Purchase's messages, carry them from the crow's-nest to the ground, and deliver them over to one of two midshipmen in waiting, who would at once scamper off with it, while I ascended the Jacob's ladder again for further information, to be transmitted by the second midshipman—if, meanwhile, the first had not had time to return. This system acted admirably, for it kept the captain fully informed of the course of events, and at the same time left him quite free to attend to such preparations for the reception of the three craft as he might deem necessary.

These preparations were beautifully simple, consisting merely in the arming of every man capable of taking part in what would probably prove to be a fairly stubborn fight, manning the boats with the fighting contingent, and then remaining concealed until the approaching craft had come up to the anchorage and made fast to the buoys,—as we fully expected that they would,—when the boats were to make a simultaneous dash at all three craft and carry them by boarding, while we invalids were left to look after the prisoners and see that they did not break out and create a diversion in favour of their friends.

Meanwhile the land-breeze was fast dying away in the offing, while the sea-breeze had not yet set in, consequently, when the approaching craft arrived within about two miles of the river's mouth they entered a streak of glassy calm, and lay there, rolling heavily, with their sun-bleached canvas napping itself threadbare against their masts and rigging, thus affording us an excellent opportunity to get breakfast at leisure, and fortify ourselves generally against the stress of the coming struggle.

We had just comfortably finished our meal, and Captain Perry had completed his final dispositions, when the look-out who had temporarily taken Mr Purchase's place in the crow's-nest came down with the intelligence that the sea-breeze was setting in, and might be expected to reach the becalmed craft within the next ten minutes; whereupon the first lieutenant and I returned to our post of observation to watch the progress of the approaching slavers, and report upon it from time to time.

Upon regaining our perch we saw that the brigantine, which was the outermost craft of the three, had just caught the sea-breeze and, having squared away before it, was coming along almost as fast as the breeze itself; then the barque and the ship caught it within a minute of each other, and presently all three of them were racing straight for the mouth of the river. But they were still a long way off, and, owing to the many twists and turns in the course of the river, would have nearly twenty miles to travel before they could reach the anchorage. And when, some time later, having safely negotiated the bar and entered the river, they arrived at the point where they would have to shift their helms to enter the N'Chongo Chine Lagoon—where we were patiently awaiting them—we saw that only two of them, the barque and the brigantine, were coming our way, while the ship continued on up the river, presumably bound to the Camma Lagoon, where poor Captain Harrison had lost his life in the attack upon the factory. This was a distinct relief to us; for although all our wounded were doing remarkably well, the number of men actually in fighting trim was so small that to tackle the three vessels simultaneously would have been an exceedingly formidable job, whereas we felt that the capture of two of them was well within our powers. Moreover it would be comparatively easy to take the ship upon her return down the river, which would doubtless happen immediately upon the discovery of the destruction of the factory to which she was evidently bound.

Despite the zigzag course that the two approaching craft would have to steer, the sea-breeze afforded them a leading wind all the way to the south-east end of the island, which we occupied; consequently after leaving the river and entering the lagoon they came along at a very rapid rate, the brigantine seeming to be rather the faster craft of the two. Meanwhile the skipper, being kept fully informed of the progress of the approaching vessels, had caused our prize, La Belle Estelle, to be warped far enough off from the wharf wall to allow of our boats being placed in ambush between her and the wharf, where they now lay, with their officers and crew already in them, waiting for the moment when the word should be given for them to dash forth from their hiding-place.

At length the brigantine, with the barque less than a cable's length astern of her—both of them flying Spanish colours at their gaff-ends—arrived within a mile of the spot where it would be necessary for her to luff up in order to fetch the anchorage, whereupon Purchase and I descended from our look-out, and, having made our final report to the skipper, went our several ways—the first to take command of the pinnace in the impending attack, and I to place myself at the head of the convalescents, my duty being to assist as might be required, and to see that the prisoners did not seize the opportunity to become troublesome.

The prisoners were all confined in outbuildings at the rear of the settlement, and it was there that my little band of armed convalescents were assembled; consequently I was obliged to station myself where I could keep an eye upon and be in touch with them. Yet I was quite determined that, even though I must keep one eye upon my own especial command, and the buildings over which they were mounting guard, I would also witness the attack upon the approaching slavers. Ultimately, after two or three unsuccessful attempts, I succeeded in finding a spot from which I could accomplish both objects, and at the same time sit comfortably in the shadow of a building.

A few minutes later, from behind the belt of trees and scrub that extended along the whole southern shore of the islet, I beheld the end of the brigantine's flying-jib-boom slide into view, with the flying-jib, recently hauled down, napping loosely in the wind; then followed the rest of the spar, with the standing jib also hauled down, and a couple of men out on the boom, busily engaged in stowing it; then her fore-topmast staysail, beautifully cut and drawing like a whole team of horses, swept into view, followed by the fore part of a very handsome hull bearing the foremast, with the topsail still set, the topgallantsail and royal clewed up and in process of being furled, and the course hanging from the foreyard in graceful festoons. Finally came the remaining length of hull with the towering mainmast supporting a mainsail as handsomely cut and setting as flat as that of a yacht.

She was a most beautiful vessel, sitting very low in the water, and therefore, perhaps, looking even longer than she actually was. She was broadside-on to me, so I could not see what amount of beam she showed; consequently it was a little difficult to estimate her size, but, judging from her general appearance, I put it down at about two hundred and twenty tons. She was painted a brilliant grass green from her rail to her copper, and showed four ports of a side, out of which peered the muzzles of certain brass cannon that I decided were probably long nines.

The vessel reached across the narrow channel and went in stays quite close to the tree-clad northern shore of the lagoon—thus at once exhibiting her own exceedingly shallow-draught of water and her skipper's intimate knowledge of the locality—just as the barque in turn hove in sight. This last vessel had nothing at all remarkable in her appearance, except perhaps that her canvas was exceptionally well cut, but she was by no means a beauty, and to the eye presented all the characteristics of the ordinary merchantman, being painted black, with a broad white band round her upon which were depicted ten painted ports. But these appearances of honesty were deceptive, for despite the general "motherliness" of her aspect she was almost as speedy a ship as the brigantine, although she had by this time shortened down to her two topsails and fore-topmast staysail. Also, with the aid of my telescope, I was able to discern, above the blatant pretence of the painted ports, six closed ports of a side, which I had no doubt concealed as many cannon.

The brigantine, tacking as smartly and handily as a little boat, came round and headed well up for the weathermost buoy, to which she made fast a few minutes later, with the barque close upon her heels. Until the latter had also made fast to a buoy—the one astern of the brigantine—a dead silence reigned over the settlement, broken only by the shouts of the people on board the two new arrivals as they went noisily about their work of clewing up, hauling down, and furling their canvas; but the moment that the barque was fast to her buoy and the men who had bent the cable to the buoy had returned on board, there arose a sudden rattle and splash of oars, and our concealed boats swept out from their hiding-place between the brig and the wharf and made a dash for the two craft, half of them going for the brigantine while the other half struck out for the barque.

The surprise, admirably managed by the skipper, was complete; for the greater part of the crews of the two vessels was aloft furling the canvas at the moment when our boats appeared; and although their appearance served as a signal for the men aloft to swing themselves off the yards and descend to the deck by way of the backstays, yet before they had time to arm themselves and prepare for an effective resistance our lads were alongside and swarming in over the low rails of the two craft; and a very brief scuffle sufficed to place them in possession of both. Upon inspection, they proved to be undoubted slavers, for they were not only fitted with slave-decks, but had a full supply of water and meal on board; in fact they were ready for the immediate reception of their human cargo, which, but for our interference, they could have shipped and gone to sea again in a very few hours.

The barque was named *Don Miguel*, of three hundred and forty-seven tons measurement, hailing from Havana; with a crew of fifty-six, all told; and she mounted twelve twelve-pounders, with an ample supply of ammunition for them in her magazine. The brigantine rejoiced in the name *El Caiman*. She was a trifle bigger than I had estimated her to be, her papers showing her tonnage to be two hundred and thirty. She carried a crew of forty; and mounted eight beautiful brass long nines on her broadsides, as well as a long eighteen pivoted on her forecastle. She hailed from Santiago de Cuba, and was quite a new ship; whereas the *Don Miguel* was nearly twenty years old, and leaked like a basket when heavily pressed by her canvas, as some of us soon discovered.

None of our people were hurt in the scrimmage which resulted in the capture of these two craft; as soon, therefore, as their crews had been taken out of them and securely confined, Captain Perry made ready to sally forth and capture the ship which had gone up the river, and which might be expected to return immediately upon discovering the destruction of the factory on the Camma Lagoon. It was regarded as just possible that, finding the up-river factory destroyed, her captain might make his way to our anchorage, in the hope of securing a cargo from our factory; but, on the other hand, it was also possible that he might get an inkling of our presence somewhere in the river, and go straight to sea again, preferring to try his luck on some other part of the coast. There was just sufficient time for our lads to get a meal in comfort before the moment arrived for them to shove off and make their way to the mouth of the lagoon in order to intercept, and prevent the escape of, the returning ship; the skipper therefore gave orders to pipe all hands to dinner, and while the meal was in progress he made his dispositions for the forthcoming expedition.

As before, I was left in charge of the convalescents to take care of the sick and see that the prisoners—now, of course, considerably augmented in numbers by our most recent captures—did not get into mischief. But although I was not permitted to participate in the fun, I was in no mood to lose it altogether; I therefore waited patiently until the little flotilla of boats had started—and my services on their account were no longer required—and then, having first gone the rounds of the place and satisfied myself that everything was perfectly safe, I slung my telescope over my shoulder and made my way aloft to the crow's-nest, wherein I comfortably settled myself, and, levelling my glass over a big branch that served admirably as a rest for it, prepared to watch the progress of the boats and, as I hoped, witness the capture of the ship.

The crow's-nest was rigged among the topmost branches of the highest tree on the islet, the view obtainable from it was very extensive, embracing an arc of the horizon of nearly one hundred and eighty degrees, which included, on my far right, the mouth of the river, some twenty miles distant, and a few miles of the offing beyond, while stretching away to the left of that point, toward the southward and eastward, could be traced the entire course of the river as far as the native town of Olomba, and thence onward to the Camma Lagoon, while the near and middle distance was occupied by the waters of the N'Chongo Chine Lagoon, with—in the present instance—the boat flotilla carrying on under a heavy press of canvas to fetch the passage giving access to the river.

I watched these for some time, observing with interest the gallant manner in which the captain's gig, under a spread of canvas that was manifestly too much for her in the roaring sea-breeze that was now blowing, struggled along and contrived to still retain the lead of the bigger and more powerful boats; and then I began to search the river for signs of the returning ship, for I calculated that by this time she must have arrived at her destination and discovered the destruction of the factory; so it was a question what the skipper of her would do upon making the discovery. That she was not in the Camma Lagoon was pretty evident, for almost the whole expanse of that sheet of water was in full view from my look-out, and I could scarcely have failed to see her, had she been there; I therefore carefully inspected the course of the river more toward Olomba, and presently I caught a glimpse of her upper canvas sliding along past the belt of mangroves and bush that bordered the river. She was beating down against the sea-breeze, with a strong current under her lee bow hawsing her up to windward, and was making very rapid progress.

Then I allowed my glances to return to the boats, and wondered whether those in them could see the ship. I came to the conclusion that they could not, being by this time too far over toward the other side of the lagoon, and consequently too close in to the mangroves to be able to see over them. I now most ardently wished that I had thought of arranging to display a signal warning them of the approach of the ship, for it would be a piece of information very useful for them to possess under the existing circumstances; but I had not, so there was no use in worrying about it. And even as I came to this conclusion the gig, still leading, disappeared within the narrow channel giving access to the river, and was quickly followed by the other boats, until the whole had vanished.

And now I could but guess what was happening in the channel, and watch the movements of the ship. By the time that the last of the boats had disappeared, and I was free to again direct my attention to the larger craft, she had worked down the river as far as the entrance of the creek giving access to Olomba; and when she next hove about I soon saw, by the length of time that she was holding on the same tack, that she was making a long "leg" down the main channel of the river. But she still had some ten miles of river to traverse before she would reach the spot at which it had been arranged that the boats should lie in ambush for her; and, fast as she was travelling, I estimated that it would take her at least an hour to cover that distance. I therefore drew out my watch, noted the time, and then set myself patiently to await the course of events, keenly watching her movements meanwhile. I noticed that, thanks to the exquisite cut of her canvas, she was looking well up into the wind, and I thought it possible that, with this advantage, she might perhaps reach the spot where the boats were awaiting her, without breaking tacks, which would be an advantage for our people, for it would throw her so close to the place of ambush that it would cause the attack almost to take the form of a surprise. And so it did, as I afterward learned; for when at length her skipper was compelled to put his helm down and go about, in order to avoid grounding on the mud of the eastern bank of the river, the ship was in the very mouth of the creek wherein our boats were lurking; and while the ship was in stays, and all hands of her crew were busily engaged in tending the tacks, sheets, and braces, our people dashed alongside and took her almost without striking a blow.

Chapter Nine.

We leave the Fernan Vaz.

Of course nothing of this was perceptible from my look-out in the crow's-nest; the only thing of a suggestive character that came to my notice was that when, looking through my telescope, I saw the ship hove in stays, I observed that the operation of swinging the after yards seemed to be only partially performed, while the head sails remained aback for an unconscionable length of time, from which I concluded that at that precise moment events were happening on board her. When, some five minutes later, I saw her yards trimmed, and presently observed her come about again and bear away for the lagoon, instead of holding her luff down the river, I was able to make a pretty accurate guess as to what had happened. I remained aloft, however, until she slid through the narrow channel leading from the river into the lagoon, when I saw that she had all our boats towing astern of her in a string; whereupon I descended, for I knew that to betoken the fact that she was now in the possession of our people.

She came along very fast, and as she drew nearer I saw that she was an exceedingly handsome vessel, by far the most handsome, indeed, that I had ever seen. She was frigate-built, seven hundred and forty tons measurement, her three masts accurately parallel, raking slightly aft, and stayed to a hair, while her snow-white canvas was more beautifully cut than that of many a yacht. She was painted black all over—hull, masts, and yards; and her royal yards hoisted close up under the trucks, like those of a man-o'-war. If she was anything like as good as she looked we had secured a prize that was indeed worth having.

The skipper had instructed me that he might possibly bring the prize directly alongside the wharf, and that I was to make all the necessary preparations to assist in the operation. I accordingly turned out my contingent and mustered them on the wharf, at the next berth ahead of that occupied by *La Belle Estelle*, with an ample supply of hawsers and heaving-lines at the bollards; and by the time that I was quite ready the ship was in sight, luffing round the point and hauling up for the anchorage. But instead of making a board across to the mainland, as all the others had done, the skipper kept his helm down until she was all a-shiver, when everything was let go at the same instant, the square canvas shrivelled up to the yards, the fore and aft canvas was brailed in, or hauled down, and then, as a strong party of men sprang aloft and laid out upon the yards, the beautiful craft came sliding along, with the way which she still had on her, straight for the wharf. The skipper had calculated his distance to a nicety, for her momentum was sufficient to bring her handsomely up to her berth, but not enough to impose any undue strain upon the hawsers in checking her and bringing her alongside; this part of the work being done by my gang, while the men who had captured her were still aloft busily furling the canvas.

As soon as she was securely moored and a gangway plank rigged, I went aboard and had a good look at our latest acquisition. There could be no doubt as to the fact that she was a slaver; for her slave-decks were already fitted, and she carried all the requisites, including meal and water, for the transport of a very large cargo of slaves. She was, in fact, the largest slaver I ever saw, and had accommodation to—I had almost said *comfortably*—carry at least eight hundred slaves. She was Spanish; named the *Doña Josefa*; hailed from Havana; was oak-built, coppered, and copper-fastened; was a brand-new ship, worth half a dozen *Psyches*; and her cabin accommodation aft was the most spacious and elegantly fitted that I had ever seen. She was armed with eighteen twenty-four pounders, and carried a crew of ninety-eight, all told. She was, in short, a most formidable ship; and, but for the fact of our having taken her by surprise as we did, she might have bade defiance to the slave squadron for years, and paid for herself twenty times over.

Naturally, the skipper was in high feather at so brilliant a series of successes as we had met with, for he had not been altogether without his anxious moments as to what might be the result of the inevitable court-martial that awaited us all for the loss of the *Psyche*; but he flattered himself that the authorities could not possibly be hard upon officers who brought in four such rich prizes as ours.

And now there began to be general talk about leaving the river and reporting ourselves at Sierra Leone; for not only had we ships in plenty to accommodate all hands, but those among us who were most experienced felt that, after having made such a clean sweep as we had, it was exceedingly unlikely that there would be any more chances to capture either slaves or ships in the Fernan Vaz for some time to come. Still, it would not be possible for us to go quite at once; for even now there remained several matters to be attended to, the most important being the disposal of the blacks whom we had captured from the slave-traders. Although these had come a long distance down from the interior, there was no doubt that they would be able to find their way back to their homes; whereas, if we carried them to Sierra Leone, the chances were that they would never see either home or relatives again. Therefore although, strictly speaking, it was our duty to take them to Sierra Leone with us, the skipper decided to strain a point, if necessary, and give the poor wretches the opportunity to decide for themselves which alternative should be adopted. Accordingly, the question was put to them, through Cupid, with the result that they decided, unanimously, to return by the way that they came rather than trust themselves to the tender mercies of the sea, which none of them had seen, and few had heard of, before. But they begged a few days longer in which to rest and recuperate before they were despatched on their long journey; and this the skipper cheerfully accorded them, although he was now all anxiety to get away.

After the negroes had been given a full week in which to recover their health and strength, they were mustered early on a certain morning, given a good breakfast, allowed to load themselves up with as much meal as they chose to take, furnished with a few boarding-pikes and cutlasses from the prizes wherewith to defend themselves on the way, and transported across the harbour and fairly started upon their journey. Then, having already completed our own preparations for departure, our prisoners were apportioned out among the four prizes, put down in the holds on top of the ballast and made perfectly secure, and the officers and men then proceeded to take up their quarters on board the vessels to which they had severally been appointed by the skipper.

The captain himself naturally took command of the *Josefa*, with Mr Purchase as his first lieutenant; Mr Hoskins was given the command of the *Don Miguel*, with Copplestone and Parkinson from our old midshipman's berth to bear him company and keep him from becoming too completely satisfied with life; Mr Marline, the master, was placed in charge of *La Belle Estelle*, with the boatswain's mate to assist him; and, lastly, the skipper was good enough to show his confidence in me by giving me the brigantine to navigate to Sierra Leone—our common destination—with the gunner's mate and Jack Keene as my deck officers.

As there was not very much room in the anchorage for manoeuvring, we got under way in succession, the *Josefa* taking the lead, followed by *Don Miguel*, after which went *La Belle Estelle*, while *El Caiman*, with her canvas set, strained at the cable which secured her to the buoy, as though she were afraid of being left behind.

But *I* had a duty to perform before I cast off from the buoy at which the brigantine was straining; therefore, while the other vessels got under way, I and my boat's crew stood on the wharf and quietly watched them go. Then, as soon as the brig was fairly clear of the anchorage, I went, with two of my boat's crew, to the leewardmost building of the settlement and set light to a little pile of combustibles that had been carefully arranged in each room, finally thrusting a blazing torch into the thatch upon quitting the building. And in the same way we proceeded to each building in turn, until the entire settlement, barracoons and all, was a roaring furnace of flame. Then, bidding my crew get down into the boat and stand by to shove off in a hurry, I proceeded to a certain spot and set fire to an end of slow match that was protruding from a box sunk into the ground near the wharf face, after which I picked up my heels and scampered off, best leg foremost, for the boat, into which I sprang, without much consideration for my dignity, and gave the word to shove off. The boat's crew, who were fully aware of my reasons for haste, lost no time in obeying the order, and the next instant we were foaming away toward the brigantine, from the deck of which the hoarse voice of Tasker, the gunner's mate, now reached us, bawling an order for those for'ard to "stand by to slip!" But before we were half-way across the intervening stretch of water a dull "boom" resounded astern of us, and a length of some fifty feet of wharf face suddenly leapt outward and fell with a heavy splash into the water, followed, about half a minute later, by a second "boom" and splash, then a third, fourth, fifth, and so on, until the entire wharf was completely destroyed and the whole place a ghastly, fire-swept ruin. Then we, too, turned our backs upon what, a short time before, had been one of the most extensive, important, and conveniently situated slave factories on the whole of the West Coast, and made sail to rejoin our companions. We overtook them about half a mile outside the bar; and when I had signalled the commodore that my mission of destruction was fulfilled, he hoisted a general signal setting a course of north-west by west for Cape Palmas; and, when this had been acknowledged, hoisted another to "try rate of sailing." This, of course, was the same thing as giving the word for a race, and, the weather being moderate at the time, we each at once proceeded to pile upon our respective commands every rag of canvas that we could find a yard, boom, or stay for.

The race proved an exceedingly interesting and exciting event, for all the vessels were fast. The wind being off the land, the water was smooth for the first three or four hours of the race; and during that time there was scarcely a pin to choose between the *Josefa* and the brigantine, first one and then the other contriving to get the lead by a length or two, while the brig and the barque also made a neck-and-neck race of it but very gradually dropped astern until, by the time that we had run the land out of sight, the *Josefa* and the brigantine were leading by nearly a mile, which lead we very gradually increased. By this time, however, the breeze had freshened up considerably, and the sea had got up, whereupon the *Josefa* displayed so marked a superiority that she had to take in all three royals and her mizzen topgallantsail to avoid running away from the rest of us. But, contrary to my expectations, *El Caiman*, which was an exceedingly beamy, shallow vessel, behaved so well under the new conditions that we also could spare the barque and brig our royal and still keep ahead of them.

The weather remained fine, and we made a very quick and pleasant passage to Sierra Leone, where our arrival under such unusual conditions, and the report of our doings and adventures, created quite a sensation. Also we happened to arrive at a most opportune moment; for there were three British men-o'-war in harbour at the time, and we were, therefore, able to undergo at once, and on the spot, our trial by court-martial for the loss of the *Psyche*, instead of being obliged to return to England for the ordeal.

The trial took place on the fourth day after our arrival; and, as a matter of course, those of us who had been away in the boats at the time of the wreck were acquitted and exonerated from all blame. But poor Purchase, who had been left in charge of the ship, was not so fortunate, the Court finding that, in the first place, he had been negligent in that he had not maintained a sufficiently careful look-out to preserve the ship from being maliciously cut adrift; and that, in the second place, he had let go the two stream anchors prematurely and before the actual necessity for such a precaution arose, but for which act he would have had the stream anchors available to let go when he discovered that the ship was adrift, and might thus have checked her shoreward drift long enough to permit of other measures being taken for the safety of the ship, even if the streams had not brought her up altogether. For these acts of negligence the prisoner was sentenced to be reprimanded, to lose two years' seniority, and to be dismissed his ship! Fortunately for Purchase, the sentence was not quite so severe as it sounded, for the *Osprey*—one of the men-o'-war in harbour—happened to have a vacancy for a lieutenant, and the Commodore, after hearing Purchase's story of the disaster from his own lips, unhesitatingly gave him the appointment.

The fact of the three ships being in port also suggested to me the possibility of getting through my examination, forthwith; I therefore ventured to speak to Captain Perry about it, who very kindly explained my desire to the Commodore. The Commodore, in turn, caused a few inquiries to be made, when it was ascertained that, among the three ships, there were sufficient midshipmen desirous of passing to justify the arrangement of an examination; and within the next fortnight I had the satisfaction of finding myself a full-blown lieutenant.

Meanwhile, the Mixed Commission had condemned all four of our prizes—as indeed they could not avoid doing—and the crews were sentenced to long terms of imprisonment with hard labour in chains upon the roads. Then there arose the question of replacing the *Psyche* on the station; and at the earnest representation of Captain Perry the Commodore was induced to take upon himself the responsibility of purchasing the *Josefa* into the service, rechristening her the *Eros*, and commissioning her under the command of Captain Perry, who at once arranged for the whole of the officers and crew of the *Psyche* to accompany him.

Then, arising out of the loss of the *Psyche*, another matter was brought to the fore which was destined to exercise a very important influence upon my fortunes. This matter had reference to the dearth of shallow-draught vessels in the slave squadron vessels capable of following the slavers in over the bars of the African rivers and fighting them upon equal terms. At the moment in question we had not a ship in the squadron drawing less than fourteen feet of water; consequently, when a slaver entered a shallow river, or a river with a shallow bar, such a course of procedure as that which had led up to the loss of the *Psyche* was imperative; and it was very strongly felt that the time had arrived for an improvement in the conditions. The result was that *El Caiman* also was purchased into the service, rechristened the *Dolphin*, and placed under my command with a crew of sixty, all told; of whom, however, Jack Keene, midshipman, and Tasker, the gunner's mate—who in his new ship held the rank of gunner—were the only individuals with whom I had already been shipmate; the rest were a motley crowd indeed, collected out of the gutters and slums of Freetown. The *Dolphin*, it was arranged, was to act in the first instance as tender to the *Eros*; but, later, might perhaps be detached for certain special work which was just then beginning to attract the attention of the authorities.

There was, however, still another matter that was at that moment forcing itself upon the attention of the Commodore; and that was the doings of two craft which were pursuing the nefarious business of slavers, with a measure of audacity that was only equalled by the impunity with which they worked. They were said to be sister ships, undoubtedly built from the same model, most probably launched from the same stocks, and made to resemble each other so absolutely in every respect, down to the most insignificant detail, that it was impossible to distinguish one from the other, excepting at close quarters. But one was an American—named the *Virginia*, hailing from New Orleans, and manned by a Yankee crew—while the other—the *Preciosa*—sailed under the Spanish flag, and was manned by Spaniards. They were phenomenally fast vessels, and simply laughed at the efforts of ships of the squadron to overtake them; but they had been caught in calms on three or four occasions, and boarded by means of boats; when, by a curious freak of fortune, if the boarding party happened to be British, it always proved to be the American that they had boarded; while, if the boarders happened to be American, it was the Spaniard that they found themselves meddling with. Thus, as there was no treaty existing between Spain and the United States of America on the one hand, and England and the United States on the other, conferring mutual rights of search and capture, the vessels had thus far escaped. But now, with two such speedy craft as the *Eros* and the *Dolphin*, it was confidently hoped that the Spaniard at least would soon be brought to book; when, there being no possibility of further confusion, it was believed that the Americans—who, in consequence of repeated disappointments, had manifested a disposition to leave both craft severely alone—might be induced to renew their interest and speedily capture the *Virginia*.

As soon as Captain Perry learned that his special mission was to put a stop to the operations of these notorious vessels, he made it his business to institute exhaustive inquiries in every direction, with the object of acquiring the fullest possible information relative to their movements. Although he had been unable to learn anything very definite he had finally come to the conclusion that at least one of them—which one he could not be certain—was now well on her way to the other side of the Atlantic; so he reasoned that if we proceeded with all despatch to the West Indies, and maintained a careful watch upon the mouth of the Old Bahama Channel, we should be almost certain to fall in with one or the other of them upon her next eastward trip.

Accordingly, on a certain day, the *Eros* and the *Dolphin* sailed in company from Sierra Leone, and, having made a good offing, caught the trade-wind, blowing fresh, to which we in the *Dolphin* showed every rag of canvas we could set, while the *Eros* kept us company by furling her royals and letting run the topgallant halliards from time to time when she manifested a disposition to creep away from us. We did the run across in the quickest time on record, up to that date, making the Sombrero in a fortnight, almost to the hour, from the moment of leaving Sierra Leone, without starting tack, sheet, or halliard—so far as the *Dolphin* was concerned—during the entire passage.

But now, with the Sombrero in sight and Anegada only about one hundred miles ahead, we felt that we were practically on our cruising ground; the *Eros* therefore shortened sail to her three topsails and jib and signalling to the *Dolphin* to do the like in proportion and to close, requested me to proceed on board for fresh orders. I was glad enough to obey these instructions, particularly the one relative to shortening sail, for the past fortnight of "carrying on" had been a distinctly anxious time for me; moreover it was a pleasant change to find myself on the comparatively spacious deck of the *Eros*, and once more surrounded by the familiar faces of my former shipmates. There was scant time, however, for the interchange of greetings, for Captain Perry was in a perfect fever of anxiety to complete his arrangements, and I was no sooner through the gangway than he hustled me off to his handsome and delightfully cool cabin under the poop, where, over a large-scale chart of the West Indies, he explained to me in much detail the course of action that he had planned for the two craft. This, in brief, consisted in the adoption of measures which enabled us, while remaining within signalling distance of each other all day, to keep an effective watch upon a stretch of sea some forty miles wide—over which we felt certain the vessel of which we were in search must sooner or later pass—while at sunset we were to close and remain in touch all night. This, of course, was an excellent plan so far as it went, but it was open to the objection that the craft for which we were on the look-out might slip past us unobserved during the night. That, however, was something that could not be helped; moreover, there was a moon coming which would help us, and according to Captain Perry's calculations one or the other of the two craft was almost certain to turn up ere that waxing moon had materially waned.

And turn up she did, shortly after midnight on the fifth night following our arrival upon our cruising ground. The moon was by that time approaching her second quarter, was well above the horizon by sunset, and was affording enough light to enable us to distinguish the rig and chief characteristics of a vessel eight miles away. To my very great gratification it was the look-out aboard the *Dolphin* who first sighted her, she being at that time hull-down in the south-western quarter and reaching athwart our hawse on the starboard tack; thus as the *Eros* and ourselves were hove-to, also on the starboard tack, she rapidly neared us. At first the only thing that we could clearly distinguish was that she was a full-rigged ship—as were the *Virginia* and the *Preciosa*—but, even so, there were certain details connected with her rig which, while not being exactly peculiar, corresponded with similar details referred to in the description of the two notorious slavers, as ascertained by Captain Perry; I therefore made a lantern signal to the *Eros*—under the shelter of our mainsail, so that the stranger to leeward might not see our lights and take the alarm—calling attention to the fact that there was a suspicious sail in sight to the south-west; and this signal was simply acknowledged without comment. But I saw that almost immediately afterwards the *Eros* swung her main-yard, boarded her fore and main tacks, and hauled to the wind with the object, of course, of preventing the strange sail from working out to windward of us; and a few minutes later I got a signal from the commodore instructing me to remain hove-to for the present, and, later, to act as circumstances might require.

The stranger was under all plain sail, to topgallantsails, and was slipping through the water like a witch; but I had very little fear of her outsailing the *Eros*, for, fast as that ship had been when she first fell into our hands, the skipper had improved her speed on a wind nearly a knot, merely by a careful readjustment of the ballast; and now she fully justified my faith in her by handsomely holding her own, and perhaps rather more, but this I could scarcely judge, for since we remained hove-to, the others rapidly drew away from us.

I waited with what patience I could muster until the stranger had worked out to a position some five miles ahead of us, and two points on our lee bow, and then I determined to wait no longer, for I felt that if, perchance, anything were to happen aboard the *Eros* - if, for example, she were to carry away or even spring a spar—and the trade-wind was piping up strongly—our unknown friend might very easily give us the slip; I therefore gave orders to swing the foreyard and make sail, piling on the brigantine everything we could show, even to the royal and flying-jib. And it was well that we did so, for half an hour later, strangely enough, my fears with regard to the *Eros* were realised, an extra heavy puff of wind snapping our consort's fore-topgallant-mast short off at the cap, and causing her to luff sharply into the wind with her big flying-jib dragging in the water under her forefoot.

That the stranger was not anxious to make our closer acquaintance at once became apparent, for no sooner did her people perceive the accident that had befallen the *Eros*—which was within a minute of its occurrence—than they put down their helm, tacked, and endeavoured to slip away out to windward clear of us both. The *Dolphin*, however, was doing exceptionally well just then, the combination of wind and sea seemed to exactly suit her, and I felt that, although I had perhaps unduly delayed taking action, we could more than hold our own with the stranger provided that it blew no harder—and I therefore held on grimly, presently receiving a signal from the *Eros* to take up the chase, which she would resume as soon as she had repaired damages.

Shortly afterward the stranger reached out across the bows of the *Eros*, beyond cannon-shot, and although the skipper fired two blank charges and a shotted gun to bring her to she took no notice, a fact which made me more determined than ever, if possible, to get within speaking distance of her.

The *Eros*, meanwhile, having cleared away her wreckage, had stowed her mizen topgallantsail, brailed up her spanker, and filled away again; and when we passed her, some three-quarters of an hour later, and about a mile to windward, they had already sent down the stump of her topgallant-mast and had prepared the topgallant rigging for the reception of the new spar.

The moment that we arrived in the wake of the stranger we tacked and stood directly after her; and we had not been on the new tack more than ten minutes when I found, to my great gratification, that the *Dolphin*, despite the exceeding shallowness of her hull, was quite as weatherly a vessel as the chase, which was now nearly four miles ahead of us. But it was not until we had been in direct pursuit of her for a full hour that I was able to assure myself that we were undoubtedly gaining on her.

Yes, we were gaining on her, but it was *so* slowly that it was not until sunrise next morning that we were within gun-shot of her; and now, in response to our first shot, she let fly her royal and topgallant halliards, flowed her jib-sheet, and backed her main-yard to allow us to come up with her.

As, still carrying on, we rapidly approached the handsome craft, I was busily engaged, with the aid of my glass, in discovering, one after the other, the various points of resemblance between her and the vessels that had been described to us, and I could have kicked myself with vexation when, in answer to the hoisting of our ensign, we saw the Stars and Stripes of the United States flutter out over her taffrail and go soaring aloft to her gaff-end. And almost at the same instant, she now being out of the dazzle of the sun, I was able to read, legibly inscribed on her stern, the words "Virginia. New Orleans!" With the usual perverse luck that had attended the efforts of the British, we had dropped upon the wrong ship of the pair; the *Virginia* was American, and we had no power to interfere with her. Nevertheless, having gone so far in the matter as to bring her to, I was determined to board her and get a sight of her papers; a Spanish vessel might hoist American colours if she happened to find herself in a tight corner and believed that she might thereby escape. While, as for the name—ah! that certainly was a difficulty not to be easily got over; a ship could scarcely change the name painted on her stern as easily as a chameleon changes his colour, without affording some indication that the change had been made. Still, the slavers were up to all sorts of extraordinary dodges, and—well, I would at least inspect the *Virginia's* papers, and satisfy myself that they were in order.

Chapter Ten.

The Virginia of New Orleans.

Having arrived within pistol-shot of the chase, we hove-to to windward of her, lowered a boat, and I proceeded to board her. As we swept round under her stern, in order to reach her lee gangway, I took a good look at the name on her counter. Yes; there was nothing of pretence or fraud about it, so far as I could see; the words were not only painted upon the wood, but were actually cut deep into it as well; and, furthermore, the paint had all the appearance of having been applied at the same time as that on the rest of her hull.

Upon our arrival alongside I was somewhat surprised to observe that the crew had not taken the trouble to throw open the gangway, or put over a side ladder; I had therefore to watch my opportunity and scramble aboard by way of the main chains. The *Virginia* was a very fine craft indeed, measuring quite eight hundred tons, and carrying a fine, lofty, full poop, by the rail of which stood a typical Yankee, eyeing me with even greater malevolence than the Yankee of that day was wont to exhibit toward the Britisher. He was tall, lean, and cadaverous, with long, straight, colourless hair reaching almost to his shoulders, and a scanty goatee beard adorning his otherwise clean-shaven face. His outer garments, consisting of blue swallow-tail coat with brass buttons and white kerseymere waistcoat and trousers—the former also trimmed with brass buttons—seemed to have been made for a man many sizes smaller than himself; for the coat was distinctly short at the waist, while the sleeves terminated some four inches above the wrist; his waistcoat revealed some two inches of soiled shirt between its lower hem and the top of his trousers; and the latter garments did not reach his bony ankles by quite three inches. He wore an enormous stick-up collar reaching almost to the level of his eyes; his head was graced by an old white beaver hat of the pattern worn by the postboys at that period, and the nap looked as though it had never been brushed the right way since it had been worked up into a hat. On his feet he wore white cotton stockings or socks and low-cut slippers; he carried both hands in his trousers pockets, and his left cheek was distended by a huge plug of tobacco, upon which he was chewing vigorously when I scrambled in over the rail and leaped down on the deck. As I did so I raised my hat and courteously bade him good-morning.

Instead of returning my greeting, he ejected a copious stream of tobacco-juice in my direction so dexterously that I had some difficulty in avoiding it, and then remarked—

"Waal, my noble Britisher, what the tarnation mischief do yew mean by firin' them brass popguns of yourn at me, eh? What right have yew to shoot at a ship flyin' the galorious Stars and Stripes? D'ye see them handsome barkers of mine?"—pointing to a fine display of eighteen-pounders, six of a side, mounted in the ship's main-deck battery. "Waal, I was in more'n half a mind to give ye a dose from them in answer to your shot; and yew may thank my mate here, Mr Silas Jenkins, for persuadin' me outer the notion! And what d'ye want, anyway, now that yew're here, and be hanged to ye?"

"I have taken the liberty to board your ship for the purpose of getting a sight of your papers," I answered. "Our information is that there are two sister ships—this vessel, and a Spanish craft named the *Preciosa* which are doing a roaring trade in carrying slaves across the Atlantic; and it is part of my duty to lay hands on the *Preciosa* if I can. Your vessel answers to her description in every particular save that of name and the flag she flies; and therefore, having fallen in with you, I felt that I should not be doing my duty unless I boarded you and inspected your papers."

"Waal, I'll be jiggered!" exclaimed the skipper, turning to his mate. "Hear that, Silas? I'll bet yew ten dollars the critter calls hisself a sailor, and yet he can't tell the difference between the *Virginia* and the *Preciosa* without lookin' at their papers! I'll tell ye, stranger, where the difference is between them two vessels. One on 'em has V-i-r-g-i-n-i-a, N-e-w O-r-l-e-a-n-s cut—*cut*, mind you—and painted on her starn, and she flies that galorious flag that's floatin' up thar," pointing to the American ensign fluttering from the gaff-end—"while t'other has the words P-r-e-c-i-o-s-a, H-a-v-a-n-a cut and painted on hern, and she flies a yaller flag with two red bars. I know, because I've seen her—ay, most as often as I've seen the *'Ginia!* Now, sonny, d'ye think ye'll be able to remember that little lesson in sailormanship that a free-born American citizen has been obliged to give ye?"

I laughed. "Thank you for nothing," said I. "And now I will trouble you for a sight of those papers that we were speaking of."

"I'll be darned if yew will, though, stranger!" he snapped. "No, sirree; not much, I don't think! Why, yew're even more ignorant than I thought yew was, and I must teach ye another little bit of yewr business. Why, yew goldarned Britisher, d'ye know that yew haven't got no right at all to stop me from pursooin' my v'yage, or to demand a sight o' my papers? Supposin' I was to report this outrage to my Gover'ment, what d'ye suppose would happen? Why, our men-o'-war would just up and sink every stinkin' Britisher that they comed across!"

"Ah, indeed!" I retorted sarcastically. "Very well; now we'll have a look at those papers; after which you may take whatever steps you deem fit."

"And supposin' I refuse?"—began the skipper. But the mate, seeing, I imagine, that I would take no denial, seized his irate superior by the arm and, leading him right aft, conversed with him in low tones for nearly five minutes, at the end of which time they both came forward to the break of the poop, and the skipper, descending the poop ladder, remarked ungraciously:

"Waal, since nothin' less than seein' my papers 'll satisfy ye, ye'd better come into my cabin, and I'll show 'em to yew."

Whereupon I followed him in through a passage which gave access to a fine, airy poop cabin, plainly but comfortably fitted up, and seated myself, uninvited, upon a cushioned locker while my companion went alone into his state-room, returning, a minute or two later, with a large tin box, the contents of which he laid upon the table.

"Thar they are," he exclaimed, pushing them toward me; "look at 'em as long as yew like! I guess yew won't find nothin' wrong with 'em."

Nor did I. I inspected them with the utmost care, and ultimately came to the conclusion that they were genuine, and that the ship was undoubtedly the *Virginia*, and American.

"Waal," exclaimed the Yankee skipper, when I at length refolded and handed the papers back to him, "are ye satisfied, stranger?"

I intimated that I was.

"Then git out o' here, ye darned galoot, as quick as you knows how," he snarled, "and thank your lucky stars that I don't freshen yewr way wi' a rope's end!" Then, suddenly changing his tune, as he followed me out on deck and saw me glance round, he remarked:

"Purty ship, ain't she? and roomy for her size. Guess I can stow away all of seven hundred niggers down below, and not lose more'n twenty per cent of 'em on an ordinary average passage. And the *Preciosa* is the very spit of this here craft—built in the same yard, she was, and from the same lines; there ain't a pin to choose atween 'em. Now, if yew was only lucky enough to fall in with *her*, stranger, I guess she'd be a prize worth havin', eh?"

"She would!" I agreed. "And, what's more, my friend, we mean to have her, sooner or later."

"Yew don't say!" he jeered. "Waal, I guess yew'll have to fight for her afore you git her. And yew'll have to find her afore yew can fight for her. won't yew, sonny? And p'rhaps that won't be so very difficult, a'ter all, for when I next see my friend Rodriguez—that's the cap'n of the *Preciosa*—I'll tell him that yew're out arter him, and maybe he'll lay for yew; for Rodriguez hates the Britishers 'most as bad as I do, and I'm sure he'd enjy blowin' *El Caiman* outer the water now that she's fallen into yewr hands. He and Morillo was great friends; and I reckon he'll feel bound to avenge Morillo's loss. Yes; I'll tell him, for sure. And I'll also tell all the others on the Coast to keep a bright look-out for the brigantine. Waal, so long, stranger. I'm bound for the Congo, if yew're anyways anxious to know."

The foregoing remarks were made as he followed me to the waist and watched my progress over the rail and from the main chains into my boat; and the last item of information was yelled after me when we had put about twenty fathoms of blue water between the boat and the ship. As I flourished my hand by way of reply to his jeers, he turned away and I heard his harsh, nasal accents uplifted in an order to his crew to "Swing the main-yard; haul aft the jib-sheet; and sway away them t'gallan' and r'yal yards."

Profoundly disappointed at my non-success, and bitterly mortified at the insults to which I had been subjected by boarding the Yankee, I moodily returned to the *Dolphin* and, upon mounting to the deck, ordered the gig to be hoisted and the helm to be put up in order that we might return to the *Eros*, the royals of which were now just rising above the horizon to the westward. Three-quarters of an hour later we were again hove-to, and I was once more in the gig, on my way to report to Captain Perry the result of my pursuit.

To say that the commodore was also deeply disappointed is only stating the bare truth; yet I was not more than half-way through my narrative before I saw that some scheme was taking shape in the back of his mind. He questioned me very closely indeed upon certain points, one of his questions having reference to the point of the possibility of effecting a change in the name of the ship displayed upon her stern, it being evident that a suspicion had arisen in his mind that the two ships might, after all, be one and the same craft, sailing under different flags as circumstances might require. To speak the truth the same suspicion had once or twice crossed my own mind, but had been completely dissipated by my visit to the *Virginia*; I was quite convinced there could be no possible tampering with the name on the stern, while the papers were undoubtedly genuine, and the crew were as undoubtedly genuine Yankee as were the papers. Yet, despite all this, the fact that such a suspicion had arisen in Captain Perry's mind caused it to recur in my own; I was therefore very glad when he finally said:

"Thank you, Mr Fortescue. You appear to have executed your mission very effectively, and to have done everything that I should have done, had I been there. Of course I should have preferred to have been there myself; but—well, I have no doubt the result would have been precisely the same. Now, having found the *Virginia*, I am minded to send you after her, to keep an eye upon her and also to drop a friendly hint to any Yankee cruiser that you may happen to fall in with; for, although you cannot touch her, they can; and they ought to be exceedingly grateful for a hint that will ensure them against making any further mistakes. Yes; you shall follow her up, every inch of the way; go into the Congo with her, and, unless there is some very strong reason against it, come out again with her and follow her right across the Atlantic to her destination, wherever it may be. And while you are doing that, I—confident that you are keeping the *Virginia* under observation— will look out for the *Preciosa*, and endeavour to nab her. Go and have a yarn with Mr Hoskins while I prepare your written instructions."

The skipper was much longer than I had anticipated over the job of drafting his written instructions to me, and Hoskins and I therefore had an opportunity to discuss the situation at some length. I ventured to voice the suspicion that, for some inexplicable reason, so persistently suggested itself to me that the *Virginia* and the *Preciosa* might possibly be one and the same vessel, despite the weighty evidence against such a supposition, but the first lieutenant laughed at the notion, which he pronounced in the highest degree fantastic.

"No," said he, "I do not think you need worry about that, Fortescue. But, all the same, you will have to keep your weather eye lifting, on this expedition upon which the captain is about to despatch you. For, from your account of him, I judge the skipper of the *Virginia* to be an exceptionally vindictive individual, with a very strong animus against us 'Britishers,' as he calls us, and such men are apt to be dangerous when provoked, as he will pretty certainly be when he discovers that you are following and watching him. Therefore, be on your guard against him, or he may play you one of those ghastly tricks that the slavers are apt to play upon the slave-hunters when the latter chance to fall into their hands. In my opinion you are rather too young and inexperienced to be sent alone upon such a job."

"Nevertheless," said I, "one must acquire one's experience in some way before one can possess it; and I suppose there is no way in which a young officer can learn so quickly as by being placed in a position of responsibility. After all, there is no danger in this forthcoming expedition, so far as I can see; it is but to follow and keep an eye upon a certain ship, and do what I can to promote her capture. But I will keep your warning in mind, never fear. And now I suppose I must say good-bye; for here comes Parkinson, the captain's steward, doubtless to say that my instructions are ready."

It was even as I had anticipated; Parkinson was the bearer of a message summoning me to the skipper's cabin, where my written instructions, having first been read over to me, in order that I might be afforded an opportunity to seek explanation of any doubtful points, were placed in my hands, and I was dismissed; the skipper's final order to me being to carry on and, if possible, overtake the *Virginia*, thereafter keeping her in sight at all costs until the remainder of my instructions had been carried out. Ten minutes later I was once more on the deck of the *Dolphin*, and giving orders to make sail, the signal to part company having been hoisted aboard the *Eros* the moment that my boat left her side.

Having braced up on the same course as that steered by the *Virginia* when last seen, and crowded upon the brigantine every square inch of canvas that her spars would bear, I sent a hand aloft to the royal yard to take a look round and see whether he could discover any sign of the chase; but, as I had more than suspected, she had completely vanished; and my first task was now to find her again. To do this, two things were necessary; the first being that we should follow precisely the same course that she had done; and the second, that we should sail fast enough to overtake her. I therefore ordered the boatswain at once to get up preventer backstays, fore and aft, to enable our spars to carry a heavy press of sail; and then went to my cabin, where, with a chart of the Atlantic spread open before us upon the cabin table, Jack Keene and I discussed the knotty question of the course that should be steered to enable us once more to bring the *Virginia* within the range of our own horizon.

The point that we had to consider was whether our Yankee friend would or would not anticipate pursuit. If he did, he would probably resort to some expedient to dodge us; but if he did not there was little doubt that he would make the best of his way to his port of destination, which, if he spoke the truth, was the Congo. Now, we were well within the limits of the north-east trade-winds, the wind at the moment blowing, as nearly as might be, due north-east, and piping up strong enough to make us think twice before setting our topgallantsail; it was therefore perfectly ideal weather for so powerful a craft as the

Virginia, which might dare not only to show all three of her topgallantsails but also, perhaps, her main-royal. We therefore ultimately came to the conclusion that, the weather being what it was, our friend the Yankee would shape a straight course for Cape Palmas, with the intention of then availing himself of the alternate sea and land-breezes to slip along the coast as far as the Congo—that being the plan very largely followed by slavers on the eastward passage—and that he would only be likely to deviate from that plan in the event of his actually discovering that he was pursued. Consequently we determined to do the same; and I issued the necessary orders to that effect. We were not very long in getting our preventers rigged, after which we not only set our royal and flying-jib, but also shifted our gaff-topsail, hauling down Number 3, a jib-headed affair, and setting Number 2 in its place, a sail nearly twice as big as the other, with its lofty, tapering head laced to a yard very nearly as long as the topmast. Then, with her lee rail awash—and, in fact, dipping deeply sometimes, on a lee roll—and the lee scuppers breast-deep in water, the *Dolphin* began to show us what she really could do in the matter of sailing when called upon; reeling off a steady eleven knots, hour after hour, upon a taut bowline; the smother of froth under her bows boiling up at times to the level of her lee cat-head, and her foresail wet with spray to the height of its reef-band. It was grand sailing, exhilarating as a draught of wine, maddening in the feeling of recklessness that it begot; but, all the same, I did not believe that we were doing more than perhaps just holding our own with the *Virginia*; it was not under such conditions as those that we were likely to overhaul her; our chance would come when, as we gradually neared the equator, the wind grew more shy and fitful. Nevertheless, I kept a look-out in the fore-topmast cross-trees throughout the hours of daylight, to make sure that we should not overtake her unexpectedly.

We carried on all through that night, and the next day, and the next, with the breeze still holding strong, yet there was no sign of the chase; and, meanwhile, the carpenter informed me we were straining the ship all to pieces and opening her seams to such an extent that the pumps had to be tended for half an hour at a time twice in each watch; while the boatswain was kept in a perpetual state of anxiety lest his rigging should give way under the strain.

At length, on the afternoon of the fourth day after parting from the *Eros*, the wind began to moderate somewhat rapidly, with the result that by sunset our lee scuppers were dry, although we still had all our flying kites aloft; and that night the watch below were able to bring their mattresses on deck and sleep on the forecastle, a luxury which had hitherto been impossible during our headlong race across the Atlantic. And now I began to feel sanguine that before many hours were over we should see the mastheads of the *Virginia* creeping above the horizon somewhere ahead of us; for I felt convinced that, in the moderate weather which we were then experiencing, we had the heels of her.

But when the next morning dawned, with the trade-wind breathing no more than a gentle zephyr, the look-out, upon going aloft, reported that the horizon was still bare; which, however, was not to say that the chase might not be within a dozen miles of us, for the atmosphere was exceedingly hazy, and heavy with damp heat which was very oppressive and relaxing, to such an extent, indeed, that the mere act of breathing seemed to demand quite an effort. After taking my usual morning bath under the head pump, I made my way below to my state-room to dress, and found Keene sitting in the main cabin, on one of the sofa lockers, attired only in shirt and trousers, perspiring freely, and in a general state of limpness that was pitiable to behold.

"Morning, skipper!" he gasped. "I say, isn't this heat awful? Worse, even, than that on the Coast, I think! And what has become of all the wind? I say, I suppose we haven't made a mistake in our reckoning, and run down on to the Line unbeknownst, have we?"

"If we have," said I severely, "the mistake is yours Master Jack; for, as you are very well aware, I have been entrusting the navigation of this ship to you."

Which, by the way, was only true in a certain sense; for while I had given the young man to understand that, for his own benefit and advantage, I intended to make him perform the duty of master, and hold him responsible for the navigation, I had taken care to maintain a strict check upon his calculations and assure myself that he was making no mistakes. Of which fact he was of course quite aware. Wherefore his reply to my retort was simply to change the subject with some celerity.

"I say, old chap," he remarked, "you look awfully cool and comfy. Been under the head pump, as usual, I suppose. Upon my word, if it were not for the possibility—not to say the extreme probability—of being snapped up by a shark, I should like to go overboard in a bowline and be towed for half an hour. And—talking of sharks—have you noticed how often we have seen the beggars following us since we have been in this ship? I suppose her timbers have become saturated, as it were, with the odour of the slaves she has carried, and so—but, hillo! what has happened to the barometer?"

I glanced at the instrument, which, together with a tell-tale compass, swung from the skylight transoms, and saw that the mercury had sunk in the tube to the extent of nearly an inch since the last setting of the vernier; and, as it was our custom in the Slave Squadron at that time to set the instrument at 8 o'clock a.m. and 8 o'clock p.m., it meant that the mercury had fallen to that extent during the night! What was about to happen? I had observed nothing portentous in the aspect of the weather, while on deck, unless, indeed, the softening away of the trade-wind and the hazy condition of the atmosphere might be regarded as portents. Yet that could hardly be, for I had observed the same phenomena before, yet nothing particular had come of it. I decided to have a talk with Tasker, the gunner's mate, and get his views on the matter; he was a man of very considerable experience, having been a sailor before I was born; I therefore at once entered my cabin, and proceeded to dress; after which I returned to the deck, where Tasker was officer of the watch. I found him sitting aft on the stern grating, replacing his socks and shoes, which he had removed from his feet at four bells in order to take a leading part in the matutinal ceremony of washing decks. I had already seen him a little earlier that morning, and exchanged greetings with him; I therefore at once, and without any circumlocution, plunged into the subject by asking:

"What do you think of the look of the weather, Mr Tasker; is there anything unusual about it, in your opinion?"

Tasker rose to his feet and cast a prolonged glance at the sky before replying. Then he said slowly:

"I can't say as I sees anything much out of the common about it, so far, Mr Fortescue. The wind's dropped a bit more than's quite usual, certainly; but I don't know as there's very mich in that. And then there's this here thickness o' the hatmosphere—well, that may or may not mean somethin', but I don't see anything alarmin' about it just yet. Why d'ye ask the question, sir? Is the glass droppin' at all?"

"It has dropped nearly an inch since it was set last night," I answered.

"Phew! Nearly an inch since eight bells last night!" ejaculated the old salt, with an air of concern. "That means, sir, that it have fallen that little lot since midnight; for I looked at it then, when Mr Keene relieved me, and it hadn't dropped nothin' then."

"Then what is going to happen?" I demanded. "Are we going to have a hurricane?"

"I should say yes, Mr Fortescue, most decidedly," answered Tasker. "And yet," he continued, again carefully scanning the sky, "I must confess I don't see nothin' very alarmin' up there at present. I s'pose the mercury bag haven't sprung a leak, by no chance, have it? This here sudden drop reminds me of a yarn a shipmate of mine once told me about a scare he had when he was in the sloop *Pyramus* in the Indian Ocean, outward bound to the China station. The scare started with a sudden fall of the barometer, just as it might be in this here present case, and it went on droppin' until the skipper began to think he was booked for the biggest blow as ever come away out o' the 'eavens. He started by sendin' down royal and t'gallan' yards and housin' the t'gallan' masts. Then, as the mercury still went on droppin', he shortened sail to close-reefed fore and main taups'ls, sent the t'gallan' masts down on deck, and housed the topmasts. While this work was goin' on the mercury kept fallin' until it sank out o' sight altogether; and the skipper had actually given the order to furl the taups'ls and send the yards and masts down when the cabin steward happened to make the discovery that the mercury bag had busted and the mercury from the barometer was rollin' in little balls all over the cabin floor! My mate told me that the time in which they got that there *Pyramus* ataunto again, that day, and the royals upon her, was never a'terwards beaten!"

I could not avoid a good hearty laugh at this quaint story of a phenomenal fall of the mercury in a barometer; for it was easy to conjure up a picture of the rapidly growing alarm and dismay of the captain as he watched the steady and speedy shrinkage of the metallic column, and of the feverish anxiety and haste with which he would proceed with his preparations to meet the swoop of the supposedly approaching typhoon, as also of his disgust at the discovery that all his alarm and anxiety had been brought about by the unsuspected leakage of a leather bag! But the story served as a hint to me; what had happened once might happen again; and I forthwith retired to the cabin and carefully examined our own instrument to discover whether, haply, such an accident had occurred in our case. But no, the bag into which the base of the glass tube was plunged was perfectly sound and intact; and, meanwhile, during my brief colloquy with Tasker a further fall of a full tenth had occurred. I lost no time in returning to the deck.

"The scare is quite genuine this time, Mr Tasker," I said; "there is no leakage in our mercury bag to account for the heavy drop; moreover, the drop has increased by a full tenth. Therefore, although the present aspect of the weather may not be precisely alarming, we will proceed to snug down at once, if you please, in view of the fact that the crew we carry is not precisely what might be called efficient, and will probably take an unconscionably long time over the work."

"Ay, ay, sir," answered Tasker. "I expect the mercury ain't droppin' exactly for nothin', therefore, as you says, we'd better be makin' ready for what's in store for us." Then, facing forward, he gave the order:

"Clew up your royal and t'garns'l, furl 'em, and then get the yards down on deck. Hurry, you scallywags; the more work you does now, the more time for play will you have a'ter breakfast."

The "snugging down" process occupied us until nearly four bells of the forenoon watch; but when at length it was completed we felt that we were prepared to face anything, our royal and topgallant-mast and all our yards being down on deck, the fore and main-topmasts and the jib-boom housed, the great mainsail snugly stowed and the heavy boom securely supported in a strong crutch, and the ship under fore and main storm staysails only.

Chapter Eleven.

The end of the Dolphin.

By the time that all this had been accomplished, the wind had fallen away to a dead calm, and the only sounds audible were the creaking and groaning of the ship's timbers, the loud rattle of the cabin doors below upon their hooks, the wash of the sea alongside and under the counter, the constant irritating *jerk-jerk* of the tiller chains, and the violent rustle and slatting of the staysails, as the *Dolphin* rolled her channels under in the long, oily swell that was now running. But, so far as the aspect of the sky was concerned, there was no more sign of the threatened storm than there had been when I first went on deck that morning—except that, maybe, the haze had thickened somewhat, rendering our horizon still more circumscribed, and the heat had increased to such an extent that, as Keene had remarked, one would gladly have gone overboard to escape it but for the sharks, several of which were cruising round us, while three monsters persistently hung under our counter in the shadow of the ship's hull, hungrily ogling those of us who chanced to lean over the taffrail to get a glimpse of them. Yet, when, for want of something better to do, Jack Keene and I got a shark hook and, baiting it with a highly flavoured piece of pork out of the harness cask, sought to inveigle one of the monsters into swallowing it, they disdained to even so much as look at it, merely glancing upward at us, when we deftly dropped the bait upon one of their broad, shovel noses, as though to say:

"No, no, my hearties! No rancid pork for us, thank you, when, by exercising a little patience, we may, with luck, get a chance to learn what one of you jokers tastes like." The enervating effect of the heat seemed to be as strongly revealed in them as it was in ourselves.

The sun still flamed in the heavens when, shortly before noon, Jack and I brought our sextants on deck with the object of measuring his meridian altitude above the horizon; but we were only able to obtain a very approximate and wholly useless result, for, when we came to try, we found that the sun appeared in our instruments merely as a shapeless glare of light, while the horizon was wholly indistinguishable. Then, by imperceptible degrees, the sun, like the horizon, became obliterated, and the atmosphere stealthily darkened, as though a continuous succession of curtains of grey gauze were being interposed between us and the sky. Meanwhile the barometer was still persistently declining, although not quite so rapidly as during the early hours of the morning.

It was about six bells in the afternoon watch when, with a sudden darkening of the sky, that came upon us like the gloom of night, it began to rain—a regular tropical deluge, sluicing down upon us in sheets, as though the bottom of a cloud had dropped out; and within less than a minute our decks were more than ankle-deep in warm fresh water, and our scuppers were running full. The downpour lasted for perhaps a minute and a half, and then ceased as abruptly as though a tap had been turned off, and we heard the shower passing away to the northward of us, leaving us with streaming decks and dripping canvas and rigging. But, although the rain had come and gone again in the space of a couple of minutes, the darkness intensified rather than otherwise, and presently we heard a muttering of distant thunder away down in the southern quarter, followed, after a while, by a further dash of rain, lasting for a few seconds only.

Then, all in a moment, and without any further warning, the blackness overhead was riven by the most appallingly vivid flash of lightning that I had ever seen, accompanied—not followed—by a crash of thunder that temporarily deafened all hands of us and caused the ship to quiver and tremble from stem to stern. Then, while we were all standing agape, our ears deafened by the thunder and our eyes blinded by the glare of the lightning, a fierce gust of hot wind swept over us, filling our two staysails with a report like that of a cannon and laying the ship over to her sheer-strake. Tasker, who was again officer of the watch, at once sprang to the wheel and assisted the helmsman to put it hard up; but almost before the ship had begun to gather way the first fierceness of the gust had passed, leaving us little more than a fresh breeze. I therefore went aft and shouted to them—for they were as deaf as I was—to bring the vessel up to her course again, when we began to move through the water at a speed of some five knots.

That first terrible flash of lightning and crash of thunder was, however, only the beginning of the most awful electric storm that it has ever been my fate to witness, the sky, now black as night, being rent in half a dozen different directions at once by fierce, baleful flashes, green, blue, crimson, and sun-bright, while the bombarding of the thunder was absolutely terrifying, even to us who were by this time growing quite accustomed to tropical storms. With it there came frequent short, sharp, intermittent bursts of rain that swept across our decks, stinging the exposed skin like shot, and enshrouding everything beyond a couple of fathoms away in impenetrable obscurity. Now, too, there came, at irregular but quickly recurring intervals, savage gusts of wind that smote the ship as though she had been but a child's toy, heeling her down until her lee rail was awash, and holding her thus for two or three minutes at a time, then easing up for a short space, the "easing up" intervals, however, steadily growing more abbreviated, while the gusts that invariably followed them rapidly grew in intensity and fury, until after the passage of one that had pinned us down for three or four minutes, with our lee sheer-poles buried in the smother, I thought that the time had arrived to heave-to, and gave the order to do so. Nor was I any too soon; for the sea was rapidly rising, and a quarter of an hour later we probably could not have accomplished the feat without having had our decks swept. The gale now rapidly increased in intensity, the gusts of wind ever growing stronger and more furious, and succeeding each other more rapidly, until at length the intervals between them became so brief as to be practically imperceptible, the strength of the wind now being equal to that of a heavy gale, and momentarily growing stronger as gust after gust swooped down upon us. The blinding, drenching showers that occasionally swept us were no longer composed of fresh water only, for there was a strong mingling of salt-water in them that was none other than the tops of the waves, torn off by the terrific blasts of wind and hurled along horizontally in the form of vast sheets of spray. The sea, meanwhile, was rising with astounding rapidity, taking into consideration the fact that, as just stated, the height of the combers was greatly reduced by the enormous volumes of water that were scooped up from the ocean's surface by the fury of the wind; moreover the sea was short, steep, and irregular, much more nearly resembling the breakers on a coast in shallow water, than the long, regular, majestically moving seas of the open ocean. The *Dolphin*, therefore, despite her beautiful model and the reduction of her tophamper, was beginning to make exceedingly bad weather of it, frequently burying herself to her foremast, and careening so heavily that during some of her lee rolls it was impossible to maintain one's footing on deck except by holding on to something.

At length, about four bells in the first watch, the lightning, which had hitherto almost continuously illuminated the atmosphere, suddenly ceased altogether, and the night grew intensely dark, the only objects remaining visible being the faintly phosphorescent heads of the seas, flashing into view and gleaming ghostly for a moment before they were torn into spray by the violence of the wind and whirled away through the air to leeward. Then, with almost equal suddenness, there came a positively startling lull in the strength of the wind, and the ship—which had for some hours been laying over to it so steeply that movement about her decks was only to be achieved with great circumspection and by patiently awaiting the arrival of one's opportunity—suddenly rose almost to an even keel. I seized the chance thus afforded me to claw my way to the skylight and glance through it at the barometer, illuminated by the wildly swaying lamp which the steward had lighted when darkness fell, but, to my intense disappointment, the mercury, which had steadily been shrinking all day, exhibited a further drop since the index had been set at eight o'clock that evening.

"We have not yet seen the worst of it," I shouted to Tasker, who, although it was now his watch below, had elected to remain on deck and bear me company. "The glass is still going down."

"I'm very sorry to hear it, Mr Fortescue," he answered. "I don't like the look of things at all. The ship has been most terrible uneasy for several hours now, and I'm afraid we shall find that she's been strainin' badly. It might not be amiss to sound the well; and if, as I fear, we find that she's been takin' water in through her seams, I'd advise—"

His further speech was cut short by a terrific blast of wind that swooped down upon us like a howling, screaming fiend, without a moment's warning. So violent was it that Tasker and I were both swept off our feet and dashed to the deck, where I brought up against the cabin companion with a crash that all but knocked the senses out of me, while the gunner's mate disappeared in the direction of the lee scuppers. The yelling and screaming of the wind was absolutely appalling, the volume of sound being such that nothing else could be heard above it; and in the midst of the din I became vaguely conscious that the ship was going over until she lay upon her beam ends, with her deck almost perpendicular, and the water up to the level of her hatchways.

For a few seconds I lay where I was, on the upturned side of the companion, listening to the water pouring into the cabin with every lee roll of the ship, and endeavouring to pull together my scattered faculties; then, dimly realising that something must be done to relieve the ship if we would not have her founder beneath us, I scrambled to my feet and, seizing a rope's end that came lashing about me, dragged myself up to the weather rail, clinging to which I slowly and painfully worked my way forward, shouting for the carpenter as I did so. At length, arrived at the fore rigging, I came upon a small group of men who had somehow contrived to climb up to windward and out upon the ship's upturned side, where they were now desperately hacking away with their knives at the lanyards of the weather fore rigging.

"That's right, lads!" I exclaimed, whipping out my own knife and lending a hand; "we must cut away the masts and get the ship upright again, or she will go down under us. Where is the carpenter? Let him bring along his axe. He will do more good in one minute than we can in ten."

"I'm afraid, sir, as Chips has gone overboard with some more when the ship was hove down. But I'll see if I can get into the fo'c's'le and lay my hand upon his axe," answered one of the men.

"Do so by all means," I returned; "and be quick about it. I would go myself, but you will know better than I where to find the axe; and even moments are precious just now."

They were, indeed; for it was easy to tell, by the feel of the ship, that she was becoming waterlogged, and every gallon of water that now poured into her seriously decreased our chances of saving her. But it was bad news to learn that the carpenter, "with some more" men, had been lost overboard when the ship was thrown upon her beam-ends; yet, when I came to recall the suddenness of the event, the surprising thing was that any of us had survived it. This reminded me of Tasker, and set me wondering whether he had been as fortunate as myself, or whether that last awful lurch had been as fatal to him as it had been to some others among us.

Meanwhile we continued to hack away with our knives at the lanyards, and presently, after what appeared to have been a terribly protracted interval, but which was probably not more than a couple of minutes, the last lanyard parted with a twang, and the next instant, with a crash heard even through the terrific hubbub of the gale, the foremast snapped close off by the deck and plunged, with all attached, into the boil to leeward.

Then we breathlessly waited, hoping that, thus relieved, the ship would recover herself, and for a moment it almost seemed that she would do so; but just at the critical moment the gale swooped down heavier than ever, and at the same instant an extra heavy sea struck her, and down she lay again, as though too tired to struggle further.

"It is no good, men," I cried, "she won't rise. Lay aft, and cut away the mainmast also. It is our only chance!" And, therewith, we all crawled along the ship's side—escaping being washed off or blown overboard only by a series of miracles, as it seemed to me—until we arrived at the main chains, where we had something to cling to, and where the channel-piece partially sheltered us. Here we at once got to work with all our energy upon the weather main lanyards, and, the man with the axe presently joining us, in a few minutes the mainmast also went over the side.

"Now, inboard with you, men, as smart as you like," I cried. "If she is going to rise at all she may do so quite suddenly, in which case we run the risk of being hove overboard if we remain here."

We all scrambled in on deck, steadying ourselves by such of the running rigging as we could lay hold of; and we had scarcely done so when the hull partially recovered its upright position, not quite so suddenly as I had expected, yet with a quick righting movement that left our decks knee-deep in water. I sprang to the companion and strove to close the burst-open doors and so prevent any further influx of water to the cabin; but the heavy washing sounds that came up from below told me that my efforts were already too late to be of any service, for the cabin seemed to be flooded to almost half the height of the companion ladder, and the sluggish motions of the ship told me eloquently enough that she was perilously near to a foundering condition. I therefore rallied the men and bade them get to work at the pumps forthwith; and it was then that I discovered, to my horror, that, of our complement of sixty, we had lost no fewer than fourteen, including my messmate, poor Jack Keene, and Tasker, the gunner's mate, all of whom must have gone overboard when the vessel was thrown down on her beam-ends! It was a most deplorable affair, and I was especially grieved at the loss of my light-hearted chum; but that was not the moment for indulgence in useless lamentation, and I busied myself in doing what might be possible to provide for the safety of the ship.

First of all I got a strong gang to work at the pumps in two relays, each taking a spell of ten minutes pumping, followed by an equal length of time for rest. When I had fairly started these, and saw the water gushing in a clear stream from the spouts of both pumps, I set the rest to work cutting away all the rigging which still held the wreckage of the masts attached to the hull, leaving the fore and fore-topmast stays untouched, my intention being that the drift of the hull should bring the wreckage under the bows, where, being held fast by the stays, it should form a sort of floating anchor to which the ship should ride head to wind and sea. Thus we might hope that she would no longer ship water in such quantities as to threaten her safety. After nearly an hour's hard labour we succeeded, during which it appeared to me that the men were making little or no impression upon the amount of water in the hold. But, as I had hoped, when once we had brought the hull head to wind she no longer shipped water in any very alarming quantities; and after watching her carefully for some minutes I came to the conclusion that we might safely venture to open the after hatchway and supplement the efforts of those at the pumps by baling with buckets.

Before starting the pumps I had taken the precaution of having the well sounded, with the result that we had discovered the depth of water in the ship's interior to be three feet ten inches, as nearly as could be ascertained; but the violent motions of the hull had rendered anything like really accurate sounding an impossibility, and the same cause now precluded us from ascertaining with certainty whether the leak was gaining upon the pumps or *vice-versa*. One thing was perfectly certain, and that was that if the pumps were gaining upon the leak at all, it was but slowly. If that should prove to be the case, it would mean that there was something the matter more serious than the mere straining of the ship; possibly a butt or a hood-end had been started.

It was by this time close upon midnight, and there were times when I almost succeeded in persuading myself that it was not blowing quite so hard as it had been, although the difference—if difference there were—was certainly not very strongly marked; the sea, however, still continued to rise, and was now running higher than I had ever before seen it. Yet the poor, sorely battered *Dolphin* rode it reasonably well, all things considered; although there were times when the water in her interior, happening to become concentrated in the fore part of her just as she should be rising to a sea, pinned her down by the head to a dangerous extent, causing the sea to come in, green, unbroken, and like a miniature mountain, over her bows. When this threatened to occur it became necessary to watch her narrowly, and if the danger seemed to be imminent we hurriedly replaced the after hatches, otherwise we should very quickly have been swamped.

When the pumping gangs had been at work for about an hour they complained of exhaustion, and I accordingly relieved them to the extent of setting them to work with the buckets and putting two fresh gangs at the pumps; yet, although these men worked pretty energetically, it soon became evident that we were not gaining anything upon the leak, and as time passed on it became exceedingly doubtful whether the leak were not rather gaining upon us. Moreover, as the sea continued to rise the vessel's movements became more laboured, and she again began to take the water aboard in such dangerous quantities that at length we were reluctantly compelled to abandon our baling operations, and close the hatches to prevent the heavy seas from reaching her interior.

In this fashion the seemingly endless night at length wore itself away and the lowering dawn came, disclosing to us the true seriousness of our condition. There we were, aweary, hollow-eyed, haggard-looking little band, sodden to the very bones of us with long hours of exposure to the pitiless buffeting of rain and sea, our flesh salt-encrusted, our eyes bloodshot, our hands raw and bleeding with the severe and protracted work at the pumps, adrift in mid-ocean upon a mastless, sorely battered, and badly leaking hulk, with her ballast shifted and a heavy list, tossed helplessly upon a furiously raging sea that seemed instinct with a relentless determination to overwhelm us, toiling and fighting doggedly against the untiring elements, in the hope that, perchance, if our strength held out, we might keep the now crazy, straining, and complaining fabric beneath us afloat long enough to afford us some chance of saving our lives. Yet the hope was, after all, but a slender one; for with the coming of daylight we were able to see that our plight was very considerably worse than we had dreamed it to be during the hours of darkness; for *then* we had believed that the loss of our masts and the springing of a somewhat serious leak represented the sum total of our misfortunes; while *now* we saw, to our unspeakable dismay, that, with the solitary exception of the longboat, the whole of our boats were so badly damaged as to be altogether beyond our ability to repair; of two of them, indeed, nothing save the stem and stern remained dangling forlornly from the davit tackles. But that, bad though it was, was not the worst; for it was no longer possible for us to blind ourselves to the fact that the leak was gaining upon us inexorably, and that, even though we should continue to toil with unabated energy, we could not keep the ship afloat longer than a few hours more, at the utmost.

And then what were we to do? The longboat, fine boat though she was, when stocked with even a meagre supply of provisions and water, would not accommodate more than twenty-five men, and I gravely doubted whether she would live ten minutes in such a sea as was then running, with half that number in her. Still, with the exception of such a raft as we might be able to put together, she was all that we had, and half an hour of daylight sufficed to show me that no time must be lost in making preparations to quit the slowly foundering ship. Yet it would not do for us to leave the pumps for a moment; one gang must, at all costs, be kept hard at work pumping out as much as possible of the water that was pouring in through the open seams, otherwise the leak would gain upon us so rapidly that the ship would settle from under us long before we were ready to face such a catastrophe. I therefore at once set about the formulating of my plans and carrying them into effect. First of all, while one gang kept the pump-brakes clanking and the clear water spouting out upon our streaming deck, I got another gang to work at launching the guns overboard as the roll of the ship permitted—and this, I was glad to see, eased the poor labouring craft quite perceptibly. This done, all hands, except those at the pumps, went to breakfast, the meal consisting of hot coffee sweetened with molasses, and ship's biscuit, more or less sodden with salt-water—for with the coming of daylight and the preparation of breakfast the unwelcome discovery had been made that the salt-water had got at the provisions and gone far toward spoiling them. Then, as soon as the first gang had finished breakfast, they relieved those at the pumps, who in their turn took breakfast and next proceeded to clear away the longboat and prepare her for launching, by providing her with a proper supply of oars and thole-pins, her rudder and tiller, masts and sails, and then carefully stowing her stock of water and provisions. But when all this was done it was still blowing too hard—although the worst of the gale seemed to be over—and the sea was altogether too rough to allow of our attempting to launch her. We therefore next got to work upon a raft, first of all lashing all our spare spars together as a sort of foundation, and then, upon the top of this, lashing the hen-coops, gratings, a few planks that the carpenter had stowed away down below, and, finally, some lengths of bulwark that we cut away for the purpose. This raft, when completed, was a fairly roomy affair, affording space enough to stow away some thirty people, together with a good supply of provisions and water, which we now proceeded to get up from below and stow; the cook, meanwhile, industriously boiling as much beef and pork as he could crowd into his coppers. Then we knocked off and piped to dinner; and while we were getting this— probably the last meal of which we should ever partake aboard the poor old *Dolphin*— our hearts were gladdened by a sudden burst of sunshine breaking through the clouds, and half an hour later the sky to windward was clear, the sun was shining brilliantly and pouring his welcome warmth upon our chilled bodies and saturated clothing, while the gale had broken and was fast moderating, having already declined to the strength of a double-reefed topsail breeze. The sea, too, was no longer raging like a boiling cauldron; yet, even so, it was still too heavy to justify us in attempting to launch either the longboat or the raft.

And now, at the very moment when it was most necessary that the crew should preserve an orderly and obedient disposition, they suddenly broke into open mutiny, flatly refusing to work any longer at the pumps; declaring that the ship was good for at least another hour, and that before that had passed we should all be safely away from her; that there was no sense in wanting to keep the ship afloat longer than there was any absolute need for; and that the time had now arrived when they must begin to think of saving their own personal belongings. When I attempted to remonstrate with them and point out the folly of their behaviour they became virulently abusive, and declared that if I wanted the pumps kept going I might keep them going myself—and this although I had already done considerably more than my fair share of that back-breaking labour. Therewith they abandoned the pumps and betook themselves forward to the forecastle, from which there shortly afterward came floating to my horrified ears loud peals of maudlin laughter, mingled with snatches of ribald songs and coarse jests, whereby I came to know, all too late, that, while getting up the provisions from below, some of them must have broken into the spirit-room and possessed themselves of a very considerable supply of rum, upon which they were now fast drinking themselves into a condition of reckless indifference to the awful danger that threatened them. Anything, I thought, was better than this; therefore, having first gone down below and brought up the chronometer, my sextant, and a chart of the Atlantic, and stowed the whole carefully in the stern-sheets of the longboat, loaded my pistols, and girded my sword to my side, I went forward to the fore-scuttle and, putting my head into it, shouted in as cheery a tone as I could summon:

"Now then, lads, tumble up on deck, all hands of you. We have still a great deal to do, and very little time to do it in; therefore let us see about getting the longboat into the water, and the raft over the side. There will be time enough to rest when we are safe away from the wreck."

"All ri', schipper, don' you worry," bawled a great hulking Dutchman in reply. "Dere's blendy of dime yet; and ve're nod going do move undil ve've vinished dhis grog."

Then another—an American this time—took up the tale, shouting, "Go 'way, little man, go 'way! Wha' d'you mean, anyway, by comin' here and disturbin' gen'lemen when they're busy? Come in and have a drink with us, youngster, just to show that you're not stuck up. I guess we're all equals in this dandy little barkie; yes, sirree! I'm a free-born 'Murican, I am, an' just as good as you or any other blamed Britisher, and don' you forget it. So, if you won' come in an' have a drink, take your ugly-lookin' mug out o' the daylight, d'ye hear?"

To emphasise this polite request the man seized a heavy sea boot from the forecastle deck and hove it at me, with so poor an aim that instead of hitting me he dashed it into the face of an Englishman who happened at the moment to be drinking rum out of a pannikin. The blow dashed the pannikin out of the man's hand, and splashed the fiery spirit all over his face and into his eyes; and the next instant, with a low, fierce growl of concentrated ferocity, he sprang to his feet and struck the free-born 'Murican a smashing blow under the chin that sent him sprawling.

"You have no time to waste in fighting, lads," I cried, for I felt that the ship was fast settling under our feet. But my voice was completely drowned in the babel of angry yells that instantly arose, for it appeared that the men were, after their own fashion, rivals for leadership in the forecastle, and each man had his own partisans, every one of whom instantly took up the quarrel of his own favourite, and in another moment the whole of them were at each others' throats, like so many quarrelsome dogs.

"Let the drunken, mutinous brutes fight it out among themselves," I muttered disgustedly as I turned and walked away. "They will get a sobering-up before very long that will astonish them, or I am greatly mistaken!"

As I walked aft I could tell, by the feel of the ship, that her race was nearly run—although I did not at that moment dream how very near to her end she was—and I paused abreast of the longboat to satisfy myself that she was quite ready for launching out through the wide gap that we had made in the bulwarks when cutting them away to provide material for the construction of the raft. The gripes, I saw, had been cast off, and the boat was supported solely by her chocks, upon which she stood upright on the main hatchway. Suddenly, stooping down, a small spot of bright light in the deep shadow under the boat caught my eye, and looking closer I saw that some careless rascal had omitted to put in the plug, and that the bright spot of light was caused by the sun shining down through the unplugged hole in the boat's bottom. With a muttered objurgation of the fellow's carelessness, I climbed into the boat and, stooping down, sought for the plug. I was seeking for perhaps two or three minutes before I found it, but as I was about to abandon the search, and hunt for a suitable cork out of which to cut another, my eye fell upon the missing plug, and I at once inserted it and proceeded to drive it tightly home. I had just completed the job to my satisfaction when I felt the ship lurch heavily. There was a sudden, violent rush and wash of water, and I sprang to my feet barely in time to see the boat caught up on the crest of a sea that came sweeping, green and solid, through the gap in the starboard bulwarks, and carried clear and clean out through the corresponding gap in the port side! The longboat had launched herself; and before I could collect my senses, or lift a hand, I found myself adrift alone, some twenty fathoms to leeward of the doomed ship, and driving farther away from her every moment.

Chapter Twelve.

Alone in the longboat.

To seize one of the long, heavy ash oars that formed part of the boat's equipment, fling the blade over the stern, and jerk the oar into the sculling notch, with the idea of sculling the boat back to the wreck was, with me, the work of but a second or two; but although I contrived, with some labour, to get the boat's head round toward the *Dolphin*, and to keep it pointed in that direction, I soon discovered—as I might have had the sense to know— that to scull a big heavy boat like the longboat to windward against such a strong wind and so heavy a sea was a task altogether beyond the power of a single man, however strong he might be; for every sea that swept down upon the boat sent her surging away a good half-dozen fathoms to leeward.

Finding this attempt useless, I at once hauled the oar inboard again, and proceeded to ship the rudder, which task I at length accomplished, with some difficulty owing to the violent motion of the boat; then I shipped the tiller; and next proceeded to loose the boat's canvas, with the idea of beating back to the ship. But here again I found myself seriously hampered and delayed by the circumstance that, when equipping the boat, the men had only half done their work. The boat was rigged as a fore and aft schooner, setting a main trysail, fore trysail, and a staysail secured to the head of the stem; and while the masts had been stepped and the shrouds set up hand-taut, I found, upon casting loose the sails, that they had omitted to obey my instructions to close-reef them, and since the wind was still blowing altogether too hard for the boat to carry anything more than close-reefed canvas I lost quite ten minutes in reefing and setting the mainsail and staysail—I dared not attempt to set the foresail also, for I did not believe that the boat could carry it. And when at length I had got the canvas set and the boat fairly under way, I found, to my consternation, that I had driven a good half-mile to leeward of the ship, by which time, their quarrel, I suppose, being over, the men had left the forecastle and, finding that I had gone adrift in the longboat, were making frantic signs to me to return.

But I soon discovered that, even now, with the boat under canvas, to beat back to the ship was an impossibility; for the boat had not been built for sailing to windward in a strong breeze; she was the ordinary type of ship's longboat, constructed to carry a heavy load in proportion to her dimensions, with a long, flat floor, bluff bows, and with only some three inches of exposed keel; and while she might possibly, with skilful management, have been made to work to windward in very moderate weather, she now, with so strong a wind and so heavy a sea to battle with, drove to leeward almost as rapidly as she forged ahead. Nor did I dare to press her with any more canvas, for she was already showing more than was at all prudent, the stronger puffs careening her to her gunwale and taxing my seamanship to the utmost to prevent her from filling. Under such circumstances, with the boat demanding my utmost vigilance to keep her afloat, it will be readily understood that I was only able at intervals to cast a momentary glance toward the ship to see how she was faring, and even then it was not always possible for me to catch a glimpse of her because of the mountainous seas that interposed themselves between her and me. At length, however, when I had been adrift about half an hour, I got a chance to take a fairly long look to windward at a moment when the longboat was hove up on the crest of an unusually lofty wave; but the ship was nowhere to be seen; nor did I again catch sight of her, or even of the raft; and the only conclusion at which I could arrive was that she had gone down and taken all hands with her.

But, in such a mountainous sea as was then running, the horizon of a person in a boat is naturally very restricted, and I knew that, although I had failed to catch a glimpse of either the wreck or the raft, the latter at least might be afloat, and my plain duty was to remain in the neighbourhood so long as there was any chance of falling in with it; I therefore watched my opportunity and, seizing a favourable moment, wore the boat round on the other tack and, again bringing her to the wind, went back as nearly over the ground I had already traversed as was possible. But although I kept a sharp look-out, and wore round every half-hour, I saw nothing, no, not even so much as a fragment of floating wreckage, to indicate what had actually happened; nor did I ever hear of any of my late crew being picked up.

It was about four bells—two o'clock—in the afternoon watch when I last saw the wreck; and I beat about, remaining as near the spot as I could, until sunset. Then, having failed to fall in with or sight either the wreck or the raft, I came to the conclusion that I had seen the last of my mutinous crew, and that the time had arrived when I was quite justified in abandoning any further effort to find them, and might look after my own safety.

The weather, by this time, had improved very considerably; the wind had been slowly but steadily moderating, and the sea, although still tremendously high, was not now breaking dangerously; the sky also had cleared and was without a cloud; there was therefore every prospect of a fine night, with a further steady improvement of the weather; the boat was no longer dangerously pressed by the amount of canvas that she was carrying, and I felt that I need be under no immediate apprehension regarding the future. Moreover my clothes had by this time dried upon my body, and I felt quite warm and comfortable. But I was both hungry and thirsty, for the so-called dinner that I had snatched aboard the *Dolphin* had been a very hasty and meagre meal. I therefore hove the boat to, by lashing the tiller hard down and hauling the staysail sheet to windward, and then, finding that she rode quite comfortably and was taking care of herself, I proceeded to rummage among my stock of provisions, and soon had a hearty meal set out before me on the after thwart.

By the time that I had finished my supper night had fallen, the stars were shining with the brilliance that they only display in the tropics, and I was beginning to feel the need of sleep; I therefore took a final look round, satisfied myself that all was right and that nothing was in sight, and then, heartily commending myself to the care of my Maker, I stretched myself out on the bottom-boards, and was almost instantly asleep.

To say that I slept soundly that night would scarcely be speaking the truth; for, although I had pretty well satisfied myself before I lay down, that the weather was improving and that therefore I had little or no cause for immediate apprehension, a sailor quickly acquires the trick of maintaining a certain alertness, even in the midst of his slumbers, since he knows that the weather is his most formidable and treacherous enemy, against which he has always to be on his guard; and this faculty of alertness is of course especially active when, as in my own case, he has only himself to depend upon. Consequently I never completely lost consciousness throughout that night, the rush of the wind, the hiss of the sea, the occasional sprinkling of spray were all mechanically noted, and whenever the heel of the boat appreciably exceeded its normal angle I at once became momentarily awake; yet, notwithstanding this, when on the following morning— the first rays of the newly risen sun smote upon my closed eyelids, informing me of the arrival of a new day, I at once arose, refreshed and vigorous, and ready to face any emergency that the day might bring.

My first act was to kneel down and return thanks for my preservation through the night and seek the protection and guidance of God throughout the day; after which I leaned over the boat's gunwale and freely laved my head, face, and hands in the clear salt-water. Then I set about preparing for myself the most appetising breakfast that my resources would permit; and while I was doing this and discussing the meal I carefully reviewed the entire situation, with a view to my arrival at an immediate decision as to my future proceedings.

The chart which I had with me showed the position of the *Dolphin* at the moment when my last observations were taken; and from this information I was able to deduce the approximate position of the spot where the vessel had foundered. This spot, I found, was, in round figures, one thousand miles from Sierra Leone, and fourteen hundred miles from the island of Barbadoes; but whereas Sierra Leone was almost dead to windward, Barbadoes was as directly dead to leeward; and a little calculation convinced me that while it would take me about thirty-six days to beat to windward the shorter distance, I might cover the longer, running pleasantly before the wind, in about twenty-four days, allowing, in both cases, for the boat being hove-to throughout the night to enable me to obtain necessary rest. Fortunately, I had with me not only the chart of the North Atlantic, but also a chronometer, sextant, nautical almanac, and boat compass; I was therefore equipped with every requisite for the efficient navigation of the boat, and had no fear of losing my way. I could consequently without hesitation choose what I considered to be the most desirable course, and it did not need any very profound reflection to convince me that this was to make the best of my way back to Barbadoes. I accordingly put up my helm, kept away before the wind, shook out all my reefs, and went sliding away to the westward, easily and comfortably, at a speed of some six knots per hour.

The weather had by this time reverted to quite its normal condition; the trade-wind was blowing steadily, the sea had gone down, and I had nothing worse than a somewhat heavy swell to contend with; I therefore felt that, unless I should be so unfortunate as to fall in with another gale, there was no reason at all why I should not reach my destination safely, and without very much discomfort. My only trouble was that, running, as the boat now was, with the wind so far over the starboard quarter, I dared not release my hold upon the tiller for an instant, lest she should broach-to and, possibly, capsize. Whenever, therefore, it became necessary for me to quit the helm for the purpose of taking an astronomical observation, or otherwise, I had to heave-to, and, occasionally, to shorten sail while doing so, which kept me pretty actively employed, off and on, all day. Thus, about nine o'clock in the morning, I had to heave-to and leave the boat to take care of herself while I secured observations of the sun for the determination of the longitude; the same procedure had to be adopted again at noon when I took the sun's altitude for the determination of the latitude; and the preparation of a meal involved a further repetition of the manoeuvre. Thus I had no time to feel lonely, at least during the hours of daylight; but after nightfall, surrounded and hemmed in by the gloom and mystery of the darkness, with no companionship save that of the multitudinous stars—which, to my mind, never betray their immeasurable distance so clearly as when one is in mid-ocean—with the sough and moan of the night wind and the soft, seething hiss of the sea whispering in one's ears, the feeling of loneliness becomes almost an obsession, the sense of all-pervading mystery persistently obtrudes itself, and one quickly falls into a condition of readiness to believe the most incredible of the countless weird stories that sailors love to relate to each other, especially when this condition of credulity is helped, as it sometimes is, by the sudden irruption of some strange, unaccountable sound, or succession of sounds, upon the peaceful quietude and serenity of the night. These sounds are

81

occasionally of the weirdest and most hair-raising quality; and while the startled listener may possibly have heard it asserted, time and again, by superior persons, that they emanate from sea birds, or from fish, he is perfectly satisfied that neither sea birds nor fish have ever been known to emit such sounds *in the daytime*, and the strain of superstition within him awakes and whispers all sorts of uncanny suggestions, the sea bird and fish theory being rejected with scorn. Moreover, those harrowingly mysterious sounds seem never to make themselves audible save when the accompanying circumstances are such as to conduce to the most startling and thrilling effect; thus, although I had now been knocking about at sea for more than three years, and had met with many queer experiences, I had never, thus far, heard a sound that I could not reasonably account for and attribute to some known source; yet on this particular night—my second night alone in the longboat—I was sitting comfortably enough in the stern-sheets, steering by a star—for I had no lantern wherewith to illuminate my compass—and thinking of nothing in particular, when suddenly a most unearthly cry came pealing out of the darkness on the starboard beam, seemingly not half a dozen yards away, and was twice repeated.

I felt the hair of my scalp bristle, and a violent shudder thrilled through me as those dreadful cries smote upon my ear, for they seemed to be the utterance of some human being in the very last extremity of both physical and mental anguish, the protest of a lost soul being wrenched violently out of its sinful human tenement, cries of such utter, unimaginable despair as the finite mind of man is unable to find a cause for. Yet, despite the agony of horror that froze my blood, I instinctively thrust my helm hard down and flattened in the sheets fore and aft; for the thought came to me that, perchance, a few fathoms out there, veiled from sight in the soft, velvet blackness of the night, some poor wretch—a victim, like myself, to the fury of the late gale—clinging desperately to a fragment of wreckage, might have caught a glimpse of the longboat's sails, sliding blackly along against the stars, and have emitted those terrible cries as a last despairing appeal for help and succour. Accordingly, as the boat swept round and came to the wind, careening gunwale-to as she felt the full strength of the night breeze in her dew-sodden canvas, I sprang to my feet and, clapping both hands funnel-wise to my mouth, sent forth a hail:

"Ahoy, there! where are you? Keep up your courage, for help is at hand. Where are you, I say? Let me but know where to look for you and I'll soon be alongside. Shout again; for I can see no sign of you. Ahoy, there! *Ahoy*!! Ahoy!!!"

The sound of my own voice, coming immediately after that terrible thrice-repeated cry, seemed somehow comforting and reassuring, and I now awaited a reply to my hail with a feeling in which there was more of curiosity than horror. But no reply came; and I once more lifted up my voice in tones of appeal and encouragement. Then, since I failed to evoke any response, I put the boat's helm down, and tacked, the conviction being strong within me that I could hit off, to an inch, the exact spot from which those dreadful sounds had come. So firmly convinced, indeed, was I of my ability to do this that when the boat came round I left the staysail sheet fast to windward, eased off the fore sheet, and stood by, leaning over the lee gunwale, in readiness to seize and haul inboard the drowning wretch who, I was fully persuaded, must be now almost under the boat's bilge. But, although the starlight was sufficiently brilliant to have betrayed, at a distance of seven or eight yards, the presence of such an object as a man clinging to a piece of floating wreckage, I could see nothing, no, not even so much as a scrap of floating weed. That I was bitterly disappointed—and also somewhat frightened—I freely admit; for I had somehow succeeded in convincing myself that those terrifying sounds had issued from the throat of a human being so close at hand that I could not possibly fail to find him; yet I had *not* found him; had failed, indeed, to find the slightest suggestion of his presence;

and if those sounds had not a human origin, *whence came they?* It was the mystery of the thing, as well as the weird, unearthly character of the cries, that sent a thrill of horror through the marrow, and made me almost madly anxious to find an explanation. I worked the boat to and fro athwart those few square yards of ocean for a full hour or more, and shouted myself hoarse, until I at length most unwillingly abandoned the search, and squared away to place as many miles as possible between myself and that unhallowed spot ere I attempted to sleep.

It must have been past midnight before I had so far thrown off the feeling of horror induced by the uncanny experience that I have related as to admit of my contemplating seriously the idea of securing some rest; and even when at length I did so, and had completed all my preparations, such as shortening sail and heaving-to, it was still some time before oblivion came to me. But when it did, it was complete, for the weather was fine and had a settled appearance, the boat lay-to most admirably and took perfect care of herself, and altogether I felt so absolutely safe that there seemed to be no need at all for that peculiar attitude of alertness during sleep to which I have already alluded; my need of sound, refreshing slumber was great, and I lay down, determined to satisfy that need while the opportunity presented itself, and let myself go completely.

Yet, although I had surrendered myself to sleep with the settled conviction of my absolute safety, and the feeling that my repose would continue until broken by the first rays of the morrow's sun, I awakened suddenly while it was yet quite dark and when, as it seemed to me, I had only been asleep a very few minutes. And my awakening was not that of a person who gradually passes from sleep to wakefulness because he has enjoyed a sufficiency of rest; it was an abrupt, instant transition from complete oblivion to a state of wide-awake, startled consciousness that caused me to leap to my feet and gaze wildly about me as my eyes snapped open to the star-lit heavens. And as I did so I became aware of a rapidly growing sound of leaping, splashing, gurgling water, and a humming as of wind sweeping through tightly strained cordage, close to leeward. There was no need for me to pause and consider what was the origin of these sounds; I recognised them instantly as those given forth by a sailing ship sweeping at a high speed through the water, and I sprang forward clear of the mainmast to where the stowed foresail permitted me a clear and uninterrupted view to leeward. The next instant three dreadful cries in quick succession—exactly reproducing, tone for tone, those terrifying sounds that had so startled and unnerved me only a few hours earlier—burst from my lips; for there, almost within reach of my hand, was the black, towering mass of the hull and canvas of a large ship bearing straight down upon the longboat, and aiming accurately to strike her fair amidships. So close was she that her long slender jib-boom, with the swelling jibs soaring high among the stars, was already over my head, the phosphorescent boil and smother from the plunge of her keen bows already foamed to the gunwale of the longboat. A startled shout rang out upon the heavy night air from somebody upon her forecastle in response to those weird cries of mine, and above the hissing wash and gurgle of the water under her bows I caught the sound of naked feet padding upon her deck-planking, as the rudely awakened look-out sprang to peer over the topgallant rail. But before the man could reach the spot for which he sprang the ship was upon me, and as her cutwater crashed into the frail hull of the boat, rending it asunder and flinging the two halves violently apart to roll bottom upward on either side of the swelling bows, I leapt desperately upward at the chain bobstay, caught it, shinned nimbly up it to the bowsprit, and made my breathless way inboard, to the terror and astonishment of some twenty forecastle hands who had evidently been startled out of a sound sleep by the sudden outcries and commotion under the bows, and into the midst of whom I unceremoniously tumbled.

The excited jabber which instantly arose among my new shipmates at once apprised me that I was aboard a vessel manned by Frenchmen. A single quick glance aloft sufficed to inform me that she was barque-rigged, and probably of about three hundred and fifty tons measurement. The excited and astonished watch crowded round me, regarding me curiously—and, methought, with looks not wholly devoid of suspicion. They were, one and all, beginning to deluge me with questions, when an authoritative voice from the poop broke in with a demand to be informed what all the disturbance on the forecastle was about. Whereupon an individual among the crowd who surrounded me, and who might have been, and indeed proved to be, the boatswain, took me by the arm, and bluntly suggested that I had better accompany him aft to Monsieur Leroy, the chief mate, and explain my uninvited presence aboard the barque.

It was, of course, the only thing to be done, and I accordingly turned and walked aft, with my arm still firmly grasped by the individual who had made the suggestion, and who seemed to regard me as his prisoner, until we reached the poop ladder, up which I was somewhat unceremoniously hustled, to find myself in the presence of a broad, sturdily built man of about middle height, who stood at the head of the ladder, with his feet wide apart, lightly balancing himself to the roll and plunge of the ship. There was a lighted lamp hanging in the skylight some two or three fathoms away, and as this man stood between me and the light, which somewhat feebly gleamed out through the skylight on to the deck, I was unable to see his features or the details of his dress; but as he stepped back and somewhat to one side to make way for me the light fell full upon me, and, feeble as it was, it sufficed to show him my uniform.

"Ah!" he exclaimed sharply, "a British naval officer, if I am not very greatly mistaken. Pray, monsieur, where did you come from; and are there any more of you?"

"I came in over the bows, a minute ago, out of a boat that—thanks to the blind look-out that your people seem to keep—you ran down and cut in two. And there are no more of us; I was the only occupant of the boat," I answered.

"The only occupant of the boat!" he exclaimed in astonishment. "You amaze me, monsieur. Is it permissible to inquire how you, a British officer, come to be adrift, quite alone, in a boat, in the middle of the Atlantic?"

Whereupon I told him briefly the story of the loss of the *Dolphin*, very imprudently adding the information that she was a unit of the Slave Squadron, and that I was her commander.

"Ah!" he commented, incisively, when I had finished. "An exceedingly interesting story. Captain Tourville will be pleased that we have picked you up when he hears the news to-morrow. Meanwhile, by lucky chance we happen to have an unoccupied state-room into which I will put you for the remainder of the night. Thoreau,"—to the man who had conducted me aft—"take this gentleman below to the cabin; then turn out the steward and tell him to put some bedding into the spare state-room, but to be silent about it lest he disturb the captain. And now, monsieur, permit me to bid you good-night. I trust you will rest well."

The man Thoreau, who seemed to be an individual of exceedingly glum and taciturn disposition, thereupon signed to me to follow him, and led the way down the poop ladder and through an open door in the front of the poop which gave access to a narrow passage, some eight feet long, at the end of which was another open door giving access to the ship's main cabin. This was a fairly roomy and comfortable apartment, plainly but tastefully fitted up, with a mahogany table running lengthwise down the middle, through the centre of which the mizenmast passed down to the depths below. A row of seats upholstered in red Utrecht velvet, and with swinging backs, was secured, on each side of the table, to the deck, between which and the sides of the cabin ran narrow strips of carpet. The sides and ends of the cabin were formed of bulkheads, the fore bulkhead being occupied by a sort of sideboard on each side of the entrance door, while against the after bulkhead stood a very handsome pianoforte, open, with a quantity of music in a stand beside it. There was a door to the right of the piano, which, I conjectured, led to the captain's state-room, right abaft; and the side bulkheads, which like the rest of the woodwork of the cabin were painted in white enamel, were each pierced by two doors, close together, which, I had no doubt, gave access to state-rooms. My surmise as to this arrangement was proved true, a few minutes later, by the steward, an ugly, shock-headed, taciturn individual, who, still more than half asleep, presently came stumbling into the cabin with a bundle of bedding, which, having with silent care opened the aftermost door on the port side, he flung into the dark state-room and then motioned me to enter; it appeared that he intended me to make up my own bed. Well, that was no very great hardship; but I should have liked a light to enable me to see what I was about, and I turned to ask my surly friend for one, but he had already turned his back upon me and was in full retreat to the forecastle to finish his interrupted night's rest. I therefore opened out the bundle and found that it consisted of a straw mattress, a flock pillow, and a pair of blankets, all of which I at once proceeded to arrange in the bunk, as best I could, by the dim light which entered the open door from the main cabin. Then I most thankfully removed my clothes—for the first time since the springing up of the gale—tumbled into the bunk, and at once fell fast asleep.

Chapter Thirteen.

In the power of a madman.

The sounds of water being freely sluiced along the deck overhead, and of the vigorous use of holystones and scrubbing-brushes immediately following thereupon, awoke me on the following morning, and I opened my eyes to find the rays of the newly risen sun flashing off the heaving surface of the ocean through the open scuttle of the state-room which I occupied. Although I could not have been asleep more than three or four hours at most, I awoke wonderfully refreshed, and the memory of what had happened to me during the night instantly returning, I at once sprang out of the berth, determined to avail myself forthwith of the renewed opportunity of starting the day by taking a salt-water bath under the head pump. It took me but a few seconds to make my way out on deck, where I found the watch, under the supervision of the second mate, as I presumed, busily engaged in the operation of washing decks, while the fresh, invigorating trade-wind, sweeping in over the port cat-head, hummed and drummed with an exhilarating note through the taut weather rigging and into the hollows of the straining canvas overhead. The weather was brilliantly fine, the clear, deep azure of the sky merely flecked here and there with a few solemnly drifting puff-balls of trade-cloud, and the ocean of deepest blue sweeping in long, regular, sparkling, snow-capped surges diagonally athwart our bows, from beneath which the flying-fish continually sprang into the air and went flashing away on either hand, like handfuls of bright silver dollars new from the Mint. Merely to breathe such an exhilarating atmosphere, and to feel the buoyant, life-like lift and plunge of the straining, hurrying ship, were joys unspeakable, and I felt in positively hilarious spirits as I danced up the poop ladder to greet the officer of the watch. and prefer my modest request for a minute's use of the head pump.

The individual whom I assumed to be the officer of the watch was a young fellow apparently not very much older than myself, attired in a somewhat dandified style of semi-uniform, bare-footed, and with his trousers rolled up above his knees. It was he who was sluicing the water about the poop so freely, while half-a-dozen of the crew vigorously plied the holystone and scrubber under his directions, and my first quick glance round the decks sufficed to show that the holystoning process was confined to the poop only, the cleansing of the main-deck seemed to be accomplished sufficiently by the application of the scrubber only. The exuberant buoyancy of my spirits suffered a sudden and distinct check as I glanced at the faces of those about me, which, without exception, seemed to belong to the lowest and most depraved class of seamen—sullen, brutal, reckless, resembling, more than anything else, in air and expression, an assemblage of wild beasts, whose natural ferocity has not been eradicated but is held in check, subdued, and daunted by the constant exercise of a ferocity even greater than their own. The aspect of the young man whom I conceived to be the officer of the watch was even more repellent than that of his subordinates; and it was in distinctly subdued tones that I bade him good-morning and preferred my request to be allowed to take a bath under the head pump.

He did not respond to my salutation, but, carefully placing upon the deck the bucket which he had just emptied, stood intently regarding me, with his feet wide apart and both hands upon his hips. He remained silent for so long a time that the men about him suspended their operations, regarding him with dull curiosity, while I felt my patience rapidly oozing away and my temper rising at the gratuitous insolence of his demeanour, and I was on the point of making some rather pungent remarks when he suddenly seemed to bethink himself, and said, in accents that were apparently intended to convey some suggestion of an attempt at civility:

"So you are the British naval officer that Monsieur Leroy told me about when I relieved him, are you? And you want a bath, do you? Very well; go and take one, by all means. And, hark ye, Monsieur Englishman, a word in your ear. Take my advice, and after you have had your bath get back to your cabin, and stay there until the captain has been informed of your presence in the ship; for if he were to come on deck, and unexpectedly see you, the chances are that he would blow your brains out without thinking twice about it. He is not quite an angel in the matter of temper, and I may tell you that he is not too well disposed toward Englishmen in general, and English naval officers in particular. Now be off, get your bath, and scuttle back to your cabin as quickly as may be."

"I am much obliged to you for your warning, monsieur," said I, "and I will act upon it. Do you care to increase my obligation to you by stating why your captain has such a— prejudice, shall we call it, against British naval officers?"

"Well," replied my new acquaintance—whose name I subsequently learned was Gaston Marcel—"for one thing, this ship, which is his own property, is employed in the slave-trade, and Captain Tourville has already suffered much loss and damage through the meddlesome interference of your pestilent cruisers. But I believe he has other and more private reasons for his hatred of your nation and comrades."

So that was it. After having suffered shipwreck, I had been run down and narrowly escaped with my life, only to fall into the hands of a Frenchman—and a slaver at that! Now, most slavers were little if anything better than pirates; they were outlaws whose crimes were punishable with death; trusting for their safety, for the most part, to the speed of their ships, but fighting with the desperation of cornered rats when there was no other way of escape; neither giving nor asking quarter; and, in many cases, guilty of the most unspeakable atrocities toward those hapless individuals serving in the Slave Squadron who were unfortunate enough to fall into their hands. This was especially true in the case of those who carried on their nefarious traffic under the French flag; for they were, almost without exception, West Indian Creoles, most of whom bore a dash of negro blood in their veins, therefore adding the inherited ferocity of the West African savage to the natural depravity of those to whose unbridled passions they owed their being. If, as was more than likely, I had fallen into the power of one of these fiends, my plight was like to be desperate indeed. I came to the conclusion that I could not do better than act upon the advice of the second mate, and abide the issue of events with as much equanimity as I could muster. Accordingly, as soon as I had taken my bath I returned to the state-room which had been assigned to me by the mate, and there remained *perdu*, awaiting the moment when that somewhat formidable individual the captain should be pleased to send for me.

The approach to my state-room was, it will be remembered, through the main cabin; and as I passed through the latter the ugly, shock-headed steward, more ugly and more shock-headed now, in the garish light of day, than he had been when he presented himself fresh from his hammock on the night before—was down on his hands and knees busily engaged in scrubbing the cabin floor, while the strips of carpet and the table-cloth were rolled up and placed upon the table, the beautifully polished surface of which was partially protected by a large square of green baize. I bade the fellow good-morning; but he took no more notice of me than if I had never spoken; so I passed on and entered my sleeping apartment, closing the door behind me. I then proceeded to dress leisurely and perform my toilet as well as the means at my disposal would permit, but when it is remembered that I had no change of linen, and owned only the clothes which I happened to be wearing when I was washed off the wreck, it will be readily understood that when I had done all that was possible to render myself presentable the result still left much to be desired.

The steward finished the washing and swabbing of the cabin deck, and then retired, returning about half an hour later—by which time the planks were dry—to relay the strips of carpet, replace the table-cloth, and arrange the table for breakfast, producing, somewhat to my surprise, a very elegant table-equipage of what, seen through the slats which formed the upper panel of my cabin door, appeared to be solid silver and quite valuable china.

He had barely finished his task when seven bells struck on deck, and prompt upon the last stroke the door in the after bulkhead was thrown open and a man issued from it, and, passing rapidly through the cabin, with just a momentary pause to glance at the tell-tale barometer swinging in the skylight, made his way out on deck.

I caught a glimpse of him, through the slats in the top panel of my door, as he passed, and judged him to be about thirty years of age. He was rather tall, standing about five feet ten inches in his morocco slippers; very dark—so much so that I strongly suspected the presence of negro blood in his veins—with a thick crop of jet-black hair, a luxuriantly bushy beard, and a heavy thick moustache, all very carefully trimmed, and so exceedingly glossy that I thought it probable that the gloss was due to artificial means. The man was decidedly good-looking, in a Frenchified fashion, and was a sea dandy of the first water, as was evidenced by the massive gold earrings in his ears, the jewelled studs in the immaculate front of his shirt of pleated cambric, his nattily cut suit of white drill, and the diamond on the little finger of his right hand, the flash of which I caught as he raised his hand to shield his eyes from the dazzle of the sun when glancing at the barometer.

I heard his voice—a rather rich, full baritone—addressing the second mate, but could not distinguish what was said, at that distance and among the multitudinous noises of the straining ship; and a few minutes later the door opposite my own, on the other side of the cabin, opened, and Monsieur Leroy, the chief mate of the ship—to whose slackness of discipline I was chiefly indebted for being run down during the previous night—emerged and followed his chief out on deck. I recognised him in part by his figure, and in part by the fact that he was evidently an occupant of one of the state-rooms adjoining the main cabin, which would only be assigned to an officer of rank and consideration. As I now gained a momentary glimpse of him he appeared to be about thirty-seven years of age, broadly built, his features almost hidden by the thickly growing beard, whiskers, and moustache that adorned them, and out of which gleamed and flashed a pair of resolute but good-natured eyes as black as the bushy eyebrows that overshadowed them. He was dressed in a coat and pair of trousers of fine, dark-blue cloth, and, like the captain, wore no waistcoat. His shirt, thus exposed, however, unlike that of his superior, was made of coarse linen woven with a narrow blue stripe in it. Also, like his captain, he wore no stockings on his slippered feet.

While I was speculating what the captain's behaviour toward me would probably be, the steward unceremoniously flung open my cabin door, and in surly tones curtly informed me that the captain desired to see me at once upon the poop. He stood aside to permit me to pass, waved a directing hand toward the passage leading out on deck, and then busied himself in putting a few finishing touches to the arrangement of the table.

When, in obedience to this summons, I stepped out on deck, the washing down had been completed and the planks were already practically dry; the running gear had been carefully coiled down; the brasswork polished; mops, swabs, and scrubbing-brushes stowed away; and the crew were mustered on the forecastle, partaking of breakfast. They glanced curiously at me as I emerged on to the quarter-deck, and one of them said something that excited a burst of sardonic laughter from the rest, disregarding which I sprang lightly up the poop ladder and found myself in the presence of a group consisting of the captain and the two mates. The countenances of the latter expressed much annoyance and some perturbation, particularly that of Leroy, the chief mate; but the look of savage ferocity on the captain's face was positively fiendish, and enough to strike terror into the heart of even the boldest who might find himself in the power of such an individual. My hopes of considerate, or even of ordinarily merciful, treatment from one of so vindictively ferocious a character as this man seemed to be at once sunk to zero; yet I was not minded that any Frenchman should enjoy the satisfaction of saying that he had frightened me. I therefore assumed a boldness of demeanour that I was very far from feeling, and bowed with all the ease and grace that I could muster. Then addressing the captain I said:

"Good-morning, Captain Tourville. I am afraid that the hard necessities of misfortune compel me to claim from you that succour and hospitality which the shipwrecked seaman has the right to ask—"

"Stop!" shouted Tourville, as, with clenched fist, he stood seeming about to spring upon me; "I admit no such right, especially of an Englishman. The English have ever been my most implacable enemies. Because, forsooth, I choose to earn my living by following a vocation of which some of them disapprove, they must needs do their utmost to ruin me, and by heaven they have very nearly succeeded, too! Who are they that they should presume to thrust their opinions down the throats of other people? If their own countrymen choose to be led by the nose and are willing to submit to their dictation, well and good, it is nothing to me; it is their own affair, not mine. But what right have they to dictate to other nations, to say you shall do this, and shall not do that? I tell you that it is nothing short of monstrous, and I am ashamed of France that she has submitted to be thus dictated to. But if my country is so weak as to tolerate interference from a foreign Power, I am not. I claim to judge for myself what is right or wrong, and to be governed by my own conscience. I am a slaver, and I care not who knows it! And I will continue to be a slaver as long as I please, despite the disapproval of a few English fanatics. But let those beware who dare to interfere with me, and especially those Englishmen who have done their utmost to ruin me! You, monsieur, are one of them; by your own confession you belong to an English man-o'-war engaged in the suppression of that trade by which I am striving to make a living; and do you suppose that because you happen to have suffered shipwreck you are entitled to claim from me succour and hospitality, and ultimate restoration to your own people in order that you and others like you may do your utmost to ruin me? I tell you no! I do not admit the claim; you are an enemy—an implacable enemy—and you shall be treated as such. The fact of your shipwreck is merely an accident that has placed you in my power, and you shall die! I will revenge upon you some few of the countless injuries that I have suffered at the hands of your accursed countrymen!"

"Shame upon you, monsieur!" I cried. "Are you coward enough to revenge yourself upon a mere lad like myself? I will not ask you what your crew will think of you, but what will you think of yourself, in your calmer moments, when you come to reflect—"

"Silence, boy!" he thundered; "silence, you English dog! How dare you speak—" Then, suddenly interrupting himself, he turned to the chief mate and exclaimed:

"Leroy, have that insolent young puppy confined below in irons until I can make up my mind how to dispose of him."

The chief mate approached and took me by the arm. "Come with me, Monsieur John Bulldogue," said he, not unkindly, as he led me away; "and do not allow yourself to be more anxious as to your fate than you can help. I tell you candidly that I cannot form the slightest idea what that fate will eventually be; many men, knowing the skipper as well as I do, would no doubt say that you will be thrown to the sharks before you are an hour older—and it may be; yes, it certainly may be; for you are the first who has ever dared to assume a defiant attitude toward him and he is an inordinately vain man, as well as a man of unbridled temper. But, somehow, I am inclined to think that your defiance, which some people would say must seal your fate, will be more likely to tell in your favour than against you. Yes; although you have the misfortune to be an Englishman, I really think I may venture to encourage you to hope for the best. Now, here we are; and here comes Moulineux with the irons. I must obey orders and see that they are put on you; but make yourself as comfortable as you can; and I will send you down some breakfast presently. And, monsieur, you may rely upon my goodwill; I admire courage wherever I see it, whether in friend or in enemy, and you have proved that you possess it. If I find it in my power to do anything to help you, I will."

The place in which I now found myself confined was a small apartment that was apparently used upon occasion as an auxiliary store-room, for there were a number of barrels and cases of various sizes in it, as well as what had the appearance of being spare sails. As the place was constructed in the depths of the ship, and considerably below the level of the water-line, there was no window to give light to it, the only light which reached it being as much as could find its way down through the partially open hatchway, some ten feet above. I was therefore able to observe my surroundings only very indistinctly even after I had been some time in the place and my eyes had become accustomed to the gloom of it. The mate was as good as his word in the matter of breakfast, a man bringing down to me a most excellent and substantial meal after I had been incarcerated for nearly an hour. I discussed the food with relish, for I was hungry, and then sat impatiently awaiting the moment when my fate should be made known to me. But hour after hour passed without word or sign from the man who held my destiny in the hollow of his hand; and it was not until late in the afternoon that the carpenter appeared and, removing my irons, requested me to follow him. He conducted me up the steep ladder leading to the main-deck and into the main cabin, where Captain Tourville was sitting alone. There was silence for a full minute after the carpenter had ushered me into the cabin and closed the door behind me. Tourville remained seated at the end of the table, with one hand clenched on the cloth before him, while with the other he plucked quickly and impatiently at his thick beard and then combed it through with his fingers, "glowering" moodily at me meanwhile, in an absent-minded fashion, as though he scarcely realised my presence. At length he pulled himself together with an effort, and, pointing to the lockers, said:

"Be seated, monsieur, and have the kindness to tell me who and what you are; and how you come to be on board my ship. I have only heard my chief mate's story as yet."

Whereupon I proceeded to give him the required information, as briefly as possible, not omitting to mention the fact of my being an officer of the Slave Squadron; for I had already stated this to the chief mate, and from what had transpired earlier in the day I knew that he, in turn, had communicated the information to his captain. That what I told him did not appear greatly to increase his state of irritation seemed proof enough that he had already learned all the material facts, and I congratulated myself upon having shown him that I was not to be frightened into the suppression of any portion of my history, no matter how damaging its effect might be expected to be upon my interests. When I had told him everything he remained silent for quite two or three minutes, drumming the table meditatively with his fingers.

At length he looked up from the table, at which he had been moodily glowering, and said:

"Monsieur Fortescue, I thank you for the evident frankness with which you have told your story; and, in return, feel that you are entitled to some explanation of what you must doubtless have deemed my very extraordinary conduct of this morning. It is unnecessary for me to enter into details, but I may inform you that I have suffered irreparable loss and injury at the hands of the English. They have chosen to regard the method by which I earn my living as unlawful, and on no less than four occasions have brought me to the verge of ruin at the moment when I was upon the point of realising a handsome competence. They have persecuted me relentlessly, confiscated my property, slain my two brothers in action, and would have hanged me ignominiously, had I not been fortunate enough to effect my escape from them; and it was an Englishman who—well, that is a story into which I need not enter with you; let it suffice to say that the injuries which I have suffered at the hands of your countrymen have been such, that the mere name of Englishman excites me to a very frenzy of anger and hate, in which I am really not responsible for my actions. Now, the question is: What is to be done with you? I tell you candidly that your life is not safe for a moment while you remain on board this ship. Even as you sit there the memory of all that I have suffered at the hands of your countrymen so strongly moves me that I find it exceedingly difficult to refrain from blowing your brains out—"

"But, monsieur," I interrupted, "pardon me for suggesting such a thing, but are you not surrendering yourself to a very childish weakness? Is it possible that you, a man in the very prime of life and apparently in perfect bodily and mental health, can be so utterly devoid of self-control that because you have suffered injury, real or imagined, from—"

"*Sacré!*" he interrupted, starting savagely to his feet; "there is no question, monsieur, as to the reality of the injuries that I have suffered at the hands of your hateful countrymen—"

"Very well, monsieur," I cut in, speaking very quietly, "for argument's sake I will admit, if you like, that your injuries are both real and deep. Still, does it not seem to you absurdly illogical that because certain persons have injured you, you must yield to this insane craving to wreak your revenge upon somebody else who has had no hand in the infliction of those injuries?"

"Quite possibly; I cannot tell," answered Tourville. "It may be that I *am* mad on this one particular point. But I do not admit the soundness of your argument, monsieur. You contend that you personally have not injured me. That may be perfectly true. But you admit that you belong to the Slave Squadron; and it is at the hands of that same squadron that I have suffered much of the injury of which I complain. Now it is impossible for me to discriminate between the individuals in that squadron who have injured me, and those who have not; and I therefore contend that I am perfectly justified in wreaking my vengeance upon any of them who chance to fall into my power. And, in any case, if I should blow out your brains I shall at least have rid myself of one potential enemy. Therefore—"

And to my immeasurable surprise the man calmly drew a pistol from his belt and levelled it across the table straight at my head. I sprang to my feet with the idea of flinging myself upon and disarming him, for I could no longer doubt the fellow was stark, staring mad upon this one particular point; but before I could get at him the weapon exploded, and the ball, passing so close to my head that I felt it stir my hair, buried itself in the panelling of the cabin behind me. With a savage snarl he raised his hand, and would have dashed the heavy pistol-butt in my face; but by that time I was upon him, and, seizing his throat with one hand, while I wrenched the weapon from his grasp with the other, I bore him to the deck, and planted my right knee square in the middle of his chest, pinning him securely down.

"You treacherous, murderous scoundrel!" I cried. "How shall I deal with you? You are as dangerous as a wild beast! If I were to beat your brains out with the butt of this pistol I should only be treating you as you deserve! And I will do it too as sure as you are lying there at my mercy, unless you will swear by all you hold sacred that you will never again attempt my life, and that you will set me ashore, free, at the first port at which we touch. Will you swear that, or will you die?"

"I swear it, monsieur," he gasped. "Release my throat and let me rise, and I swear to you by the Blessed Virgin that I will declare a truce in your favour, and that you shall leave this ship as soon as a suitable opportunity offers."

I relaxed my grasp upon his throat, and permitted him to regain his feet, whereupon he looked at me for some moments with an expression of surprise, not altogether unmingled, methought, with fear. Then, bowing profoundly, he said:

"Leave me, monsieur, I beg of you. I will send for you again, a little later."

I passed out of the cabin, and made my way up on to the poop, where I found Monsieur Leroy, the chief mate, in charge of the watch. He nodded to me as I ascended the poop ladder, and when I joined him in his fore-and-aft promenade of the weather side of the deck, jerked his head knowingly toward the skylight and remarked:

"In his tantrums *again*? Ah! quite as I expected. It is rather unfortunate for you, monsieur, that you happen to be an Englishman, for the mere mention of the word to him has the same effect as exhibiting a red rag to a bull: it drives him perfectly frantic with rage."

"So it appears," remarked I dryly. "What is the cause of it? Have you any idea?"

"No," answered the mate. "I doubt whether anybody knows; perhaps he does not even know himself. Of course I have heard him speak of the losses which he has sustained through the interference of the ships of the Slave Squadron; but we who elect to make our living by following a vocation which civilised nations have agreed to declare unlawful must be prepared to be interfered with. For my own part I have no particular fault to find with those who have undertaken to suppress the slave-trade. We go into the business with our eyes open; we know the penalties attaching to it; and if we are foolish or unskilful enough to permit ourselves to be caught we must not grumble if those penalties are exacted from us. I like the life; I enjoy it; it is full of excitement and adventure; and when we succeed in outwitting you gentlemen the profits are handsome enough to amply repay us for all our risk and trouble. It is like playing a game of skill for a heavy wager; and I contend that no man who is not sportsman enough to bear his losses philosophically should engage in the game. But that is not precisely what ails the skipper; he takes his ill-luck grievously to heart it is true, but he insists that he has other grievances against the English as well; and, whatever they may be, they seem to have partially turned his brain."

"Partially!" I objected. "Why, the man is as mad as a March hare. He absolutely loses all control of himself when he allows his temper to master him, and becomes more like a savage beast than a man!"

"Ay, that is true, he does," agreed Leroy. "But, hark ye, monsieur, let me give you a friendly hint—you have escaped unharmed thus far, therefore I believe you may consider yourself reasonably safe; but in case of any further outbreaks on the captain's part, take especial care that you give him no reason to suppose that you are afraid of him; that is the surest road to safety with him."

"Upon my word I believe you are right," said I. "At all events that is the road which I took with him just now, for I pinned him down to the cabin deck, and threatened to beat his brains out. Yet here I am, alive, to speak of it."

"Good!" ejaculated the mate. "If you did that you are all right; I believe that if there is one thing he admires more than another it is absolute fearlessness. Show him that you do not care the snap of a finger for him and he will forgive you anything, even the fact that you are an Englishman."

I walked the poop with Monsieur Leroy for a full hour, chatting with him and learning many things very well worth knowing; and while I was chatting with him I kept my eyes about me, carefully noting all the particulars and peculiarities of the barque, with a view to future contingencies. Among other things I learned that she was named *La Mouette*; that she was of three hundred and sixty-four tons register; that she mounted fourteen twenty-eight pound carronades on her main-deck and four six-pounders on her poop; that she carried a complement of one hundred and seventy men; and that she was then bound into the river Kwara for a cargo of slaves to be conveyed to Martinique, or Cuba, as circumstances might decide.

At the end of about an hour I was once more summoned to the cabin, where I found Tourville sitting at the table. The man had now completely regained his self-control; he was perfectly calm, and waved me courteously to a seat on the cabin sofa, which I took.

"Monsieur Fortescue," said he, "I shall not mock you or myself by pretending to excuse or apologise for my recent outbreak of violence, for it is due to a weakness which I am wholly unable to conquer, and which may, quite possibly, get the better of me again. If it should, I must ask you to kindly be patient and forbearing with me, and to keep out of my way until the fit has passed. What I particularly wish to say to you now is that you are from this moment perfectly safe so long as it may be necessary for you to honour my ship with your presence. But, since you will naturally desire to rejoin your own ship as speedily as possible, I propose to tranship you into the first vessel bearing the British flag which we may chance to fall in with—provided, of course, that she is not a ship of war. Should we happen to fall in with a British man-o'-war, my course of action will be guided by circumstances; I shall not feel myself justified in trusting to her captain's magnanimity to let us go free after delivering you safe on board her; but should the weather be fine enough to allow of such a proceeding without risk to you, I will give you a boat in which you may make your own way on board her. Meanwhile, I beg that you will regard yourself as my guest, free to come and go in this cabin as you please, and to take your meals at my table; and I have also made arrangements for your greater comfort in the state-room which Leroy assigned to you when you came aboard last night. I trust that these plans of mine will be agreeable to you."

I replied that they were not only perfectly agreeable to me, but that I regarded them as exceedingly generous—taking all the circumstances of the case into consideration; that I regretted his violent antipathy to Englishmen, as I feared that, in consequence of it, my presence could never be otherwise than exceedingly disagreeable to him, but that during my enforced sojourn aboard *La Mouette* I would strive to render my nationality as little obtrusive as possible, and that I trusted we might very soon be fortunate enough to fall in with a craft of some sort into which he could transfer me. To which he replied that he fervently hoped so too, for both our sakes; then directing my attention to a case of books attached to the after bulkhead, on the opposite side to that occupied by the piano, he rose, bowed, and retired to his own cabin. As for me, I went out on deck and resumed my conversation with Leroy, telling him what had passed, and begging him to keep a sharp look-out for vessels; for that since Captain Tourville made no attempt to disguise his uneasiness at my presence on board his ship I was quite determined to tranship into the first craft that we might happen to fall in with, provided, of course, that she did not happen to be of questionable character—for I had no inclination to jump out of the frying-pan into the fire by going aboard another slaver.

The mate fully agreed with me as to the wisdom of leaving the ship as soon as possible; indeed I soon discovered that, even after what had passed between Tourville and myself, he was still very far from satisfied that there might not be further trouble ahead. "If such should unfortunately come," said he, "you must maintain a bold front, and show him that you are not to be so easily frightened. When his fits are upon him he very strongly reminds me of a wild beast which hesitates to attack so long as one faces it boldly, but springs the instant that one's back is turned."

I considered this very excellent advice, singularly applicable to the circumstances, and determined to act upon it. At eight bells I was summoned below to supper, and found the cabin brilliantly lit, and the table a picture of dainty elegance in the matter of equipage and of choice fare. Captain Tourville was evidently no ascetic in the matter of eating and drinking, and the meal to which we immediately sat down was quite as good as many that I have partaken of ashore in so-called first-class hotels.

Tourville seemed at first to be in imminent danger of relapsing into one of his black moods, for he was distrait and inclined to be silent; but I was determined not to permit this if I could help it. I therefore persisted in talking to him, trying him with subject after subject, until I discovered him to be an enthusiast upon the arts of painting and music—in both of which I also dabbled, in an amateurish way. As soon as I spoke of these his brow cleared, he threw off his gloom, and spoke fluently and with evident knowledge of his subject, with the result that the meal which had begun so inauspiciously ended quite pleasantly. Nay, more than that, as soon as the cloth was drawn this extraordinary man opened the piano and, sitting down to it, played piece after piece, sang several songs, and finally invited me to sing, the result being that, on the whole, the evening passed with far less constraint than I had anticipated.

The next morning, while Tourville was engaged in taking his sights for the longitude and working them out, he suddenly complained of feeling ill, sent for Leroy, gave him certain instructions, and then took to his bed. By noon it became evident that he was in for a smart attack of malarial fever, to which it appeared he was very subject; and when I turned in that night the mate volunteered the information that he feared the skipper was going to be very ill.

Tourville's condition on the following morning amply justified Leroy's foreboding; he grew steadily worse, became delirious, and at length grew so violent that about mid-day the mate considered it necessary to remain with him constantly, lest in his madness he should rise from his bed and fling himself through the stern windows into the sea. One result of this was that I offered to take Leroy's watch, from eight o'clock to midnight, an offer which was gratefully accepted; but as we were running down before a fair wind there was nothing for me to do beyond maintaining a good look-out, and I thus found it unnecessary to give the crew any orders or to interfere with them in any way. For the next three days Tourville's condition was such that the constant presence of some one in his cabin, night and day, to watch over him and guard against the possibility of his doing himself an injury, became an absolute necessity, and Leroy, the chief mate, and Thoreau, the boatswain, shared this duty between them. I volunteered to assume nursing duty in the place of Leroy, but my offer was declined, the chief mate rather drily remarking that the presence of an Englishman by the captain's bedside was scarcely likely to accelerate the patient's recovery, while some of his ravings were of such a character that it was better for all concerned that I should not hear them. But, he added, if I would be complaisant enough to keep his watch for him, he would esteem it a very great favour. Of course I could do no less than accede to this suggestion with a good grace.

Chapter Fourteen.

H.B.M.S. Gadfly.

I had been on duty as Leroy's deputy for two whole days when it fell to my turn to keep the middle watch, that is to say, the watch which extends from midnight to four o'clock in the morning.

When, upon being called by Marcel, the second mate, I went on deck to relieve him, he informed me that the wind had been steadily dropping all through the first watch, and expressed a fear that we were about to lose it altogether. This did not in the least surprise me, for we were now at about our lowest parallel, and on the border at least of, if not actually within, the belt of practically perpetual calms that exists about the Line, which are the sources of so much delay, vexation, and hard work to the mariner. That the wind had dropped very considerably since I had turned in was evident to me even before I reached the deck, for, upon turning out of my bunk to dress after being called, I had immediately noticed that the ship was almost upon an even keel, while the inert "sloppy" sound of the water alongside that reached my ears through the open port of my cabin told me that we were sailing but slowly.

The night was intensely dark, for the moon was but one day old, and had only barely revealed herself as a thin line of faint pearl in the evening sky for about half an hour before she followed the sun beneath the horizon, there was not a star to be seen in the whole of the visible firmament, and there was a feeling of hot, muggy dampness in the air that made me shrewdly suspect the presence overhead of a pall of rain-charged vapour, which would account for the opacity of the darkness which hemmed us in and pressed down upon us from above.

As Marcel curtly bade me good-night and went below upon being relieved, after giving me the course to be steered, and expressing his forebodings concerning the weather, I walked aft, glanced into the binnacle, and inquired of the helmsman whether the ship still held steerage-way, to which he replied that she did, and that was about all, the man whom he had relieved at eight bells having informed him that the log, when last hove, had recorded a speed of barely two and a half knots. He also volunteered the opinion that we were booked for a heavy downpour of rain before long, significantly glancing at the same time at the oilskins and sou'wester which he had brought aft with him.

As the time dragged slowly along the heat seemed steadily to grow more oppressive, and the difficulty of obtaining a full breath greater; the perspiration was streaming from every pore of my body, and I felt almost too languid to drag one foot after the other as I moved about the deck. That the sick man also was affected unfavourably was evident, for his shouts came up through the after skylight with positively startling distinctness as his delirium grew more acute.

At length, just after two bells had struck—and how dreadfully clamourous the strokes sounded in that heavy, stagnant air—the helmsman reported that the ship was no longer under command; and presently she swung broadside-on to the swell, rolling heavily, with loud splashing and gurgling sounds in the scuppers, with a swirling and washing of water under the counter, frequent vicious kicks of the now useless rudder, accompanied by violent clankings of the wheel chains, loud creakings and groanings of the timbers, heavy flappings and rustlings of the invisible canvas aloft, with fierce jerks of the chain sheets, and, in short, a full chorus of those multitudinous sounds that emanate from a rolling ship in a stark calm. The helmsman, no longer needed, lashed the wheel and, gathering up his oilskins, slouched away forward, muttering that he was going to get a light for his pipe; and I let him go, although I knew perfectly well that he had no intention of returning uncalled; for, after all, where was the use of keeping the man standing there doing nothing? I therefore contented myself by calling upon the hands forward, from time to time, to keep a bright look-out, and flung myself into a basket-chair belonging to the skipper.

Sitting thus, I gradually fell into a somewhat sombre reverie, in the course of which I reviewed the events that had befallen me during the short period that had elapsed since the *Dolphin* and the *Eros* had parted company. I went over again, in memory, all the circumstances connected with the loss of the brigantine, the hours I had spent alone in the longboat, her destruction and my somewhat dramatic appearance among the crew of *La Mouette*, my reception by her mad captain, and then fell to conjecturing what the future might have in store for me, when I was suddenly aroused to a consciousness of my immediate surroundings by a sort of impression it was no more than that—that I had heard the sound of a ship's bell struck four times—*ting-ting, ting-ting*—far away yonder in the heart of the thick darkness. So faint, such a mere ghost of a sound, did it seem to be that I felt almost convinced it was purely imaginary, an effect resulting from the train of thought in which I had been indulging; yet I rose to my feet and, walking over to the skylight, peered through it at the cabin clock to ascertain what the time might actually be. *It was on the stroke of two o'clock*! Therefore if, as I had assured myself, the sounds were imaginary, it was at least a singular coincidence that they should have reached me just at that precise moment. I walked to the fore end of the poop, upon the rail guarding which the ship's bell was mounted, and sharply struck four bells, after which I again called to the crew forward to maintain a sharp look-out.

"Now," thought I, "if those sounds originated outside my own imagination some of those fellows for'ard will certainly have heard them, and will mention it." But my call elicited nothing more than the stereotyped "Ay, ay, sir!" and a faint momentary shuffling of feet—meant, no doubt, to convey to me the impression that the look-outs were on the alert and then deep silence, as before, so far as any report of suspicious sounds was concerned. I stood for quite two minutes listening intently for any further sounds out of the darkness, but none came to me, nor could I detect any light or other evidence of another craft in our neighbourhood. At length, fully confirmed in my conviction that my imagination had been playing a trick with me, I returned to the chair in which I had been sitting, and there finished out the watch, merely leaving my seat to strike six, and finally eight, bells. But I placed my chair in such a position that while still sitting in it I could keep my eye on the clock, and as the hands crept round its face, marking first three and then four o'clock, I strained my listening powers to their utmost in the hope that those elusive bell-strokes might again come stealing across the sea to me, but without result. When four o'clock came round, after striking eight bells with perhaps a little more vigour than usual, I called Marcel, resigned the deck to him, and went below.

Yet, although I had felt drowsy enough on deck, and although Tourville's ravings had ceased and he seemed to have fallen asleep, when I flung off my clothes and stretched myself on top of the bedding in my bunk, expecting to instantly drop off to sleep, I found, to my annoyance, that I had never been less inclined to slumber than I was just then. The fact was that in spite of myself those ghostly tinklings were still worrying me. Were they, or were they not, imaginary? If they were—well, there was an end of it. But if they were not imaginary; if, as I now perversely began to think, they were actual sounds, then it followed, of necessity, that there must be a craft of some sort not very far from us.

If this were the case, what, I asked myself, was she likely to be? She could but be one of three things—either a trader, a slaver, or a craft belonging to the Slave Squadron; the chances, therefore, were about even that on the morrow I might be able to effect my escape from *La Mouette*—always provided, of course, that those strokes of the bell had been real. For if the craft on board which they had been struck happened to be a trader, the odds were in favour of her being British; and the same might be said presuming her to be a man-o'-war. On the other hand, she might of course be a slaver; in which case I was fully resolved to endure the ills I had, rather than fly to others which might conceivably be worse.

Thinking thus, and worrying myself as to the best course to be pursued in certain eventualities, I lay there restlessly tossing first to one side, then to the other, until at length, sitting up in my bunk and putting my face to the open port in quest of a breath of fresh air, the fancy took me that the darkness was no longer quite so opaque as it had been, nay, I was sure of it, for by putting my face right up against the circular opening I was enabled to catch an occasional transient gleam of faint, shifting light that I knew was the glancing of the coming dawn upon the back of the oily swell that came creeping up to the ship; while, by directing my glances higher, I found that I was able to make out indistinctly something of the outline of the great black cloud-masses that overhung us.

In those latitudes the dawn comes as quickly as the daylight vanishes, day comes and goes with a rush—thus within five minutes of the time when I first glanced out through the port there was enough light abroad to reveal a louring, overcast, thunder-threatening sky, an inky, oil-smooth, sluggishly undulating sea, and a long, low schooner with tremendously taunt masts raking over her stern, and not an inch of canvas set, lying broadside-on to us at a distance of some two miles to the eastward. When I caught my first glimpse of her she was very little more than a black blur standing out against the background of scarcely less black sky; but even as I sat looking at her the light grew, her outline sharpened and became clear and distinct, and my heart gave a great bound of delight as the conviction forced itself upon me that I knew her. Yes, that long low hull, with its abnormal length of counter, and its bold sheer forward, the high, dominating bow with its excessive rake of stem, and the peculiar steeve of the bowsprit were all familiar to me. I had seen and noted them before while in Sierra Leone harbour, and I was convinced that the craft was none other than the British man-o'-war schooner *Gadfly*, armed with eight 12-pound carronades and a long 32-pound pivot-gun on her forecastle, with a crew of eighty men under the command of Lieutenant Peters, than whom there was not a more dashing and enterprising officer on the Coast.

I had just arrived at the above conclusion when I heard one of the barque's crew hailing the poop; I could not distinguish what was said, but I presumed that it had reference to the schooner, for immediately upon the hail I heard the creaking of the basket-chair on the poop, as though Marcel was just hoisting himself out of it, and presently his reply came floating down through the skylight, "Ay, ay; I see her." Then I heard the soft shuffling of his footsteps overhead and guessed that he was getting hold of the telescope wherewith to examine the schooner.

Ten minutes later, perhaps, I heard the second mate leave the poop and enter the cabin, and I concluded that he had come down to report the schooner to Leroy; but, to my surprise, instead of doing that, he came straight to my cabin door and knocked softly. I at once guessed that he wished to question me about the stranger, but it was no part of my policy to let him know that I had already seen and made up my mind about her, I therefore feigned to be sound asleep, and did not reply. Then he knocked a second time more sharply, whereupon I started up and responded in a drowsy tone of voice, "Hillo! who is it? What's the matter?"

"Monsieur Fortescue," Marcel responded, murmuring through the slats in the upper panel of the door, "I want you on deck, quick!"

"Oh, indeed," I replied, still affecting drowsiness; "what for? Is there anything wrong?"

"Please come up at once, monsieur," he returned, with a note of impatience in his voice. "When you come on deck you will understand why I want you."

"Very well," I grumbled, "I will be up in a brace of shakes;" whereupon my disturber departed.

But his conversation with me, brief as it had been, and quietly as it had been conducted, had evidently aroused Leroy, for as I emerged from my cabin he stepped out of his and we proceeded to the poop together, the chief mate expressing his surprise that Marcel should have called me instead of him. Of course I had a very shrewd idea as to the reason, but it was my cue to feign ignorance, and I did so.

By the time that Leroy and I reached the poop the sun must have risen—although there was no sign of him to be seen through the dense canopy of cloud that completely obscured the heavens—for the light had strengthened so much and the atmosphere was so clear that every detail of the distant schooner was plainly distinguishable even to the unassisted eye. Marcel was again examining her through the glass; it was therefore only natural that Leroy's and my own glances should turn toward her as soon as our heads rose above the level of the rail. Neither of us said anything, however, until Marcel took the glass from his eye, when, seeing Leroy, he said:

"What d'ye think of her, monsieur? I have taken it upon myself to turn out Monsieur Fortescue to see whether he can tell us anything about her?"

"*I?*" I ejaculated. "What the dickens should I know about her? That she is a slaver anybody can tell with half an eye,"—as a matter of fact the *Gadfly* had been a slaver in her time, but having been captured, had been purchased into the Service—"but her skipper is a sensible fellow, evidently; he doesn't believe in threshing his canvas threadbare in a calm, so he has furled it."

"Permit me," said Leroy, taking the telescope from Marcel and placing it to his eye. He looked long and anxiously at the distant schooner, and at length, with an "Ah!" that spoke volumes, passed the glass over to me.

I understood at once from that expressive "Ah!" that Leroy knew and had recognised the vessel, and that my pretence of ignorance would no longer serve any good purpose. I therefore determined to abandon it and to make a virtue of necessity by frankly admitting my knowledge. For if Leroy recognised the schooner, as I was certain he had, he would be fully aware of the fact that I, as an officer of the Slave Squadron, must necessarily know her too. After regarding her attentively through the lenses, therefore, for more than a minute, I passed the glass back to the chief mate with the quiet remark:

"Yes, I believe I recognise her now that I come to see her distinctly. If I am not mistaken she is the British man-o'-war schooner *Gadfly*, and her presence yonder affords Captain Tourville an opportunity to fulfil his promise of transhipping me. He promised me that, should such a case as this occur, he would give me a boat in which to transfer myself; and that small dinghy of yours will be just the thing."

"Y–es," returned Leroy meditatively. "He promised you that, did he? I remember your telling me so. But, unfortunately for you, he never said a word upon the matter to me, and he is far too sick just now to be worried about that or anything else. I am very much afraid, therefore, Monsieur Fortescue, that you will be obliged to let this opportunity pass; for, you see, I could not possibly take it upon myself to release you and give you even the dinghy without first receiving definite instructions from the captain."

"Oh, come, I say, Leroy, you surely don't mean to insinuate that you doubt my word, do you?" I remonstrated. "I hope you don't pretend—"

"I do not pretend or insinuate anything," Leroy retorted, somewhat impatiently; "I merely state the fact that I have received from Captain Tourville no such instructions as those you mention, and without such instructions I dare not comply with your wishes."

"Ha, ha!" jeered Marcel. "You will have to curb your impatience, Monsieur Englishman. It is evident that we are not yet to lose the pleasure of your society."

To this I replied nothing, but turned remonstratingly to the chief mate, urging him to at least do me the favour to go down and see if the captain chanced to be awake, and if so, to put the matter to him. But he would not listen to my suggestion, insisting that, even if Captain Tourville happened to be awake, he was far too ill to be troubled over any such matter. Suddenly it came to me that, despite all his past apparent friendliness, he was, for some unknown reason, anxious that I should not be released. Seeing, therefore, the utter uselessness of further argument, I desisted, and turned away, bitterly disappointed.

Not, of course, that with Leroy's refusal all hope of deliverance was to be abandoned. By no means. So long as the *Gadfly* remained in sight there was always a chance; for if I knew anything of Lieutenant Peters, he was not the man to let us go without giving us an overhaul, and then my chance would certainly come. It was the duty of the ships of the Slave Squadron to stop and examine the papers of *every* ship encountered in those waters, and I was certain that Peters would not be likely to make an exception in our favour; while, if Leroy resisted, as, of course, he would—well, it would simply mean that *La Mouette* would be captured.

Meanwhile Leroy and Marcel were eagerly consulting together, and presently the second mate left the poop, went forward, and quietly called all hands. Then, as soon as the crew were all on deck, they were ordered to clear for action, the guns were cast loose, the magazine opened, and powder and shot were passed up on deck; the arms' chests were brought up, cutlasses and pistols were served out—a brace of the latter to each man; pistols and muskets were loaded, pikes cast adrift and distributed, and, in short, every preparation was made for a fight, except that the guns were not then loaded. The second mate had been the moving spirit in all these preparations, Leroy, meanwhile, remaining on the poop and intently watching the schooner through the telescope.

By the time that the preparations for battle were complete it was close upon seven bells, and the order was given for the crew to get breakfast, and for that meal to be also served in the cabin. A few minutes later the steward came along with a pot of cocoa in one hand and a covered dish in the other, and Leroy, coming aft to where I stood moodily pondering, thrust his hand under my arm and said, with all apparent good-nature:

"Now, don't sulk, *mon cher*, but come down and have some breakfast. Unless I am greatly mistaken the *Gadfly* is about to send us her boats, and then you may perhaps be able to return in them. But do not build too much upon the chance, for as soon as they come within range I shall open fire upon them with round and grape; and if we cannot sink them before they get alongside, why, we shall deserve to be hanged, that's all."

"Thank you, monsieur," I answered, "but I have no appetite for breakfast just now, and, with your permission, will remain on deck rather than go into that suffocating cabin, merely to watch you and Marcel eat."

98

"*Eh, bien*! as you please," he returned, with a shrug of the shoulders. "I will not ask you to keep a look-out for me, because I can do that quite well from the windows of the captain's cabin; and," looking round, "I do not think you can do any mischief up here. You are sure you will not come down? Very well, then, *an revoir!*"

Now, to be left on deck, practically alone, was a bit of luck that I had not dared to hope for; and the fact that I had been, coupled with what Leroy had said about the boats, gave me an idea upon which I immediately acted. We were still lying broadside-on to the *Gadfly*, and I had not the least doubt that on board her a constant watch was being kept upon the barque; glancing round hurriedly, therefore, and observing that all hands on the forecastle were busy with their breakfast, I slipped over the side into the mizzen chains, where I could stand without being seen from inboard, and, removing my jacket, so that my white shirt-sleeves might show up clearly against the barque's black side, I forthwith began to semaphore with my arms, waving them up and down for about a minute to attract attention. Then, without knowing whether or not I had been successful, I proceeded to signal the following message:

"*La Mouette*, slaver, armed with fourteen 28-pound carronades and four 6-pounders. Carries one hundred and seventy men. Attack with your long thirty-two; boats too risky!"

Then, donning my jacket again, I returned inboard just in time to see Marcel's head appear above the level of the poop.

"Hillo!" he exclaimed; "I was wondering what had become of you. What have you been doing over the side? Considering whether you should attempt to swim across to the *Gadfly*?"

"Yes," answered I boldly, seizing at once upon the suggestion thus given. "But I have thought better of it," I continued. "There are too many sharks about. Look there!" and I pointed to a dorsal fin that was sculling lazily along half-a-dozen fathoms away.

The man looked at me suspiciously for several seconds, then walked to the side and looked over into the chains, but of course there was nothing to be seen. Then, muttering to himself, he returned to the cabin, presumably to finish his breakfast.

He had scarcely disappeared, and I was looking round for the telescope, when a flash of flame and a cloud of white smoke suddenly burst from the schooner's forecastle, and presently a 32-pound shot dashed into the water within half-a-dozen fathoms of our rudder. "Good shot, but not quite enough elevation!" muttered I, delighted at this indication that my message had been noted and was being acted upon; and then came the sullen *boom* of the gun across the water. I went to the skylight and quite unnecessarily reported, "The schooner has opened fire!"

"*Sacré-e-e!*" I heard Leroy exclaim between his teeth. "The one thing that I was afraid of! He has thought better of sending his boats, then!"

Marcel answered something, but what it was I could not catch, and then the pair of them came racing up on deck. They had scarcely arrived when another shot came from the schooner, crashing through the bulwarks just forward of the fore rigging, dismounting a gun, and playing havoc with the men who crowded that part of the deck. Five were killed outright and nine wounded by that one shot and the splinters that it created. Leroy at once called the crew to quarters and ordered them to return the schooner's fire; but the latter was too far off for either the carronades or the 6-pounders to reach her; and my spirits began to rise, for if the schooner could only continue as she had begun she would soon compel *La Mouette* to strike. And there was every prospect of this happening, for the *Gadfly* had now got our range to a nicety, and shot after shot hulled us, playing the very mischief with us, dismounting another gun, strewing our decks with killed and wounded, and cutting up our rigging, but, most unfortunately, never touching our spars.

Leroy stamped fore and aft the deck, cursing like a madman, shaking his fist at the schooner, glowering savagely at me, and whistling for a wind.

"Give me a breeze!" he shouted; "give me a breeze, and I will run down and blow that schooner out of the water!"

Presently his prayer was answered, but not quite as he desired; for, while we watched, the clouds broke away to the eastward, and presently we saw a dark line stealing along the water toward the schooner. Ten minutes later all hands aboard her were busily engaged in making sail, and by the time that the wind reached her she was all ready for it. Then, as it filled her sails, she put up her helm and squared away for us, running down before the wind and yawing from time to time to give us another shot. But it was a fatal mistake; she should have continued to play the game of long bowls, in which case she could have done as she pleased with us; by keeping away, however, and running down to us, she gave Leroy just the chance he wanted; he waited until she was well within range of his carronades, and then, double-shotting them and watching his opportunity, he gave her the whole of his starboard broadside, and down came her foremast and main-topmast. At the same moment another shot came from the schooner, badly wounding our main-topmast above the cap, and the breeze reaching us almost immediately afterward, the spar went over the side, dragging down the mizzen topmast and the fore-topgallant-mast with it. The result of all this was that while the schooner broached to and rode by the wreck of her foremast as to a sea anchor, *La Mouette* fell broad off and refused to come to the wind again; consequently the distance between the two vessels rapidly widened until both were out of range, and the firing ceased.

Thus ended the fight; and I presume that the two craft soon passed out of sight of each other and did not again meet, during that voyage at least, for there was no more firing from *La Mouette* while I remained aboard her. But what transpired during the rest of the voyage I was destined to know very little about, for scarcely had the firing ceased when Captain Tourville, thin, weak, and emaciated, crept up on the poop. He had a pistol in his hand, and no sooner did his gaze fall on me than he levelled the weapon at me and fired it point-blank.

Fortunately for me, the man's hand was so unsteady that the ball flew wide; but the report brought the mates and half-a-dozen men to us with a rush to see what was the matter.

"Take that young scoundrel," exclaimed Tourville, pointing at me with a finger that trembled with rage as much as with weakness, "put his hands and his feet in irons, heave him down on the ballast, and leave him there until I give you further instructions."

Chapter Fifteen.

In the hands of savages.

The order was promptly obeyed; and in a few minutes I found myself, heavily ironed, in the pitchy darkness of the lower hold, squatted disconsolately upon the bed of shingle which constituted the ballast of the vessel.

And what a situation for a young fellow of less than twenty years of age to be in! The ship of which I had been placed in command lost—foundered in mid-ocean, and, only too probably, all hands lost with her. Our fate would never be known; it would be concluded that one of the mysterious disasters that so frequently befall the seaman had overtaken us; we should be given up as lost; and there would be an end of us all, so far as our fellow-men were concerned. For whatever hopes I might once have entertained of escaping from this accursed ship, I had none now.

That Tourville would not be satisfied with anything short of taking my life, I was convinced; and very soon I began to feel that I did not care how soon he sated his vengeance; for confined below in the heat and darkness of the stifling hold, with no resting-place but the hard shingle for my aching body, breathing an atmosphere poisonous with the odour of bilge-water, with only three flinty ship-biscuits, alive with weevils, and a half-pint of putrid water per day upon which to sustain life, and beset by ferocious rats who disputed with me the possession of my scanty fare, I soon became so miserably ill that death quickly lost all its terrors, and I felt that I could welcome it as a release from my sufferings.

How long I remained in this state of wretchedness I cannot tell, for I soon lost count of time and indeed at last sank into a state of semi-delirium; but I think from subsequent calculations it must have been about ten or twelve days after the date of my incarceration that I was aroused once more to a complete consciousness of my surroundings by observing that a change had occurred in the motion of the ship. She no longer pitched and rolled as does a vessel in the open sea, but slid along—as I could tell by the gurgling sound of the water along her bends—upon a perfectly even keel except for the slight list or inclination due to the pressure of the wind upon her sails. I conjectured that she must have arrived at the end of her voyage and entered the Kwara river, a conjecture that was shortly afterward confirmed by the sounds on deck of shouted orders and the bustle and confusion attendant upon the operation of shortening sail, soon followed by the splash of an anchor from the bows and the rumble of the stout hempen cable through the hawse-pipe. Then ensued a period of quiet of several hours' duration, broken at length by the appearance of the carpenter and another seaman who, having removed my irons, gruffly ordered me to follow them up on deck.

I felt altogether too wretchedly ill, and too utterly indifferent respecting my fate, to ask these men any questions, but contrived, by almost superhuman exertion, to climb up the perpendicular ladder which led to the deck; and when I presently emerged from the foetid atmosphere of the hold into the free air and dazzling sunshine of what proved to be early morning, I was so overcome by the sudden transition that I swooned away.

I must have remained in a state of complete unconsciousness for several hours, for when at length I again opened my eyes and looked about me the sun was nearly overhead, and I was lying unbound in the bottom of a long craft that my slowly returning senses at length enabled me to recognise as a native dug-out canoe. She was about forty feet long by four feet beam and about two feet deep; and was manned by thirty as ferocious-looking savages as one need ever wish to see. They were stark naked, save for a kind of breech-clout round the loins, and squatted in pairs along the bottom of the canoe, plying short broad-bladed paddles with which they seemed to be urging their craft at a pretty good pace through the water. A big, brawny, and most repulsive-looking savage, who was probably the captain of the craft, sat perched up in the stern, steering with a somewhat longer and broader-bladed paddle, and urging his crew to maintain their exertions by continually giving utterance to the most hair-raising shrieks and yells.

It was the fresh air, I suppose, that revived me, even as, after my long sojourn in the noisome hold of the slaver, it had prostrated me by my sudden emergence into it, and I presently became conscious that I was feeling distinctly better than I had done for some time past. For a minute or two I lay passively where I was, in the bottom of the canoe, blinking up at the pallid zenith, near which the sun blazed with blinding brilliancy; and then, no one saying me nay, I slowly and painfully raised myself into a sitting posture and looked about me.

We were in a typical African river, about three-quarters of a mile wide, with low bush-clad banks bordered by the inevitable mangrove, while beyond towered the virgin tropical forest, dense, impenetrable, and full of mystery. The turbid current was against us, as could be seen at a glance; I therefore knew at once that we were paddling up-stream. But whither were we bound; of what tribe or nation were the negroes who manned the canoe; and how had I come to be among them? Had Tourville, with a greater refinement of cruelty than even I gave him credit for, handed me over to work their bloodthirsty will upon me, instead of himself murdering me out of hand? If so, what was to be my ultimate fate? I shuddered as I put this question to myself, for I had been on the Coast quite long enough to have heard many a gruesome, blood-curdling story of the horrors perpetrated by the African savages upon those unhappy white men who had been unfortunate enough to fall into their hands.

But I was not going to allow myself to be frightened or discouraged by dwelling upon stories of that kind; I was feeling so far better that the desire to live had returned to me. I even experienced some slight sensation of hunger, and there was no doubt at all as to the fact that I was parched with thirst. I therefore turned to the savage who was flourishing the steering paddle and, first pointing to my open mouth, went through the motions of raising a vessel to it and drinking. The man evidently understood me, for he shouted a few—to me quite unintelligible—words, whereupon one of the paddlers about the centre of the canoe laid in his paddle for a few moments, did something dexterous with a spear and a brownish-grey object the size of a man's head, and a minute later my lips were glued to a luscious cocoa-nut, the extremity of which had been deftly struck off with the blade of the spear, disclosing the white-lined hollow of the cup within brimming with a full pint or more of the delicious "milk," which I swallowed to the last drop. Then, breaking off a strip of the husk and using it as a spoon, I proceeded to scrape out and hungrily devour the soft creamy fruit that lined the shell, and thus made the most satisfying and enjoyable meal that had passed my lips for many a day. Shortly afterward, the strength of the ebb current increasing so greatly that we were able to make scarcely any headway against it, our steersman headed the canoe in toward the western bank of the river, and we presently entered a narrow creek up which we passed for a distance of about a quarter of a mile until we reached a practicable landing-place, when the canoe was secured to a stout mangrove root, and all hands stepped out of her, the steersman taking the precaution to draw my attention to the spears and bows and arrows with which his party were armed, as a hint, I suppose, of what I might expect should I be foolish enough to attempt to escape. We pushed our way through the thick bush for a distance of about a hundred yards, and then reached a small open space, where we bivouacked; a party of ten disappearing into the bush, while the rest remained to kindle a fire and, evidently, to look after me and make sure that I did not give them the slip. At length, after the lapse of about half an hour, the party who had vanished into the bush returned, singly or by two's and three's, some bringing in a monkey or two, others a few brace of parrots, one man a big lizard like an iguana, another a fine deer, until each of the ten had contributed something to the common larder, when the fire was made up, a plentiful supply of food cooked, and all hands set to with a will, each apparently animated by a determination to show all the others how much solid food he was capable of putting out of sight at a sitting. They very civilly offered me a choice of their dainties, and I accepted a tolerably substantial venison steak, broiled over the fire by being suspended close over the glowing embers upon the end of a stick. Off this I contrived to make a fairly hearty meal, after which, following the example of the others, I stretched myself out in the long grass under the shadow of a big bush, and quickly fell into a deep sleep.

I was aroused from my slumbers, some hours later, by my savage companions, who intimated to me, by signs, that the moment had arrived for us to take our departure, and we accordingly wended our way back to the canoe, taking our surplus stock of food with us, and, embarking, soon found ourselves once more afloat on the placid bosom of the broad river, the downward and opposing current of which had by this time greatly slackened under the influence of the flood tide which was evidently making fast.

Keeping well out toward the centre of the stream, and paddling steadily, we now made rapid progress in a northerly direction, the river gradually widening and shoaling as we went, until, by the time of sunset, we found ourselves progressing up a comparatively narrow deep-water channel with wide expanses of shallow water on either side of us, dotted here and there with dry patches of mud or sand upon which crocodiles lay basking, in some cases in groups of as many as six or eight together, while occasionally the great head of a hippopotamus appeared for a moment, only to vanish again with a little eddying swirl of the mud-charged water as the creature dived.

While the sun still hovered a degree or two above the tree-tops on the western bank of the stream, the moon, now nearly full, sailed gloriously into view above the clumps of vegetation that shrouded the eastern bank; and the gradual transition from the ruddy, golden light of the dying sun to the flooding silver of the brilliant moon, with the ever-changing effects that accompanied the transition, presented a spectacle of enchanting beauty such as I had never up to that time beheld, even at sea. But, beyond a low muttered word or two and a grunt, apparently expressive of deep satisfaction at the appearance of the unclouded moon, the savages took no notice of the magical loveliness of the scene; and while I sat entranced and practically oblivious of everything else, they merely paddled the harder, conversing in low tones among themselves. Of course I did not understand a single word of what was said, yet, so much did I gather from the glances that they flung about them, and the emphasis and accent of their speech, that I shrewdly suspected them of anticipating the possibility of attack from the shore.

This suspicion was strengthened, a little later on, by the fact that as we approached a certain bend in the river our timoneer edged the canoe in toward the eastern bank, until we were completely plunged in the deep shadow of the vegetation that grew right down to the water's edge, as though he were desirous of escaping observation; at least there was no other reason that I could think of for such a manoeuvre, for by this time the current was running up quite strongly, and under ordinary circumstances it would have been to our advantage to have remained in mid-channel, where the full strength of it would be felt. But if this was his object he was only partially successful; for we presently arrived abreast of a bay, or it may have been the wide entrance of a creek, many of which branched off the main stream on either hand, where the forest receded so far that, for the distance of fully half a mile, we were compelled to traverse a space of water completely flooded by the brilliant rays of the moon, and before we had accomplished half the passage a quick ejaculation of mingled annoyance and dismay from the steersman caused me to glance toward the western bank, from an opening in which half-a-dozen canoes were darting out with the evident determination to intercept us if possible. Fortunately for us, however, we had already passed the spot from which the pursuing canoes were emerging, this spot now bearing well upon our port quarter; but, on the other hand, our pursuers would presently obtain an important advantage over us, since they would soon reach the deep channel, where the upward current was now running strongly. I feared that when they arrived in that channel they would turn the bows of their craft up-stream and avail themselves of the advantage afforded by the strong current to endeavour to pass ahead of us and cut off our retreat; but in the eagerness of their pursuit they seemed to lose sight of this advantage, for they continued to head straight for us, while we, impelled by the full strength of our thirty paddles, now plied with desperate energy by our freely perspiring crew, gradually drew out and threw our pursuers still further on our quarter.

Yet they were steadily nearing us, and I did not see how we could scrape clear without something in the nature of a fight.

All this time we were heading straight for a low, heavily timbered point which marked another turn in the course of the stream, and I could see that our people were straining every nerve to get round this point before being overtaken. At length, with a mighty stirring up of the mud by our deep-plunging paddles in the shallow water, we shaved close round this point and almost immediately afterwards darted into a narrow creek so completely overgrown with vegetation that the boughs of the mangroves and other trees united over our heads, forming a sort of tunnel, the interior of which was so opaquely dark that it was scarcely possible to see one's hand before one's face. Yet our helmsman seemed to know the place perfectly, for he stood boldly on, urging the crew to continue their exertions. At length, after we had traversed a full hundred yards or more of the creek, we sighted a spot ahead where, doubtless in consequence of a wind-fall, or some similar phenomenon, the dense bush had been levelled, leaving room for a patch of clear moonlight, some ten yards in circumference, to fall full upon the channel of the creek, revealing every object, even the smallest, within its boundary with a clearness and distinctness that was positively startling. Arrived here, the canoe was sheered in alongside a spot where the mangroves grew thickly, and some twenty of our crew, laying in their paddles, hastily seized their bows and arrows and, springing ashore, swiftly vanished into the adjacent deep shadow, while the canoe, with the remainder of us on board, pushed across the patch of moonlight into the darkness beyond, where she was forced beneath an overhanging mass of foliage, in such a manner as to lie perfectly concealed.

Hardly had this been accomplished when we heard from the river the exclamations of our pursuers, startled at our sudden and, at first, inexplicable disappearance. But it did not long remain inexplicable; some sharp eye soon detected the entrance of the creek and suspected that we were concealed therein, for, after a few minutes spent in animated discussion by the occupants, the pursuing canoes were heard cautiously approaching. It was evident that their knowledge of the creek was not nearly so complete as that of our own steersman, for whereas we had contrived, despite the pitchy darkness, to navigate the crooked channel without running foul of anything, we could hear the continual swishing of foliage and the bumping of the canoes as they encountered the overhanging branches or collided with the mangrove roots on one side or the other. We were thus able to follow the progress of their approach with the utmost precision, and the moment that the leading canoe—a craft manned by some twenty most villainous-looking savages—emerged from the darkness into the patch of brilliant moonlight, she was greeted with a murderous discharge of arrows at short range which put the greater part of her crew *hors de combat*. She was closely followed by another canoe of about the same size, the occupants of which were treated to a similarly warm reception. A warning shout from one of the survivors of this second discharge was raised in time to save those behind from pushing forward to meet a similar fate, and now the quick twanging of bowstrings and loud shouts from those ashore and afloat told that a fierce battle was raging. But our people, from the advantage of their position, had very much the best of it, and at length the pursuers were beaten off and compelled to retreat precipitately, with the loss of nearly two-thirds of their number and two canoes, which, with their wounded occupants, were left in our hands, while our party escaped absolutely unscathed. The wounded of the enemy, numbering eleven, would have met with but short shrift at the hands of their captors, but for the interposition of the man whom I have termed our timoneer, who seemed to be a petty chief. This individual carefully examined his prisoners and found that three of them were so severely wounded as to afford little hope of their recovery; these three he therefore despatched with the most callous sang-froid by driving his broad-bladed spear into their throats, after which they were flung over the side; the remaining eight, who appeared to be only temporarily disabled, were trussed up, hand and foot, with thin, tough, pliant creeper, cut from the adjacent jungle, and bestowed, without much consideration for their comfort, in the bottom of our canoe. The captured canoes were then sunk by means of a few large stones placed in them to take them down, and then heeled until the water flowed in over their gunwales, when they quickly vanished beneath the turbid, foetid waters of the creek. This done, our people made preparations for the continuation of their journey.

But our leader, whose knowledge of the river seemed intimate enough to entitle him to a certificate as branch pilot, had no inclination to incur the risk of leaving the creek again at the point where we had entered it, and thus very possibly falling into a cleverly arranged ambuscade. On the contrary, he proceeded to push boldly on up the creek for a distance of several miles, much to my astonishment, for the waterway generally was so narrow as scarcely to afford room for two canoes to pass abreast, and I was momentarily expecting that this creek, like so many others of the African rivers, would abruptly end in a mud-bank overgrown with mangroves. Contrary to my anticipations, however, when a dozen times or more the banks closed in upon us in such a manner as to suggest that our further progress was about to be stayed, we would suddenly emerge into a comparatively wide channel, and push merrily on for a mile or more ere we encountered our next difficulty. In this manner we must have traversed a distance of nearly twenty miles when, to my amazement, and also that of most of the canoe's crew, I think, we suddenly emerged from the tunnel-like channel that we had been navigating for something like five hours, and found ourselves once more in what was undoubtedly the main stream of the river, and so far away from the spot at which we had diverged from it that it was nowhere to be seen. The moon had by this time risen so high in the sky as to be almost directly overhead; there was therefore little or no shadow on either bank of the river to shroud us from observation, nevertheless we continued to cling closely to the eastern bank for several miles further—the tide having now turned and being against us—until at length, the current becoming too strong for us, our leader found a practicable landing-place, and all hands, except the unfortunate prisoners of war, scrambled ashore and, hastily lighting a fire, disposed ourselves to sleep around it.

Now, it will probably be thought by many that I was submitting to my uncertain fate with far greater philosophy than wisdom; but this was by no means the case. The fact was that I had no sooner awakened to the consciousness that I was a prisoner in the hands of African savages than I made up my mind that I could not too soon effect my escape from them; for although I have just spoken of my fate as uncertain I felt that, in reality, there was very little uncertainty about it. It was so rarely that a white man fell into the hands of the negro savages that when one had the misfortune to do so they generally made the utmost of him. And that "utmost" was usually something in which prolonged and agonising torture figured largely. But it would obviously be worse than useless to attempt to escape until an opportunity occurred of at least a fair prospect of success; for to attempt and *fail* meant the extinguishment at once of all further hope. And, up to the present, I had not had a ghost of an opportunity. My captors had taken good care of that, although they had been kind enough to leave me unbound. But now, when all hands must be feeling the effect of fatigue after several hours of strenuous labour at the paddles, and were likely to sleep soundly, it was possible that, by biding my time, I might be able to steal off to the canoe and cut the bonds of the captives who had been so callously left in it, when it would be strange indeed if, out of gratitude for my release of them, they were not willing to help me to make my way back to the mouth of the river, where I should of course have to take my chance of finding a ship the master of which would be willing to receive me on board. It was not, perhaps, a very brilliant prospect, but I felt that it was at

105

least preferable to that to which I might look forward if I remained in the company of my present owners; and accordingly when my sable companions disposed themselves to sleep, I apparently did the same, but summoned all my energies to aid me in the task of resisting the tendency toward somnolence that I felt stealing over me.

But this was not nearly so easy as I had believed it would be. If I closed my eyes for a few seconds a delicious languor seized me, my thoughts began to wander, and it was only by an almost painful effort that I succeeded in, as it were, jerking myself back to full consciousness. My intention was to remain awake until all my companions had become wrapped in slumber, and then effect my escape from them; but to my chagrin I found that while it was almost impossible for me to remain awake, my captors or owners—I scarcely knew which to consider them seemed restless, watchful, and all more or less upon the alert. Finally, while waiting and watching for signs that they were succumbing to the influence of the drowsy god, I lost all control of myself and sank into a profound and delicious slumber.

Chapter Sixteen.

King Banda.

How long I remained steeped in that delightful and refreshing sleep I did not then know; but when at length I awoke with a violent start the embers of the fire were merely smouldering, while the snorts and snores that were emitted by the recumbent figures grouped around it seemed to indicate that the fateful moment had arrived when I might make a bid for liberty with some prospect of success. It was now very much darker than it had been when I sank into involuntary slumber, for the moon had swung so far over toward the west that at least two-thirds of the small clearing which we occupied were enveloped in deep shadow, but I observed with some dismay that my path to the canoe lay directly across the patch that was still bathed in the moon's rays. That, however, could not be helped; I could not afford to delay until the moon had sunk low enough to throw the entire clearing into shadow, for with the setting of the moon would come dawn and sunrise. I therefore determined to start upon my attempt forthwith, and, as a first step, rolled myself over, away from the fire, as though stirring in my sleep.

I was now lying with my back to the fire, and could therefore not see my companions or observe what effect, if any, my movement had had upon them; but I resolved not to fail for want of caution, so I made no further attempt to withdraw myself for the next ten minutes, but confined myself simply to a few restless movements, as though—which was actually the case—I was being worried by the swarms of minute creeping and biting things with which the spot abounded. Then, at the end of about ten minutes from my first movement, I ventured again to roll over in the same direction as before, which once more brought me with my face toward the fire. I now opened my eyes cautiously and carefully surveyed my surroundings. Not one of the black figures about the fire appeared to have altered his position in the slightest degree, so far as I could perceive, while the snoring and snorting still proceeded as vigorously as ever. I lay quite still for two or three minutes, and then, as everything seemed perfectly safe, and I had not too much time to spare, I decided that I might venture upon a somewhat more rapid mode of progression. I accordingly raised myself upon my hands and knees, and proceeded to crawl very cautiously toward the canoe, looking back from time to time to see if I were observed.

It was while I was thus engaged in looking back, while still creeping forward, that, as I put forth my right hand, it fell upon something cold and clammy that stirred beneath my touch, and the next instant I felt a sharp pricking sensation in the fleshy base of my right thumb. Like lightning I snatched my hand away, threw myself backward and sprang to my feet with an involuntary cry; and as I did so I indistinctly caught sight of a small wriggling object in the long grass that seemed to vanish in a flash. It was a snake, and it had bitten me! Yes, there was no mistake about that, for as I lifted my hand to my eyes there was light enough for me to see two drops of blood, about a quarter of an inch apart upon my right hand. Upon the spur of the moment I clapped the wounded part to my mouth and sucked vigorously, spitting out such blood as I was able to draw from the wound, and this I continued to do industriously for the next hour or more. But my chance of escape was gone for that night at least; for my cry brought the whole of the savages to their feet as one man, with their weapons grasped and ready for instant use. Some half-a-dozen of them, seeing me upon my feet, sprang toward me and surrounded me with angry cries, but I did not of course make the slightest attempt to run; on the contrary, I showed them my wounded hand, and, with two fingers of my left hand extended, made a motion as of a snake striking his fangs into my flesh. The individual whom I took to be the chief of the little party thereupon led me back to the fire, and thrusting two or three dry twigs into the smouldering ashes, fanned the latter into a blaze with his breath, thus causing the twigs to ignite. Then, using these twigs as a torch, he carefully examined my wounded hand, shook his head as though to indicate that I had no chance, cast the blazing twigs to the ground, and saying a few words to his companions, lay down and again composed himself to sleep, an example at once followed by his companions. I, however, remained awake, diligently sucking my wounded hand, which soon began to swell and grow acutely painful, the throbbing pain extending all the way up my arm, right to the shoulder. The pain at length became so acute that I could sit still no longer, I therefore sprang to my feet and began to pace to and fro; but I had no sooner done so than half-a-dozen of the savages were beside me, not exactly interfering with me—for I think they understood pretty clearly what was the matter with me—but making it perfectly plain that they were watching me, and that only a certain amount of freedom would be permitted me. Whether they really understood that I was actually attempting to effect my escape when the snake bit me, I was never able to determine.

At length the dawn arrived, day broke, the sun rose, and a few of the savages, taking their bows and arrows, went off into the bush to forage, as I surmised; and a little later they returned, one after the other, each bringing some contribution to the common larder, while others busied themselves in collecting fresh wood and rebuilding the fire. While they were thus engaged, one of the party, who happened to pass near the spot where I had been bitten, suddenly uttered a most dreadful yell, grasped his left foot, looked at it a moment, and then began with furious haste to search about in the long grass, which he pushed apart with the blade of his spear. A few seconds later he fell to stabbing the ground, as it seemed, savagely, finally stooping down and picking up the still writhing halves of a snake that had been cut clean in two by a blow of his spear. It was not at all a formidable-looking creature, being not more than eighteen inches long and perhaps three inches girth about the thickest part of its body. But it was an ugly, repulsive-looking brute, its head being heart-shaped, and its body almost the same thickness for the greater part of its length, terminating in a short, blunt tail. Its ground colour was a dirty grey, upon which occurred large, irregular blotches or markings of dull black with a few splashes of brilliant red here and there. The fellow who had fallen upon it with such ferocity, and who had evidently been bitten by it, brought the two writhing fragments and flung them into the fire, in the midst of which they writhed still more horribly. Then seizing a good, stout, brightly-glowing brand from the fire, he coolly sat down and applied the almost white-hot end to the wound, which was in his left instep. I do not think I ever saw anything more heroic than this act of the savage, for though the flesh hissed and smoked and gave forth a most horrible odour of burnt flesh, the man never winced, but calmly and deliberately cauterised the bite with as much care and thoroughness as though he had been operating upon somebody else. But that he was not insensible to his self-inflicted torture was very evident from the fact that in a few seconds he was literally drenched with the perspiration that started from every pore of his body.

While this was happening, the leader of the party had hurriedly raked from the fire the scorched and blistered half of the snake to which the head was attached, and, seizing it by the neck, squeezed it until the jaws were forced open, revealing two long, slender, needle-like fangs projecting from the upper jaw. Holding this horrible object between the finger and thumb of his right hand, he approached me, and, before I had the least idea of what he intended to do, seized my wounded hand and approached the head of the still living reptile so closely to it that it was easily to be seen that the two tiny punctures in my flesh were exactly the same distance apart as the snake's fangs, the inference being that this was the identical reptile that had bitten me. Having satisfied himself of this, the man flung the loathsome object back into the heart of the fire, where it was soon consumed.

I was by this time suffering the most dreadful agony, my hand and arm were so terribly swollen that they had almost lost all semblance to any portion of the human anatomy, while the two punctures made by the poison fangs were puffed up, almost to bursting, and encircled by two rings of livid grey colour. The throbbing of the limb, as the blood forced itself through the congested passages, can only be compared to the pulsing of a stream of fire, and I am certain that, had I been within reach of qualified surgical assistance at the moment, I should have insisted upon having the limb removed, as I was convinced that the pain of amputation would have been less acute than that from which I was suffering. Needless to say, I had no appetite for food when it was offered me a little while afterward; but I felt thirsty enough to drink the river dry, and quaffed several cocoa-nuts with an ecstasy of delight that almost caused me to forget my pain—for the moment.

Breakfast over, the word was given to re-embark, and we all wended our way back to the canoe. I do not know whether it was deliberate intention, or merely the result of accident, but I could not help noticing that during the short journey from our camping-place to the spot where the canoe had been left, there were always three or four savages quite close to me, who appeared to be keeping a very careful watch upon my movements, as though they more than half suspected me of a desire to give them the slip; but I was by this time suffering such excruciating agony that, for the time being at least, all thoughts of escape were completely banished from my mind. I had become quite convinced that the bite was going to prove fatal, and my only subject of speculation was how many more hours of torture I was doomed to endure before merciful death would come to my relief. But after we had been afloat for about half an hour, and were once more speeding up the river as fast as the sturdy arms of the paddlers could urge us, I suddenly became violently sick, the paroxysm lasting for nearly ten minutes; and when I had in some degree recovered from the exhaustion attendant upon this attack, I was equally surprised and delighted to find that the pain and throbbing in my arm were distinctly less acute; and from that moment, as much to the astonishment of the savages as of myself, my symptoms rapidly improved, until by evening I was so far free from pain as to be able to sleep for several hours, although the swelling did not entirely subside until nearly forty-eight hours later. But meanwhile my fellow-sufferer, the savage who had also been bitten, and who had resorted to the heroic method of cauterising his wound, had been all day steadily developing symptoms similar to my own before the curative attack of sickness, his foot and leg, right up to the hip, had swollen to an enormous size and become so stiff that when the moment arrived for us to disembark for the night he was unable to move, and begged most piteously—as I interpreted the tones of his voice and his actions—to be left in the canoe all night, to fight out the battle between life and death alone and undisturbed.

The next morning, when we went down to the canoe, the poor fellow was not only dead, but his whole body was swollen almost out of human semblance, presenting in that and other respects a most shocking and revolting spectacle. We took the corpse with us until we had reached the main channel of the river, and there flung it overboard. We had scarcely left it fifty fathoms astern when there arose a sudden violent commotion in the water about it, and a second or two later it disappeared from view, dragged down by the voracious crocodiles with which the river swarmed.

I was by this time quite free from pain, and apart from a feeling of extreme debility, which I had endured for some hours on the previous day, I was not much the worse for the alarming experience that I had undergone. The death of the savage who had been bitten after me, and undoubtedly by the same reptile, conclusively proved how very narrow had been my escape from a similar fate; and I naturally fell to wondering how it was that he had succumbed to his injury while I had recovered from mine. For it seemed to me at the moment that the remedial measure which he had adopted ought, from its very severe and drastic character, to have proved much more efficacious than my own; whereas the opposite was the case. But upon further reflection I came to the conclusion that while I had proceeded to suck the poison from the wound *at once*, or within a second or two of its infliction, the savage had wasted at least a minute in pursuing and slaying his enemy before cauterising his wound, and that this minute of delay, accompanied as it was by somewhat violent action on the part of the injured man, had sufficed for the poison to obtain a strong enough hold upon his system to produce fatal results. Whether or not this is the correct explanation I must leave to those who are better qualified than myself to judge.

Day after day we steadily pursued our course up the river, which, for the most part, retained the same dreary, monotonous aspect of low, bush-clad, mangrove-lined banks, and practically the same width, save where, at occasional intervals, it widened out and became dotted with islands, some of considerable size. At length we arrived at a point where the land on the western bank rose into a range of hills some eight or nine hundred feet high, densely clothed with vegetation to their summits. This range of hills extended northward for a distance of about thirty miles before it once more sank into the plain; but before it sank completely out of sight astern more high land was sighted ahead, and two days later we found ourselves navigating among some very picturesque scenery, with high land on both sides of us, some of the peaks being twelve to fourteen hundred feet high. Late in the evening of the second day after entering upon this picturesque stretch of the river we arrived at a point where the stream forked into two of apparently equal width and depth, one branch striking away to the eastward, while the other continued its northerly course. Here my savage companions proceeded with the utmost caution, frequently landing and sending one or two of the party away to reconnoitre, and otherwise behaving as though they feared attack; but after a slow and anxious progress of some twenty hours' duration they seemed to consider the danger as past, and once more pressed boldly forward.

By this time I had completely recovered, not only from the effects of the snake-bite—at which my companions seemed greatly astonished—but also from the hardship and privation which I had experienced during the latter part of my voyage aboard *La Mouette*, and had begun to think very seriously of how I was to effect my escape from those who held me captive. Not that I was ill-treated by them, far from it; I enjoyed the same fare as themselves, and was never asked to share their labours, and that, I take it, was as much good treatment as I could reasonably expect under the circumstances. But I knew that they were not hampering themselves by taking me and their other prisoners this long journey up the river—much of the paddling being done against the stream—merely for the pleasure of enjoying our society. My intuition assured me that their action had a more sinister motive than this, and in any case I had no desire to penetrate the interior of equatorial Africa; therefore so soon as I felt that my health and strength were sufficiently restored to allow of my attempting the long and perilous journey back to the sea alone, I began to consider the question of escape. But the longer I thought of it the less became my hope of success; for I very soon discovered that under no circumstances whatever were my custodians disposed to allow me to stray a yard out of their sight. Without imposing any actual restraint upon me, they invariably so contrived that, if I made the slightest attempt to withdraw myself from them, three or four of the most active of the party, always well armed, had occasion to go in precisely the same direction as myself. That, however, was not my only difficulty; for, assuming for a moment the possibility of my being able to give the savages the slip, how was I, a white man, alone, unarmed, and with no means of obtaining food, to make my way down more than two hundred miles of river, flowing through a country every inhabitant of which would undoubtedly be an enemy, whose delight it would be to hunt me to death? I told myself that if I could obtain a small, light, handy canoe and weapons, even though they should but consist of a bow and arrows, the situation would not be altogether hopeless—for I possessed a very fair share of pluck and resource; but I felt that before I could effect my escape from my watchful custodians, and obtain these necessities, I might find myself in so dire a strait as to render them and all else valueless to me. Yet I would not suffer myself to feel discouraged, for I recognised that to abandon hope was to virtually surrender myself tamely to the worst that fate might have in store for me, and this was by no means my disposition; I therefore continued to keep my eyes wide open for an opportunity.

But, watch as I might, the opportunity never presented itself, nor, thanks to the watchfulness of my companions, could I make one; so the time dragged on until, after a river voyage of more than three weeks, we one evening, about two hours before sunset, entered a creek important enough to suggest the idea that it might possibly be a small tributary of the main river. After paddling up it for a distance of about two miles we suddenly hove in sight of a native town of considerable size built upon the north bank of the creek, upon an area of ground that had been completely cleared of all undergrowth, but was well shaded by the larger trees which had been allowed to stand. That the town was of some importance, as well as of considerable size, I surmised from the fact that, with a few exceptions, the habitations, instead of being of the usual circular, bee-hive shape common to most native African towns, were of comparatively spacious dimensions and substantial construction, being for the most part quadrangular in plan, with thick walls built of substantial wattles, interwoven about stout poles sunk well into the ground and solidly plastered with clay which, having dried and hardened in the sun, had become quite weather-tight, protected as they were from the tropical rains by a thick thatch of palm leaves, with which also their steep sloping roofs were covered. The average size of these huts was about twenty feet long by twelve feet wide and eight feet high to the eaves; but there were others—about fifty of them altogether—surrounded by and cut off from the rest by a high and stout palisade—the points of the palisades being sharpened, in order, as I took it, to render the fence unclimbable—which were not only considerably larger and more substantial in point of construction, but which, as I afterward had opportunity to observe, evidenced some rude attempt at decoration in the form of grotesquely carved finials affixed to the roofs. This part of the town, situated in its centre, and covering, perhaps, a space of forty acres, was, I afterwards learned, the habitation of King Banda, his Court, the principal officers of his army and household, and the priests, whose temple, or fetish-house, stood on the opposite side of the square to that occupied by the "palace" of the king.

Our appearance did not at first attract very much attention, or create any very great amount of excitement; but when we arrived within hail of the beach in front of the town—upon which were hauled up some three to four hundred canoes of various sizes— our skipper suddenly sprang to his feet and, placing his hands trumpet-wise to his mouth, began, in a curious, high-pitched voice, to shout a somewhat lengthy communication. Before it was half finished there was a very distinct commotion upon the beach; half the naked children, who had been playing in the water, were racing up to the town as fast as their legs would carry them, shouting as they went, while from every hut the inhabitants came pouring out, like ants from a disturbed nest, and began to hurry down to the beach. By the time that we arrived there must have been at least two thousand people assembled to meet us, and others were hurrying down in crowds.

I soon found that I was the cause of all the commotion, for no sooner did I step out of the canoe than, although my travelling companions formed themselves into a cordon round me, and the headman or chief who had me in charge strove by virtue of his authority to prevent such a happening, there occurred a wild rush on the part of the crowd to get at least a sight of me, while those who could get near enough to me insisted upon touching my skin, apparently with the object of satisfying themselves as to the genuineness of its colour; and from their eagerness and their exclamations of astonishment I came to the conclusion that although they might have heard of, they had never actually seen a white man before, a conclusion which I afterwards found to be correct.

Using the butts, and occasionally the points, of their spears freely in order to force a passage through the steadily growing crowd, my escort slowly made their way toward that part of the town which was enclosed by the palisade; and, as they did so, I studied the faces of those who thronged about me, with the object of forming some idea, if I could, of the fate that I might expect at their hands.

I must confess that the results of my inspection were by no means reassuring. The first fact to impress itself upon me was that these people among whom I now found myself were of an entirely different race from the negro, properly so-called—the woolly-pated, high cheek-boned, ebony-skinned individual with snub nose and thick lips usually met with aboard a slaver. To start with, their colour was much lighter, being a clear brown of varying degrees of depth, from that of the mulatto to a tint not many shades deeper than that of the average Spaniard. But this difference, marked though it was, was not so great as that between their cast of features and that of the negro; the features of these people were, for the most part, clean cut, shapely, and in many cases actually handsome, their noses especially being exceedingly well formed. Then their head covering was hair, not wool, that of the men being worn close-cropped, while the women allowed theirs to grow at will and wore it flowing freely over the back and shoulders, the locks in many cases reaching considerably below the waist. It was invariably curly, that of the men growing in close, tiny ringlets clustering thickly all over the head, while that of the women, because it was worn longer, I suppose, took the form of long graceful curls. In colour it was a rich glossy black. They were certainly an exceptionally fine race of people, the men being lithe, clean-limbed, muscular fellows, every one of them apparently in the pink of condition, while the faces and figures of the women, especially the younger ones, would have excited the envy of many an English belle. But there was a something, very difficult to define, in the expression of these people that I did not at all like, a hardness about the mouth, and a cruel glint in the eyes—especially of the men—which looked at me in a manner that suggested all sorts of unpleasant possibilities, and excited within me a distinct longing to be almost anywhere rather than where I was.

The party who had brought me to this remote spot were of an entirely different race from those among whom I now found myself, and the fact that we were making our way toward what was obviously the aristocratic part of the town, coupled with the expressive conversation carried on by the leader of my custodians with three or four individuals who had joined us, led me to surmise—although of course I did not understand a word of what was said—that I had been brought up the river as a peace-offering or something of that sort, which conclusion was again the reverse of reassuring.

As we drew near to the exceedingly narrow gate in the palisade, which had been thrown open to admit us—and which, I presently saw, was strongly guarded by a number of warriors armed with heavy, broad-bladed spears, murderous-looking swords, and small round shields, or targets, of wood covered with what looked like crocodile hide—I became sensible of a horrible charnel-house smell; but it was not until we had passed through the gate, and were inside the palisaded enclosure, that I discovered from whence it emanated. Then, observing the direction of the wind which wafted this dreadful odour to my nostrils, I looked that way and presently noticed a large dead tree standing in the middle of the square that formed the centre of this part of the town. It was the immense number of birds that wheeled and screamed about this tree that first caused me to regard it with particular attention, but even then I could not, for the moment, see anything to account for either the birds or the odour. But a minute or two later, as we drew nearer the tree, the stench meanwhile becoming almost overpoweringly strong, I detected fastened to the trunk of the tree, in a manner that was not at first apparent, nine human corpses, some of them so far advanced in decomposition that even the birds would not approach them! Then I understood that I saw before me that detestable thing of which I had often heard as the most prominent object in the typical African native town or village, the "crucifixion tree," upon which the petty despot who rules over that particular community is wont summarily to put to a cruel and lingering death such of his subjects as may be unfortunate enough to offend him! In some cases, I believe, the monarch is content to cause his victims to be securely lashed to the crucifixion tree by stout lianas, there to perish slowly of hunger and thirst; but King Banda, the potentate whose will was law in this particular town, had carried his cruelty to its utmost limit by adopting the time-honoured method of nailing his victims to the tree with spike nails driven through the hands and feet into the tough timber.

The enormous crowd who had followed us up from the beach were not permitted to enter the palisaded enclosure, which was strictly taboo to the common herd; our party therefore now consisted solely of those who had brought me up the river, four individuals who had joined us outside the gate—and whom I took to be officials of some sort—and my unworthy self; and, for my own part, I would very willingly have waived the distinction of forming one of the party. Marching up to what I conjectured to be the king's house—from the fact that it was not only by far the largest dwelling in the enclosure, but was also distinguished by an exclusive embellishment in the form of a row of a dozen poles, each surmounted by a human skull, planted upright in the ground before it—we halted at a distance of some twenty paces from the entrance, with our backs turned toward the crucifixion tree, the leafless branches of which overshadowed us, and waited.

Ten minutes, twenty minutes, passed, and the sun was within a hand's-breadth of the horizon when a man emerged from the "palace," bearing a massive chair of ebony, quaintly-carved, and draped with a magnificent leopard's skin, which he placed immediately before the open door, midway between the house and ourselves, and departed. A moment later another man appeared—this time from the fetish-house on the opposite side of the square—also with a chair, decorated with most gruesome—looking carvings, which he placed beside the first. Then a tall and enormously stout man, clad in a leopard-skin *moucha*, and with a handsome leopard-skin cloak on his shoulders, came forth from the palace, leaning upon the shoulders of two other men, and advanced toward the chair which had first been placed in position, into which he subsided heavily, casting a strongly disapproving glance at the second chair as he did so. Then there arose a sudden tramping of bare feet upon the dry earth, and from somewhere in the rear of the palace there swung into view a hundred picked warriors, armed like those who had mounted guard at the palisade gate, who formed up behind and on each side of the chairs with very commendable military precision. Simultaneously with the appearance of the guards—for such they were—there emerged from the fetish-house a man who appeared to be incredibly old, for his hair and beard were as white as snow, and his once stalwart form was now bowed and wizened with the passage of, as it seemed to me, hundreds of years. Yet, although in appearance a very Methuselah in age, this individual had a pair of piercing black eyes that glowed and sparkled with all the fire and passion of early manhood, and, bowed as he was, and decrepit as he appeared to be, he tottered across the intervening space with extraordinary agility, and seated himself in the second chair. Thus I found myself in the presence of the two most powerful men in the district, namely, King Banda and Mafuta, the chief witch-doctor.

The contrast between these two men was most remarkable, for whereas Mafuta appeared to be the living embodiment of extreme age, King Banda could scarcely have been forty; and while Mafuta was an image of decrepitude, Banda, despite his excessive corpulence, appeared to be—what in fact he was—a man of immense physical strength. Yet, notwithstanding this marked dissimilarity in their appearance, there was one point of strong resemblance between them: the expression of their faces, and particularly of their eyes, was ineffably cruel.

Chapter Seventeen.

King Banda's daughter.

For the space of nearly a minute there now prevailed an intense silence while King Banda sat glowering at our party, and especially at me, in a manner that caused cold chills to run down my back, as I reflected that this was the man who was responsible for the gruesome fruit borne by the tree, the branches of which overshadowed us, and that if he should by any chance take the fancy into his head to further decorate that tree by nailing a white man to it, there was nobody but myself within some hundreds of miles who would dream of saying him nay; and I somehow had a conviction that my disapproval of such a course would not very strongly influence him.

At length, when the prolonged silence was beginning distinctly to get upon our nerves, the king spoke to the headman of our party, addressing to him a few curt words in a decidedly ungracious tone of voice; whereupon the headman, taking the precaution first to conciliate his Majesty by prostrating himself and rubbing his nose in the dust in token of abject submission, rose to his feet and proceeded to spin a long yarn, of which I was evidently the subject, since he repeatedly pointed to me. He must have included in his narrative the incident of the snake-bite, for at one point he seized my right hand and, turning the palm upward, pointed out the spot where the two tiny punctures of the poison fangs were still faintly visible. It appeared as if this part of his story was received with grave suspicion by both Banda and Mafuta, for I was led forward in order that each in turn might examine the marks; and after this had been done, several of the savages who had been present at the time were invited to give what I took to be corroborative testimony. When at length the headman had told his story, Banda issued a brief order to his guards, two of whom at once advanced toward me and laid their hands upon my shoulders as though to lead me away. But, whatever the order may have been, Mafuta evidently objected to it, for no sooner had it been spoken than he sprang to his feet, and with quite marvellous agility, hurried to me and seized me by the left arm, saying in an angry voice something to the guards that I interpreted as an order to release their hold upon me. But Banda promptly intervened, reiterating his order to his guards; whereupon there ensued between the two great men a most unseemly altercation, the hubbub of which had the effect of bringing the entire royal household to the door of the palace, when, catching sight of me, they unceremoniously swarmed out and crowded round me with every expression of the most unbounded astonishment, particularly on the part of the women, who apparently could not persuade themselves that the colour of my skin and hair were real, for they not only took my skin between their fingers, but gently pinched it. When they found that my shoulders and other parts of my body which had been protected from the sun were quite white, whereas the exposed parts were by this time quite as dark as their own skins, there was no limit to their amazement and delight. I thought that the women-folk seemed rather well disposed toward me, I therefore did the best I could to strengthen this feeling by smiling at them and speaking to them in a gentle tone of voice, with the result that before another five minutes had passed we were all gabbling and laughing together like so many children, although neither side understood a word of what was said by the other. In the midst of it all Mafuta sprang from his chair in a towering rage, and, addressing a few remarks to the king which seemed to make the latter feel rather uncomfortable, took himself off to his fetish-house, within which he vanished. Then the king shouted something to his women-folk which caused them to scuttle back into the palace like so many rabbits; and the next moment the two guards who had me in charge marched me off to an empty hut behind the palace—which was, luckily, to windward of the crucifixion tree, the odour from which therefore did not reach as far as my lodging—and, having signed to me to enter, mounted guard, one on each side of the door.

My prison—if such it was—was a tolerably spacious affair, measuring about twenty feet long by fifteen feet wide, and it was absolutely empty; also, there being no windows to the building, and the light entering only by the open door, the obscurity, on entering, seemed profound, although a few minutes sufficed to enable one's eyes to grow accustomed to it, when, at least during daylight, it was possible to see clearly enough for all practical purposes.

I had not been in my new quarters above five minutes when two elderly women entered, each bearing upon her head a large bundle of dry fern, which they cast down in one of the two corners of the hut most distant from the door and proceeded to spread there in such a fashion as to form a most comfortable bed, upon which I at once flung myself, for I was very weary. But before I could compose myself to rest two other women entered, one of whom bore, upon a thick biscuit-like cake the size of an ordinary dinner-plate, two roast ribs of goat and a generous portion of boiled yam, while the other carried a calabash full of what I took to be some kind of native beer. Evidently, whatever was to be my fate, they did not intend to starve me; and, gratefully accepting the viands, which gave forth a most appetising odour, I sat down and made a hearty meal, after doing full justice to which I composed myself to sleep upon my bed of ferns, and enjoyed a long and most comfortable night's rest.

I may here mention that I never again saw the party of savages who brought me up the river, and I was therefore strengthened in the conclusion at which I had arrived that they had gone to all the trouble of conveying me that long distance in order that they might make a present of me, possibly as a peace-offering from their tribe, to King Banda, who, I soon had reason to believe, was a decidedly formidable potentate, as African kings went.

For nearly a week I was kept closely confined to the hut which had been assigned to me, never being permitted to go beyond the door of the building, where, when the sun had worked round far enough to cause the building to cast a shadow, I soon got into the way of sitting for an hour or two, doing my best to ingratiate myself with the inhabitants of the place, many of whom used to come and stare at me with never-ceasing curiosity and wonder, and with whom I used to laugh and chat, although of course neither party understood a word of what was said by the other. That is to say, neither understood the other *at first*; but in the course of a few days I found that, with the more intelligent of the natives, it was possible for me to convey by signs, and by speaking with much emphasis, some sort of general idea of my meaning. It was undoubtedly by diligent practice in this direction that, after strict confinement to the interior of my hut for some five or six days, I was permitted, first of all, to wander at will about that portion of the town which was enclosed by the palisade, and ultimately to pass outside and go practically whither I would, always accompanied, however, by two armed guards.

One of the greatest discomforts from which I suffered at this time was the outcome of the peculiar musical taste of King Banda's subjects. Though I was then happily unaware of the fact, the period of the great annual festival, or Customs, was approaching, and the joy of the populace began to find vent in nocturnal concerts inordinately prolonged, the musical instruments consisting of tom-toms, each beaten by two, three, or four performers—according to the size of the tom-tom—with a monotony of cadence that soon became positively maddening, further aggravated by the discordant squealing of a number of flageolet-like instruments made of stout reeds.

Now, although I have not hitherto had occasion to mention the fact, I was passionately fond of music, and rather fancied myself as a performer upon the flute; one night, therefore, when one of these hideous concerts was in full blast, and when, consequently, it was useless to attempt to sleep, I sallied forth, accompanied as usual by my guards, and made my way round to the great square in front of the king's house, where, squatted round a huge fire, some twenty of these enthusiasts were tootling and thumping with a vigour that I could not help regarding as utterly misplaced. I stood watching them for a few minutes, and then approaching one of the flageolet players I held out my hand and pointed to his instrument, signifying that I desired to examine it.

With some show of hesitation the man surrendered the thing, and upon inspection I found it to be a reed of about a foot in length, with a mouthpiece shaped something like that of a whistle, and with four small holes drilled in the length of the tube, whereby an expert performer might produce seven distinct tones; but the tones were not consecutive, and the instrument was altogether a very poor and inefficient affair. It furnished me with an idea, however, and on the following day, by dint of much suggestive gesticulation, I contrived to intimate to my guard my desire to obtain a reed similar to those from which the native instruments were made. They offered no objection, but conducted me some distance beyond the town, through the bush, to a spot on the bank of the river where the reed was growing in abundance. I had resolved to make myself either a flute or a flageolet, whichever might prove easiest, and I accordingly selected with great care half-a-dozen of the most suitable reeds that I could find, and, borrowing his spear from one of my guards, cut them, taking care that they should be of ample length for my purpose.

Then I hunted about for some soft wood wherefrom to make mouthpieces and the stopped end of the flute; and it was while I was thus engaged that I made a most important discovery, which was nothing less than that there were several very fine specimens of the cinchona tree growing in the jungle quite close to the town. This was a singularly fortunate and opportune discovery, for I had already observed that fever and ague were very prevalent among the inhabitants, and I hoped that if by means of a decoction of cinchona bark I could effect a cure, I might be able very materially to improve and strengthen my position in the town. I therefore collected as much of the bark as I could conveniently carry, and took it back with me to my hut, where I lost no time in preparing a generous supply of tolerably strong solution of quinine. This done, I sallied forth on the look-out for patients, and soon found as many as I wanted. But it was one thing to find them, and quite another to persuade them to swallow my medicine, and it was not until at length I administered a pretty stiff dose to myself that I prevailed upon a man to allow me to experiment upon him. That, however, was quite sufficient; for it did him so much good that not only did he come to my hut clamouring for more, but brought several fellow-sufferers with him, with the result that before the week was out I had firmly established my reputation as a powerful witch-doctor. I very soon found, however, that this reputation was by no means an unmixed blessing; for the people jumped to the conclusion that if I could cure one disease I could of course cure all; and I speedily found myself consulted by patients suffering from ailments of which I did not even know the names, and expecting to be cured of them. Yet, astonishing to say, I was marvellously successful, all things considered, for when at a loss I administered pills compounded of meal dough and strongly flavoured with the first harmless substance that came to hand, and so profound was the belief of these people in my ability that at least half of them were cured by the wonderful power of faith alone.

All this, however, was exceedingly detrimental to the reputation of Mafuta, the chief witch-doctor of the community, who found his power and influence rapidly waning, and he soon discovered means to make me understand that I must cease to trespass upon what he deemed his own exclusive sphere of operations, on pain of making him my mortal enemy. This of course was bad, for I was in no position to make any man my enemy, much less an individual of such power and influence as Mafuta; nevertheless I continued to prescribe for all who came to me, trusting that if ever it should come to a struggle between Mafuta and myself, the gratitude of my patients would suffice to turn the scale in my favour.

Meanwhile I devoted my spare moments to the construction of a flute, and, after two or three partial failures, succeeded in producing an instrument of very sweet tone and a sufficient range of notes to enable me to tootle the air of several of the most popular songs of the day, as well as a fairly full repertoire of jigs, hornpipes, and other dance music. And it was particularly interesting to observe how powerfully anything in the nature of real music, like some of the airs of Braham, Purcell, Dr Arne, and Sir H. Bishop, appealed to these simple savages; a sentimental ditty, such as "The Anchor's weighed" or "Tom Bowling," would hold them breathless and entranced; "Rule, Britannia!" or "Should He upbraid" set them quivering with excitement; and they seemed to know by intuition that "The Sailor's Hornpipe" was written to be danced to, and they danced to it accordingly a wild, furious, mad fandango in which the extraordinary nature of the gambols of the performers was only equalled by the ecstasy of their enjoyment. Such proceedings as these could not of course long exist without the fame of them reaching the ears of the king, and I had only given some three or four performances when I was summoned to entertain his Majesty and his household, which I did in the great square before the palace, my audience numbering quite two thousand; Banda and his numerous family being seated in a huge semicircle—of which I was the centre—in front of the palace, while the rest of the audience filled the remaining portion of the square.

It was now that I first began to grow aware of the fact that there was a certain member of the king's household who seemed to be taking rather more interest in me than any one else had thus far manifested. She was a girl of probably not more than sixteen years of age, but for all that a woman, and, as compared with the rest, a very pretty woman too; quite light in colour, exquisitely shaped, and with a most pleasing expression of countenance, especially when she smiled, as she generally did when my eyes happened to meet hers. I had seen her many times before, but had never taken very particular notice of her until now that she appeared determined to make me understand that she was friendly disposed toward me. I endeavoured to ascertain who she was; but although I had contrived to pick up a few words of the language, my ignorance of it was still so great that I had experienced the utmost difficulty in making myself understood, and all I could then learn about her was that her name was Ama. It was not until later that I discovered her to be King Banda's favourite daughter. And the discovery was made in a sufficiently dramatic manner, as shall now be related.

It happened that one night, when, as now was frequently the case, I had been summoned to entertain the king and his household by "obliging them with a little music," I was playing some soft, plaintive air—I forget what—when, chancing to glance toward Ama, who, seated on the ground on the extreme left of the semicircle, was well within my range of vision, I fancied I saw some moving object close to her left hand, which was resting lightly on the ground. At the moment I took but scant notice of the circumstance, for the flickering flames of the fire which was always kindled upon such occasions played strange pranks with the lights and shadows, and often imparted a weird effect of movement to stationery and even inanimate objects; but presently, happening to again glance in that direction, my eye was once more caught by the same queer wavering movement. There was something so strange and uncanny about it—for I by this time knew the ground well enough to be fully aware that there *ought not* to be any moving thing there—that I stopped playing and sprang to my feet so suddenly that my movement appeared to startle Ama, who uttered a little cry of alarm, or surprise, and made as though she too would spring to her feet.

At that instant the thing upon which my gaze was fixed, and which looked like half a fathom of stiff tarred lanyard, darted with lightning swiftness at the girl and coiled itself about her shapely bare arm, while a piercing scream rang out from her pallid lips. I of course knew in an instant what it was—a snake, that very possibly had been attracted to the spot by the notes of my flute, and, startled by the sudden cessation of the music and Ama's quick, involuntary movement, had instantly coiled itself round her arm and struck at it in its blind and panic-stricken rage. Acting upon the impulse of the moment, and scarcely knowing what I was about, with a single bound I flung myself upon the terrified girl and, guided more by instinct than reason, seized the reptile immediately behind the head in so vice-like a grip that its jaws at once opened wide, when I tore its hideous coils from the girl's arm and flung it far from me into the very heart of the blazing fire. Then, gripping the wounded limb, I turned it toward the light of the fire, and saw two marks close together upon the inner part of the arm, just below the elbow, from which, as I gazed, two drops of blood began to ooze slowly.

Without wasting a moment, I applied my lips to the double wound, intending to suck the poison from it, even as I had done in my own case; but another startling scream from the girl caused me to look up, and, following the direction of her terrified glance, I looked behind me and beheld the king himself, his eyes ablaze with demoniac fury, in the very act of raising a spear that he had snatched from the hand of one of his guards, to drive it through my body. Whether it was that he had not seen just what had happened—as might very well have been the case, since the whole thing seemed to have occurred in the space of a single instant—and was under the impression that I had suddenly gone mad and was attacking his daughter, I know not, but it is certain that Ama's scream, and certain hasty words uttered by her, only barely saved me from his fury. But no sooner did he lower the threatening spear than I once more glued my lips to the wound, sucking hard at it with the object of extracting the poison before it had contaminated the blood; and in this effort I was happily successful, for although there was a slight swelling of the limb, and some pain for an hour or two, that was all that happened; and before morning my patient had quite recovered from all the effects of her alarming adventure.

The result of this was that I immediately became a prime favourite of the king. There was no further pretence of treating me as a prisoner, but, on the contrary, I was loaded with honours. A large house was assigned to my use, with a complete staff of servants to attend to my wants; an abundant supply of food was daily sent to me from the royal table; and, as I understood it, I was appointed physician in ordinary to the royal household. Another result—to which I did not attach nearly sufficient importance at the moment—was that I made an implacable and deadly enemy of Mafuta, the chief witch-doctor.

I have said that there was no further pretence of treating me as a prisoner, and this was true, but only within certain limits, as I discovered the moment that I set about taking measures to effect my escape. I was allowed to go freely where I pleased, it is true, even to the extent of making long hunting or exploring excursions into the adjacent country, but—whether or not by the king's orders I could never satisfactorily ascertain—I soon found that I could never manage to steal off anywhere alone. If ever I attempted such a thing—and I did, very frequently—a party of the king's guards was certain to turn up, in the most exasperatingly casual and unexpected manner, and join me, under the pretence, as they made me understand, that it was extremely dangerous to venture alone beyond the confines of the town, if I pretended that I was engaged in hunting for animals, or plants to be used in my medical practice. Or, if I attempted to go anywhere by water, I could take any canoe I chose, but two or more men always insisted upon accompanying me, that I might be spared the labour of paddling. It was always the same, no matter what the hour of day or night that I might choose to start upon my expeditions; no surprise was ever displayed at my eccentricity in the choice of times, but I simply could not contrive to elude notice; and at length it was borne in upon me that if I wished to effect my escape I must adopt tactics of a totally different kind. I therefore very gradually curtailed my excursions, and when I undertook them was careful that there should be nothing in the nature of secrecy connected with my movements.

Meanwhile, without any effort on my part, I now seemed to see a good deal of Ama, the king's daughter, who appeared to have assumed the responsibility of seeing that my house was kept in order, and that the servants were faithfully performing their duty. She was frequently in and out, as often as three or four times a day, and very seldom indeed less than twice; moreover, she seemed exceedingly anxious to become my instructress in her own language, and as I had already felt heavily handicapped on several occasions by my inability to converse freely with those around me I made no demur, although I must confess that I at length began to view with vague disquietude the extreme freedom of intercourse thus instituted by the young woman. Yet I scarcely knew precisely what it was that I feared, but I certainly had a feeling that the situation was not altogether devoid of peril, one of the most obvious of which was foreshadowed in the question which I frequently asked myself, What would the king think of the intimacy of his daughter with one of totally different race and views of life, should the matter chance to come to his knowledge? Therefore I kept a very close watch upon myself, and was careful never to allow my manner to relax in the slightest degree from the strictest formality, although to preserve consistently this attitude of extreme reserve was sometimes exceedingly difficult with a companion of so amiable and altogether winsome a manner and disposition as that of Ama.

Under the zealous and indefatigable tuition of this young damsel I made astonishingly rapid progress as a student of the language spoken by those around me, and was soon able to converse in it with a very fair amount of freedom. Meanwhile I had practically abandoned my attempts to effect my escape, for the time being at least; for the conviction had at length been forced upon me that neither Banda nor his people would ever willingly let me go, and that, therefore, before engaging in any further attempts, I must contrive to disarm suspicion completely, and create the impression that I had at length resigned myself to live out my life in this remote African town, and with savages only for my companions.

118

It was while matters were in this very unsatisfactory state that I became aware that some event of extreme importance was imminent in the town; for upon sallying forth from my residence on a certain morning and crossing the great square, in the centre of which stood Banda's crucifixion tree, I saw that a number of men were engaged in setting up some forty stout, quaintly-carved posts in a circle round about the tree. The arrangement somehow had a sinister, suggestive appearance that made me feel vaguely uncomfortable; and abandoning the intention, whatever it may have been, that took me to the spot, I returned to my house, and, as soon as Ama made her appearance, asked her what it meant.

"It means, my dear Dick," said she, laying her hand upon my arm, and looking very serious—she had insisted upon knowing my name, and calling me by it, early in our acquaintance—"that the Customs begin six days hence; and those men you saw setting up the posts round the crucifixion tree are making preparations for them."

"The Customs!" I exclaimed, in horrified accents, for I had heard of these grim and ghastly festivities before. "And pray, Ama, what is the nature of these Customs under your father's beneficent rule?"

"Oh, they are horrible; I hate them!" answered the girl. "They last six days—six whole days, in which the people abandon themselves to every kind of licence and cruelty, in which human blood is shed like water. I do not think *you* will like them, Dick—at least I hope not!"

"Like them?" I ejaculated indignantly. "I should think not, indeed. But I suppose a fellow is not obliged to watch them, is he? I shall go off into the forest, or up the river, during those six days—"

"Nay, Dick, you will not be able to do either of those things," answered Ama. "In the first place I am not at all certain that the king would give you leave; and, even if he did, you would not be permitted to go alone; and where would you find men willing to absent themselves from the Customs for the sake of accompanying you? There is not a man in the town who would consent to do so. No, I am afraid that we shall both be obliged to witness them."

"No," I said. "We must devise some scheme whereby we may both be exempted. You say that they take place six days hence; it will be strange indeed if our united ingenuity is not equal to the task of devising some simple yet efficacious plan. But, tell me, Ama, where do the victims come from, and how many of them are usually sacrificed?"

"The number sacrificed depends, of course, upon how many can be found," answered Ama; "but generally there are at least three hundred; this time it is hoped that there may be many more. As to where they come from, a good many are 'smelled out' by Mafuta and his assistants, and the rest are made up of such prisoners as may happen to be in our possession at the time. There are five hundred hunters out now securing prisoners; we expect them back to-morrow or the next day. And that reminds me, Dick," she added, with a sudden access of gravity, "if you had not been clever enough to save my life when the snake bit me, you would most certainly have been one of the victims; indeed it was with a view to sacrificing you at the Customs that my father accepted you from the Igbo."

"The dickens it was!" ejaculated I, in some dismay. "Then who is to say that I shall not be still included in the batch?"

"Nay," answered Ama; "you saved my life, and for that my father will spare you. It is not he whom you have to fear, but Mafuta. Mafuta hates you, I know, and would willingly 'smell you out' if he dared; but the people will not let him; for where would they get any one else to play beautiful music to them if you were to die? Besides, do you think *I* would allow any one to hurt you? My father is the king; no one, not even Mafuta, dare dispute his will; and I have more influence than any one else with the king. Nay, fear not, Dick, none shall hurt you while I live."

"I would that I could feel as fully assured of that as you appear to be, Ama," answered I. "With all due respect to your father, I may perhaps be permitted to remark that he has impressed me as a man of singularly short and uncertain temper; and if I should ever chance to be so unfortunate as to offend him—"

At this moment two guards presented themselves at the door of my hut and, saluting, one of them curtly remarked:

"The king is ill, and commands the presence of the white man at the palace *at once*!"

"The king—my father—ill!" ejaculated Ama, in a tone of greater consternation than seemed quite called for. "Let us go at once, Dick. And—oh, you must cure him—you must, *for your own sake*, Dick!"

Chapter Eighteen.

Doomed to the torture.

"You must cure him—you *must, for your own sake, Dick*!" Exactly. In uttering those words Ama unconsciously disclosed how slight was her confidence in the influence over her father, of which she had been boasting only a moment or two before the arrival of the summons for me to attend that father on his bed of sickness. It was all very well for her to tell me that I *must* cure him; but suppose that I could not, suppose that the sickness—whatever it might be—should run its course and fail to yield to my treatment, what then? The reason, so urgently expressed by her, why I must effect a cure—"for your own sake, Dick,"—was significant enough of the direction in which her apprehensions pointed; there was no necessity for me to inquire what she meant. I *must* cure the king, or it would be so much the worse for me! And how was I to cure him? My knowledge of disease was of the slightest and most amateurish kind, and, for aught that I could tell to the contrary, might not even be sufficient to enable me to diagnose the case correctly, much less to treat it successfully! However, there was no use in meeting trouble half-way; the only possible course was to obey the summons forthwith, and do my best, leaving the result in the hands of Providence. I accordingly rose to my feet and, motioning the guards to lead the way, followed them to the palace, with Ama walking by my side and holding my hand in a protective sort of way.

The distance from my hut to the palace was but a few yards; and we quickly arrived at our destination, being at once conducted into the presence of the king, who, stretched upon a couch, and evidently suffering severe pain in his internal organs, was surrounded by the somewhat numerous members of his family.

As I approached the side of his couch he gazed at me with lack-lustre eyes and groaningly said:

"I am very sick, O Dick; my entrails are being burnt up within me! Cure me at once and I will give thee my daughter Ama as thy wife and make thee a powerful chief!"

"I thank thee, Banda, for thy magnificently generous promises," answered I, "but I will gladly do my utmost for thee without reward. Tell me, now, how long hast thou been like this?"

"Not very long," answered the king; "perhaps while the sun has been climbing thus far,"—describing with his hand the arc of a circle measuring about seven degrees, or, say, half an hour—"I had just finished my breakfast when the pains seized me."

"Ah!" remarked I, trying to look as though I knew all about it; "and of what did thy breakfast consist?"

"Of very little, for I am but a moderate eater," answered the king. Let me consider. There was, first, a broiled fish, fresh from the river, with boiled yams; then a few roast plantains—not more than a dozen, I think; then the roast rib of a cow; a few handfuls of boiled rice; and—yes, I think that was all, except a bowl of jaro'—the latter being a kind of native beer.

It occurred to me that, probably, after this very "moderate" meal, his Majesty might be suffering from indigestion, although the "burning" pains in the stomach puzzled me a bit. I therefore came to the conclusion that if vomiting could be freely induced almost immediate relief ought to follow; and I accordingly prescribed the only emetic which I could think of at the moment, namely, copious draughts of warm water, followed by tickling the back of the throat with a feather. These means were so far successful that the patient acknowledged a certain measure of relief; but after a time the burning pains recurred and seemed to become more acute than ever, to my profound dismay; for, goaded almost to madness by the intensity of his suffering, the king was rapidly growing as dangerous as a wounded buffalo, and, between the paroxysms of his anguish, began to threaten all and sundry with certain pains and penalties, the mere enumeration of which made my flesh creep and plunged me into a cold perspiration.

At length, after a more than usually intense paroxysm of pain had passed, Gouroo, Banda's favourite wife, who was present, and whose virulent animosity I had been unfortunate enough to arouse, bent over the patient and whispered something in his ear, the purport of which I could not catch. But it was a suggestion, the nature of which I was able to divine without difficulty, for, by way of reply, Banda ejaculated between his groans:

"Yes, yes; let Mafuta be instantly summoned. And as for the white man, let the presumptuous pretender be closely confined in his own hut until I can decide upon the nature of his punishment. Away with him at once; and if he is allowed to escape, the guards who have him in charge shall be nailed, head downward, to the crucifixion tree!"

Gouroo smiled a smile of triumphant malice as, in reply to her summons, two guards entered, and, seizing me roughly, hurried me away; while Ama, bathed in tears, flung herself upon her knees beside her father's couch and vainly besought him to have mercy upon me. As I passed out of the room I saw the king, writhing in agony, rise upon his couch and strike the poor girl a violent blow, while he bellowed a fierce command to her to withdraw from his sight.

It was nearly noon when I was conducted back to my hut after my futile attempt to cure the king; and it was not until close upon sunset that I got any further news, when one of the guards who had me in charge informed me, as he brought in my supper, that Mafuta had completely cured the king within an hour of the moment when he was first summoned to his Majesty's bedside; that Banda had already risen from his couch; and that, in requital for his service, Mafuta had claimed—and been granted—the right to dispose of me as he pleased upon the occasion of the forthcoming festival of the Customs! Which meant, of course, that I was to die by some exquisite refinement of torture, the nature of which would probably be too dreadful for description. For I very shrewdly suspected that Gouroo and Mafuta were equally interested in my downfall— might, indeed, have conspired in some mysterious manner to bring it about—and would probably take care that it should be as complete and disastrous as savage vindictiveness could make it.

The days now dragged themselves away upon leaden feet, yet—apparent paradox— with frightful rapidity; for I now no longer had a household to attend to my wants; my

121

meals were brought to me with unfailing regularity by my guards, but they had apparently been forbidden to communicate with me, for not a word could I get out of them, good, bad, or indifferent. I was not permitted to show myself in the doorway of my dwelling, or even to approach it nearly enough to see what was going on; and in this dreadful solitude, waiting and hoping for I knew not what impossible happening to occur and effect my deliverance, each day seemed to drag itself out to the length of a month—until the darkness came; and then, with the realisation of the fact that I was so much nearer to a hideous fate, the hours seemed suddenly to have sped with lightning swiftness. The excited buzz and bustle of preparation pervaded the town all day, and every day, while night again became a pandemonium of barbarous sounds—for the tom-tom and flageolet concerts had been resumed with tenfold virulence since my incarceration—and on one occasion a terrific uproar announced the arrival of the unhappy prisoners who had been captured, in order that the festival might lose nothing of its importance or impressiveness through lack of a sufficient tale of victims; but I could not detect any indications of an attempt on the part of any one to communicate with me; and at length the latent hope that Ama's boast of her influence with her father might be verified, and that she might succeed in inducing the king to spare me, died out, and I began to prepare myself, as best I could, to meet whatever fate might have in store for me with the fortitude befitting a Christian and an Englishman. But do not suppose that all this while I was supinely and tamely acquiescing in the fate that awaited me. Far from it. For the first few days of my captivity my brain was literally seething with schemes for effecting my escape, most of them wildly impossible, I admit; but some there were that seemed to promise just a ghost of a chance of success—until I attempted to put them into effect, when the vigilance of my guards—with the fear of crucifixion, head downward, before their eyes—invariably baffled me.

Thus the time passed on until the first day of the Customs dawned, when, having received a more than usually substantial meal, I was stripped of the few rags that still covered my nakedness, and, with my hands tightly bound behind me by a thin but strong raw-hide rope, was led forth to the great square wherein the Customs were celebrated, and firmly bound to one of the posts, the erection of which I had witnessed a week earlier. Of course I was but one of many who were to gasp out their lives in this dreadful Aceldama; and in a very short time each post, or stake, was decorated with its own separate victim, some of whom, it seemed, were to perish by the torture of fire, for after the victims had been secured to the stakes, huge bundles of faggots, composed of dry twigs and branches, were piled around some of them. What the fate of the rest of us was to be there was nothing to indicate, but I had no doubt that it would be something quite as dreadful as fire; and I had fully made up my mind that when my turn came I would endeavour, by insult and invective, to goad my tormentors to such a state of fury and exasperation as should provoke them to finish me off quickly.

All being now ready, the gate in the palisade was thrown open, a conch-shell was blown, and the waiting inhabitants began to pour into the enclosure with all the eagerness and excitement of an audience crowding into the unreserved portions of a theatre, and in a very short time the great square was full, the front ranks pressing close up to a cordon of armed guards that had been drawn round the circle of posts. Then, while the air vibrated with the hum and murmur of many excited tongues, shouts and a disturbance in the direction of the palace proclaimed the approach of the king and his household, and presently the entire party, numbering some three hundred, passed in and made their way to a kind of grand-stand, from which an admirable view of all the proceedings was to be obtained. I looked for Ama, but could not see her; Gouroo, however, was present and favoured me with a smile of malicious triumph. Banda himself took not the slightest notice of my presence.

No sooner were the royal party seated than a commotion on the opposite side of the square portended another arrival; and in a few minutes, through a narrow lane that had been formed in the dense mass of people, Mafuta and his myrmidons, to the number of nearly a hundred, came leaping and bounding into the open space beneath the crucifixion tree. Daubed all over their naked bodies with black, white, and red paint, with their hair gathered into a knot on the crown of the head, and decorated with long feathers, strings of big beads, and long strips of scarlet cloth—obtained from goodness knows where—with necklaces of birds' and animals' claws about their necks, and girdles of animals' entrails round their waists, they presented as hideous and revolting a picture as can possibly be imagined as they went careering madly round the circle, each man waving a long spear over his head. Now I noticed a curiously subdued but distinct commotion among the spectators of the front rank, each of whom seemed anxious to surrender his apparently advantageous position to whomsoever might be willing to accept it. But, singularly enough, no one seemed desirous to avail himself of his neighbour's generosity; and the reason soon became apparent; for presently, in the midst of their wild bounding round the inner edge of the tightly packed mass of spectators, they came to a sudden halt, and Mafuta, advancing alone, proceeded to "smell out" those who were supposed to be inimical to the king's or his own authority, or against whom either of them had a secret grudge. With his body bent, his head thrust forward, and his nostrils working, he slowly passed along the inner face of the crowd, his shifty eyes darting hither and thither, until his gaze happened to fall upon one of the individuals for whom he was looking, when he would come to a halt, appear to be following a scent, and finally stretch forth his spear and lightly smite some man or woman on the head with it. The unhappy victim, thus "smelled out," would thereupon be instantly taken in charge by Mafuta's followers, and the process would be repeated until all those whose removal was desired had been gathered in. In the present case the victims numbered nearly a hundred, and the finding of them consumed the best part of two hours.

The process of "smelling out" being at an end, and those who had passed the ordeal unscathed being relieved of all further apprehension, the enormous crowd which had gathered to witness the "sports" settled down to thoroughly enjoy itself. And certainly there was a very commendable celerity manifested by those who had the direction of affairs; there was no disposition to keep the holiday-makers waiting; the unhappy victims were led up, one after the other, before King Banda, and their supposed crimes very briefly recited to him, whereupon his Majesty, with equal brevity, pronounced their sentence—in all cases that of death—which was at once carried out, the only difference consisting in the mode of execution; some of the unfortunate wretches being secured to the crucifixion tree in one way, some in another; but it was very difficult for a mere onlooker to decide which of the plans adopted inflicted the most suffering. These victims, it should be explained, were doomed to remain fastened to the tree until death should ensue from hunger, thirst, exposure, and the agony of their wounds.

Then, in batches of ten at a time, forty more victims were triced up to the boughs of this accursed tree by raw-hide ropes fastened to one wrist or one ankle, in such positions that their bodies showed clearly against the bright background of sky; and, while thus suspended, whosoever would was at liberty to shoot at them with bows and arrows, the great object being, apparently, to pierce the body with as many arrows as possible without inflicting a mortal injury. King Banda evidently prided himself upon his skill in this direction. But there were a few bunglers among the crowd, for some of the shots went so far astray that instead of hitting the mark at which they were supposed to be aimed, they hit and *slew* some half-a-dozen of the crucified ones. I wondered whether by any chance the fatal wounds were actually inflicted by interested persons who desired to put as speedy an end as possible to the sufferings of their unfortunate friends; and if so, whether the idea would occur to Ama to enlist the services of a few good marksmen in my behalf when my turn should come.

When all those who had been condemned to die in the above manner had perished, a further variety was imparted to the proceedings by compelling some fifty victims to "run the gauntlet." This is a very favourite form of pastime among savages, and is carried out in a variety of ways. In the present instance a narrow circular course was arranged round the great square, a lane of about a yard in width being formed through the mass of spectators, and into this lane the victims, stripped naked, were introduced, one at a time, to run round and round until beaten to death by the bare fists of as many as could get in a blow at them. And, since the lane was so exceedingly narrow, it happened that practically every individual on either side of the lane was able to get in at least one blow. To the uninitiated this may seem a not particularly inhumane form of inflicting the death punishment; but I, who saw the whole remaining part of the day spent in doing some fifty poor wretches to death in that fashion, can tell a very different story; there is no need to enter into details, but I may say that those who were weakest, and who succumbed most quickly, were to be most envied.

The day had opened with a cloudless sky and brilliant sunshine; but, as the hours dragged themselves slowly away, clouds, light and filmy at first but gradually growing more dense and threatening, began to gather, until toward evening the sun became blotted out and the whole vault of heaven grew overcast and louring, as though nature, horrified and disgusted at the orgy of human cruelty being enacted here on this little spot of earth, were veiling her face to shut out the shameful sight. By the time that the proceedings of the day were over and the enormous crowd began to disperse, it became evident that a more than usually violent tropical thunderstorm was brewing, although it might be some hours yet before it would burst over the blood-stained town. Naturally, I was very thankful that the awful day had passed over, and that its end found me still in the land of the living; for "while there is life there is hope," and in the course of my somewhat adventurous career I have seen so many extraordinary escapes from apparently inevitable disaster that the one piece of advice above all others which I would give to everybody is "Never despair!" I can recall more than one occasion when, if I had abandoned hope and the effort which goes with it, I should not now have been alive to pen these words. No man can ever know what totally unexpected happening may occur to effect his deliverance at the very moment when fate looks blackest and most threatening. But although I had passed through the day unscathed, so far as actual bodily injury was concerned, it had nevertheless been a day of suffering for me, growing ever more acute as the hours dragged wearily away, for, apart from the feelings of horror with which I had witnessed the display of so much unimaginable cruelty and torture, the bonds which confined me to my post had been drawn so tightly as greatly to impede the circulation of blood through my extremities, until by the time that the great square was empty of its crowd of bloodthirsty revellers, the anguish had become so great that I was almost in a fainting condition and could give but scant attention to anything beyond the pangs that racked every nerve of my tortured body; in fact I observed, with feelings of envy, that many of my fellow-sufferers had already succumbed and become unconscious, if indeed they were not dead. However, since we had been spared thus far, I concluded that we might reasonably hope to be reprieved at least until the next day, and I looked with impatience to be released and conveyed back to my place of confinement until dawn should again summon me forth to witness and, peradventure, be the victim of accumulative horrors.

But I soon discovered that even this small measure of mercy was to be denied me; food and drink were indeed to be served out to us—in order, as I surmised, that we might meet the ordeal in store for us with unabated strength—but the night was to be passed, as the day had been, secured to the sacrificial post, exposed, naked and helpless, to the elements and to the myriad insect plagues that attacked us unceasingly. I noted that while those who had not succumbed to their sufferings were fed as they stood still bound to their posts, those who had become unconscious were temporarily released, and revived by being copiously soused with water, and, further, were allowed to eat and drink while seated on the ground, before they were lashed up afresh; and I took the hint, feigning insensibility for the sake of the few minutes of temporary relief that I hoped thus to win.

By the time that the attendants reached me I was so near to swooning that very little pretence was necessary, and when at length they released me I sank to the ground in a heap with a low groan. I gathered from their remarks that they were seriously concerned at my condition, for it seemed that I was reserved for some very especial refinement of torture, the satisfactory application of which demanded that I must come to it in the possession of my full strength, which they feared had been seriously sapped by the suffering which I had already endured, and they freely expressed their concern lest, under existing circumstances, I should not furnish quite so much sport as was being expected of me. They therefore displayed real solicitude in their efforts to revive me, which I took especial care they should not accomplish too quickly. But, oh, what exquisite torment was mine when, my bonds being released, the blood once more began to circulate through my benumbed members! I could have screamed aloud with the excruciating agony, had not my pride prevented me; and it was a full hour before I had sufficiently recovered the use of my hands to enable me to convey food and drink to my lips. The food and drink provided for me were of an especially nourishing character, and when at length I had partaken of as much as I could force down my throat I was again lashed to my stake, but this time so carefully that, while for me to loose my bonds was an impossibility, the circulation of blood was in nowise impeded; and for even this small mercy I was inexpressibly grateful.

Meanwhile the night had fallen so intensely dark that the completion of the task of feeding us unfortunates had to be accomplished by torchlight; and we had not been very long left to ourselves before the faint flickering of distant lightning and the low muttering and grumbling of thunder warned us to expect a storm of more than ordinary violence. Everything portended it; the atmosphere was absolutely still, not a twig or even a leaf stirred, all nature seemed to be waiting in breathless suspense for the coming outbreak; even the insects had ceased to attack us, and had retired to their leafy retreat, and the air was so heavy and close that, naked as I was, I perspired at every pore. Not a sound broke the unnatural stillness save when, at irregular intervals, a low groan broke from some poor wretch upon the crucifixion tree in whom the life still lingered. But even to them relief was promised, for with the impending downpour of rain their wounds would quickly mortify, and then their sufferings would soon be at an end.

Very slowly and gradually the storm worked its way toward the zenith, gathering intensity as it rose, and at length—probably about ten o'clock—the first drops of rain, hot and heavy, like gouts of blood, began to fall, quickly increasing to a drenching downpour, accompanied by lightning, green, rose-tinted, violet, sun-bright, that lighted up the town until every object, however minute, was as clearly visible as in broad daylight, while the ceaseless crashing of the thunder was unspeakably appalling.

In the very height of the storm, when thunder, lightning, and rain together were raging in a perfect pandemonium, a stream of steel-blue lightning darted straight from the zenith, struck the crucifixion tree, and shattered it into a thousand fragments, leaving a great hole in the ground where it had stood! The storm continued to rage in full fury for about an hour, and then the flashes of lightning, with their accompanying peals of thunder, gradually became less frequent, although the rain continued to beat down upon the parched earth in a perfect deluge which formed rivulets, ay, and even brooks of quite respectable size, flowing in every direction.

My weary and aching frame soothed and refreshed by the pelting rain, I must have fallen into a kind of doze, for I was suddenly startled into full consciousness by the feeling that some one was meddling with my bonds, which, the next moment, severed by a sharp knife, fell from my limbs. Then a small soft hand seized mine and dragged me swiftly away from the stake to which I had been bound. It was so intensely dark just then, however, that I was quite unable to see where I was going, and was obliged to trust implicitly to my unknown guide. For two or three minutes we twisted hither and thither, blindly, so far as I was concerned, and then another flash came which enabled me to see that my companion was, as I had already suspected, my faithful little friend Ama, and that she was conducting me, by a somewhat circuitous route, toward the gate in the palisade.

"A thousand thanks to you, Ama, for coming to my help," I murmured in her ear as I squeezed her hand. "But whither are you taking me? To the gate? We can never pass it! The guards—"

"They are not there; they are sheltering in the houses close at hand, I expect; I took care to find out before coming to release you. And now, Dick, we must be silent," answered Ama, as we cautiously approached the spot where I knew the gate must be.

Suddenly my guide halted, and pressed herself and me close up against the wall of a building of some kind, at the same time feeling for my face in the darkness, and laying her finger on my lips to enjoin perfect silence. Here we waited for nearly five minutes until another flash of lightning came, when my companion, having caught a glimpse of her surroundings, again hurried me forward, and a few seconds later we had passed through the unguarded gate, closed it behind us, and were rapidly making our way through the streets of the outer part of the town, in the direction of the beach. About half-way down, however, we turned sharply aside and plunged down a narrow lane, which, after some twisting and turning, at length brought us out clear of the town into a plantain grove. And all this time we had not seen a single living creature, no, not so much as a dog; every living thing, save ourselves, had taken shelter from the fury of the elements, and was not likely to venture abroad again until it was over.

Still hurrying me forward, Ama led the way through the grove and along its edge, until we eventually reached a narrow bush path, through which it was necessary to wend our way circumspectly, for it was now as black as a wolf's mouth, save when an occasional flicker of lightning from the now fast-receding storm momentarily lit up our surroundings. We traversed this path for about half a mile, still maintaining perfect silence, and at length emerged, quite suddenly, upon a tiny strip of beach, beyond which hissed and gurgled the stream, already swollen by the rain. A flash of lightning, that came most opportunely at this moment, revealed a small light canoe hauled up on the beach, with a couple of paddles, a sheaf of spears, bows and arrows, and a few other oddments in it.

"Get in quickly, Dick, and let us be going," murmured Ama hastily. "The storm is passing away, and it cannot now be long before some one will visit the prisoners to see how they have fared; indeed, that may have happened already. And, whenever it occurs, your absence will certainly be discovered, and a search for you will be at once begun. It will take a little while for them to ascertain that you are nowhere concealed in the town, but when that has been determined they will at once think of the river, and a party will be despatched in pursuit; therefore it is imperative that we should secure as long a start as possible."

"Of course," answered I, as I laid hold of the light craft and ran her afloat; "I quite understand that. But, Ama, you speak of 'we,' as though you intended to accompany me. That must not be, my dear girl; you have already done nobly in freeing me, and in providing me with the means of flight, and I must now do the best I can for myself; I cannot consent to implicate you by permitting you to accompany me. Therefore let me now bid you adieu, with my warmest and most grateful thanks, not only for what you have done for me to-night, but also for the friendship which you have shown me from the moment when I first came to know you. Now, hasten back to your own quarters as quickly as possible, I pray you; I think you can be trusted to find your way back to them without permitting your share in this night's doings to be discovered. Farewell, dear Ama, and may God bless and keep you! I shall never forget you, or your goodness to me. Good-bye!"

And, in the fulness of my gratitude, I took her in my arms and kissed her.

For a moment the gentle girl resigned herself to my embrace; then, freeing herself, she said, "Thank you, Dick, for thinking of my safety at such a moment, dear, but I cannot return; I *must* go with you, not only for your own sake but for mine also. You do not understand the ways of my people, as I do, and therefore without my help you could never make good your escape. As for me, my father knows that there is only one person—myself—who would dare to do what I have done for you to-night; and even were I to succeed in returning to my own quarters undetected—which is exceedingly doubtful—his anger at your loss will be so great that he would assuredly condemn me to take your place at the stake. Therefore, Dick," she concluded pleadingly, "I must either go with you, or undergo the tortures that were destined for you."

"But surely,"—I protested, and was about to argue that, she being her father's favourite daughter, he would never be so inhuman as to sacrifice her to his anger, when a sound of distant shouting came faintly to our ears.

"Hark!" exclaimed Ama, "do you hear that, Dick? It means that your absence has been discovered, and that the hunt for you has already begun. We must not waste another moment. Will you take me with you; or must I go back to face a cruel and lingering death?"

"Not the last, certainly," answered I. "Jump in, little one, and let us be off without further parley."

Giving her my hand to steady her in entering the crank little craft, I waited until she had seated herself aft and taken the steering paddle in her hand, then, with a powerful push that sent the canoe, stern-first, far out into the rapidly flowing stream, I sprang in over the bows, seized a paddle, and proceeded to force the craft off-shore into the strength of the current.

Chapter Nineteen.

The tragic death of Ama.

We now had leisure to observe that the storm had so far passed away that there were big breaks in the canopy of cloud overhead and away to the eastward, through which the stars were beginning to show themselves, affording enough light just to enable us to discern the two banks of the stream, but not sufficient to betray our presence to an observer at a greater distance than, say, a quarter of a mile. There was therefore not much fear of our immediate discovery, since I now learned from Ama that our starting-point was at least three-quarters of a mile below the town, while, apart from our own exertions, the swollen current was sweeping us along at a speed of about six knots. In little more than ten minutes from the moment of starting we swept out of the tributary stream into the main river, the current of which was also flowing pretty rapidly, though not, of course, so swiftly as that of the lesser stream; and now, as we pushed off into mid-channel, we found time to exchange a few remarks. For my own part I was anxious to know what had first suggested to my companion the idea of effecting my rescue, and by what means, after she had conceived the idea, she had contrived to carry her plans to a successful issue. I put the question to her; and by way of reply she related to me the following story:

"From the moment when I first became aware of my father's illness I was not entirely free from suspicion; and when at length I saw that your efforts to cure him were only partially successful, and that his symptoms persistently recurred, I was convinced that there was foul play somewhere, though why, I could not at first imagine. But when Gouroo whispered to my father, hinting at your incapacity, and suggesting that Mafuta should be sent for, my suspicions began to take definite shape, and, although I was not able to verify those suspicions, I finally made up my mind that the whole occurrence was the outcome of a plot between Gouroo and Mafuta—your only enemies—to ruin you. And these suspicions were confirmed when, after you had been carried away and imprisoned, my father began to mend, even before the arrival of Mafuta upon the scene, while it seemed extraordinary to me that the witch-doctor should know so well the character of my father's ailment, that he was able to bring with him precisely the right remedies for administration.

"Now, as I told you just now, Dick, I was quite unable to verify my suspicions, but in my own mind I have not the slightest doubt that Mafuta gave Gouroo poison of some kind to administer to my father and make him ill, knowing that you would be summoned to cure him, and knowing, too, that your failure to cure would result in your condemnation to a death by torture. I tried to intercede for you, not once but many times; but my father had suffered horribly, and had been terribly frightened. He believed that, but for Gouroo's suggestion, you would have allowed him to die; and he refused to show you any mercy. Your fate seemed sealed—unless I could contrive a scheme to save you; but I could think of nothing; and the anticipation of your death made me feel so utterly wretched, that at last I entreated my father that, if he would not spare you, he would at least not compel me to witness your sufferings. He was still dreadfully angry with me for interceding in your behalf, but I persisted; and at length he told me that if I did not wish to witness the Customs I might remain at home, and of course I did so, although I knew that you were not to suffer until to-morrow. I spent all my time trying to devise some plan for effecting your deliverance, but could think of none; nevertheless, as soon as everybody was in the square and the Customs had begun, I went down to the river, got my canoe ready, and paddled it down to the place where we found it to-night. And it was while I was returning, and searching for a way to pass inside the palisade without entering by the gate, that I first saw the storm working up, and I knew that if it delayed its coming long enough I might be able to save you. As it happened, circumstances could scarcely have arranged themselves more favourably; and the result is that I have now the happiness to have you here with me in safety. Now, Dick, we must push on as fast as we can, travelling all through the night, and concealing ourselves and resting during the day; for if we are to escape it must be by stratagem, and not by strength, or speed."

"Yes," said I; "I can quite understand that if they should take it into their heads to pursue us—as you seem to think they will—we should have small chance of running away from one of your big canoes, manned by forty or fifty paddlers. But where do you propose to take me, Ama?"

"Where do you wish to go, Dick?" demanded my companion, answering one question with another.

"Why," replied I, "of course I am anxious to get down to the coast again, and aboard a ship. But I am puzzled to know what is to become of you when we part."

"*Must* we part, Dick?" murmured Ama softly. "Cannot I always remain with you?"

"Quite impossible, my dear girl," answered I hastily, beginning at last to have some faint suspicion of what was in this savage beauty's unsophisticated mind. "I owe a duty to my King; and that duty imperatively demands that I shall return at once to the ship in which I am serving him—and where, Ama, I may mention, no place could possibly be found for you. But I do not forget that you have saved my life, Ama; and therefore, come what will, I will not leave you until you have formed some definite plan for your own safety and happiness. What did you think of doing when the time comes for us to part?"

The girl was silent so long that I was obliged to repeat my question before I could get an answer, and when at length she replied, I feared I could detect tears in her voice, and could have execrated myself for a stony-hearted wretch.

"I have never looked so far forward as that," she answered in quavering tones; "but we need not think of that yet, Dick. When the time comes I have no doubt that I shall know what to do. And now, we really *must* cease talking, and push on as fast as we can, or we shall not reach our place of concealment before the dawn comes to reveal our whereabouts to our pursuers."

I was not sorry to have the conversation closed, for I wanted a little time for reflection. It was clear to me that this unsophisticated young savage had been dominated in her actions by one idea alone, that of saving me from a death of unspeakable horror; she knew that, in so doing, she was cutting herself off for ever from her own people, to whom it would be impossible for her to return; and, in her absolute simplicity, she had evidently thought that it would be the easiest thing in the world for her to throw in her lot with mine. How was I to undeceive her; how make her understand the absolute impossibility of such a thing? I greatly feared that to convince her of this would be wholly beyond my power. Yet what was to become of her? I could not abandon her, alone and unprotected, to her fate; nor could I take her with me. The problem seemed absolutely insoluble; and at length I came to the conclusion that the only thing to be done was to leave the issue to destiny.

Hour after hour we paddled on in absolute silence, making excellent progress, for the current was running strong in our favour; and at length, just as the eastern horizon was beginning to pale with the first hint of dawn, Ama gave the canoe a sheer in toward the eastern bank, looking anxiously about her as she did so. She was not long in discovering the landmarks of which she was in search, and a few minutes later the canoe was threading its tortuous way among a tangled mass of mangrove roots toward the solid bank of the river, landing upon which, we drew our light craft bodily up out of the water, concealing her beneath a broad overhanging mass of foliage which hid her so effectually that I would defy anybody but ourselves to find her. Then, taking a bow and quiver of arrows, together with a brace of spears, out of the canoe, and signing to me to do the same, Ama led the way through the dense growth bordering the river bank, until we reached an open grassy space of about twenty acres, sparsely dotted here and there with magnificent trees; and here Ama signified that we were to camp for the day. She further mentioned that, as she felt sure her father would have despatched a party in pursuit of us, which, she expected, would by this time be, not far behind us, it would be very desirable to keep a watch for them, since it was important that we should know as much as possible of their movements; and she accordingly suggested that I should climb a particularly lofty tree which she indicated, and keep a look-out for them, while she went off into the forest to seek the wherewithal to furnish a breakfast. She was very quiet and subdued in her manner, and I greatly feared that she was feeling deeply mortified and hurt because I had pointed out the impossibility of her remaining with me after our arrival at the coast—should we be so fortunate as to get there.

As Ama, taking her bow and arrows, tripped lightly away toward the forest, I proceeded to shin up the tree, and presently, after some labour, found myself among its topmost branches, which towered high above those of all the other trees in the neighbourhood, and—it being by this time broad daylight—obtained a magnificent view of the surrounding country, extending for, as I estimated, some forty miles toward the south and east, while toward the north and west the view was shut off by high hills, through which the river wound its way. To my surprise I found that our camping-place was much nearer the river than I had supposed, and I was thus able to obtain a clear and unobstructed view of its surface for many miles north and south, except a width of a few yards on its eastern side, which was shut off by the mangroves and low scrub which grew along its margin. I most carefully searched the shining bosom of the stream for signs of our expected pursuers, but saw none; nor had they hove in sight when, about half an hour later, Ama returned with some seven or eight wood-pigeons which she had brought down with her arrows. She did not call to me, or announce her return in any way, but set to work to mow a circle of about ten feet in diameter in the long grass; and then, having produced fire by rubbing two pieces of wood together, she proceeded very carefully to burn off the short grass left inside the circle, setting fire to it, allowing it to burn for a few seconds, and then beating it out again with a branch, in order that the fire might not spread and burn us out, to say nothing of betraying our presence by the smoke that it would raise.

Then, when she had at length cleared a sufficient space she lighted her cooking fire, taking care to use only dry wood, and thus make but little smoke, after which she proceeded to the margin of the river and brought back a large lump of damp clay, pieces of which she broke off and completely encased the birds in, and this she did with considerable care, I noticed. When she had completed her task, she consigned the whole to the fire, placing the shapeless lumps in the centre of the glowing embers, and piling more dry wood on the top, so as to maintain a brisk blaze. In about half an hour the lumps of clay, baked hard by the heat, began to crack and break open, when Ama carefully raked them out of the embers and set them aside. Then, and not until then, did she hail me, asking whether the expected pursuers were in sight; and upon my replying in the negative, she informed me that breakfast was ready, and invited me to come down and partake of it. I felt somewhat curious to see how Ama's primitive style of cooking would turn out; but it was all right. We simply broke open the lumps of baked clay with our spears and took out the birds—minus the skin and feathers, which adhered to the clay—and, splitting them open, removed the interior organs and devoured the flesh, which I found done to a turn, and particularly rich and juicy in flavour. Then, after we had finished eating, Ama again disappeared, to return shortly afterward with four fine cocoa-nuts, which we opened with our spear-heads and drank.

"Now, Dick," said Ama, when we had finished our meal, "you need rest badly, and must have it; therefore compose yourself to sleep near the fire, where I can watch over you; and I will take your place in the tree and look out for our pursuers. They will be sure to be along very soon now; and it is important that I should see upon what plan they are conducting their search for us. I want them to get well ahead of us before we resume our journey to-night."

"Yes," said I, "that is all very well, Ama. But what about yourself? You need rest fully as much as I do—"

"No, I do not," she retorted. "I took plenty of rest yesterday, in anticipation; while you were exposed all day to the scorching sun and the flies, and have been awake all night. So please lie down and sleep; for in any case I must watch the river until our pursuers appear. I promise you that when they have passed, and I have seen all that I can of them, I will come down and sleep too."

I attempted to dissuade her from this resolution; but she was in an obstinate mood, and would not be dissuaded; recognising which, at length, I gave in; for it was true that I needed rest. Accordingly, flinging myself down in the long grass, I fell, almost instantly, into a deep sleep.

It must have been about four o'clock in the afternoon, judging from the position of the sun, when I awoke to find Ama crouching over the fire, busily preparing another meal which—even as I rose and stretched myself luxuriously, feeling immeasurably refreshed and invigorated by my long sleep—she pronounced ready. As we sat down to partake, of it together, Ama informed me that one of her father's largest canoes, manned by forty paddlers, and commanded by a chief whom she had recognised, had passed slowly down the river about an hour after I had composed myself to rest, the chief in charge intently scrutinising both banks, as they went, evidently in search of some indication of our presence, and had finally passed out of sight to the southward; after which Ama had descended and taken a few hours' rest. She further stated that, upon awaking, she had again gone aloft to take another long and careful look round, but had seen nothing more of our pursuers, and was therefore inclined to believe that we were now reasonably safe, provided, of course, that we did all our travelling at night, kept a sharp look-out, and were careful not to allow ourselves to be fallen in with by other users of the river.

The supply of food which Ama had provided for our afternoon meal was so bountiful that, when we had finished, enough remained to furnish us with a good substantial meal about the middle of the night. Our wants for the next few hours were consequently supplied, we had therefore no need to do anything further than just to wait for nightfall and then resume our voyage; which we did, passing the intervening time in chatting together and discussing the various precautions which we must take in order to elude our pursuers, who, by the way, were now several miles ahead of us. We remained where we were until close upon sunset, when I again climbed our look-out tree and carefully scanned the whole surface of the river, as far as the eye could reach. There was nothing of an alarming character in sight, and therefore, as soon as I had descended to the ground, we both set out for the spot where we had hidden our canoe, launched her, and made our way out through the labyrinth of mangrove roots to the margin of the river, where we lay *perdu* until the darkness had completely fallen, when we boldly pushed off into the strength of the current, and steadily pursued our way. I soon found that travelling down-stream, with the current in our favour, was a very different matter from travelling up-stream against it; and within the next twenty-four hours I was able to estimate that we were now proceeding about three times as rapidly as was the case when I was making the upward journey. I calculated, therefore, that a full week ought to suffice us to reach the sea. And then what was to become of poor Ama, my gentle and loving companion? Alas, destiny was soon to answer that question, and most tragically, too, had we but known it.

Thanks to Ama's foresight and admirable judgment, our progress down the river was uneventful. We travelled during the night, resting and refreshing ourselves during the day, and never again saw a sign of our pursuers, nor indeed of anybody else, for our journey was begun when the moon was past her third quarter, and rose late; and Ama explained that the natives of that region never travelled through the darkness, if they could possibly avoid it.

It was on the sixth day of our journey that, having landed as usual at the first sign of dawn, we were resting in a secluded and shady spot after having partaken of an excellent and substantial breakfast. I had been sound asleep for some hours, for the sun was well past the meridian, when I was startled into sudden and complete wakefulness, and sprang up with the sensation that I had heard Ama screaming and calling upon me for help.

I glanced at the spot where she had lain, a short distance from me. She was not there; and I at once concluded that, having awakened before me, she had gone off into the forest to obtain the wherewithal for our mid-day meal. I listened intently, but the silence of noontide had fallen, and everything was deathly still; there was not the faintest zephyr to stir the foliage; and even the very insects that so persistently attack one in the African jungle seemed to be indulging in a mid-day siesta. Yet I could not divest my mind of the conviction that my abrupt awakening had been caused by a cry for help from Ama having reached my ears; and, seizing my weapons, I set out in search of her. The "form" in the grass where she had lain was plain enough to the sight, as also were her tracks in the direction of the forest, and these I followed for some distance without much difficulty, coming out at length into an open glade, through which a tiny streamlet made its way. And here, among an outcrop of immense granite rocks, I came upon the signs of a tragedy. The long grass was disturbed and beaten down, as though a desperate struggle had taken place; the ground was smeared and splashed with blood; and in the midst of it lay one of Ama's spears, and the broken shaft of the other. And, leading away from this, there was a broad, blood-stained trail, as though a body had been dragged along through the grass and over some rocky ground, further on, toward another and much bigger outcrop of rock. It was not difficult to read the signs: Ama, intent upon her hunting, had been surprised and overpowered by some ferocious beast; and now all that remained was for me to follow and rescue the unfortunate girl, or avenge her death. I accordingly fitted to my bow the stoutest arrow in my quiver, and dashed forward in a fury of rage and grief, absolutely reckless of consequences to myself, and animated by but one impulse— the determination to slay the beast, whatever it might be, that had wrought this evil to my faithful and gentle companion.

For a hundred yards or more the trail led over uneven rocky ground toward an immense rock, upon rounding which I found myself face to face with, and within half-a-dozen yards of, a splendid full-grown male leopard who was crouching over poor Ama's motionless body, snarling savagely as he strove with his claws to remove a broken spear, the head of which was buried deep in his neck. As I rounded the rock and came in sight of him he rose to his feet, with his two front paws on Ama's body, and bared his great fangs at me in a hideous grin, as he gave utterance to a snarling growl that might well have struck terror to the boldest. But my heart was so full of rage and grief at the dreadful sight before me that there was no room in it for any other emotion, and, halting short in my tracks, I gazed the brute steadfastly in the eye, as I slowly raised my bow and drew the arrow to its head. Never in my life had I felt more deadly cool and self-possessed than I did then as I aimed steadily at the animal's right eye; I felt that I *could not* miss; nor did I; for while we thus stood motionlessly staring at each other, I released the string, and the next instant the great lithe beast sprang convulsively into the air, with the butt of my arrow protruding from his eye and the point buried deep in his brain. As he fell back, and struggled writhing upon the ground, moaning horribly for a few seconds ere his great limbs straightened out in death, I dashed forward, and, seizing poor Ama's body, drew it out of reach of the beast's claws. But a single glance sufficed to show me that the unfortunate girl was beyond the reach of further hurt. Yes, she was quite dead, this gentle, faithful, savage girl who, in return for a comparatively slight service, had unhesitatingly abandoned home, kindred, everything, to save me from a cruel and lingering death; and now the only thing that I could do to show my gratitude was to make sure that no further violence should be offered to her remains.

My first impulse was to carry the body down to where the soil was softer, and there dig a grave for it; but while I was considering this plan, it occurred to me that, with no more efficient tool than a spear to serve as a shovel, it would be practically impossible for me to bury the body deep enough to protect it from the jackals and hyaenas; and I therefore determined that, instead of burying it, I would burn it. There was an abundance of fallen boughs and twigs in the adjacent jungle to enable me to build a funeral pyre; and I should have the melancholy satisfaction of actually watching the reduction of the body to impalpable ashes. I therefore took all that remained of poor Ama in my arms and carried it to the top of a bare rocky plateau close at hand, upon which I intended to build my pyre, and then diligently set to work to collect the necessary wood.

It took me the remainder of the day to collect as much dry and combustible material as I considered would be needful to accomplish the complete incineration of the body, and to build the pyre; but it was done at last; and then, once more raising the corpse in my arms, I gently placed it on the top. Then, making fire, as I had seen Ama do, by rubbing two pieces of wood together, I ignited a torch and thrust it deep into the heart of the pyre, through an opening which I had left for the purpose. The dry leaves and grass which I had arranged as kindling material instantly caught fire, and in a few minutes the flames were darting fiercely upward through the interstices, and wreathing themselves about the corpse. Then, placing myself to windward, clear of the smoke, I knelt down on the hard rock and—I am not ashamed to admit it—prayed earnestly that God would have mercy upon the soul of the simple, unsophisticated, savage maiden who had lost her life while helping me to save my own. I was doing a most imprudent thing to linger by the side of the pyre, for the smoke, in the first place, and the light of the flames when it fell dark, could scarcely have failed to attract to the spot any savages who might have been in the neighbourhood, when my plight would probably have been as bad as ever; but at that moment my sorrow at the loss of my companion overcame every other feeling, and, for the moment at least, I was quite indifferent as to what befell me. As it happened, no one came near me, and I remained, unmolested, watching the fire until it had burnt itself out, leaving no trace of the body that had been consumed.

Meanwhile, since I was almost naked, and was hoping soon to find myself once more among civilised people, it occurred to me that the skin of the leopard which had wrought this dire tragedy might be of use to me as material out of which to fashion some sort of a garment; and, therefore, while the flames of the pyre were still blazing brilliantly I utilised their light to enable me to strip the pelt off the great carcase. When the fire had entirely died down, and I had satisfied myself that there was nothing left of poor Ama to be desecrated by fang of beast or beak of bird, I sorrowfully retired from the fatal spot, carrying the leopard's skin with me, and making my way with some difficulty to the place where the canoe lay concealed, sprang in and shoved off.

Four days later I arrived at the mouth of the river, without further adventure, and was fortunate enough to find a fine slashing brigantine flying French colours riding at anchor there. It did not need a second look at her to tell me that she was a slaver; but beggars must not be choosers. I could not afford to wait about for the arrival of a more honest craft, at the risk of being again seized and carried off by the natives, and therefore, putting a bold face upon it, I paddled alongside and, with my leopard-skin wrapped round me petticoat-fashion, climbed up the side and inquired for the skipper. It appeared that he was ashore at the moment making arrangements for the shipment of a cargo of slaves on the next day; but the chief mate was aboard, and upon representing myself to him as a shipwrecked Englishman who had been carried away captive into the interior, and had just effected my escape, he gave me permission to remain, saying that he had no doubt Captain Duquesne would receive me if I were willing to work my passage to Martinique. This was not at all what I wanted; but even Martinique was better than King Banda's town, and I therefore consented. Some hours later the captain returned, and upon my repeating to him the yarn which I had spun to the mate he not only very readily consented to my working my passage, but also offered me two excellent suits of clothes, two shirts, two pairs of stockings, a pair of shoes, and a worsted cap in exchange for my leopard-skin, which offer I gladly accepted; and that night found me domiciled in the forecastle of *L'Esperance* as one of her crew.

My companions, although a sufficiently lawless lot, were nevertheless genial enough among themselves, and—let me do them justice—made me heartily welcome among them. Naturally enough, having heard that I had been a captive among the savages, they insisted upon my relating to them my adventures; and this inaugurated an evening of yarn-spinning in the forecastle, the incidents related having reference for the most part to the slave-trade. There was one grizzled old scoundrel, in particular, nicknamed— appropriately enough, no doubt—"Red Hand," who was full of reminiscence and anecdote; and by-and-by, when the grog had been circulating for some time, he made mention of the names *Virginia* and *Preciosa*, at which I pricked up my ears; for I remembered at once that those were the names of the two slavers that our own and the American Government were so anxious to lay by the heels, and which had hitherto baffled all our efforts and laughed at our most carefully laid plans. Not altogether to my surprise, I now learned that the *Virginia* and the *Preciosa* were one and the same craft, manned by two complete crews—one American and one Spanish—and furnished with duplicate sets of papers. Thus, if by any chance she happened to be overhauled by a British ship, she hoisted American colours, her American skipper, officers, and crew showed themselves, and her American set of papers was produced, the result being that she went free, although she might have a full cargo of slaves on board—for the British were not authorised to interfere with American slavers. And, in like manner, if an American cruiser happened to fall in with her, she showed Spanish colours, mustered her Spanish crew on deck, and produced her Spanish papers for inspection if she were boarded, there being no treaty between America and Spain for the suppression of slavery. What she did if she happened to encounter a French cruiser I did not learn; apparently such an accident had not yet happened, she being a remarkably fast sailer while the French cruisers were notoriously slow-coaches. This was a most valuable piece of information for me to get hold of, and I carefully laid it away in the storehouse of my memory for use when occasion should serve.

On the following morning we began to ship our cargo of slaves—three hundred and forty of them; and that same night, about an hour before sunset, we weighed and stood out to sea, securing a good offing by means of the land-breeze which sprang up later on, and finally bore away for Cape Palmas. As it happened, the weather was light and fine, and our progress was consequently slow, Cape Palmas not being sighted until our sixth day out. Here Captain Duquesne secured an excellent departure by means of three carefully taken bearings of the cape, observed at intervals of two hours, by means of which he was able to establish our position on the chart with the utmost accuracy; and, this done, we held on a westerly course, the skipper's intention being not to haul up to the northward until he had arrived at the meridian of 20° west longitude, lest he should fall in with any of the cruisers of the Slave Squadron. But, as luck would have it, the weather fell still lighter at sunset on our ninth day out; and on the following morning at daybreak we found ourselves becalmed within three miles of a British cruiser, which promptly lowered her boats and despatched them to overhaul us; and by breakfast-time I had the pleasure of finding myself once more under the British flag, our captor proving to be the corvette *Cleopatra*, by the captain and officers of which I was most kindly received when I had related to them my strange story. The prize was promptly provided with a prize crew and sent into Sierra Leone in command of the third lieutenant, and I was given a passage in her. Four days later we arrived at our destination; and, to my great joy, among the vessels at anchor in the harbour I recognised the *Eros*. I pointed her out to the prize master; and he, good-hearted fellow that he was, kindly let me have a boat to go on board her as soon as our own anchor was down.

Chapter Twenty.

Our crowning exploit.

"Come on board, sir," remarked I, touching my cap as I passed in through the gangway of the *Eros* and found myself face to face with Captain Perry and the master, who were walking the quarter-deck side by side and conversing earnestly, while the first lieutenant, from the break of the poop, was carrying on the work of the ship.

"Good heavens!" exclaimed the skipper, stopping short and staring at me as though he had seen a ghost—"is it possible? It can't be—and yet, by Jove, it *is*—Mr Fortescue! Welcome back to the *Eros*, Mr Fortescue; I am delighted to see you again. But where on earth have you sprung from? From that fine brigantine that has just come in, I imagine, since I see that the boat which brought you is returning to her; but I mean before that. You look as though you have been having a pretty rough time of it lately. And what of the *Dolphin* and her crew? We gave you all up for lost, long ago."

"And with good reason, sir," I answered. "She foundered in a hurricane in mid-Atlantic; and I have only too much reason to fear that I alone have survived to tell the tale."

"Ah," said the skipper, "that is bad news indeed; but the fact that you never turned up at our rendez-vous, and that no intelligence could be gained of you, has prepared us for it. Well, Mr Fortescue, I am afraid I am too busy to listen to your story just now; you must therefore dine with me and the officers of the ship to-day, and then spin us your yarn. Meanwhile, since you seem to have returned to us flying light, without any 'dunnage,' I would recommend you to get hold of the ship's tailor and see what he can do for you in the matter of knocking you up a uniform. For the rest, you may take a boat and go ashore to replenish your wardrobe, which you had better do at once, for we go to sea again to-morrow. I have no doubt the purser will be able to let you have such funds as you need. Now, run along and renew your acquaintance with your shipmates; I see Mr Copplestone and one or two more glancing rather impatiently this way, as though they were anxious to have a word or two with you."

Touching my cap, I slipped up on to the poop, as in duty bound, to report myself to the first lieutenant, who gave me as hearty a welcome as the skipper had done, and then joined Copplestone, the surgeon, and one or two others who were obviously waiting to have a word with me, and retired with them to the gunroom, where my return was celebrated in due form. Of course they were all exceedingly anxious to hear the story of what had befallen me since the *Dolphin* and the *Eros* had parted company; but I steadfastly refused to tell them anything beyond the bare fact that the *Dolphin* had gone down with all hands, explaining that the skipper had invited me to dine with him that day, and that they would learn all particulars then, as I gathered that it was his intention to invite them all to meet me. Then, having had a satisfactory interview with the tailor and the purser, I went ashore and laid in a stock of linen, etcetera, together with a chest, all of which I brought off with me.

As I had quite anticipated, the captain invited everybody to meet me at dinner that day, even to Copplestone and Parkinson, who were now the sole occupants of the midshipmen's berth. And very attentively everybody listened to the story, as I told it in detail, of how, after parting from the *Eros*, we had carried on in the hope of overtaking the *Virginia*; of how we had been caught in and overwhelmed by the hurricane; of how I came to go adrift, alone, in the longboat; of how I had been run down by *La Mouette*, and of my treatment on board her; of my adventures in King Banda's town, and my escape therefrom with the aid of poor Ama; of the death of the latter—at which all hands expressed their sincere regret; and, finally, of how I had reached *L'Esperance*, and the extraordinary story I had heard while aboard her. It is not to be supposed that I was allowed to spin my yarn without interruption; on the contrary, I was bombarded with a continuous fire of questions for the elucidation of points that I had failed to make quite clear; and when I had finished the captain was pleased to express himself as perfectly satisfied with all that I had done, and that the loss of the *Dolphin* was due to causes entirely beyond my control. Regret was expressed for the loss of Tasker and Keene, both of whom were highly esteemed by all their shipmates; and then the conversation diverged to the topic of the audacious *Virginia-Preciosa*, which, protected by the very ingenious fraud of the double sets of papers and the double crews, was still merrily pursuing her way and bidding defiance to everybody.

"Ah!" ejaculated the skipper, with a deep sigh of satisfaction; "thanks to your friend Red Hand's garrulity in his cups, Mr Fortescue, we shall now know how to deal with that precious craft. We go to sea to-morrow, and it shall be our business, gentlemen, to bring her to book; and a fine feather in our caps it will be if we should be successful."

The first thing after breakfast, on the following morning, Captain Perry went ashore, remaining there until close upon eight bells in the afternoon watch; and when at length he came off, he looked uncommonly pleased with himself. I saw him talking animatedly with the first lieutenant for some time, and then he beckoned to me.

"I suppose, Mr Fortescue," he said, when I joined him, "you will not have very much difficulty in identifying the *Virginia* should we be lucky enough to fall in with her?"

"None at all, sir," answered I. "I believe I should be able to identify her as far as I could see her. I boarded her, you will remember, and I took full advantage of the opportunity to use my eyes. Oh, yes, I shall know her if ever I clap eyes on her again."

"Which will be before very long, I hope," answered the skipper. "For by a most lucky chance I have to-day obtained what I believe to be trustworthy information to the effect that she was sighted four days ago, bound for the Gaboon river—or perhaps it would be more correct to say that she was sighted steering east, and identified by the master of a brig who knows her perfectly well, and who has since arrived here, and that there is authentic information to the effect that she is this time bound for the Gaboon."

"In that case, sir," said I, "there ought not to be very much difficulty in falling in with her when she comes out."

"That is what I think," returned the skipper. "Are we quite ready to go to sea, Mr Hoskins?"

"Absolutely, sir, at a moment's notice," answered Hoskins.

"Very well, then, we will weigh as soon as the land-breeze springs up," said the skipper.

And weigh we did, a little after seven o'clock that evening, securing a good offing, and clearing the shoals of Saint Ann by daybreak the next morning. We knew that it was customary for the slavers coming out of the Gulf of Guinea to endeavour to sight Cape Palmas, in order that they might obtain a good "departure" for the run across the Atlantic, also because they might usually reckon upon picking up the Trades somewhere in that neighbourhood. The skipper therefore carefully laid down upon his chart the supposititious course of the *Virginia* from the Gaboon to Cape Palmas, and thence onward to the Caribbean Sea; and then shaped a course to enable us to fall in with her on the latter, at a spot about one hundred miles to the westward of Palmas. Having reached this spot, we shortened sail to our three topsails, spanker, and jib, and slowly worked to windward along that course, tacking every two hours until we had worked up to within sight of the cape, and then bearing up and running off to leeward for a distance of one hundred miles again, keeping a hand aloft on the main-royal yard as look-out from dawn to dark. It was weary, anxious work; for of course our movements were being regulated by a theory that, for aught we knew to the contrary, might be all wrong; and as day succeeded day without bringing the expected sail within our ken there were not wanting among us those who denounced the skipper's plan as foolish, and argued that the proper thing would have been to go direct to the Gaboon, and look there for the *Virginia*. But Captain Perry, having carefully thought the whole thing out, stuck to his guns, refusing to budge an inch from his original arrangement, in response to the hints and insinuations of those who disagreed with him. And the result proved the soundness of his theory, for on the sixteenth day of our quest, about seven bells in the afternoon watch, the look-out hailed the deck with:

"Large sail two points abaft the weather beam, steerin' to the west'ard under stunsails!"

"How far away is she?" hailed the skipper.

"Her r'yals is just showin' above the horizon, sir," answered the man.

"Ah! that means that she is about twenty miles distant," remarked the skipper to me—I being officer of the watch. "Too far off for identification purposes, eh, Mr Fortescue?"

"Well, sir," answered I, "it is a longish stretch, I admit. Yet, with your permission, I will get my glass, go aloft, and have a look at her."

"Thank you, Mr Fortescue. Pray do so, by all means," returned the skipper.

Hurrying below for my own private telescope, which was an exceptionally fine instrument, I slung it over my shoulder and wended my way aloft to the main-royal yard.

"Whereabout is she, Dixon?" I asked, as I swung myself up on the yard beside him. "Ah, there she is; I see her. Mind yourself a bit and let me have a peep at her."

The man swung off the yard and slid down as far as the cross-trees, while I unslung my glass and brought it to bear upon the stranger. The rarefaction of the air bothered me a good deal, producing something of the effect of a mirage, and causing the royals of the distant vessel to stand up clear of the horizon as though there were nothing beneath them; yet, as she rose and fell with the 'scend of the sea, shapeless snow-white blotches appeared and vanished again beneath them occasionally. She was coming along very fast, however; and presently, when she took a rather broad sheer, I caught a momentary glimpse of *two* royals and just the head of a third—the mizzen—proving conclusively that she was full-rigged—as was the *Virginia*. But, as the skipper had surmised, she was still much too far off for identification. I thought rapidly, and an idea occurred to me which caused me to close my glass, re-sling it, and slide down to the cross-trees.

"Up you go again, Dixon, and keep your eye on that vessel, reporting any noticeable thing about her that may happen to catch your eye," said I. And swinging myself on to the topgallant backstay, I slid rapidly down to the deck.

"Well, Mr Fortescue, what do you make of her?" demanded the skipper, as I rejoined him.

"She is a full-rigged ship, sir," said I; "but, as you anticipated, she is still too far off for identification. But she is steering the course that we have decided the *Virginia* ought to be steering; and it has just occurred to me that, should she indeed be that craft, she may give us a great deal of trouble if she discovers us prematurely, seeing that she is to windward.

I would therefore suggest, sir, that we bear up and make sail, so as to keep ahead of her until dark, and then—"

"Yes, I see what you mean, Mr Fortescue," interrupted the skipper; "and doubtless there are many cases where the plan would be very commendable; but in this case I think it would be better to close with her while it is still daylight and we can see exactly what we—and they—are doing. Therefore be good enough to make sail at once, if you please."

"Ay, ay, sir," answered I. "Hands make sail. Away aloft and loose the royals and topgallantsails. Lay out and loose the flying-jib. Board your fore and main tacks!"

In a moment all was bustle; the watch below tumbled up to lend a hand without waiting to be called; and in five minutes the noble ship was clothed with canvas from her trucks down, and shearing through the deep blue water with her lee channels buried.

"Now, Mr Fortescue," said the skipper, "we will 'bout ship, if you please."

We tacked, accordingly; and as soon as we were fairly round and full again the skipper hailed the royal yard to know how the chase bore. The answer was, "A point and a half on the weather bow!"

"Just so!" commented the skipper. "We will keep on as we are going until she bears dead ahead, and then we will edge away after her."

Presently eight bells struck, and Hoskins came up to relieve me, whereupon I made another journey aloft, to the fore-topmast cross-trees this time. We were raising her very fast now that both ships were steering upon converging lines; I could already see nearly to the foot of her topsails; and I settled myself comfortably, determined to remain where I was until I could absolutely identify her, although even at this time I had scarcely a shadow of a doubt that it was the long-sought *Virginia*, or rather the *Preciosa*, that I held in the field of my telescope. Another twenty minutes and she was hull-up from my point of observation, by which time there was no further room for doubt, and I descended to the deck to acquaint the captain with the success of his strategy. She was by this time dead ahead of us; and the skipper thereupon gave orders to bear away four points and set the larboard studdingsails; at the same time instructing the look-out to give us instant warning of any change in the stranger's course or amount of sail set.

Both ships were now travelling very fast; and by the time that we had got our studdingsails set, the stranger was visible from our poop for about half-way down her topsails, and rising higher even as we watched. In a few minutes more we had lifted the heads of her courses above the horizon, still edging away and keeping her about four points on our port bow; and presently, as we watched her, we saw the Stars and Stripes go soaring up to her gaff-end. Not to be outdone in politeness, we hoisted our colours also; and for the next quarter of an hour the two craft continued to close, the chase stolidly maintaining her course, while we, under the skipper's skilful conning, continued to edge very gradually away, as the other vessel sped to leeward, checking our weather braces by a few inches at a time until our yards were all but square. At length, when we had brought the chase fairly hull-up it became apparent that, thanks to the pains taken by the skipper to improve our rate of sailing, the *Eros* was now a trifle the faster vessel of the two; and that, consequently, nothing short of an accident could prevent us from getting alongside the chase. Still, at sea there is always the possibility of an accident, therefore as soon as we were near enough the captain gave orders to clear away the bow gun and pitch a shot across the fellow's forefoot, as a hint that we wanted to have a talk to him. This was done; but no notice was taken aboard the chase; the next shot therefore was let drive slap at her, care being taken to fire high, with the result that the shot passed through the head of her fore-topsail and only very narrowly missed the topmast-head. This seemed to rather shake the nerve of her skipper, for the next moment her studdingsails collapsed and came down altogether, regular man-o'-war fashion—showing her to be strongly manned; but instead of rounding-to and backing her main-yard, as we thought she intended, she braced sharp up on the port tack and endeavoured to escape to windward. But we were every whit as smart with our studdingsails as she was, and instantly hauled our wind after her, she being now about one point on our lee bow. For the next hour we held grimly on, firing no more meanwhile, but by the end of that time we had neared her sufficiently to risk another shot, which, aimed with the utmost care by the gunner himself, struck the main-topmast of the chase, sending everything above the main-yard over the side to leeward. This settled the matter, and the next moment the beautiful craft hove-to.

"Mr Fortescue," said the skipper, "you know more about yonder vessel than any of the rest of us, therefore you shall take the second cutter, with her crew fully armed, and proceed on board to take possession."

"Ay, ay, sir," answered I; and running down the poop ladder I gave the order for the boatswain to pipe the second cutter away while I went below to buckle on my sword and thrust a pair of pistols into my belt. By the time that the boat's crew were mustered, and the boat made ready for lowering, we were hove-to within biscuit-toss of the other vessel's weather quarter, and were able to read with the naked eye the words "Virginia, New Orleans," legibly painted across the turn of her counter.

"D'ye see that, Mr Fortescue?" questioned the skipper, pointing to the inscription. "I hope there is no mistake as to the accuracy of your information; because, if there is, you know, we shall have got ourselves into a rather awkward mess by firing upon and winging that craft!"

"Never fear, sir," answered I confidently; "I know the secret of that trick, as you shall see very shortly."

"Very well," said he, "off you go. And as soon as you have secured possession let me know, and I will send the carpenter and a strong gang aboard to help you to clear away the wreck and get another topmast on end before it falls dark."

Five minutes later I was alongside the prize, which, as on the occasion of my previous visit, I was compelled to board by way of the lee main chains, no side ladder having been put over for my accommodation. My Yankee friend and his mate were on the poop watching us, and I thought the former turned a trifle pale as he noted the strength of the crew that I had brought with me.

"All hands out of the boat, and veer her away astern!" ordered I as we swept alongside; and the next moment I and my party were over the rail and on deck. I had already made my plans during the short passage of the boat between the two vessels; consequently the moment that we were all aboard young Copplestone, who had come with me, led a party of men forward to drive the slaver's crew below, while I, with a couple of sturdy seamen to back me up, ascended to the poop.

"Look 'e hyar, young feller," began the Yankee skipper, as I set foot on the poop, "I wanter know what's the meanin' of this outrage. D'ye see that there flag up there? That's the galorious—"

"Stars and Stripes," I cut in. "Yes; I recognise it. But I may as well tell you at once that I know this ship has no right to hoist those colours. She is the *Preciosa*, a slaver hailing from Havana, and sailing under Spanish colours; consequently she is the lawful prize of his Britannic Majesty's ship *Eros*; and I am here to take possession of her."

I saw the man turn pale under his tan, and for a moment he was speechless, while his mate Silas whispered something in his ear. But he would not listen. Instead, he pushed the man roughly away, angrily exclaiming, "Hold yer silly tongue, ye blame fool!" Then, turning to me, he demanded:

"Who's been makin' a fool of ye this time, stranger?"

"Nobody," answered I curtly. "I acknowledge that you did the trick very handsomely when I boarded you on a former occasion; but there is going to be no fooling this time I assure you."

"Well, I'll be goldarned!" exclaimed the man, suddenly recognising me. "If it ain't the young Britisher that—jigger my buttons if I didn't think I'd seen yer before, stranger. Well, you know, you've got to prove what you say afore you can do anything, haven't ye?"

"Yes," I answered; "and if you will be good enough to hand me over your keys I will soon do so, to my own satisfaction if not to yours."

"Very well," he said, producing the keys; "the game's up, I can see, so I s'pose it's no use kickin'. There's the keys, stranger. But I'd give a good deal to know who let ye into the secret."

"No doubt," returned I, with a laugh. "Adams and Markham, just mount guard over these two men, and do not let them stir off the poop until I return."

So saying, I descended the poop ladder and, entering the cabin, made my way to the skipper's state-room, and, opening a desk which I found there, soon discovered the genuine set of papers declaring the ship's name to be the *Preciosa*, her port of registry Havana, and her ownership Spanish. Her Spanish crew we soon found snugly hidden away in spacious quarters beneath the lazaret; and, as to the name on her stern, we found that the piece of wood on which it was carved and painted was reversible, having Virginia, New Orleans, carved on one side of it and Preciosa, Havana, on the other, and that it could be unbolted and reversed in a few minutes by lifting a couple of movable planks in the after cabin. I called a couple of hands into the cabin and had this done forthwith, much to the relief of Captain Perry, as I afterward learned. She had a full cargo, consisting of seven hundred and thirty negroes, all young males, on board; and as she was a remarkably fast and well-built ship she was a prize worth having, to say nothing of the credit that we should win by putting a stop to her vagaries. We transferred her double crew to the *Eros*, where they were carefully secured in the hold on top of the ballast, and, a strong prize crew being put on board by Captain Perry, we were not long in clearing away the wreck and putting everything back into place again, being ready to make sail by one bell in the first watch.

Being a prize of such exceptional value, Captain Perry decided to accompany her in the *Eros* to Sierra Leone, where we arrived without adventure five days later. In due course she was adjudicated upon and condemned by the Mixed Commission; but I did not remain at Sierra Leone for that to take place; for upon our arrival we found that a packet had come in from England a few days previously bringing letters for me, acquainting me with the sad news of my father's death and urging me to proceed home immediately to supervise the winding up of his affairs, and to assume the management of the very important property that he had left behind him. I therefore at once applied for leave, and, having obtained it, secured a passage in a merchant vessel that was on the point of sailing for Liverpool, where I duly arrived after an uneventful passage of twenty-seven days. I discovered, upon reaching home, that it would be quite impossible for me to manage my property and at the same time follow the sea; at my mother's earnest entreaty, therefore, I gave up the latter; and am now a portly grey-headed county squire, a J.P., M.F.H., and I know not what beside, to whom my experiences as a Middy of the Slave Squadron seem little more than a fevered dream.

Made in the USA
Coppell, TX
27 February 2023